THE COUNT OF THE SAHARA

WAYNE TURMEL

THE
BOOK
FOLKS

The 1925 Franco-American Sahara Expedition

Prologue

Hoggar Province, Algeria
February 20, 1926

The Commandant stuck the tip of his little finger in the bullet hole and spit a curse between his teeth. "C'est des conneries." It was, indeed, bullshit. In the old days, the Tuaregs would stage a raid, wave a few swords, put the fear of God into the locals, and disappear back into the desert. Now they had rifles and a disturbing lack of respect for French authority.

Commandant Beaumont examined the hole in the fender of the truck and its twin punched into the door panel. Another couple of years, he thought, and they'll learn how to use them. Then the real trouble will start.

Squinting into the sun, he saw the culprit waving his rifle in the air and shouting his war cry. It never seemed to occur to these idiots that if they were close enough to shoot at the Legion troops, they could shoot back.

"Should I?" asked a fat Belgian sergeant. The muzzle of his rifle lay flat against the hood and he had a clear shot, clearly itching to take it. A six foot man in bright blue robes and a foot-high turban atop a seven foot camel made an awfully tempting, and almost unmissable, target.

"Hell, no. You'll probably hit the camel, then we're really screwed. Just let him do his little dance and go home."

That's what this job had come down to. If you killed a man out in the desert, no one said much of anything—it was the natural order of things. Kill a camel, though, and you have to listen to the bureaucrats and the local tribesmen and their women wailing and whining until you ended up paying reparations to the very people trying to kill you. It might be tempting to teach the idiot a lesson by making him trudge home in the sand and heat, but it wasn't worth the aggravation or the paperwork.

Commandant Count Henri de Beaumont allowed himself a moment of nostalgia for the days when the Foreign Legion could do its job like men, instead of pansy shop clerks, then sighed and barked out, "The show's over. Let's get back".

His men were spoiling for a fight, and he heard them grumble as they climbed aboard the two vehicles. Complaining was one of the few rights Legionnaires were free to exercise, as long as it didn't reach the level of true insubordination. He was tired of these nuisance raids, too, but that's all they were, just a flea bite. Let them gripe.

His head hurt, and he laid it back against the seat in hope of catching a nap on the way back to the fort. The young driver, a skinny, almost toothless private named Lemonde, wasn't about to let that happen.

"Monsieur le Commandant, can I ask you something?"

"Of course. What is it?"

"Why stir up trouble now? Things have been pretty quiet for a while. Is it the Communists?"

Beaumont chuckled. The idea of King Akhamouk believing anyone the equal of a Tuareg, let alone sharing anything with others, was ludicrous. There was no danger of the Red Menace extending this far into the Sahara. "No. It was the Americans."

"What did they do?"

"Grave robbing, mostly. But they managed to piss off every tribe, Arab and inbred Pied-Noir between here and Algiers."

"So why are they shooting at us?"

"Who else?" Beaumont's shrug ended the conversation.

Lemonde slowed the car to twenty as they approached the village of Abalessa. Then he dropped to ten as he saw the herd of scrawny, scabby goats in the middle of the road. Hoping he wouldn't have to come to a complete halt before the goats got out of the way, he let out a long blast of the horn. The animals just stopped in their tracks and looked up, annoyed at the soldiers' impertinence.

Beaumont looked around him, bored. There was nothing special about this collection of dry brown huts and sullen dark faces. Like so many other villages in this part of Algeria, Abalessa was made up of share croppers; the descendants of slaves captured in blacker parts of Africa. Now they worked their own mostly useless land, paying a percentage to the Tuareg King and considerably less to the legal Algerian authorities. In many ways their status hadn't changed one iota, although everyone seemed happy enough to pretend the tribute was now simply a condition of employment, and not actually indentured servitude.

He sat up straighter as Lemonde ground the car to a stop. He could hear the rumbling engine of the troop transport behind them, but not much else. Usually at this time of day it was mostly women and children in the village. The men should have been out hunting or inside the huts drinking and smoking, rather than out in the sun. As a rule, the soldiers were greeted with mild interest when they passed through places like this. Today, though, Beaumont saw something too much like defiance in their eyes.

Two long, slow, baritone blasts on the horn failed to scatter the livestock. "Goddammit." Lemonde wrenched on the door handle and stepped out of the truck.

"Private, stop right there." Lemonde froze where he was, with one boot still on the running board.

The commandant winced as doors slammed behind him. The second truck was already emptying out. He slid over to the driver's side and leaned out the door to see half a dozen soldiers with rifles at the ready.

"Back in your vehicle. There's no problem," he shouted. The men, led by the fat Belgian sergeant, hesitated for the briefest moment, then reluctantly turned back to their truck. Looking back only a moment to ensure obedience, Beaumont glared at Lemonde. "Get your ass in here."

The soldier shot the goats and their owner one last dirty look. From behind the crowd, Beaumont thought he heard a faint shout.

Lemonde must have heard it too. As the young private looked behind him, his eyes suddenly darted upwards and a jagged stone bounced off the side of his head. He fell to his knees in the dust next to his blood-stained kepi.

Beaumont heard the screaming of women and the angry roars of soldiers erupt around him as he climbed down from the vehicle to check on Lemonde. The skinny soldier was already rising and dusting himself off, oblivious to the blood streaming down his temple.

"I'm okay, I think."

Beaumont nodded, but grabbed the young man by the chin and took inventory. Dust and sand mixed with blood in a muddy brown mess, but it wasn't gushing. Lemonde's eyes were as clear as they ever were, and he had as few teeth as he started with. He'd be okay.

The commandant turned his attention to the rest of his men. Five of them stood in a semi-circle, guns waving back and forth at the assembled villagers. He didn't see the sergeant, Baldewijns. Where was that fat, Flemish bastard?

"Monsieur le Commandant", came a shout from forty meters away, "I've got him."

The soldier stood next to a reed-thin boy of no more than twelve who thrashed like a fish on a line. The lad broke free for a moment, but the older soldier reached out with a his ham-sized hand and, not having a shirt to grab onto, wrapped his fist in the boy's black hair until there was a single yelp, and no more resistance.

Beaumont waved him over, then took a close look at the black faces surrounding him. Most showed surprise, a few appeared legitimately horrified. Only a handful of men actually looked angry and that was probably aimed as much at the little troublemaker as the Legionnaires. This wasn't an insurrection; it was just a kid playing big-shot. That was easier to deal with.

Huffing and sweaty, Sergeant Baldewijns brought the rock thrower to his commander. He curled his fist to tighten his grip on the young man's hair and pulled him to his knees. "Stay there, you little bastard."

The young African knelt in the dust, trying to lock eyes with Beaumont in a warrior's death stare, but his defiance was too mixed with fear to be convincing, and his gaze finally dropped to the ground in front of him. Something—tears or snot or both—made coin-sized wet patches in the sand.

"If you want to fight soldiers, you have to act like a man." Baldewijns swung the butt of his rifle into the back of the kid's head.

"Sergeant!" The fat soldier grudgingly stood to attention, offering a conciliatory salute.

From behind him, a woman wailed. Beaumont turned to see an emaciated figure, likely the mother, sobbing into the shoulder of another, older female. A tall, grey-haired man stood next to her with his arms crossed. He gave her a withering look that shut her up, then returned his gaze to the Legionnaire.

Beaumont addressed the crowd in French, knowing that only a handful of people would understand him, but hopeful the village chief was among that number. "You saw, he attacked us unprovoked. He has to come with us." He locked eyes with the older man. "Yes?"

The boy's mother began another round of wailing, eliciting sympathetic murmurs from the other women. The chief said nothing for a moment, and then gave a single, silent nod.

"Bring him with us," Beaumont told the Sergeant. Baldewijns gave an ugly sneering smile.

"Get up, scum." Taking the skinny youngster by the neck with his meaty hands he turned towards the troop truck. With a shove, he bounced the boy off the rear fender of the Commandant's car, then led him towards the half dozen or so grinning soldiers waiting there.

"Baldewijns, he can come with us in the car." The fat soldier hesitated only a disappointed moment before leading his charge back to the commandant. His eyes challenged the officer but he obeyed and took two steps back.

Beaumont opened the rear door and pointed. The lad hung his head, took a brief look back to his mother, and climbed inside without another word. The heavy door slammed behind him.

"Are you okay, Lemonde?"

The soldier nodded unconvincingly. Beaumont ordered him back to the truck with the others, and called for another driver. Then he climbed in his own side of the vehicle, his eyes continually scanning the crowd for more trouble, but gratefully saw nothing worth worrying about.

"Let's get out of here. But pull out slowly," he ordered the driver.

"Oui, Commandant."

As they pulled away, Beaumont stole a glance over at the sniffing, huddled youngster rocking silently in the back seat. On top of everything else, now he had to figure out what to do with this rock throwing brat that wouldn't make things worse.

Brooding silently most of the way back to the fort at In Salah, he thought about what a complete cockup this had become. Who could have known? The Americans seemed harmless enough, but in a few short weeks they'd left a trail of chaos and damage no sandstorm could match. The tribes were dangerously unruly again. Every week new creditors crawled out of the dunes demanding satisfaction. The regional authorities, always a boil on his ass, would be even whinier and more demanding, if that were even possible.

In his mind's eye, he saw the face of the expedition's leader. If he ever met the arrogant son of a bitch again, he'd wipe that smug grin right off his face. What was his name? It was the Count something or other. Then he remembered.

The bastard's name was de Prorok. Count Byron de Prorok.

Brooklyn, New York
January 18, 1926

Dearest Byron,

I actually mailed this letter the day before you left, in the hope that it will be waiting for you when you arrive in Cedar Rapids. That is, if the Pony Express is still running that far west. Ha Ha.

You've only left, and the girls and I miss you already. Please be safe, and come home to us in one piece. Seeing my folks is wonderful and all, but I think I'd go mad if I had to live in Brooklyn again and can't wait to be back in Paris with just our own petite famille. See, I am really learning French, no matter how much you nag me about it.

I know you'll be brilliant. You are so smart and you are so talented. You're too good for those Iowa bumpkins, but I know that you have to "break in the act" so that it's perfect. I guess it's like how Broadway plays open in Hartford or Buffalo before becoming smash hits. Those people will love you as much as I do. Watch out for those Professors' wives, I'm not there to protect you from them. Ha Ha.

Marie Terese is waving to her Papa, and little Alice is missing her big strong daddy, as am I. Come home to me soon, my darling. And dress warmly, I hear it gets really cold in the Midwest this time of year, even colder than New York, although I don't know how that's possible.

Lots of love and kisses,
Your adoring wife (how I love saying that)
Alice
P.S. Mother and Daddy say hello.

Chapter 1

Grinnell, Iowa
January 23, 1926

The lecture hadn't even started, and my cousin Bob and I were already in awe of Count de Prorok. After all, not everyone could use a grey chunk of rock to score some co-ed tail, but he was doing it. The girl— all dewy eyes and virginal goose bumps—hung on every word. So did we from the comfort of our hard wooden chairs on the end of the aisle.

"You see, even three thousand years ago, women knew that men were... susceptible to their charms. Quite at a disadvantage. Not much has changed." De Prorok gave her a boyish smile and leaned forward intimately. She leaned into him, a total goner. It was like Lillian Gish falling prey to some cad in the pictures.

With a smoothness born of practice, the Count offered her a vaguely rounded chunk of fossilized clay and she took it, her eyes asking permission first. He nodded paternally, perfect teeth gleaming. She cupped it in both sweaty hands as if it was the good holiday china, instead of some old piece of rock. The way she oohed and aahed you'd think it was the Crown Jewels or something.

I'm surprised Bob didn't pull out a steno pad and take notes. He was quite the ladies' man, if he did say so himself and frequently did, but he was in the presence of a master. "Geez, this guy's good," he said, emphasizing it with an elbow to my ribs when, as usual, my attention wandered.

Count Byron Khun de Prorok was something to behold. He was tall, as tall as me probably. Six feet at least, but lean where I was beefy, and... graceful I suppose. Not in a sissy way. He was more Douglas Fairbanks than Valentino, if you know what I mean. The pith helmet he wore certainly added to the whole look, as did the khaki jacket, complete with jodhpurs poofing out at the knees and gleaming black boots.

It wasn't what you'd call normal attire for a bitterly cold January night in the middle of Iowa, but that exotic look was why the auditorium was so crowded. Every respectable person within driving distance of Grinnell stewed in their heavy coats and sweaters waiting to see "the Discoverer of Ancient Carthage", the "Scourge of the Saharan Tuaregs," the "Finder of the Legendary Queen Tin Hinan", and he came exactly as advertised.

I was there because my aunt sent me to deliver a care package of cookies, clean laundry and, I suspect, money my uncle knew nothing about to Bob at school. I made the drive in their Ford from Cedar Rapids, was supposed to spend the night in Bob's dorm room, and come back the next morning with another bag full of dirty laundry. The lecture was a way to kill time—Grinnell's only movie theater was showing some programmer I'd already seen half a dozen times. The price of all that service was Bob had to host his poor idiot cousin for the night.

My original plan, before my Aunt decided to make me useful, was to see "That Royle Girl" at the Strand. At least that was a D. W. Griffith picture and had W.C. Fields in it. It was a serious movie, not really my thing, but it had to be better than some boring lecture at a college I wasn't even attending. Worse, I had to tag along with Bob. But, the alternative was going back to Milwaukee with my tail between my legs and without a job, so here I was. At least until my burns, and my feelings, healed.

A distinguished old guy in a blue suit came over and politely "harrumphed" in the Count's ear. Without taking his eyes off his prey, the younger man nodded politely, whispered something back and patted the old guy's back as if dismissing a servant. The older gent started a bucket brigade of waves and nods... he to the kid at the projector, the kid at the projector to the guy in the back who flicked the auditorium's lights off and on.

Showtime.

With great dignity, the old guy climbed the stairs to the stage and an expectant hush fell over the crowd. From the smile on his puss they obviously knew who he was, and he knew that they knew, and it made him very happy.

"That's President Main," Bob whispered out of the side of his mouth. "Real stick up his ass." Bob felt the need to sprinkle cuss words into his speech periodically so he didn't look like a snob to the poor relations like me. Since I assumed everyone with money had a stick of some size lodged somewhere— Bob and his folks included—I wasn't much surprised.

The old guy's voice was lighter than I expected, but he perched his glasses on his nose which made him look more president-like. "Good evening everyone. As you know, I'm the president of Grinnell College..." a smattering of applause was quickly doused with a benevolent, upheld palm and a satisfied smirk. "Thank you, but that's certainly not why you're here tonight. No, we are honored to be the first audience this year outside the Eastern Seaboard to host tonight's speaker."

A satisfied murmur rippled through the crowd. Iowa, especially Podunk towns like Grinnell didn't often host famous people, and when it did, it was usually in between stops at bigger, more important cities like Chicago and Des Moines. This was big doings indeed, and explained the size of the crowd on a snowy Thursday. They were going to get their money's worth this evening, and something good to rub in the noses of their snobbier friends in Ames and Dubuque.

"As you no doubt know, the Count is justly famous for his explorations throughout North Africa, especially his findings at Carthage. Well, he has led an expedition—a joint venture of the French Government and our colleagues at Beloit College..."

Bob and some of the other students let out a great "Boo" at the mention of the rival school. Main shot a withering look down at us, which made my cheeks burn and Bob beam with pride. "Save that for the playing field, this is a great honor for us here at Grinnell. I should think you want to show we're worthy of it."

While I tried to figure out what the big deal was, the speaker scanned his notes to take another run at it. "...Ah, yes...at Beloit College. You may have read his exploits in uncovering one of the greatest archaeological sites ever found in the heart of the Sahara Desert. It was covered by the New York Times." That got another ooh from the percentage of the audience who'd at least heard of the New York Times, even if they'd never actually read it.

"He's brought actual filmed footage with him tonight." The president made a grand sweeping gesture, pointing to the heavy black film projector and the smaller magic lantern atop a small table at the front of the stage. I craned my neck to see. It was old equipment—a hand cranked Campbell instead of an electric one, but reliable enough. There was also a new electric Victor magic lantern. The stacks of film reels and boxes of slides told me we were in for a long night.

"And so, without further ado, it is my honor to welcome to Grinnell, and indeed to all of Central Iowa, that world traveler and distinguished archaeologist, Count Byron Khun de Prorok."

The bandage on my right hand made applause difficult, so I sat back with my arms crossed. I watched the Count give his walking stick a slight toss in the air then he strode forward, caught it with a flourish and a quick baton twirl, and glided onto the platform. His eyes shone almost as brightly as his teeth.

"Good evening, everyone, I'm truly humbled at the greeting you've afforded me. It proves I was right. I said to myself, 'Byron, you've just returned from the heat and dangers of the Sahara. You've been feted in Paris and New York... what's next?' Then it occurred to me... Grinnell... Iowa." The crowd laughed good-naturedly. "In January," he added to wild applause. How lucky these yokels were he'd graced them with his presence. Not that they didn't deserve it, of course, they were every bit as good as city folks. Still, it was really white of him to come, and they let him know it.

His voice boomed out of his skinny frame, louder than I expected. It didn't just get to the back of the hall, it reached out and grabbed the people in the cheap seats by their ears. He had an accent, but a slight one that I can only describe as vaguely European, but not from anywhere specific. It sure wasn't from here, and it wasn't so foreign you had to work at deciphering it. It was a strong voice, deep and resonant, and it held the crowd of upscale bumpkins spellbound.

"I'd especially like to thank the lovely Miss Thompson for her hospitality in showing me around this institution today. A most charming young lady…" A gangly, bucktoothed girl leaned over and whispered in the co-ed's ear, and they dissolved into giggles. The speaker paid them no mind and moved to the center of the stage.

"But we're here tonight to talk about another young woman—a legendary queen some thought to be mere myth. Was Tin Hinan just a figment of overactive, superstitious, primitive imaginations? You'll learn the answer tonight."

He went on about his trip, and most of it I didn't get. It was the first trip on pneumatic tires, which mattered to somebody for some reason, and involved some tribe called the "Toregs," or "Tuaregs," or something like that who were murderous, sword-wielding tribesmen, and treasure. That made me sit up straighter. Jewels, gold, swords… maybe this would be better than the pictures, or at least not as bad as I feared.

"Yes, my friends," he continued, "This is the story of what the New York Times dubbed the 'Prorok Expedition', although officially it was the 'Franco-American Sahara Expedition of 1925'. Mine was only the honor of leading the team. Maestro, if you please…" He grandly gestured to a redheaded college boy in an argyle sweater who squatted beside the magic lantern. There was a loud click, and a slide filled the screen.

It was a picture of the expedition in front of their three trucks. At least I think that's what it was. It was hard to tell because it was upside down.

The audience laughed nervously. The Count launched a lightning bolt out of his eyes at College Boy, then popped off a quick, "As you can see, we really stood on our heads to make this trip a success."

While the crowd clapped appreciatively, the speaker hissed at the assistant, who was now redder than ever. "The slide is upside down... fix it," as if the poor kid was too thick to recognize the fact. He muttered an apology and fumbled around; trying to pull the offending picture out of the hot frame and burning his fingers in the process.

I've been there myself often enough. Those magic lanterns, especially the new electric ones, burned awfully hot. It was easy to burn yourself, and if you didn't turn them off periodically the bulbs would flare out in a hurry. This one wasn't going to last the night. I felt bad for the kid and squirmed a bit on his behalf.

At last we heard the reassuring metal click of the carriage return and another picture loomed over the audience. It was the kind of snapshot you've seen a hundred times in newspapers or newsreels: a bunch of guys trying to show how important they are, and only succeeding in looking uncomfortable.

The Count was dead center, of course; dressed for the desert heat with his pith helmet at a jaunty angle. You wouldn't get any points for guessing who the Americans were. A tall, good looking older gent sucked on a pipe, and next to him was a much shorter guy who looked far less comfortable with the proceedings. The Frogs were represented by a short, ferret-faced joker with a thin moustache and a military uniform covered in ribbons and medals. On either side were some really unhappy specimens; two guys in native getup, two in matching mechanic's outfits, and an arm, shoulder and right cheek that belonged to someone cut off by the frame.

"This picture is in Constantine, Algeria in October of last year. This very important gentleman with the medals is Monsieur Maurice Reygasse, the director of the Bibliothèque National d'Algiers, who represented the French government. As you can see, he was a decorated hero of 'La Guerre Mondiale'." He effortlessly bounced between English and French, at least seamlessly enough to knock the socks off anyone in Grinnell. French sounded a whole lot classier than the languages usually heard in the Midwest—German, Swedish, various Slavic grunts and the odd, usually extremely odd, Italian, not to mention the Scots and Irish who allegedly spoke English but you couldn't make out what they said half the time.

He droned on. "The two Americans came courtesy of the Logan Museum at Beloit College. Representing the Logan was Mr. Bradly Tyrrell, and the shorter gent was Alonzo Pond, although everyone called him Lonnie. Like all graduate students, he proved invaluable doing the mundane research that is so often the lot of young men in college. Not that you'd know anything about that." The student body chuckled knowingly. You had to hand it to him—this guy knew his audience.

"We had at our disposal three brand new vehicles, straight from the Renault factory in Paris. These were built especially for the brutal conditions we'd encounter in the Sahara. They had twelve pneumatic tires, and each vehicle its own factory-trained driver. Let me show you our modern age chariots…" He nodded to College Boy, who clicked another slide into place that showed the heroic team driving off. It would have looked like that, at least, if we were hanging from the rafters. It, too, was upside down.

A groan rose from the crowd, and even Bob mustered up a "Poor son-of-a-bitch".

"It's easy to d-d-do. They have to b-b-be upside down and backwards or they don't show right." Damn. My stutter was in rare form tonight.

"Really? That seems ass-backwards," Bob replied. I shrugged. It had to do with mirrors and reflections and stuff, but I couldn't really explain it worth a damn, I just knew it. Like I knew it wasn't the kid's fault since he was just clicking the buttons. Whoever loaded the slides after the last show put them in wrong. It was a bad deal for the poor idiot who had to show them this time, and College Boy wasn't dealing well with the pressure, and looked like he might explode any minute.

The Count soldiered on, though. "Believe it or not, the tires were in contact with the ground the whole time. Perhaps the first of our moving pictures will give you a better idea." He locked eyes with the flustered assistant, and jerked his head to the film projector.

"Join me as we set off on our journey into the deepest Sahara." Like I feared he would, the assistant cranked the handle much too hard and the first few frames ran through too quickly. Everyone looked like they were running around with their heads on fire.

Before getting struck by another lightning bolt from the stage, he rewound it and ran the film again, slower. Those hand-cranked projectors are the devil's own time, but once you have the rhythm it's not so bad. It just takes practice, and it was obvious Red didn't have much of that.

Onscreen, a gang of folks, some native others—obviously local muckamucks—gathered around the trucks. I recognized the Count, smiling and waving. An older man shook his hand then a woman, obviously Madame Big Shot, kissed the Count on each cheek. He gallantly kissed her hand, just like in the movies, pleasing her no end and really ticking off the old guy.

In the background, the natives did what natives always do on film; they jumped around, cheered the white men and fired their guns in the air. The trucks rolled off-screen amid puffs of white smoke. Then the screen burst into bright, blinding white as the film broke and College Boy was left turning the crank uselessly.

I was already out of the seat before Bob could moan, "Oh come on". It was none of my business, but it was going to be a long night if someone who knew what they were doing didn't step in. Plus I felt bad for the poor sucker. I heard Bob ask, "Willy, where you going?" but I was already on my way.

The Count continued speaking as I crouched next to the projection table. The redhead's panicky eyes silently asked who the hell I was and what I was doing there. "Relax. I'm just going to help. You have to keep the tension even on the film, or it'll b-b-b-unch up and b-break on you." I may as well have spoken Swahili from the blank stare I got.

"Get the next one loaded and I'll show you."

"Can you do it for me?" This guy was a pip. I just held up my bandaged right hand in response.

"Right, okay," he said. He took the old reel off and set it on the table next to the empty canister. This guy was completely Amateur Night. I snatched the reel with my left hand and must have been a little noisy, because the Count shot us a dirty look from the stage, and I heard a distinct "Shush" from behind us. My cheeks burned red. Jeez, I was just trying to help.

You always put the old reel in the tin right away, otherwise it can unspool on you. At best you'll have to go back and do it all later, and there was no way to do that with these reels unmarked. How the heck were you supposed to know what went where? This setup was totally bush league.

The Voice of God commanded another movie and my apprentice cranked the wheel like he was starting a car—sure to snap it again. I pushed him out of the way and, without thinking, grabbed it with my injured right hand. The burns had healed enough it didn't hurt too badly. Good thing it didn't take too much force to crank one of those old machines, just the right touch.

I hissed at him. "Keep the rhythm smooth, so the tension's tight. What's next?" He squinted at the sheet of foolscap in front of him.

"More slides," he said as if it was a death sentence.

"Start flipping them over. They have to go in upside d-d-d-own. Whoever did this last didn't do it."

"It wasn't me..." Jesus, this guy.

"Doesn't m-m-matter. It'll be you who gets his ass chewed out. I'll handle the projector, you just get the lantern right."

He set to work with agonizing slowness, flipping over each slide and putting it back in the carriage. He only had a couple done when the film I was showing ended with the flip-flip-flip of the film. The Count droned on, but I paid him no attention. Fortunately, he didn't seem to notice me either.

Even with one good paw, it wasn't much of a chore to flip the release, pull off the reel, drop it in the can, and grab the next one so it was ready to go. Old Man Mayer would be none too happy with the timing, but it was good enough for this glorified tent show. Plus, I was doing it one-handed, and my left at that. It wasn't too shabby, if I really thought about it.

"And now, we find ourselves on the rim of the civilized world. Imagine being at the edge of a sea made entirely of sand, with not a tree, rock or landmark for miles. This was the fearsome Sahara, our home for the next five weeks." A purposeful stare and a rap of his walking stick said this was Red's cue.

We held our breath until the picture appeared right side up and an ironic "hooray" arose from the college pukes. The kid beside me let out a shaky sigh of relief while I settled to my knees on the other side of the table. I was there for the evening, apparently. Being a big guy for nineteen, I was plenty used to people whining, "down in front". It wasn't my fault or anything, but I always felt bad when I blocked someone's view.

My father told me often enough I was good for nothing, but it wasn't completely true; I knew how to do this. As the Count's stick went "rap rap rap" on the wooden stage, my hand went round and round. In the background, I heard people whispering excitedly, just like at the Odeon back home. And just like when the pictures ran, I was so busy tending to the job I didn't see or hear much. I just cranked away, mindful of the speed people crossed the screen to make sure it was as natural as possible, but not much caring what they were doing up there.

"Hey, pssst, hey." My assistant was so wrapped up in the lecture I had to push him to get his attention. "Get two spare bulbs ready."

"Why? These are fine." Yes they were, but who knew for how long. It was a sure thing they'd burn out at the worst possible time. He meekly slipped away and came back with the bulbs, handing them over. I placed them between the projectors within easy reach.

"Thanks." I nodded to the box of slides. "Those done?" He gave me the "oops" face and went back to work. Then he stopped again and held his hand out.

"I'm Reggie." The pest was persistent, you had to give him that.

"Willy." Maybe that would shut him up. There was a show on, and a good projectionist never put himself above the show. The audience hated that, and it was more than your job was worth to have them complain. I could hear Meyer's voice, "vat if dey never come back?"

Somehow we made it through the next hour. Like I knew it would, the bulb went out in the Campbell first with a loud "pop" and a small cloud of smoke. With all that practice under my belt, I got it done before anyone could even yell "lights." It wasn't that tough if you knew what you were doing. The problem was most people, like Reggie the College Boy, didn't have clue one.

It also helped if you didn't mind getting the tips of your fingers scorched a bit. The bulbs were less dangerous than the commercial projectors in the movie houses, but being smaller, they burned out more often and took a finer touch to replace. Especially left handed.

I have no idea what the Count talked about that night. I was too busy watching the sheet for cues and nudging Reggie to pay attention, sometimes a little too forcefully, but hey it was his job, not mine. He should be paying attention.

It was easy to get caught up, though. I learned that the hard way my first few days working at the Odeon back home. At first, I'd be so busy watching Fairbanks, or Garbo, or Theda Bara, or pretty much any of the comics, that I'd start cranking too fast or miss a reel change. Then I learned to block it all out. In fact, someone would ask me what a picture was like, and I couldn't really tell them despite having shown it four times that day. Sometimes I'd stay late, just so I could actually watch the darned thing.

I paid just enough attention to hit my cues. That certainly wasn't the case with the rest of the audience. When I could look around, I saw Bob on the edge of his seat, uncynically hanging on every word. The Lovely Miss Thompson was in raptures by the door, and as were the rest of Grinnell's hoi polloi. They held their breath before releasing it in gasps, or chuckles, or whatever other response the speaker demanded of them. My experience with college lectures was exactly zero, but I could tell this guy knew his stuff.

"And in conclusion…" That snapped me back, because the first rule of surviving any speech is to hear when it's about to end. That way you're not caught napping, and if you have to, you have at least one thing you can repeat if really pressed.

A dramatic final meeting of the cane and stage floor sent Reggie into spasmic action. The last slide appeared, upside right and focused. It was a headline from the New York Times, 6th December, 1925: "De Prorok Expedition Arrives in Paris, Treasure in Tow."

With just the right balance of humility and bragging, the Count finished up. "Our mission ended in Paris, with Queen Tin Hinan and her treasure ready to return home to the Sands of Africa, and yours truly headed home to America to share this adventure with you fine people, and prepare for our next adventure, wherever it leads us."

He nodded to the schmo in the back who darkened the stage just long enough for the audience to erupt into applause and leap to their feet. To be fair, some leapt, most kind of creaked to their feet after sitting for an hour and a half on hard wooden chairs in heavy winter coats and sweaters.

The house lights came up, and the Count stood there for ten seconds. I know it was ten because I caught him counting, his lips barely moving before he raised that voice again. "Ladies and Gentlemen, if you'd like to take the opportunity to take a look at some of these relics up close, please approach the stage in an orderly fashion, and you may examine them for yourselves. Step right up please."

"Oh, crap. I have to take care of those exhibits," Reggie squeaked and off he went. I saw Bob over to the side, holding our coats and tapping his foot. Probably had some frat boy party I was keeping him from attending.

I stood up, letting the blood flow back into my legs when I felt, more than heard, someone beside me. "Young man, thank you very much." I looked up and there was the Count himself, for Pete's sake.

He was sweating profusely and his makeup—Christ, he was wearing makeup—was streaked and puddled along the back of his collar and his eyes were all raccoon-looking. Even though he called me "young man," he couldn't have been much over thirty. He had the voice and confidence of an Old Testament prophet, but wasn't actually much older than I am. Maybe ten years on me at most.

He smiled a rich guy's smile at me, the kind of smile I imagine you'd give the servants when they don't really have a choice but are being benevolent. He stuck his hand out. "Byron de Prorok. Nice to meet you."

"Willy. Uh, sir." Of course, it was really Wilhelm, but only my father still called me that, so Willy it was. I turned to leave, but he wasn't going to let me off that easily.

"Willy?" the Count asked. "Just Willy?"

Oh, shit. Here it was. Willy B-b-b-braun." My own name once again betraying me. Without thinking, I stuck my bandaged right hand into his.

"Brown?" he asked and I nodded. Technically speaking, it was Braun. It was spelled German, but I always pronounced it American.

"Well, Willy Brown, you saved me tonight. Thank

you." He gave my hand a quick squeeze, then pulled back suddenly, and let out a braying laugh. "God, even one handed you were more help than that other idiot. You really saved me tonight; I'm in your debt."

My hand throbbed a bit, but not too badly as I pulled it back. A stupid shrug was all the eloquence I could muster. "It was nothing."

"It was hardly nothing. I hate those blasted things. I'd do without them if I could, but of course the audience loves the movies and the pictures." With a wink, he slipped me a bill. My eyes nearly popped out of my head when I saw it was a fiver.

"That's too m-m-m-uch. Really. I didn't do anything..."

"Jeez Willy, Don't be an idiot." Bob, tired of waiting, had snuck up on me. De Prorok grinned.

"That seems to be the majority opinion, so you're outvoted. Take it. Are you a student here?"

I was trying to figure out a polite reply to such a silly question, when Bob jumped in. "Nah, he's visiting from Wisconsin. He's my cousin. I'm Bob." He stuck his hand out. "Bob Muller." He deliberately pronounced it Muller, like mulling something over. Not a hint of an umlaut or the Old Country on that side of the family. "I'm a student here. He's just visiting for the night."

"A lucky man. What are you studying, Bob?"

"Business. I don't usually go for all this history jazz. Not much percentage in it, you know?"

The Count smiled. "Indeed I do. Very practical of you."

Bob took the compliment at face value. There were a lot of differences between Bob and I, and the ability to shut up was at the top of a long list. He just kept yakking. "Of course, what you do makes it interesting. I wish you were my professor."

"Oh no you don't, believe me." With a laugh de Prorok turned his back dismissively. "Mr. Brown, could you help me pack all this up? I suspect we've seen the last of your predecessor for today."

Bob was neither getting paid nor paid attention to, and was getting antsy like he always did when ignored. "Come on Willy. We have to get out of here."

"You go. I'll catch up as soon as I'm done."

"You know I'm not supposed to leave you alone." And there it was. His was the burden of babysitting the poor, lunk-headed, stuttering cousin from Milwaukee. He didn't want the responsibility, but I had to hand it to him, he took his duty seriously. He was probably more worried about the guff he'd take from his mother if he didn't, but he looked out for me in his own way.

"N-n-nah. Go ahead. I'll just go back to your room when I'm done." His relieved sigh told me he and his frat buddy friends had plans that would be better implemented without me dragging them down.

While I refused the Count's money, I really needed it, and a little honest work might make me feel better. The reason I was in Iowa in the first place was to find a job. Old Man Meyer felt bad after what happened to my hand, and suggested several theaters in Cedar Rapids that were looking for projectionists, or were before I blew into town. Now they were all hired up, and I was left sleeping on the Muller's davenport and cramping Bob's style.

Mostly, it had been an excuse to get away from my father and Milwaukee, in that order. A full time job out of town would help me escape both. Aunt Gertie professed love for her sister's only boy, but didn't want me here a moment longer than absolutely necessary. She loved that poor abused sofa more than her Milwaukee relatives. As for Uncle Thomas, well I was just one more of many indignities heaped on him when he married beneath his station. The sooner I either got employment or left, the better, and he didn't much have a preference. Truthfully, neither did I, except failure meant going home. The sofa, and even the floor of Bob's dorm room, were better than that.

The Count worked the crowd like a reception line. There was a long line of sincere well-wishers and plain old sycophants. Mr. So-and-so from the Chamber of Commerce, and Mrs. Whosits from the Ladies Auxiliary and dozens of others lined up for their chance to touch someone who'd touched the exotic. That was really as close as any of them really wanted to come. The problem with those strange places and people in the news reels is they were so unlike America, and who really wants that? It probably sounded more interesting than it really was. It was especially interesting when the news was delivered by someone as downright fascinating as a Count.

Ignoring everything around me, I set to work starting with the last reel on the projector, gently cranking it backward.

"What are you doing?" The Count looked at me, puzzled. It should have been obvious. You always rewound the reel before putting it in the can. That way you know it was packed right, and it's ready to go for next time. Everyone knows that. I figured there was a trick question in there, so I must have sounded like a jerk.

"Rewinding it? So it's ready to go next time?"

The count was mildly confused. "Without threading it?"

"Well, yeah. If you thread it and run it backwards you'll damage the print, and it'll break sooner. Plus you can make sure it's wound tight."

"Well, naturally. Of course. It's just so rare to find

someone who knows his stuff." Jeez, this guy had no clue, did he? And no extra points for guessing who loaded the slides for the lantern either. For someone so smart, he sure was a dummy about his tools. Did he think this stuff just happened by magic?

I overheard some of the conversation while I worked, but didn't really pay much attention. People cooed over the objects he handed them, but they seemed like a poor excuse for treasure. That clay jar he claimed was a two thousand years old makeup kit could have been made in shop class, for all they knew. One fat guy in a brown hat asked about treasure, and was disappointed to learn that the arrowheads were as good as it got. He seemed disappointed. So was I, to be honest.

As usual when I worked, I didn't notice how much time had passed until I realized that the hall was echoingly empty. A janitor whistled through his teeth, shoving a wide broom along the floor. The disappointed treasure seeker in the brown hat sat in the last row, flipping through a notebook, oblivious to anything or anyone else.

De Prorok leaned against the wall, sucking noisily on a long-stemmed pipe. Clouds of blue smoke swirled in the light as he examined me, the way I suspect he looked at Arabs or some exotic tribesman; like I was another species altogether and he was taking notes.

Damned if I'd let him stare at me like that, I made myself look into his eyes. What the hell did he want from me? Finally, taking the pipe from his mouth, he pointed the stem at me. "Are you looking for work, Brown?"

Of course I was looking for work. I sure hadn't come to Iowa in January for the climate. "M-m-maybe. What did you have in mind?" I hoped I sounded more casual than I felt.

"Well, I have a number of lectures here in the Middle West before I return to New York, then home to Paris. I'd rather not have to rely on the tender mercies of the host to get me more help like I got tonight. I could use a good man to run the technical side of things. It would only be three weeks, to start at least. We'll see what happens after that."

My head spun as he laid out the plan. The good news is he had more engagements this week; Des Moines, Ames and Moline. Then there were two weeks he would be back East, but then Milwaukee, Beloit, Madison, probably Chicago. I might even get to see St. Louis if I was lucky.

The rational side of me tried to get a grip. "I really need something full t-t-time."

"It's only three weeks, true. But you won't have to stay with Cousin Bub and your Auntie. It might even be fun if your..." he gestured to my bandages.

I shook my head. "Almost healed, just a little b-b-burnt, but it's healing." He nodded in approval, then paused. Obviously he was waiting for me to say something. Then I figured out what it was.

"What's it pay?" I hoped I sounded grown up and responsible, rather than flustered and panicky.

"Let's say twelve a week." I hoped he couldn't hear my heart pounding. That was more than I'd made working full-time for Meyer, and almost what projectionists in the big cities pulled in. True, there were two weeks in between, and I'd probably have to go home, since once I was out of the Muller's house they'd probably change the locks, but I could do two weeks if I kept my nose clean and my head down.

I took a deep breath to calm myself, which I guess he took as a brilliant negotiating ploy, because he quickly added, "alright, fifteen dollars. But you pay for your own meals."

Fifteen smackers would buy a lot of ham sandwiches, which was mostly what I'd been subsisting on. Hell, put cheese on the darned things. I was rich.

I noticed the guy in the beat up brown hat leaning forward. I don't think he was intentionally listening, but de Prorok spoke every sentence like he was on stage. I don't think he ever learned to whisper. When he realized I'd seen him, the eavesdropper crammed his notebook into a coat pocket, wrapped the scarf around his face and headed out of the auditorium, kicking over a chair in the process.

"Right then. Finish packing up and meet me at the Montrose in Cedar Rapids at nine AM tomorrow. No, wait. This bloody mixer thing is going to go on a while, and they have real liquor. Make it ten. You know the Montrose?"

Of course I knew the Montrose. Everyone in Cedar Rapids knew the Montrose Hotel. I'd never been inside, of course, because that was for the Swells—or as swell as they came in that burg, but I knew where it was. I rode by it on the street car every day looking for work.

"Yes sir."

"Good. We'll talk then. Be prepared to be gone a week. Give my love to Auntie." With a flourish, he plunked his sweat stained and pancake make-upped pith helmet on his head, spun on his heel and strode off to face the savages at the Grinnell College Faculty Mixer.

Just like that. Big, dopey, Willy Braun from Milwaukee was working for Count Byron Khun de Prorok.

Chapter 2

Constantine, Algeria
October 12, 1925

Madame Rouvier lifted the champagne bottle over her head, almost bursting out of her tight dress, and wished them all well. "And God bless your journey and grant you safe return." Then she swung it down, and the bottle bounced unharmed off the hood of the truck. Mortified, she tried again, this time striking the corner above the headlights, and the bottle exploded in a shower of white bubbles all over the bonnet of the lead truck and her official occasion dress to the cheers of the crowd.

Byron kept a smile frozen on his face as Monsieur Rouvier, the highest French official in all of North East Algeria, plucked a green shard off his wife's considerable décolletage and carelessly flicked it way into the sand, oblivious to all the bare feet around him.

"Monsieur le Governeur, thank you once again." De Prorok offered his hand once more, and Rouvier shook it with no more enthusiasm than he had the last two times. The older man said something, but Byron didn't hear it. He was looking over the speaker's shoulder at the cameraman, Henri Barth.

The pudgy Swiss photographer shook his head and gestured wildly, making half-circles in the air. Byron nodded and took Rouvier by the elbow, turning him towards the camera and face first into the hazy African sun. Rouvier squinted, scrunching his face into an even less attractive blob than normal and endured another hearty handshake until they heard Barth yell, "Good. Great!"

The Count immediately dropped his hand, wiped his palm on the leg of his pants and turned towards Madame. Sliding next to her, he placed a long fingered hand on her hip and deftly navigated her towards the cameraman. Barth immediately cranked away as Byron whispered, "Adieu, Madame. I will be back sooner than you know." Then he took her fingertips and raised them to his lips giving them a brief kiss that seemed both formal and intimate at the same time.

He hoped Barth caught the tears gleaming in her eyes. It would look perfect on camera and the audiences would lap it up. Americans generally believed colonials to be degenerates, the French constantly in heat, and French Colonials the worst of the bunch. Mme Rouvier, that sausage casing of a dress, and her impressive breasts would be immortalized—fairly or not—as another of the Count's amorous conquests for the amusement of the crowds in dreadful places like Binghamton and Omaha.

He felt a fleeting twinge of guilt about Alice and the two babies but this was business, and it wasn't like anything had actually happened, despite the lady's best efforts. The flirting, toasts, pictures and all this hullabaloo were all a cost of doing business in Algeria. He wondered if in this case the cost wasn't too high, but desperate times called for desperate measures. He was doing all this for the girls, after all, and he did get those last minute permits. Alice was a realist about such things. Plus, she was in Paris.

Three brand new olive-green Renault vehicles

shone in the sun. The cars, each with three rows of seats, three double rows of tires and removable doors with canvas covers, idled in the road in front of the Hotel Cirta. The first, nicknamed Sandy, was reserved for the Count and the press contingent; Hal Denny of the Times and Henri Barth, the photographer, along with their driver, Escande.

The second car, Hot Dog, was the domain of Marshall Maurice Reygasse, as official representative of the local authorities, their guide, Louis Chapuis, and Belaid the translator. Everyone called Belaid "Caid", which was actually a title meaning Chief, but whether that was a real or self-selected title no one really knew for sure. A petulant Renault man named Chaix piloted that vehicle.

Bringing up the rear was Lucky Strike. It contained the two Americans, most of the equipment, and a little Italian driver named Martini. One of the passengers, Bradley Tyrrell blew "Oh Suzanna" softly on his harmonica. The other was not so sanguine.

"Come on, we should have been out of here an hour ago. Is he still flirting with that lady?" Alonzo Pond spent most of the last hour cursing the heat, his life, and the Count in rotating order, and was ready to move on. The October rains had been plentiful this year. It was great for the crops, of course, and welcome after two years of drought, but not so good for the humidity. He was used to the Midwestern stickiness of Wisconsin summers, but this was a whole new level of dank Hades.

"Relax, Lonnie. The Sahara's been here a while. It's not going anywhere. Besides, he's doing business."

"You call that business?"

The older man smiled. "There's always a price to be paid for doing business, son. Here they call it baksheesh, in Chicago it's called doing someone a favor. The price he's paying with Madame over there might be the steepest of all. Higher than I'd want to pay, anyway." He gave a single blast on his Hohner.

Pond didn't feel much pity for the Count and didn't push the matter. Instead he turned to the driver and asked in reasonably good French, "Martini, you're sure we have enough fuel?"

"Oui. Yes, of course. We make sure before we go. The Count sees to everything."

Pond sniffed, hardly reassured. He leaned back and closed his eyes. One thing he learned in the War, enjoy the calm while you can. Alonzo had been in the ambulance corps, and studied briefly at the Sorbonne. He *"parle français"* well enough that, along with Martini's deeply Italian-accented French they could converse, with Pond translating for the unilingual American, Tyrrell. It made for good company at least.

"Who does this guy think he is?" Pond asked, not for the first time.

"The Boss," was Tyrrell's explanation. "Every project needs one, and better him than us. Trust me, it's not as glamorous as you think."

Pond wasn't sure he believed that. "What's he bringing to the party, anyway? I'm more qualified, you've run million dollar businesses, the Museum is paying most of the freight and the Algerians and the French are paying the rest of it. What exactly does he do?"

"He brings attention. You think the New York Times cares about Beloit College? Would Renault donate three trucks and drivers for free if this was just another dig?"

"These trucks are more like overgrown cars. And they look ridiculous." He knew he was being petty, but couldn't help himself. The trucks meant press coverage for the College, and room for lots more arrowheads and flint tools than he'd be able to strap to the back of some stupid humpbacks. It just all seemed a bit… disappointing.

Pond had spent the last six months fantasizing a long, slow, camel trek through harsh conditions to undiscovered Stone Age sites, risking sandstorms and death by scimitar along the way. Instead he got brand new trucks, hotels for the first and last legs of the journey and less than a month of real field work. On top of all that, he had to put up with de Prorok's shenanigans.

Maybe, he thought, the real age of exploration was over and done. Camels were being replaced with cars and pneumatic tires. Proud warrior tribes were fast becoming tame subjects of anthropological studies, as if the depths of the Sahara were no more mysterious than a day trip to the Wisconsin Dells. Still, it beat Beloit and another semester in the classroom.

The tribes were still a little bit of a concern, as evidenced by the machine gun bracket mounted to the roof frame. Between Algerian malcontents and Tuareg tribes that had bent the knee in name only, it was better to have it and not need it than the other way around. Algeria was no picnic at the best of times, and even with more rain and the best crop in years, this was far from the best of times. Maybe Brad was right, he thought. Leave everything to the Count and just do your job. If, of course, they ever left town.

Finally, the last hand was kissed or shaken, and the final palm greased. The Count turned to the assembly and raised his pith helmet in salute. "Adieu, adieus— allons nous en," which was the cue for several burnoose-clad locals to fire their muskets in the air to the cheers of the restless crowd.

Byron couldn't fully hide his satisfaction as Madame Rouvier waved her handkerchief and bravely fought back tears. He strode to Sandy's passenger side, flung open the door, gave the crowd a final exultant flourish with his helmet, and the Franco-American Sahara Expedition of 1925 was well and truly away, heading towards the Sahara on the last paved road they'd see for a while.

At the edge of town was the Sidi Rached Bridge, a marvel of engineering in a place where camel dung bricks were considered quality construction material. It ran 330 feet high over the Gorge du Rhumel in a graceful swoop over multiple Romanesque arches. It was the first sign of civilization desert visitors saw when arriving in Constantine, and the last thing they saw—perhaps forever—as they headed into the barren wastes of the Sahara desert. Pond admitted it was a dramatic departure point, and must have made quite a picture. Before he could really enjoy it, though, the cars coasted to a halt at the very end of the bridge.

"Now what?" he groaned. Tyrrell just shrugged and the two men craned their necks out the windows to see Barth and two porters shooing a donkey loaded with camera equipment while the photographer held his hat on his head with one hand. Apparently, Count de Prorok also thought of what a dramatic sight it would make and had arranged for the whole vista to be filmed in all its glory. Now they had to wait for him to catch up.

The three cars and their inhabitants simmered in the heat at the end of the bridge, blocking traffic and enduring the honks and curses of those trying to enter the city. Finally, after ten minutes of agony, equipment and photographer were unceremoniously stowed in the back of the lead car, and they were truly, finally, off to their first destination. Next stop would be a little oasis called Batna.

The cars were unevenly loaded—most of the gas

and water had been strapped to the Marshall's car, Hot Dog. Lucky Strike carried the Americans, food, water and barrels for the archaeological samples, along with the machine gun. Sandy, the lead car, contained the Count's precious film equipment and not much else, so it was no surprise to Pond that they were becoming separated from each other. The lighter cars were able to travel a rather impressive thirty-five miles per hour, as opposed to their vehicle that chugged along at only twenty-five or so.

Going slower at least allowed for more sightseeing. They passed through a few small hamlets. One even had a small gas station, which they passed. It was only a short run and, as Martini said, the Count had made all the arrangements.

Nine miles from Batna, Lucky Strike caught up with Reygasse's car, Hot Dog. It sat at the side of the road, with a very perturbed looking driver kicking at the door and exhibiting a rather impressive vocabulary of French curses. A stoic Marshall Reygasse sat upright in the car, staring straight ahead. Louis Chapuis and Belaid squatted in the dirt in the shade of the vehicle.

"Chaix, que c'est que passe?" Martini asked as he stepped from the car.

"Manque d'essence." Pond winced, recognizing the phrase from his own days as an ambulance driver. Hot Dog had run out of gas. He grinned as he saw the frustrated driver kicking the front bumper as if that would solve the problem.

Louis Chapuis strode over to the car. "The Count and the others went on ahead to Batna and they're sending back some gas. Chaix, there, wouldn't leave his precious truck so we stayed with him. Renault probably wouldn't like anything to happen to it."

Pond agreed. "Well, hop in, no sense all of you

sitting around."

"I'll stay with Chaix. Algeria is no place to be alone," the guide offered.

Reygasse and Belaid, though, were happy to accept a ride, crowded though it was. It was unpleasantly warm and sticky before the extra bodies were added. Now it was downright fragrant. With the windows open, though, nine miles wasn't such a long haul. Off they went, Brad Tyrrell playing his harmonica to lighten the mood.

They were almost to Batna when Pond heard Martini muttering to himself, "Non… non… God damned stupid machine…" and he slammed his fist on the steering wheel.

Pond heard the engine utter a sad "chucka-chucka-pawwwww" and Lucky Strike coasted to a stop. Everyone sat quietly for a moment. Finally he couldn't take the suspense. "What's wrong?"

"Manque d'essence," offered the stoic driver, who got out and lifted the truck's bonnet to ensure that's all it was. He dropped it with an echoing "thunk". "Si, that's all it is. We're out of gas too."

Brad Tyrrell pulled his pipe out of his pocket and tamped down some of the good American tobacco he always carried. "How far is it into Batna?"

Belaid knitted his eyebrows. "Not far. Two, maybe three kilometers." When he saw the puzzled look the American gave him, he added, "A mile, mile and a bit."

Tyrrell remained upbeat. "Well, that's easy then. Lonnie, Come on, we're hoofing it. Martini, you stay here and we'll send some gas back for you. Marshall, are you joining us?"

Reygasse's cool had deserted him. He impatiently waved them away. "I'll wait. I'm not entering Batna like some god-damned beggar."

The big American gave a suit-yourself shrug. "Lonnie, you coming?"

Pond grabbed his knapsack and shouldered it in resignation. Offering a passable impression of Martini, he groused, "Monsieur le count say everything is good... The Count see to everything." Brad patted his shoulder paternally.

"Explorer's lesson number one. Never trust those city experts for anything, and don't take anything for granted. Let's go."

"What's that?" Alonzo pointed to an ancient heap of a car rattling towards them, geysers of dust shooting up in its wake. The car pulled up short and two disreputable looking Arabs immediately engaged Belaid in an animated mix of French, Arabic and wordless but explicit gestures.

Pond followed the babble as best he could. Apparently de Prorok arrived at the hotel safe and sound—of course he did—and sent this bunch with gasoline. Of course, they only expected one bunch of Kafir idiots to run out of gas. They weren't sure they had enough for two groups.

"Are there any more of those idiots out there?" one of them asked, unaware or uncaring that the Americans might hear what was said.

"No, only two groups of morons. We'll only need a splash of gas to get into town. You can take the rest to the others down the road," Belaid told them. Pond thought he could have been a little more diplomatic about it all.

Without asking permission, Martini grabbed a can of gas from the back seat, made sure the funnel was clean and poured out a few glug-glugs of petrol into the tank. Then he added one final glug for good measure, splashed some on the carburetor, recapped the jug, and handed it back. With much thanks and salaaming from all involved, the drivers headed further north to rescue Chaix and Chapuis, and the unfortunate Hot Dog.

Five minutes later, Lucky Strike pulled in front of the Hotel Batna. What was left of the welcoming committee was still there, most of them squatting and smoking in what little shade the hotel's awnings offered. The owner, a frighteningly skinny Pied-Noir with an equally thin moustache tried to rouse the staff to their feet and give an appropriate hero's welcome to the brave—and obviously rich—travelers.

Pond watched, disgusted, as Barth directed the reluctant locals to stand and applaud the arrival. When he had them looking enough like a cheering mob, Reygasse emerged from the car straightening his hat as his medals jingled like wind chimes on his chest. The local headman greeted him with a kiss on each cheek and a hearty handshake, then the owner welcomed him to the grand vision that was the Hotel Batna.

Tyrrell and Pond crawled out of their vehicle on the street side, stretching their legs. They were immediately accosted by a frazzled porter, who gestured and shouted that he would do it all. "Leave it to Mahmoud, Sir.... I am Mahmoud." He pointed to himself and bowed deeply, just to make sure there was no confusion on that point. He grabbed a crate of digging tools, promptly dropped them on the ground, then smiled apologetically, hoping his tip wasn't in the balance.

A voice boomed from the doorway, "Ah, the prodigal sons arrive." De Prorok stood in the doorway, arms spread in welcome and motioned them to come in out of the heat. His hair was perfectly groomed, and there wasn't a speck of dust on him anywhere. Pond glared sullenly. Had he had time to bathe and change already, or did the son of a gun just not sweat like normal people? "Lonnie, let's get you something cool to drink before you combust. Brad, this way…"

Inside the lobby, a combined reception, café, bar and luggage storage depot, ceiling fans clunked noisily overhead. Pond tilted his head up towards them. The breeze felt wonderful, even if the way they rattled in their brackets left their ability to stay up there very long in serious doubt.

Reygasse had regained some of his dignity, and grandly gestured for the Americans to meet his "very good friend," and "this most honored gentleman," and other prominent locals, none of whom had actual names, it seemed. Pond smiled and shook hands, muttering greetings in French. Tyrrell, who always seemed to make himself at home despite being unapologetically unilingual, managed to make "good to meetcha" a universal language.

Long after the others finally dragged themselves in, the Count held court in the middle of the room, his voice honking out stories, jokes and bonhomie in a bewildering mix of French, Arabic, English and pantomime to include every living thing in the hotel. His long-stemmed pipe was alternately a baton, a sword, and a perfectly plausible excuse to pause and bask in the appreciation of the locals.

Pond looked around and envied Hal Denny, who was dead asleep in a chair removed from the main salon. The Times reporter snored softly, his notebook dangling from his lap.

"You okay, Monsieur Pond?" Chapuis asked twice before he got a response.

"Mmm, yeah. Fine."

The guide nodded. "It'll be fine. I've worked with him before. In Carthage and other places. He's a good man."

"If you say so." Pond regretting sounding so petulant, but it was getting late, and he wasn't feeling particularly diplomatic.

After dinner, they retired for the night. Tyrrell and Pond shared a room with three narrow cots. The whitewashed mud brick walls were unadorned except a couple of iron hooks for clothes and a crude crucifix that had been hastily added once the owner was reassured the occupants weren't Muslim.

The third cot was for Martini, when he finally showed up. The driver had ducked out the back as soon as dinner was over to inspect Lucky Strike. It showed a remarkable sense of duty, especially since it meant he'd get the cot furthest from the window and the fresh air.

The Americans moved their cots as close to the window as possible and pulled the mosquito netting into place. If the insects were blind enough, maybe they wouldn't see the gaping holes along the seams and let them get some sleep. It would get cool at night, but the breeze might eliminate some of the smell, and most of the vermin. Sleeping in their clothes seemed a reasonable precaution as well.

After a few minutes of quietly sucking his pipe, Brad spoke up. "Okay, Pond. Out with it."

"I didn't say anything."

The older man chuckled. "You say nothing louder than just about anyone I've ever met. Give."

Pond leaned up on one arm. "Do you think Prorok knows what he's doing?"

"He knows what he knows, that's for sure. The College couldn't get this trip off the ground before he got involved. We wouldn't have gotten out of Constantine without him playing Madame Rouvier like a fiddle—and don't think she's done with him yet. We wouldn't be driving these pretty new trucks, and we sure as heck wouldn't have the New York Times tagging along. So, yeah. I think he has some idea of what he's doing."

Pond lay back, head behind his hands. "But the gas…"

"Not his shining moment, I'll grant you. You know this is his first command, right?"

"That's no excuse," the younger man said, fully aware of how petty he sounded, but past caring.

"Not an excuse, maybe, but a pretty good reason. He's always had someone older or smarter to take care of the details, and he could just focus on the work and take the credit. Lots of guys are like that, especially salesmen…which is what he is, let's face it. First thing I learned in business, Lonny: being good at your job doesn't make you a good boss. I know plenty of bosses who wouldn't know their ass from their elbow if they actually had to do the dirty work, but they get things done."

Tyrrell lit his pipe, then added, "Being in charge looks awfully tempting and easy from the cheap seats. You'll find out some day."

That was the longest speech he'd ever heard Brad Tyrrell make and the young student lay there silently wondering why the older man wasn't as angry about them running out of gas as he was. The Tyrrell money certainly wasn't made tolerating stupidity.

Eventually Pond fell asleep imagining himself at the head of his own expedition; making world shaking discoveries while demonstrating perfect judgment and unfailing courage. Then he'd tour like the Count did, only his lectures would be accurate and profound, at a hundred bucks a pop. Brad said he'd find out some day, he sincerely hoped his friend knew what he was talking about. His last waking thought was, *I will sure have earned it.*

Chapter 3

Cedar Rapids Iowa
January 22, 1926

When I stepped off the streetcar my eyeballs nearly froze solid, but it was January in Iowa, so what did I expect? The wind that had followed me up Third Avenue finally caught me full in the face as soon as I turned towards the Montrose. The blinding winter sun added to the discomfort, and it took a moment to stop blinking and focus. I was wearing my good clothes, so I didn't dare button my coat. Sure, I was risking frost bite, but at least I looked good.

I dashed across the street and up to the front door of the hotel. First I was greeted by an unimpressed looking doorman who took his own sweet time opening up for me, then by a blast of stale, hot air. The Montrose did its best to keep its guests insulated from the deprivations of the great outdoors. And, I presumed, riffraff like me.

I caught a glimpse of myself in the lobby mirror. What looked back at me was presentable enough, if you didn't count the bright red patches in my otherwise pasty German face. I straightened my bow tie, tugged my vest down, and remembered to pull my cap off my head and shove it in my pocket like Mama taught me I should do when going amongst my betters.

The desk clerk—a foreigner of some kind judging

by the size of his schnozz and the grease holding his hair down—checked me out in a hurry.

"May I help you?" His tone suggested that was highly unlikely. I noticed he had an oversized white carnation in his lapel and perfectly manicured hands. It threw me off, I don't think I'd ever seen such perfect fingernails on anyone, man or woman.

"Yes, Count de Prorok's room please." I hoped I sounded properly business-like. I waited as he processed the question, and whether or not he'd deign to comply.

"And your business with the Count?"

"I have an appointment at ten o'clock."

"Just a moment." He picked up the phone and asked for room 324. He appraised me from head to toe then back again as he waited, obviously displeased with his findings.

"Count de Prorok, this is Gerard at the front desk. There is a young man here to see you. I told him you were very busy but..." he flinched and covered the phone. "Your name sir?" He called me sir, although he'd probably rather choke to death on a fishbone.

"Mr. Willy Brown," I said, wondering if he'd bite on it.

"It's a Willy, Brown, sir." Nope, he wasn't going to give me the Mr. just an "a", but I did get the room number and a begrudging, "The elevator is around the corner. Have a good day, sir."

"Thanks, Pal." I slapped the front desk and spun on my heel like Harold Lloyd. Elevators no less. Walking up three flights was nothing when you lived in our part of town, but when in Rome... I decided not to take the stairs.

The elevator operator in his black uniform and pillbox hat gave a polite nod. He didn't have to ask where I was going, because I couldn't wait to tell him like the big old rube I was.

"Third floor please. I have an appointment with Count de Prorok." He seemed less impressed with that knowledge than I was, and pushed the button. The cage door slid shut with a clank, and he checked the clasp, stabbed the "3" and up we went. His eyes never left the door. For such a simple job, he sure gave it all he had.

I wondered about that job. Were people so bewildered by trusting themselves to push a button and navigate two floors without getting lost? Or were rich people just so used to having someone else do everything for them they'd never developed the skill? Either way, I couldn't imagine ever being an elevator operator. It would be like driving the world's shortest streetcar route.

We got to three and the door opened. "Thanks, don't want to keep the Count waiting."

All that got me was a monotone "Mmm hmm, haveagoodday" and the door clanked shut on me.

Amber lights in glass sconces lined the hall. The rug was softer and prettier than anything I'd ever walked on. Geometric patterns led away from the elevator and down either end of the corridor. I counted off, "Three eighteen, three twenty," right up to three twenty-four. I tugged my vest down over my gut and knocked.

"Un moment," boomed a familiar voice. The door flew open and there he stood. The same hair perfectly coiffed, the same wrinkle-free appearance. This time he wore a grey double breasted and a snow-white shirt with a school tie of some sort perfectly knotted. He grinned around the pipe in his teeth. He began to reach out to shake my hand, but caught himself and he clasped my shoulder in a friendly greeting.

"Good to see you, Brown. Right on time. Welcome

to my home away from home."

I gave the room a quick scan as I stepped inside. I'd never actually stayed in a hotel room, but I could tell this was probably a pretty swell specimen. The bed was already made, or at least the spread pulled back into place. The wardrobe door hung half open, with hangers full of perfectly pressed shirts, a pair of loafers placed dead center on the bottom shelf. Further left, the windows would have offered a panoramic view of the glory that was downtown Cedar Rapids, but the drapes were still drawn.

It had its own bathroom. Pretty swanky. I scoped out a shaving kit and toiletries perfectly arranged on the vanity. The mirror was still a little foggy, with big drops running down it. This is what the son of a gun looked like straight out of the shower, apparently. How did he do that?

Then I saw the pile of equipment in the corner. Partly hidden behind the chair, the projector lay on its side, the magic lantern up on end. The crate of relics and props lay ajar and the contents were simply thrown inside in a big jumble. An extension cord was just bunched up and left loose on the floor; an accident waiting to happen.

I resisted the urge to pick it up and rewind it immediately. I was worried it might annoy him. Plus I wasn't on the clock yet. Never say I didn't learn anything from the Old Man.

"May I offer you a glass of water? It's all I've got at the moment. Well, not all, but it's awfully early in the morning, and this *is* Iowa."

"N-n-o sir, I'm good." While I tried to strike a balance between speaking too quickly and letting my stutter get the best of me, or taking too much time and sounding like an idiot, I just rocked back and forth uncomfortably.

"Well, at least sit down." He directed me to the overstuffed brocade armchair by the window while he plunked down on the edge of the bed in a perfectly casual way that I guess came from spending so much time in hotel rooms. Who conducts business from a bed?

He paused to light his pipe. "You can smoke if you'd like."

"No sir, I'm good." I never understood smoking, and once I started working around film at Old Man Mayer's, I learned it was probably the worst habit you could develop.

The fire that left me unemployed started because O'Malley decided it was too bloody cold to go outside to smoke, and it wouldn't do any harm to light up in the projection room. By the time I saved most of Mary Pickford's "Little Annie Rooney" my hand was burnt, O'Malley was fired, and the theater closed 'til further notice. It was probably smarter not to take up the habit. A lot less money, too. A pack of cigarettes was a ridiculous fifteen cents a pack, two for a quarter if you got the cheap ones, and a little less if you rolled your own.

"Wise man, a filthy habit really. I started smoking a pipe to look older, now I can't put the damned thing down. At least it keeps the mosquitoes away." He put it in the ashtray. "So, what did you think of last night?"

Think of what? Him? The lecture? The weather? "People seemed to like it a lot."

He nodded. "They usually do. What did you think of it?" I couldn't think of a thing to say. "You didn't see much of it, did you?"

"Not really… I mean, I was too busy. It looked real swell, though," I added, hoping I wasn't blowing my chance.

"Too busy saving my bacon, you mean. Every place I go, I get assigned some idiot assistant who's too busy watching the lecture to actually do their job. I've considered being less 'swell', but I can't help it— I'm too marvelous for my own good sometimes."

That laugh was infectious. I tried not to join in, but wound up giving a queer sort of snort, which set us both off.

"How old are you, Willy?"

"N-n-nineteen, sir." Eighteen had been easier to say. Anything starting with a N, an M, a B or a P was a nightmare. I couldn't wait to be twenty and I could answer a simple question without sounding like a moron.

"Well, I'm only thirty—barely—so you can stop with the sir nonsense. Call me Byron. The whole Count thing is good for business and all, but it's quite ridiculous. I'm American you know."

I didn't know. You sure couldn't tell by his snobby voice, which sounded nothing like the American I was used to hearing. In fact, nothing about this guy passed for normal in Milwaukee, or Cedar Rapids. I'd never been anywhere else so I didn't really know.

"Mmmm," he nodded as he relit his pipe. "Raised in England and so on, but my parents were both from Philadelphia. How did you get so good with that equipment?"

I started to give an "I dunno" shrug and forced myself to answer. "It's just equipment. People act like it's voodoo or something, but if you just let it do what it does, it's just fine." I could tell I wasn't making my point very well, so I took another run at it. "If you try to get a m-m-machine to do something it can't, it'll go haywire on you. Like that kid last night, shoving the lantern carriage…" I mimed him forcing the works back and forth. "You just knew something bad would

54

happen."

I debated whether to continue, but the pile in the corner was mocking me, and I pointed to it. "If you took b-b-better care of the equipment, you'd have less trouble with it. Like this cord..." I reached down and grabbed the offending line. "If you leave it like this, it'll kink up and make knots. P-p-plus it'll break and short out on you."

I bent my arm, took the plug in my wounded hand and wrapped the cord from elbow to fist, over and over quickly. "If you just wrap it like this every time, it'll last longer and be ready to use when you need it." I wrapped the female plug around the coil and knotted it in on itself, while trying to ignore how much that sounded like one of my father's lectures.

"You're very good with all... that. You *are* looking for work? And you're not in school?"

I shook my head. "N-n-nah. I graduated last year. Like I said, I'm nineteen."

"Not high school, university. Oh, sorry, you call it college here, don't you?"

"I'm not exactly college material."

"And that genius last night was? And your cousin... Bob was it? Prime college material I suppose?" My only response was another stupid shrug, proving my case.

"Where did you say you were from?"

"Milwaukee."

He looked confused. "Muhwokee, where's that? Oh you mean Mill Wau Kee. Wisconsin. Yes, I believe I'm going there soon. Is that how they pronounce it? Muh instead of Mill?"

Rather than let on I had no idea what he was talking about, I just said, "Spose so."

"Do you know how to drive?"

"I don't have a car, but I know how to drive,

yeah."

"I have the use of a car for the rest of this leg. Supposed to drive myself but I'd like to live long enough to see my children again. I have another week here, then off to Washington and Atlanta, but will be back in February and probably into March. I need someone to take care of my equipment, get me where I'm going alive, and free me up to do what I do best. Plus you look like you can take care of yourself." He made the same mistake a lot of people make, confusing my size with any kind of athletic ability. I let him think it. What was there to keep secure other than some rocks and old clothes?

"Can you do all that, Willy?"

"For fifteen a week?" Hell yes. I'd shine his shoes and kill his landlord for that kind of money.

"So one week, starting yesterday, then two more when I'm back. After that, the sky's the limit."

I should have shut up then, but I couldn't help asking. "Why pay so much? You can get someone to do it for a couple of bucks a night. P-probably for free."

He took a sizzling pull on his pipe while he thought, then got up and went to the box of slides. He rummaged around, completely undoing last night's work. It didn't seem to bother him, though, because he took one of the slides and held it out to me.

I held it up to the lamp. It was the picture of the expedition from last night. "The gentleman on the end is Louis Chapuis. He's one of the best engineers in Africa—and the most expensive. He was our guide. Cost us, well our patrons, nearly double what a local would have run. Same with the little man in the kepi—the cloth hat with the tail, there. Caid Belaid speaks seven languages I'm aware of. We could have found someone with three and probably even gotten along with just French and Arabic. Believe me, he didn't come cheap either. Do you know why I paid them so much?

My old man would have said because you're rich and stupid, but I kept my yap shut.

His voice softened. "Because it was my first time in charge of an expedition. The New York bloody Times was watching. The Logan Museum, the French government, all of them relying on me and I had no idea what I was doing. So I paid people who did. In life, you get what you pay for. I knew Louis would keep us out of trouble, and he did. Same with Belaid. When you scrimp on the front end you wind up paying for it eventually."

"So why me?"

"I need to focus on my presentation. That's what I'm good at... it's what people come to see. When the projector goes down, or the trucks are upside down— although that was a good line, maybe we'll keep it in— the audience gets restless and disappointed. The smoother everything runs, the better time the audience has, and the smarter I look. The better I look the more people ask me to lecture, and the more money I can charge. I literally can't afford to look like an idiot."

"And," his tone became conspiratorial, "a big-shot Count shouldn't be lugging his own equipment around like some kind of...stevedore. I am not paying you to run a projector. I'm paying you to keep me out of hot water and make me look good."

My confusion must have been obvious, and he was getting exasperated at my thick-headedness. I knew the tone well. "Look. It's like with that cord. You knew that if you wound it a certain way, and handled it right, it would work when I needed it. You can see those things and you just do them. I don't see them, and when I do them, it's half-arsed. It bites me in the backside every time. It's the same with people. Understand?"

I knew it was that way with machinery, but I'd never heard the idea applied to human beings. Going cheap on a projector, or bad carbons for the lamps, meant you'd spend more time replacing them than watching movies. Everyone knew that, or should. I was unconvinced real people worked the same way, and I wasn't entirely sure I was a good investment, but what the hell. It was his money.

"So a couple of stops, we'll finish up in Moline, and you bring the car back here. Then we'll meet up the twentieth of February. After that it's two weeks... so far. Chicago, Muhwaukee, Madison, probably Saint Louis, and I have a very important stop in Beloit..."

He had me at St. Louis, even if he pronounced it Saint Looey. Given that Cedar Rapids was the farthest I'd ever been from home the idea of even Beloit and Madison sounded exotic. To think he went all over the world—even to Atlanta and St. Louis—like it was nothing. The job sounded better and better.

He set the hook with the final question. "Will your aunt and uncle mind if you left tomorrow?"

They'd probably do a jig. They weren't the problem. The hole in the schedule left me with two weeks or so with no work. I'd have to go home, but after that I'd be gone for good. Mama could probably buy me that much time. It wouldn't be fun, but I could tough it out, especially when I knew I'd be able to make my escape permanent.

"N-n-nope, it's fine." I stuck out my hand, bandages and all, and he used a two-hand shake on it.

"Done. Okay, we leave tomorrow for the bustling metropolis of Des Moines, Ioway," he said in a surprisingly convincing Hawkeye accent. "What do we need to get up and running?"

I'd have to realign those slides, and maybe put a lock on the box so he couldn't muck them up anymore. None of the boxes was properly labeled, that would make things a whole lot easier. We'd need some stuff from the hardware store.

"Not much. I can get most of it at Martinek and Son's, it's just down Third Avenue."

"Great, make a list and we'll get it while we're having lunch. I believe I've recovered fully from last night. I'm starving."

Chapter 4

Batna, Algeria
October 13, 1925

Pond gave his ankle an early morning scratch through his sock, then his arm through his sleeve. Then his nails scraped over most of the rest of his body. The mosquitoes they'd been so worried about were merely decoys for the fleas that ambushed him while he slept.

It was barely dawn, and everything in the room was bathed in a cool grey. Tyrrell snored away on one cot under a mound of blankets. Martini, like any other old desert hand, lay on top of the blankets, sleeping the sleep of the just and uneaten.

Pond got out of bed, slopped some water from a pitcher into a chipped white bowl, then palmed it against his face. He combed his fingers through his hair in a vain attempt to tame it and quietly slipped out of the room. He always enjoyed early mornings. Whether it was the North Woods of Wisconsin or the hills of southern France, there were few things he loved more than being alone with Mother Nature at sunrise. He was in a hurry to experience the feeling of dawn over the desert, but there were at least two more nights of flea-bag inns before then. No sense complaining about it.

He took his notepad and writing stationery to the lobby. He had time to dash off a short letter to Dr. Collie at the Logan Museum, and hoped it sounded professional. He'd calmed down a little since yesterday, but only a little. Running out of fuel on the first day was annoying. If it happened out in the true desert it could be fatal.

Surprisingly, de Prorok was already awake, if a little the worse for wear from the brandy he'd consumed. Hungover or not, he was fully operational, sitting slouched in a raggedly upholstered chair with his back to the rest of the lobby, jotting notes in a leather-bound notebook. The Count gestured to the silver urn on the table in front of him.

"Ahh, Pond, good morning. Everything up to scratch?" He chuckled at his own joke as his nails raked at his own shirt sleeve.

"Funny," Pond grunted, and gestured towards the coffee. He always thought cowboys and loggers back home drank thick coffee, then he'd gone to Europe. And even that sludge couldn't prepare him for how the Arabs drank it. It was so thick and strong, you could use it for medicinal purposes rather than recreation. There was no way you could spend the morning lingering over these little thimbles that passed for cups. A good American diner mug of this mud would have you awake and crapping for a week. Thank God sugar was in good supply.

Taking that first scalding sip, Pond studied the other man. The Count was two years younger than he was—they celebrated the Count's thirtieth birthday in Constantine—and the nearness in age was about the only similarity between them. Pond was short. At best he was five two or three depending on who he was talking to and how straight he stood, while the other man towered over him, literally looking down at him most of the time. While the American was stocky, Byron de Prorok was wiry, and deceptively strong.

Pond blew a stray wisp of hair from his face. That

was another thing that bothered him. De Prorok's dark hair was always molded into a crest of wavy perfection at any time of the day or night. Even when the Count removed his pith helmet after a day in the sun, it was still pristine, not a hair out of place. Pond hated those stupid hats, preferring a floppy safari-style, but it didn't seem to matter what he put on, his hair would fly about and stand on end. Sometimes that made him look taller. Mostly it made him look like he'd just crawled out of bed.

De Prorok's booming voice shook him from his thoughts. "I'm awfully sorry about yesterday. Not the most auspicious start was it?"

"No, I suppose not. What happened?"

"I had the cans filled and loaded as soon as Rouvier granted permission for us to leave. I'm afraid I underestimated the amount of evaporation they'd undergo in such a short time. I've seen it happen before. I remember one time outside Carthage…"

"Evaporation? You're telling me the gas was there and just, uhh, poof? There's no chance you underestimated what it would take?"

This drew a smiling shrug in response. "Oh, it's possible, of course. Math isn't exactly my strong suit, and ultimately, of course, it's on me. Still the boys from Renault told me what they needed and they should know, so that's what I ordered. Reygasse's people assure me we have plenty of supplies for the trip. I mean, it's basically a walk in the park isn't it? Especially this first leg."

Pond thought his derisive snort at the mention of Reygasse had been kept to himself, but de Prorok obviously caught it. "Lonnie, what is your issue with Reygasse?"

"That toy general routine gets on my nerves."

"I understand. He does look a bit like a Gilbert and

Sullivan character doesn't he? But without him and the Musée we wouldn't be able to dig here at all. And his contacts with the government and the local tribes have secured our supplies all along the route. I don't know what I'd do without him."

Pond just took another sip of coffee. One thing they'd do, he thought, is save a lot of money. Every time they turned around he was renegotiating some detail of the trip, usually placing the blame on the local officials or the tribes. "Greedy bastards," he'd say while extorting yet more cash for the permits, extra materiel or whatever else they needed.

"What happened back in Tangiers with you two?"

"I don't like the way he treats his wife," Pond said simply.

"You're not… I mean it's not a…"

"No, oh Christ no. I have a girl, and…. It's just, he…." Pond tried to find a diplomatic way out of this. Maybe he needed more coffee after all. The trouble started when the poor mousey little woman had dared to correct Monsieur le Marshall on some detail in a story he was spinning, and Reygasse would have none of it. He grabbed her roughly by the arm and escorted her to the door to the accompaniment of some of the vilest language Pond ever heard directed at a respectable woman. Being in the ambulance corps, he knew most of the really good French epithets, but he learned a few more that night. "He manhandled her, in front of people. I don't trust a man who treats a woman that way."

"Quite right. Still, not ours to judge what goes on in a marriage is it?"

"No, I suppose not. But there's the way he's treating the College. Did you hear that nonsense with Brad's expenses?"

"Yes, something about what they'd pay for and

what they won't. That's all between the Logan and the Musée of course, not exactly our business. I try to keep my nose out of it."

"You mean you don't want to tick him off, and so you take his side, no matter the cost to the College or to Brad."

"Without Maurice Reygasse, we have no digging rights. We need to remember that." Sometimes Byron wished he could forget himself, but the reality was omnipresent, and made cooperation between the Logan and the authorities absolutely imperative.

"Oh, he manages to bring it up occasionally." Pond was getting worked up again. Since the War it was like there was a rich American surcharge on everything. If, like Brad Tyrrell, you actually were a rich American, you were fair game. Pond was not rich, and frequently used local intermediaries to get the things he needed at a fair price.

"Have some coffee, Lonnie. We're underway now. Smooth sailing from here on out." Byron toasted him with his tiny coffee cup. Pond poured himself some and toasted back with considerably less enthusiasm.

The two men silently wrote in their journals as the coffee burned its way through the morning fog, the scratch-scratch of pencil on paper interspersed with the more muted scratching of fingernails through cloth.

Pond's writing was small and precise, although much neater than the man himself. De Prorok's notebook was full of what could have been hieroglyphics – a mix of French and English, his script large, full of curlicues and swooping "L"s and "S"s.

The hotel began to stir around them as staff and travelers emerged, blinking and scratching, into the sunlit café. Hal Denny, already sweating and looking like he hadn't slept more than a few minutes, came in from outside. The Count called him over with that honking voice and a broad smile. "Ahhh, our Boswell. Did you get your story filed, Hal?"

"Well, it's written. Whether it will get out of here in one piece is another question." Byron knew he had to do something. The reporter had been singularly pessimistic and miserable since the moment he arrived in Algeria. An unhappy reporter was likely to write unflattering stories, and that was no good for business.

He certainly wasn't the movie version of a foreign correspondent, either. Denny wasn't much taller than Pond, and looked like he'd spent the night fully clothed and wadded into a ball, rather than in a semi-comfortable hotel bed. He seldom smiled, and seemed to consider sighing heavily a natural part of the respiratory process.

Soon the whole party was caffeinated, fed and packed. On the Count's signal, Barth ran outside to set up his tripod and camera to capture their glorious departure to the half-hearted cheers of a handful of sullen hotel employees. No sooner were they off then they stopped, waited for Barth to catch up and climb aboard the lead vehicle, and took off again. Sandy led the parade, as always, followed by Hot Dog with Lucky Strike bringing up the rear.

Byron looked out the window. So far, the trip had been a disappointment, especially to the Americans. Instead of a dangerous adventure in the mighty African desert, they were in comfortable automobiles, leaving one hotel on the way to another, on roads that wouldn't have been out of place in most of America outside the big cities. Every few miles they'd pass another hamlet, usually containing a gas station, a market of some kind, an inn, and the life-giving town well. True, the pictures could be manipulated, but somehow all this was missing the sense of drama he and his audiences craved.

The terrain rose slightly as they neared a ridge up front, and Martini cursed.

"What is it?" Pond asked. "They can't be out of gas again, can they?"

De Prorok stood beside Sandy happily waving his walking stick. The occupants of the other trucks got out, stood and stretched, curious as to the source of the excitement. "Everything okay?" Tyrrell shouted.

"Couldn't be better, but I thought you'd want to see this." The road peaked at a narrow gap between two stones, then dipped sharply downwards. The Count stood atop the rock to the left, making a majorette's twirling baton out of his walking stick.

"Get your good first look at the real Sahara gentlemen." He spread his arms wide in welcome. The clicking of Barth's camera drifted by them on the breeze, almost drowned out by the dull grumble of the three engines. Byron noticed that Reygasse chose not to share in the moment, staying in Hot Dog, feigning sleep and moping.

Pond, Tyrrell and Denny came forward to look over the crest of the hill. Ahead of them lay a vast, flat plain. Despite what the travel books said, the first expanses of the Sahara from the North weren't sandy, but rock strewn and brown, broken up by small patches of light colored sand. The plain lay two hundred feet below them and stretched infinitely southward.

"Isn't it wonderful, Pond?" De Prorok prodded for an elusive sign of happiness from the American.

Alonzo wasn't sure he could provide it. "It doesn't look very, I don't know, Sahara-like, does it?"

Byron wondered what it would take to make the American happy. "Oh, you'll get your sand and your camels. Not to worry. The rain will stop, too."

Along the southern and western horizons, Pond could make out the green blots indicating a well or spring, surrounded by date trees. Some of those trees grew over eighty feet tall, but from their vantage point they were smudges of green on an unending flat, tawny canvas.

Looking directly past de Prorok and down the mountainside, Alonzo could see a thin, curved goat track of a road carved in the side of the mountain. A steep switchback led downwards and, assuming they survived that, a single straight line led southwest towards the horizon and El Kantara. It looked for all the world like God, or Allah, or whoever ruled here simply dragged his finger in the dust to show the way.

The little ceremony over, they jumped back in the cars and Sandy disappeared over the ridge first, followed closely by Hot Dog. Martini and the Lucky Strike sat for a few minutes. Pond and Tyrrell shot silent questions back and forth until Tyrrell couldn't take it anymore.

"Martini, why aren't we moving?" Martini turned with a sly grin.

"I've driven this road before. They haven't. They're going to go down too slowly, and maybe burn out their brakes. That one in the lead, Escande? He's probably pissing his pants right now," and he chuckled a little harder than Pond thought tasteful or appropriate.

"I give them a head start so we can do it right and spare the brakes."

"So you're actually going to go down faster than they are?" Pond was delighted Martini was looking after the brakes but then thought about the sharp turns snaking down the mountainside. The part about doing so faster than everyone was considerably less comforting.

At long last, Lucky Strike lurched into action and they headed up the hill, then sharply down and to the right. The view out the right window by Pond was a sheer wall of crumbling grey and brown rock and the occasional sere bush. On Tyrrell's side, there was a lot of air, then the brown expanse of the desert floor.

The big truck slowed, maneuvered a sharp left turn, and the passengers traded views. Pond watched Martini nervously. The driver's left hand locked onto the wheel, the right alternated between the gear shift and the hand brake. His eyes were fixed on the dusty track ahead of him and the herculean task of keeping all twelve tires on the ground at the same time. For the most part, he succeeded.

Right, left, right, left, they wended their way down to the valley floor. Pond caught himself holding his breath on every switchback. No one said anything until they'd completed the final left turn when Martini let out a bellowing, "Merde!"

He slammed on the brakes, sending American passengers and equipment bouncing around the cabin. They narrowly missed ramming into Hot Dog at the bottom. Martini slammed on the brakes and brought his vessel to a skidding stop just short of the crates strapped to the other vehicle's rear.

Terrified the crazy Italian would ram him from behind, the French driver hit the gas and bounced onto the main roadbed with a gut-tightening scrape Pond could feel in his bones, and took off. Martini never even slowed down, he just put his charge in the middle of the track and pointed southwest. Byron and the occupants of Sandy were already speeding towards El Kantara.

The Hotel El Kantara was much nicer than the hotel in Batna. The café boasted white tablecloths and plenty of ice. The only fleas were the ones who'd made the trip with the expedition. Pond ignored all that, and set to writing his daily report to the Logan. The real work was still days away, and he hoped his impatience didn't show too much in his correspondence. Dr. Collie was always telling him to slow down and relax but Pond wasn't here to relax, and the company didn't exactly entice him.

Tyrrell did finally convince him to go for an exploratory walk after dinner, and on their return they were surprised to find de Prorok sitting in a chair surrounded by yards of black ribbon and wooden stakes. He puffed away on his pipe, muttering softly, as he wrestled to create some kind of memorial wreath.

"Did someone die?" Tyrrell asked.

"Actually yes, about 50 years ago, Cardinal Lavigerie…" He excitedly waited for some sign of recognition. Not finding any, he went on, his voice shifting to full lecture mode. "Founder of the White Fathers of the Desert…?" Still nothing.

Monsieur le Cardinal had been the founder of a sect of hermits who'd followed up the discovery of the Sahara by promptly finding a hole to live in and stayed there, tending to the spiritual, and occasionally the hydration needs of desert travelers. Byron happily rattled on. Tomorrow was the 100th anniversary of the good Father's birth. He wanted to place a wreath on his tomb.

"Never heard of him. Was he important?" Brad asked.

"Not unless you were really thirsty and he got to you in time," laughed the Count.

"Then why bother? Seems like a waste of time to me."

De Prorok nodded. "I know, Lonnie, it's not a

particularly historic event, but I need the film for my lecture tour. Americans love missionaries. They'll even respect the Catholics as long as they're not settling in their neighborhoods. The only thing they like better than a white man going where he isn't wanted or needed, is if he dies doing it. They eat that stuff up."

"How long will it take?"

"Twenty minutes, half an hour maybe. Long enough to say a prayer, get it on film, and get some proper snaps. Oh, and dress nicely. Reygasse will be in full uniform." He continued winding the black ribbon around the upright stick.

"Reygasse sleeps in full uniform." Pond thought he said that to himself, but the Count's laugh bounced around the empty hotel lobby, followed by a hissed "God damn it..." as he dropped the cross piece and the ribbon unspooled to the floor. "I swear I am all thumbs..."

The two men left de Prorok to his arts and craft project and went upstairs for a flea-free rest.

Chapter 5

Cedar Rapids, Iowa
Afternoon of January 22, 1926

Appraising the pile of equipment in the corner, a few things were obvious. I knew the lantern was all right, although we'd need more carbons, and better stuff than he'd been using so far. We probably should do the same for the film projector. From the feel of the crank last night, a new cotter pin wouldn't be a bad idea. That was literally two cents worth of prevention.

I picked up a couple of items just to see what was under them. Two black crates were unlabeled and I asked, "What's in there?"

"You'd best take a look for yourself, since you're in charge of it now. Basically it's souvenirs of my trips and props for the lectures. You saw most of it last night."

I opened it slowly and peered inside. "Go ahead," he urged. "Some of that stuff has lasted two thousand years, I doubt you can do much damage."

He obviously didn't know who he was dealing with, but I took him at his word. I clicked open the hasp and lifted the lid. Everything was thrown inside haphazardly, and looked like a magpie nest. For every item that looked like it might be important, there was a shiny campaign button, or a picture post card or a hotel ashtray. The one I picked up read "Waldorf Astoria", but there were others. I'd have to sort through this dog's breakfast before making any rash decisions.

The second box was full of robes and things from his last expedition in the Sahara. He tried to explain it, though it was all gobbledygook to me; "burnooses" and "fezzes" and a dark blue robe and turbans, plus some bracelets and arm jewelry. Hardly anything resembling treasure, and I wondered exactly what he thought he needed security for. Anyone who stole this crap was harder up than I was.

Two larger items lay wrapped in newspaper at the bottom of the trunk. I held up the first one and unwrapped it. It looked like one of those crazy swords Rudolph Valentino used in the pictures. "It looks like it's from the Garden of Allah, or something."

He nearly jumped off the bed. "You've read Garden of Allah?" He sure didn't know me very well yet.

"N-n-no, I saw the movie, though."

The Count seemed disappointed but tried to hide it. "Well the author is a dear friend, you know. Hichens, Robert Smythe Hichens. A terrible writer, and a worse influence on me. Still, makes a good living writing that stuff and living out in the middle of nowhere. So you're a movie fan, did you know I was in a movie? Dreadful thing. Played a Red Indian... Rose France, it was called."

I only half listened, too busy examining the sword. It was obviously a bad fake. The blade was pasteboard, and the handle wasn't camel skin or whatever it should have been, just brown ribbon wrapped around a wooden dowel. I weighed it in my hand and said, "Doesn't look like much."

He pouted a bit at that but let it slide. "It looks better on stage. Certainly good enough to get the point across. I had a real one, quite a lovely example of a Tuareg flyssa, but it was confiscated when we were leaving Algeria. Quite unfairly. Claimed I stole it, but it was a gift from a friend."

I picked up the other package. This got him really worked up. "Open it, Brown, open it. This is my greatest possession. I take it with me wherever I travel." Well, that was sufficient motivation. I flipped open two pieces of newsprint fully prepared to be dazzled.

It was an old piece of wood, probably a one by four with broken ends and some faded writing scribbled on it. "It's a piece of a sled Ernest Shackleton took to the South Pole." My blank expression inspired more explanation. "He gave it to me when I was in school, for helping raise money for one of his expeditions." I hoped for some spark of interest to register, but nope, I still didn't give a hoot. He wasn't about to let go, though. He was like a dog with a sock.

"Oh come on, Brown. This humble piece of wood was part of a sled. That sled went somewhere no one else on earth has ever gone. Men may well have died while sitting on that sled. Someone famous once used it to do something amazing, then took the time to offer a piece of that story to a lonely fourteen year old boy thousands of miles away. Every time I look at it, I imagine myself being on that adventure with him, and I have a piece of it all to myself and can relive it any time I want. Isn't that amazing?"

I didn't exhibit enough excitement, I guess, because he began to pace back and forth. "Everyone thinks history is dull and drab... dates they can't remember, and battles they weren't in, and names they can't pronounce." I couldn't argue with him there.

"The important part of history, though, is the story..." He reached back and picked up the makeup pot. His voice changed, becoming deeper, smoother, more insistent. "Like this jar, for instance."

He held it out to me, waving his hand over it like a carnival magician. "This isn't just a jar of face powder, you can get that at any drug store in any town. No, it's Carthaginian face powder, from before the time of Christ. Who knows, maybe Queen Dido herself owned it, and it was part of her last heroic effort to convince Aeneas to stay with her. She tarted herself up and threw herself at his feet, only to be abandoned anyway. Maybe, this was the very last thing she touched before throwing herself on that funeral pyre and turning herself to ashes for the sake of love." He paused dramatically.

"You got all that from a chunk of rock?"

He laughed. "You're a tough audience, Willy Brown. The point is, it's a really good story. That's what I do, I tell stories that people want to hear, and can't hear anywhere else. I travel where they can't—or mostly won't—and bring the tales back so they don't have to leave their dreary little houses and their horrid jobs, and their boring spouses to have adventures of their own. That's why they pay me, to bring the adventure to them."

It seemed like a mug's game to me, but he wasn't paying me to think.

At the bottom of the case was a black metal box, about ten inches by six and three inches deep, held shut by a delicate silver padlock. "What's in here?"

His hand shot out and snatched it from my hand. "Nothing you need concern yourself with. Purely personal." Then, after a deep breath, his smile reappeared and he handed it over. "Please don't touch it, and keep it secure. It's not part of the lecture materials, but it's very important to me."

I took it back with a shrug and placed it at the

bottom of the crate. "Sure."

I don't know how long it took me to sort through everything and figure out what we'd need. Thirty minutes later, maybe, I had a list of about seventy-five cents worth of doodads that would make the whole shebang easier to deal with. Creating order out of chaos wasn't all that difficult. People just don't give it enough thought. Mind you, some of us didn't have the seventy-five cents to start with.

"Enough, Brown. Lunchtime." I looked up from my work and he was at the door; a long camelhair coat, thick felt hat, and what I could only assume was a cashmere scarf loosely wrapped around his neck. I quickly gathered my things and joined him in the hallway.

The elevator doors clanged open, and the sour-pussed operator was still on the job. De Prorok's eyes dropped to the man's chest for a moment, then a smile crept across his mug from one corner of his mouth to the other like a zipper. "Martin, how are you today?"

The operator straightened up and actually smiled, "Just fine, Count... uh, your honor. Button up, it's cold out there." He apparently had no concern for my health, because he roundly ignored me. I gave him the once-over. Sure enough, on his chest was a small brass nametag that read, "Martin".

On reaching the lobby, Martin tipped his hat—to the Count—who tipped his back and wished Martin a pleasant day. As the doors closed, I could hear him tell his newest passengers, "See that guy, he's a real Count... French or something."

Byron never seemed to notice or miss a step. He nodded to the doorman with a quick "Johnson," and we were on the sidewalk. "Where to?" he asked.

Where do you take a Count for lunch in Cedar

Rapids? "Brown, I'm freezing. Where would you go if you were by yourself?"

"I'd probably just get a bowl of soup at the Top Hat. It's on the way to the hardware store, but you don't want to eat there."

"I don't want to freeze to death, either. Which way?" I pointed down Third Avenue and he set off, cursing the cold all the way to the Top Hat Diner.

The place was full of men in outdoor gear, along with a few low-level bank clerks who decided to splurge on a quarter's worth of soup instead of a cold sandwich at work, just because it was Friday.

De Prorok looked around. "This place looks fine, why didn't you think I'd like it?"

"It's probably not what you're used to. I mean…"

"What I'm used to," he snapped, "is eating what people eat wherever I am. The fastest way to learn anything about people is to see what they eat. When I'm at the Waldorf, it's shrimp cocktail and aspic. In the desert, I've eaten fried crickets and millet porridge. I doubt there's anything as exotic as that on the menu here." He paused and looked over to the next table. "Although I might want to check the provenance on that meat loaf."

Throughout the meal, he peppered me with questions. What was I doing in Iowa (looking for work), what was Milwaukee like (okay, I guess) and what exactly was a Hawkeye and why did it matter so much (it beat me all to hell)? Finally, the inquisition ended and the check came.

"Okay, so sixty cents… You had the soup so that's twenty-five. Plus your share of the tip."

I guess I expected him to pick up the tab, because he waited a moment, then gave me a very stern look. "Our deal is fifteen a week, and you pay your own meals. This was a meal, ergo, you pay your share.

Were the conditions of employment unclear?"

"N-n-o sir." He was paying me more than I was worth, a quarter for a cup of soup wasn't a big deal. If that's how this was going to be, well a deal's a deal. Fortunately, I had the money he paid me last night. The waitress broke the fiver, making a point of informing me she could only do it because it was Friday, and they were flush.

I handed over thirty cents which he took with a smile and passed it on to the waitress with a tip of his hat. "Thank you, Patricia, it was divine. Perhaps it was the company."

She blushed right through the sweat and rouge. "Sure thing, honey. Come back any time," she said but he'd already turned his back and we were out the door.

At the hardware store, the inquisition continued.

"What's this thingamee do?" It was a toilet ballcock.

"How does this work?"

"Why so many sizes of screws?" Each question was in that honking baritone, and it was drawing attention. The clerk shook his head in sad disbelief. An older lady gave me a sympathetic look, as if I were escorting a disobedient child or a senile old man. As my cheeks got redder, my answers got shorter and crankier.

He stood in front of a drawer full of cabinet pulls, fingering each one like it was some jewel pulled from a sarcophagus. "Do you ever wonder what someone would think this place was if they found it two hundred years from now?" That was easy. No. And why would it cross any normal person's mind at all? I just shook my head and finished getting the stuff on my list.

I was making my way to the counter when I heard a braying, "Brown, over here." I followed the echoes to where he stood in front of a bunch of mechanics overalls. "What size are you?"

"Large. No, probably extra-large…. Why?" Then I knew why. "I'm not wearing those."

"Why not?"

"B-b-because I have clothes. I'm running a projector, not fixing the boiler."

"You are not 'running the projector,' you are my… presentation technician." He seemed overly pleased with the choice of words. "A trained monkey can work a projector, although it seems beyond the grasp of the college educated. You, my friend, are a trained professional, and part of a highly organized…"

"F-f-forget it. Unh uh. What's wrong with what I'm wearing?" His look implied there was more than I thought.

"Like it or not, you're part of the show. People know you work for me, and I want them to know I hire only the best. The best guide, best translator, best presentation technician… or projection engineer. Which do you prefer?"

Jesus, who did this guy think he was? Worse, who did he think I was? "The presentation one, I guess."

"Done. You are my presentation technician. And a technician should have a uniform that says you're not just some mug off the street. This'll serve until we find something more creative."

That night, I told my aunt and uncle I'd be out in the morning. Uncle Bill said nothing at all, as expected. Aunt Gertie made all the appropriate clucking noises but seemed relieved. I made them feel better by explaining this was not some fly-by-night outfit. I was to be the by-God official Presentation Technician to the Count de Prorok.

Getting off their couch was the easy part. Telling my folks was going to be harder. It was only for two weeks, and Momma would be heartbroken it wasn't for good. The Old Man would be furious I was back at all, without a full time job in hand. He might put up with me for two full weeks work, but not a day longer. We might be able to make it work. Maybe.

Chapter 6

Hassi Khalifa, Algeria
October 15, 1925

When Chapuis knocked on his door a little before six, Alonzo was already awake. He tried not to wake Brad and Martini as he asked, "Louis, what's going on?"

"I've got a surprise for you, 'Lonzo. Come on."

"What is it?" the American asked groggily.

"That's why they call it a surprise, come on. And be quiet. Oh, and bring a coat, it's colder than a whore's heart this morning."

Twenty minutes, and one small very insufficient cup of coffee later, the two men stood at the base of a large boulder just outside the village. On the north side, a deep hole tunneled deep beneath the striated stone. This early in the morning, it looked even more insignificant than it would most other times. Pond was getting irritated with Chapuis' mysterious attitude.

"I'll bite. What am I looking at?" The guide gave him an indulgent smile, dipped his hand in a puddle and smeared the water across the lower edge of the rock and shone his electric torch on the wet spot. Barely discernible, three lines formed an arrow aimed at an even fainter circle with four lines emerging from it.

Pond looked closer and whistled. "No, really?"

Louis eagerly nodded. "I asked someone last night if there were any stories about this place. I knew most of them, but then they mentioned this rock. Everybody knows about it, but nobody cares much."

He bent down and picked up a stone, darker than the rest of the shards and gravel, and held it out to Pond whose eyes widened. Only someone with a well trained eye would appreciate this as he could. It was a projectile head, probably a spear tip, crudely but effectively chipped by hand and stone a long, long time ago.

"Who knows about this?"

"Besides you and me? Everyone around here but no one who matters. Reygasse knows about the site but hasn't pissed on it yet because he doesn't think it's worthwhile. Not enough shiny things for him, and the drawings are too faint to bring in tourists."

Pond only half listened as he ran his hands through the gravel. He squatted as low as he could without actually sitting in the muddy water that pooled around their feet. Without a torch of his own, it was more a symbolic gesture than an attempt to see very much. "How deep?"

"Deep enough to eat and sleep in, maybe skin your catch."

Eagerly, Alonzo ran his fingers through the gravel, where he found another sharp stone, this one definitely an arrowhead. He also found the telltale tiny shards of flint that indicated the weapons had been fashioned here, not just brought from somewhere else. This had once been a full-fledged hunting camp. Flint told a lot of stories, if you knew what you were looking at, and even as a graduate student, Pond had a far better eye than most.

Louis stood up wiping the grime from his hands. "When we're done, it might be worth coming back. Probably a lot of good work to be done here, and you can get a decent cup of coffee and sleep indoors every night."

Pond wasn't sure proximity to the village was much of a selling point, but he nodded. "Sure might. Merci, Louis. Thanks so much." The anthropologist in him itched to grab his tools and start digging, but he knew there was no time. It took weeks, maybe a lifetime to search, catalogue and really analyze a site like this properly. The best he could do in the next month and a half was collect the best scraps for the Logan Museum, and create a wish list of potential digs for the Santa Clauses in Beloit to grant.

"Not at all. And the Count will probably give you a discount on the digging rights."

Pond froze in place. "What do you mean?"

"Next year. You know. When this is all over, Reygasse is going to give de Prorok the rights for this corner of Algeria. All the permits will go through him. That should be a good deal for you and the Museum, no?" He paused. "Oh, Christ, you didn't know. I just thought... well, you're partners and all..."

Pond just shook his head. No, he had no idea. He wondered if Dr. Collie and the big shots back in Beloit knew about this. The excitement of the morning's discovery dissipated like fog in a stiff breeze.

"We should go back," the guide suggested.

"Yeah. Time's awasting." Pond put the two flint relics in his pocket, and they walked back to the inn in silence.

They were back at their lodgings in plenty of time to warm up and help pack for the easy straight run to Touggart. The clouds were lighter today, although still gray, and Pond thought the cold wind felt more like the Dakotas than the Sahara.

They left Hassi Khalifa a bit later than planned, but it was such a short, straight run to the next town where Reygasse's friends were planning a big banquet nobody really cared much. They gave the rain a chance to blow through, then set out again.

As usual, Martini and Lucky Strike played caboose to the train of cars. Soon enough, Pond noticed, there was a lot of room between the cars, and finally the other two vehicles couldn't be seen at all. Cautiously, he broached the subject to Martini, who had woken up in a foul mood, which didn't help the coherence of his French. "Why are we going so much slower than the others?"

Martini sucked the long hairs of his moustache. "Monsewer Pond. We no go slow. They go fast."

"Shouldn't we go fast, too?" he offered.

"You wanta run out of gas again? Twenty-five. We go twenty-five alla the time. Save fuel, get inna no trouble."

"Let the man do his job, Lonnie." Pond fumed. Tyrrell's advice always seemed to be to let people do their jobs. But what if they didn't do them? What then? He idly wondered if Brad had always had that attitude, and if so, how the Tyrrell knit company ever made its millions. He peered ahead, unable to see anything but the occasional puddle or tread mark in the road ahead.

Finally, he lay back, pulled out some paper and began composing another letter to Dorothy, describing yesterday's foolishness with the truck, and hoping it sounded amusing instead of whiney. He thought he had an excellent sense of humor about things, but it didn't seem to be appreciated by everyone equally.

Lost in his work, he was jolted to attention by Martini shouting, "Porco Vacca!" and Lucky Strike nosed into a sudden halt. Brad stopped blowing his harmonica and craned around the back of the driver's head. The driver pounded his palm on the steering wheel. "Ah… ah…. What I tell you Monsewer Pond?"

Up ahead, Hot Dog, the pride of France's glorious *Société des Automobiles Renault*, and the state of the art in desert travel was buried to the axles of its rear eight precisely engineered pneumatic tires in gooey muck. Sandy, driven by the company's very best chauffeur/ingénieur was twenty feet further down the road, sat mired almost as deeply.

Caid Belaid stood at the dry edge of the swampy roadbed frantically waving and shouting, "Don't come any closer. We're stuck."

They were, indeed, stuck. The rains the last few days had washed what little real topsoil there had been into the deepest dips and valleys of the road, turning the dirt into a slurping, sucking sponge, capturing whatever dared cross it like a mosquito in amber.

As Martini, Tyrrell and Pond approached the other vehicles, de Prorok high-stepped towards them, wiping his hands on his trousers. "Damned worst luck, isn't it?"

Pond wasn't a firm believer in luck, but didn't intend to hash it out here. "Can we tow you out?"

The Count looked a bit abashed. "Well, actually, that's how Sandy got into this pickle. We got through fine, then Chaix got caught. The winch is on Hot Dog there, and we thought, oh, we'll just brace our car, and when the winch tightens…. It kind of sucked us in, instead. Now we're both stuck. Damned bad luck."

"It's not luck. What idiot thought up that idea?"

"Well it wasn't me was it, Pond? Bloody professional drivers are supposed to know what they're doing. Apparently the Sahara desert is nothing like the streets of Paris. Who'd have guessed?"

"Well, I suppose we'd better help if we ever want dinner tonight," Pond said, stripping off his coat and immediately missing its warmth. Grabbing spades meant for more careful digging, the Americans, Martini and de Prorok joined the occupants of the lead vehicles in the slop.

Byron noticed that everyone, including Denny and a very unhappy, shivering Barth, dug frantically, and futilely, with the small archaeological tools. For a moment, he thought he was seeing things. An Arab was digging with them, alternately shoveling and swearing in perfect French. The strange sight was actually Maurice Reygasse, who'd thrown the cape on in an attempt to keep his uniform presentable for their arrival in Touggart.

For hours they dug, slipped, smoked and cursed. At first the oaths were directed at Escande for leading them into the quagmire. Then they blamed, in turn, the Renault Brothers, the idiot who thought twelve tires a good idea, the Count, Chapuis (for not alerting them to the danger in time) and then, since mudslides weren't high on the list of common desert perils, they settled on God himself. The less pious among them cursed with gusto, the rest under their breath on the off chance God was listening and made things worse.

At last, Martini drove off the road and circled around to the relatively dry road ahead, getting close enough to haul Sandy back onto terra firma. Then Martini managed to link enough rope and chain for both vehicles to haul Hot Dog out of the mud and onto the road bed.

The rain had stopped, and the sun finally elbowed its way through the clouds, although far too low on the horizon for comfort. The daylight was almost gone, and they were still over two hours to Touggart where baths, a warm bed, and a full blown feast awaited them. Pond heard a stomach growl, and guessed—correctly—it was Barth.

Caid Belaid squinted into the sun. "Maybe we should spend the night in Stil, and go on in the morning.

"What's in Stil?" Byron wanted to know.

"Not a damn thing," Chapuis spoke up. "There's no hotel, it's a water station for the railroad. Just a water tank and a poor excuse for a market. We might be able to camp for the night and scrounge dinner."

Reygasse shook his head emphatically. Byron looked at him. Stripped of his burnoose, his uniform was actually clean from the knees up. The Marshall kept repeating, "No, no. We have to push on."

"Maurice, it might be for the best," De Prorok offered mildly.

"Absolutely not. First of all, we have people waiting for us in Touggart, and they'll be worried. Our hosts have been cooking for us. And these are people you don't want to disappoint." Reygasse directed that last statement directly at Byron, who took his meaning.

Chapuis coughed. "Messieurs, if I may, it's getting close to dark…"

"Yes it is, Chapuis, that happens at night. Especially when you're not prepared for the road you're on. The faster we get on the road, the sooner we'll be there, no?" Reygasse looked to Byron for support he wasn't yet prepared to give.

"What do the rest of you think?" Byron really hoped they'd reach consensus so he wouldn't have to cast the deciding vote.

Belaid, Chapuis and the Americans were in favor of spending the night at Stil and pressing on in the morning. On hearing, "spend the night outdoors," Barth and Denny immediately sided with the Marshall. Of course it would bloody be up to me, he thought. He sighed and voted with the New York Times. Best to push on.

"Dark be damned," he said, clapping his hands. "We've earned a hot meal and a soft rack, and both those things await us in Touggart. Let's go. Louis, why don't you and Hot Dog take the lead?"

After all the rain a glorious sunset taunted them as they headed off to the southeast. After about ten minutes, they passed the hamlet of Stil. Byron cupped his hand over his eyes to see the water tower, a couple of date palms and a few dilapidated houses. Reygasse is right, probably worth skipping he thought.

The ground was mostly hard-packed sand now, making traction reliable and travel much safer. As the bumps became less jarring, their speed increased. He watched Escande confidently navigate. He wondered how he could tell the difference between the official track of the road, and the desert floor. That's what separates professionals from the rest of us. Sooner than expected, night fell and everything was coated in thick inky blackness.

After an hour, de Prorok became seriously concerned. Chapuis' plan had been to follow the railroad tracks, which was fine providing one could actually see the tracks in question. Instead the only thing they could make out in the direct glow of the headlights was ten to twenty yards of rock and scrub brush.

Ten minutes after he began to worry the caravan came to a halt. They were, exactly as he feared, completely lost, and had been for about thirty minutes.

The Count heard everyone's opinion then nodded. "Nothing for it, then. We'll backtrack to Stil and spend the night." Reygasse began to protest, but the Count held up his hand. "End of discussion." Both Pond and Reygasse appeared thunderstruck, but the

Count had made a decision, one he sounded like he would actually stand by.

"Signor Martini. Allez-vous." They turned the cars around, Lucky Strike in the lead this time, and headed back even slower than they'd come, desperately keeping the faint tire tracks framed in the weak headlights. At last they heard the comforting ca-chunk of rubber on real road bed, and a few minutes later they saw the welcoming fires of Stil.

The parade of filthy cars came to a halt in front of a ramshackle telegraph office. Three carloads of hungry, shivering men stepped out, flaking mud everywhere. The temperature climbed once the rain stopped, and was actually becoming warm, but the afternoon's exertion and wet filth made that irrelevant. Every member of the party was shivering, tired and ravenous.

The Count stretched his long legs and climbed out of the car. Curious faces peered out at them through rough doorways and tent flaps. Mostly children at first, then they heard a voice greeting them warily. "Qui est la?"

The Station Master emerged from the largest shack, a rifle in his hand; the way it shook in his grip he could have been aiming at any one of them. Everyone nodded to each other in silence, each party waiting for the other to speak.

Chapuis offered a brief explanation of their trouble, leaving out the most embarrassing parts, and politely asked if they could park their vehicles and camp until morning. This drew a grudging accommodation from the locals who pointed to a dry, flat spot just off the road.

As Chapuis negotiated this, Escande whispered to Byron, "Ask about food."

Chaix chimed in. "What about dinner? Is there a

restaurant?" Like ornery children up past their bed times, they just wanted their supper.

Like children, de Prorok quickly shushed them. "Just hold on, damn you."

The slam of a car door drew their attention to Reygasse, who'd removed the burnoose and stood in front of them in his uniform and medals. He looked the very picture of the French authority, at least from the shins up. Below that, his pants and boots were a solid brick of desert mud, but the sight of him sent a buzz through the crowd. Byron groaned.

"Have you a telephone? I must tell the authorities in Touggart where we are. I'm sure they're looking for us already."

"I'm afraid not, but we have a telegraph, I can wire for you," squeaked Costans, the manager.

"I'd be most grateful. Thank you."

"Ask them about dinner, Monsieur," came two voices, almost in chorus.

"Have you anything extra you can spare for us? We haven't eaten since noon, you see. We were supposed to have a great banquet…"

The station master, Costans, bit his lip and shook his head sadly. "You'll have to ask the wife about that, but I doubt it. The supply train is a day late, and everyone is already eating scraps."

De Prorok stoically took it all in. Taking a deep preparatory breath, he barked an order to Belaid. He needed to do something before Reygasse got them all shot. "Start camp, Monsieur Belaid. Let's make the best of it. Maurice, wire Touggart and tell them we aren't coming and they can call off the hunt til morning. Chapuis, see what you can do about food, if you will."

"Can I go with him?" asked Pond.

Lonnie didn't know much about the desert

although he'd heard of the desert code of hospitality, and how no one would ever let a guest starve, even a stranger. He sincerely hoped that was more accurate intelligence than the geography books and maps had provided so far. He did know he hadn't starved in France during the war, though, even in places where there was precious little to spare, and had talked more than one housewife out of an egg or a chicken in time of need. This situation warranted his best efforts, before the Renault drivers tried to eat poor Martini.

As Costans led the Count and Reygasse to the telegraph office, the rest of the expedition maneuvered the cars into a wide triangle, shining their headlights into the center to illuminate their workspace.

Tyrrell, Chapuis and Pond conferred, then headed towards the largest, most European-looking house. There they were met at the door by the chatelaine, Madame Costans, a thin, hawk-faced woman with no discernible sense of humor. The three men all bowed. Chapuis took his cap in his hand and offered a meek "Bonjour Madame." The others chimed in as well, hoping to get in her good graces. They got a single, suspicious nod in reply.

"Only one of you is French."

Chapuis admitted that the other visitors were American, which elicited an arched eyebrow. Pond came forward, twisting his hat in hand and offered a small bow. "We're surprised to find such a lovely French woman out here. It makes the trip almost worth it." Both parties smiled at the lie. "Madame, is it possible that you might spare some dinner tonight? We've not eaten all day, you see. We were supposed to be in Touggart tonight. As you can see, we didn't make it and we have to spend the night here."

"How many are you?"

Pond shrugged, "Not many at all. Only twelve of us."

"Twelve, how am I supposed to feed twelve of you? I'm afraid I can't help you, I'm sorry."

Tyrrell's shoulders sagged in disappointment. Chapuis and Pond grinned. This was only the first salvo of what could be a long back and forth battle. "I know it's a huge imposition, Madame," Louis said, "and it shames me that I've led my people into this situation. Are you sure you can't help us just a bit?"

"I've never known a French woman yet who couldn't make a miracle out of an egg—like the loaves and fishes," added Pond.

"Eggs," she spat, "we don't even have chickens." Just then a clucking squawk erupted from behind the house. "Just one stupid old rooster…not a hen left," she hastily explained.

"Perhaps just some porridge, or a couscous?" Pond asked again. This was an unexpected turn, and Madame Station Agent raised a skeptical eyebrow.

"That's native food. You'd eat that?" Pond smiled. The game was afoot.

"What's couscous?" Tyrrell asked out of the side of his mouth as he smiled and nodded as if thrilled with the notion.

"It's hard to explain," Pond said in English. "It's kind of like grits only edible. Usually made with meat, if they have it. It's not bad and a little can feed an army."

He turned back to the lady who was trying to understand the foreign conversation. Pond switched back to French. "It may be peasant food, but in your hands it would be a feast. We'd be ever so grateful. Thank you so much."

"I'll see what I can do. It will take an hour or so." She looked at their clay encrusted pants and boots.

"I'll bring it out to you when it's ready."

"Merci, Madame," and the three backed away bowing, as if to a Queen. This brought both a contemptuous snort and a giggle from the woman as she hustled into the shack, shouting at someone, either a servant or a child.

"Good work, Pond." Chapuis clapped him on the shoulder. Tyrrell pulled out his pipe and stuffed a pinch of tobacco inside, spilling most of it as they walked. "Did those charms work on all the French women when you were there?"

"Unfortunately only ones that looked like that, and only when it came to food."

"Maybe we won't tell Dorothy about this, huh? Hey, not that I'm ungrateful, but do they have meat in this couscous or is it just like a porridge?" Just then, a shrieking squawk could be heard, accompanied by the hysterical flapping of wings.

"I suspect this one will have some chicken in it," Pond said, very pleased with himself.

A long hour later, Monsieur and Madame Costans arrived, bearing a huge platter on which was couscous with bits of stewed chicken. Another family came bearing a bowl of local olives, and a third brought some dates as dessert. Along with the little bit of bread left over from lunch and the rest of the wine, it turned into quite a feast.

Reygasse, his mood improved considerably and still hell-bent on having a banquet tonight, invited their hosts to sit and join them. After the appropriate refusals, they sat down on the ground with a smile. The crew would have dived right in, but there was a lack of utensils, which caused a moment of consternation and confusion before Belaid explained what they were eating, and how one ate it with one's fingers without seeming like savages.

Madame Costans' concern that fancy people like Frenchmen and Americans didn't eat peasant food was well founded. It turned out that Tyrrell, Barth, Denny and the drivers Chaix and Escande, had never eaten native cuisine. It struck none of their party as odd that they'd been in Algeria two weeks already, and this was their first local meal. Hunger proved a good teacher, though, and they quickly figured out that the process of getting food to one's mouth with fingers was universal.

Now that the rumbling in his stomach had quieted down, de Prorok could think again. He stood and called for attention. First he toasted Madame Costans for her beauty and generosity, then M. Costans for allowing them the pleasure of a safe place to sleep and the company of his charming wife and friends.

The wine seemed to be working wonderfully well on empty stomachs, because it wasn't long before the teasing and story-telling began. One of the Constans' neighbors shouted that since they were eating like Arabs, it was Muslim custom to sing for one's supper.

"Ah yes indeed. A song. Allow me, if you would." De Prorok started off by bowing deeply to his audience, drawing up all his dignity. He stood with a very serious look on his face, taking an opera singer's stance. He cleared his throat, folded his hands professionally across his chest, and then launched into a mildly profane but very funny French folk song, complete with a silly, wiggling dance. The audience erupted in applause and laughter.

Then he turned to the drivers with a cold smile. "Gentlemen, I believe some gratitude is in order. See if you can find your way through a song, at least, will you?" Moping, they stood up, conferred, then Chaix and Escande sang a song popular with French soldiers during the war that got polite applause. Caid Belaid contributed an Arab ballad which few people understood, but contained enough trills and ululations to impress.

Brad Tyrrell spared everyone from his singing voice by playing his mouth organ which greatly amused everyone who hadn't spent the last three days in a car with him. The locals had never seen such an instrument and clamored for more, which pleased the American mightily. Maurice Reygasse leaned over to the Count and whispered, "Maybe he's good for something besides babysitting the Museum's money after all." Byron let the uncharitable remark pass. Everyone was tired and a little grumpy.

Pond was getting nervous. It was almost his turn, and flattering housewives was as close as he came to a talent for poetry or music. Eyes turned to him, expectantly.

"Brad, what am I supposed to do? You've heard me sing… it will start an international incident," he asked the older American.

"Hell, kid, I don't know. Just do something. What did you do at school?"

The musicales and skit nights at Beloit College were largely the province of fraternity boys and rich kids who didn't have to work, hardly Pond's world. He stood up and sheepishly explained that while it wasn't a song, exactly, the school cheer did go something like this. He then threw his arms in the air and waved them back and forth in time to a chant:

"Ole Olson, Yohnny Yohnson, Go Beloit…Wisconsin." He repeated it twice, giving it the old college try and entreating others to join in. After a couple of half-hearted attempts, he slunk back to his place by the fire, embarrassed, while Byron explained to the confused audience as best he could the notion of a school cheer and why Americans were so attached to them.

To shake him out of his funk, Tyrrell nudged Pond in the ribs. "Let's teach them, 'How do you do Harry Jones?' You'll have to translate, though." Pond regained his feet and explained in French that it was a song many groups sang to welcome visitors. You sing the song and put the visitors name in it. Then you sing another chorus saying *that* person's name, and adding the next name to it and try to get through it by including everyone.

He demonstrated by singing, "How do you do—and pointed at Tyrrell, who sang back 'Brad Tyrrell'." He led a few brave souls in echoing it back. Then he sang "How do you do….and pointed at the Count, who quickly added in his lush baritone, "Byron Prorok" a few more people joined in singing, "How do you do Byron Prorok," then Pond pointed back to Brad, and a few people managed to utter a mangled "Brahd Teerell," and on it went until everyone was properly introduced and the audience dissolved into giggles, falling over themselves in both French and English.

The night air and plentiful food finally warmed the travelers, and morning would arrive early so the party drew to a close. De Prorok thanked everyone profusely, kissed Mme Constans' bony hand adieu and the expedition settled down to a few hours of sleep on the hard ground.

The day's stresses had sapped the team's energy. Everyone, even Denny, who hated sleeping outdoors more than most New Yorkers, fell fast asleep with a minimum of grousing. The night was warmer and dryer than the day had been, and surprisingly comfortable.

It was also extremely pleasant, it turned out, for the mosquitoes which were usually dormant for the year by now but with all kinds of wet places to spawn, they used them as a base of attack. They spent the night tormenting the members of the team and waking each of them in turn with either their incessant humming or stinging.

Eventually, dawn broke and the team straggled to their feet. The Costans, or some other locals, had left dates and bread for their breakfast. The team broke camp as quickly as possible and headed alongside the now visible railroad tracks to Touggart, arriving mid-morning in an itching, scratching, mud-bedraggled caravan.

God help us, Byron thought to himself as they pulled into Touggart. *This was supposed to be the easy leg of the trip.*

Chapter 7

Ames, Iowa
January 26, 1926

I squatted near the stage in my new white overalls, looking for all the world like a giant snowball, in plain view—and earshot—of everyone. As I did all the necessary last-minute puttering, I could hear snatches of conversation behind me.

"Who's this galoot?"

"He must be part of the show."

"Ooh, I didn't know there'd be movies. So it's not just all some joker talking?"

"Yes, Marv, there's movies. God's sake, you're like a little boy. It wouldn't kill you to have a little culture."

Behind me, I could hear Marv defending himself. "What? I like the pictures. Makes it more interesting. What's wrong with that?" I was on Marv's side.

Marv was going to get his pictures, alright. I knew, because I'd gone through every one of them that morning, ensuring they were upside down and backwards. I also carefully wiped them with a tiny splash of vinegar and water and an old silk shirt of de Prorok's to remove the accumulated fingerprints, sweat and God knows what. My eyes almost crossed by the time I was done, but it was worth it.

I flexed my right hand. It felt good not to have the bandages on any more, even if it wasn't a hundred percent healed. A patch on the back of my hand was shiny and smooth, completely devoid of hair or wrinkles. It still felt tight when I flexed it, but no one could really see. Maybe they were too dazzled by the stupid monkey suit I was wearing. Small blessings.

The cue sheet was in place, large block letters on foolscap so I could read it, and the little Niagara flashlight handy, so I could read in the dark. Somehow, in all the lectures he'd given, it had never occurred to the Count to actually write down what came when so someone could actually read it. I felt a little sorry for all his past assistants. No wonder it was usually such a train wreck. The film canisters were neatly stacked and legibly labeled to the right of the table, the magic lantern and the slides to the left. I guessed I was as ready as I was going to be.

I looked over to the wings of the stage. The Count stood alone, muttering to himself. He cut quite a figure. We'd swapped out the sweat-stained cloth that covered his pith helmet so it was whiter than the Iowa snow. I'd spent almost an hour polishing his boots— my old man would choke if he knew—to an onyx shine. Relaxed and confident, he idly twirled his walking stick and paced back and forth, muttering to himself. He looked up, caught my eye and gestured me over.

I "pardoned," and "excuse me-ed" my way to the edge of the stage. He leaned down and whispered, "Everything ready, Brown?"

"Yeah, it's all set up."

"You're sure?" A fleeting moment of doubt flashed across his face. I nodded again. He turned away and muttered reassuringly to himself, "Good, very good." I thought I heard a vague 'thank you' but his back was to me.

"So you're our speaker, are you ready?" That perfect smile reappeared in the split second it took to turn to the speaker, a distinguished looking older guy.

"President Pearson, isn't it? Yes, indeed. Ready when you are, sir. Just checking with my presentation technician that everything's ship shape."

Raymond Pearson, president of Iowa State College seemed suitably impressed. "Well, if your technician says we're good to go, let's begin shall we?" He checked his note cards. "And it's pronounced de Proke?"

"De Pro... rock... actually."

Pearson wrote it phonetically on a note card, gave a curt nod and walked away muttering to himself. "Prorok. De. Pro. Rok."

According to one of the knowledgeable voices behind me, Pearson was leaving to take over some big school in Maryland, and only came out now for big sporting events. The Des Moines papers were here tonight, though, so he came out to absorb some reflected glory.

I returned to my position, apologized to the people whose view was suddenly obstructed by this giant white blob, and got ready. The house lights dimmed, the stage lights popped on, and the Honorable Raymond Allan Pearson emerged to polite applause. I guess everyone knew he was a short timer, and didn't need to ingratiate themselves.

There were the obligatory kind words of thanks, blah blah blah, yakkety yakkety, and something about auspicious occasions. Then he told everyone how proud and pleased he was to introduce the discoverer of Tin Hinan's tomb, the world's most renowned archaeologist and his personal friend, Count Byron de Prock. I tried to suppress a laugh that turned into a snort and launched a booger onto the sleeve of my white overalls.

The Count never missed a beat. He shook

Pearson's had warmly, gave him a friendly upper arm squeeze and strode to the edge of the stage. The silver tip of his stick struck the ground. Every eye turned to him expectantly. "Thank you, Ray... President Pearson, I'm sorry. This is a formal occasion." Pearson beamed and magnanimously forgave him.

"Good evening everyone. I'm truly humbled at the greeting you've given me. It proves I was right. You see, I said to myself...." It was the same spiel as last time, only last time it was Des Moines, and just like last time when he got to, "That's when it occurred to me... Ames Iowa," they laughed just as hard as they had in Grinnell and Des Moines.

Then he turned to the chubby little brunette who'd escorted us around that afternoon. "I'd like to thank the lovely Miss Angelica Carter for her hospitality..." I was a little surprised that the words hadn't changed at all. It just seemed so effortless and natural that the notion he wasn't just making everything up as he went along never occurred to me.

The words drifted back to me, "...The Franco-American Sahara Expedition of 1925. Maestro, if you please..." I was so caught up watching him I almost forgot I was the Maestro in question. I snapped to attention long enough to slide the first picture into place. There was pause and a look of surprised relief on my boss's face as the members of the expedition and their trucks were displayed with their feet and tires pointing in the proper downward direction.

I mentally shouted at myself to pay attention dammit, and focused on the task at hand. The next slide was the entrance to the desert. I checked my notes, clicked the button on the lantern and... right on cue.

"Our first three days were without incident. I'd like to show you something you don't often associate with the arid Sahara…" Click, whir and the film showed one of the trucks rolling effortlessly across a wide river.

"We were honored at a banquet of local foods in a little village called Stil…" Another click, another picture. This time it was the Americans shoving something in their mouths with their fingers. Another click, and a snapshot of the Count singing to the gathered audience. As much as the Algerians seemed to have a good time, the good people of Ames enjoyed it just as much.

The time flew by. Snatches of his speech were nothing more than cues for me to start a movie or click a new image into view.

"The grave of Pere Lavigerie…"

"The village of Touggart…"

"Machine gun practice," that one caused quite a buzz.

"They call this Love Mountain…"

The films were actually quite interesting, the little I saw of them. The natives in the movie looked a little like they do in Hollywood films, only more real. And scary. Not like Valentino or Tom Mix, or any of those guys who didn't look like they'd ever been in a real fight in their lives.

De Prorok's voice boomed out to the crowd. "They're not actually Arab or Negro at all. In fact, many experts think the Tuaregs are a lost white race. They're taller than their neighbors, and infinitely stranger. The men dress in veils and bright blue robes, while the women are unveiled and run the village. The men can't be bothered with mundane issues, they're too busy hunting and fighting… and they all are quite expert in this…"

He pulled the blue robe thingy, I remember it was called a *burnooz,* out of the box and struggled to put it on. "Just a moment…" the more he wriggled, the more tangled up he got, like a backwards Houdini. You could hear a chair scraping impatiently on the floor as someone shifted on their seat.

Finally, he managed to yank it over his clothes, more or less. Then he put on the *tagelmus*, a big blue turban, and grabbed the phony sword, giving it a couple of crisscrossed swipes in front of him, slicing the air to ribbons. That drew some uncomfortable laughter from the crowd.

From my position the sword—he called it a *flyssa*—didn't look nearly as cheap and fake as it did up close, but it sure wasn't threatening. The way the pasteboard blade wobbled, I knew it wouldn't last many more performances. I'd have to take care of that.

A flustered Count de Prorok finally admitted defeat. "And then they would dance with their swords. If you would, please…" That was my cue to start the film of the Tuaregs dancing. It didn't look like much, just a lot of moving back and forth, waving swords then leaning back, kind of an Arab Hokey Pokey.

It actually made them seem less terrifying. Then I imagined what they'd think if they saw my father and his friends jumping around in their lederhosen and Tyrol hats, wielding nothing more dangerous than steins of beer. Maybe it wasn't so silly and embarrassing after all.

Shedding the robes proved easier than putting them on. They fell in a heap on the floor, and he unceremoniously kicked them aside as he continued. "Finally, we reached the resting place of the great Berber Queen, the Mother of all Tuaregs, Tin Hinan…" I cranked carefully and the screen burst into light.

The tomb didn't look much like a movie set, just a small pit with a stone slab room. The Count, and damned if he didn't look good even after digging in the desert, wore a floppy French hat that drooped over to one side. One of the other guys kneeled beside a tiny, darkened skeleton. Jewels or beads or something were scattered all over the platform. A metal—gold I guess—armband and necklace adorned the bones. The Count lovingly caressed the skull as they all shook hands and smiled to the camera.

For a moment, we were no longer in snowy, Methodist, Iowa, but a big budget Ronald Coman movie. Any minute now, Vilma Bánky would scream for help and our heroes would have to run to her rescue. The spell stayed cast until the film ran out, and the screen erupted into white light accompanied by the flap-flap-flap of the trailer against the projector.

I clicked off the light, and the place was completely dark except for the row of stage lights. The Count, eyes flashing happily, took two steps forward. His eyes scanned the crowd back left to front right, then front right to rear left. Every audience member was convinced he looked straight at them. Slowy he tilted his head upwards and opened his arms wide. The tip and handle of his walking stick caught the light and glinted in his right hand.

"The New York Times called it…" and he went into his finishing speech. "…With you, the good people of Ames, Iowa, tonight." He paused, taking in each face in silence. After a short, wordless pause, he placed his hand over his heart and gave a small, elegant bow.

The place went crazy. Everyone applauded. Even Marv behind me risked his wife's displeasure by breaking decorum and putting two fingers in his mouth, whistling his shrill appreciation. The 'pictures' really had made things better.

I rocked back on my heels and began rewinding the

film. I was so busy it took me a moment to catch onto what he was saying from the platform, but finally it filtered through.

"And if you notice that we didn't suffer the slings and arrows so often associated with projectors and equipment, it's because of the unsung hero of the evening…" Oh Christ no. He wasn't really going to do it. Of course he was. "My presentation technician and aide de camp, Willy Brown." He extended an open palm my way and several hundred eyes locked on my burning red face.

I managed a weak wave in acknowledgment, then returned to my equipment. I wished I could have crawled into one of the crates until everyone was gone. Ignoring the good wishes of the crowd, I set to work while my employer finished up with the usual question time.

Inevitably the first question was, "is there a Countess?" Then "What's your next trip?" Something was different about the next question, though.

"Count de Prorok, the New York Times reported there's some controversy with your discovery. Some even claim the body you say is Tin Hinan isn't even female…" The young woman, a pretty enough redhead with a perfect triangle of a nose was interrupted by the surprised muttering of the crowd. It didn't seem to faze the Count.

The perfect smile stayed perfectly in place as he raised a hand to shush the audience. "What paper do you work for, my dear?" Turns out she worked for the Ames Daily. "And has the Register ever said one of your stories was untrue?"

The audience cracked up at that. The Register and its ruthless bastard of a publisher Cowles spent as much time trying to disprove anything the State's other papers wrote as they did putting out news of their own. She smiled politely and conceded that it had. She was about to follow up, but never got the chance.

"There is always going to be a healthy skepticism about any find like this, and of course some unhealthy jealousy. There should be—it's how we guard against frauds and charlatans. But surely, you also know that an independent pathologist from L'Institut Scientifique d'Algier has cleared all that up." He moved forward, taking each member of the audience into his confidence.

"The challenge, you see, is that Tin Hinan's pelvis was smaller than the average female, leading some to wrongly conclude it might have been the body of a male. What's been scientifically, unequivocally proven, is that her pelvis," and here he made a large circle with the tips of his fingers barely touching, "made it impossible for her to have children. Ironic, isn't it, that the Mother of the Tuaregs was unable to fulfill the normal destiny of women everywhere and have children of her own?" This drew a sympathetic clucking from the audience.

"Like Joan of Arc, or Elizabeth the Virgin Queen, she took that pain and turned it to power. In fact," he turned to the crate of props and pulled out a snowman-shaped rock with a hole bored through what should have been its head. "This was found next to her body. It may have been a fertility fetish designed to help her conceive in the next world." He turned to the reporter, "You may, all of you, come take a look afterwards, if you wish. Although, I must warn you there are markings on the lower part of this that make it, uhhhh, undeniably female. Let your sensibilities be your guide." I smiled at that. They'd be lined up around the block now.

The reporter admitted defeat and closed her

notebook. The crowd surged forward to shake the hand of the mighty explorer, and take a look at the titillating hunk of stone. The pudgy Angelica Carter used her sorority organizing skills to herd them into a line. The crowd looked the same as it did in Grinnell, right down to a guy in the same brown hat and coat as I'd seen the other night.

The car idled outside for half an hour before de Prorok appeared. Standing by the door, I watched as he kissed Miss Carter's hand adieu and gave a quick wave to the stragglers. He pulled on his overshoes, coat and scarf, but didn't seem to know what to do with his white desert helmet. Finally, he put it on his noggin, hunched down and made a dash for the car.

The temperature had dropped about twenty degrees while we were inside and he uttered a muffled, "Good Christ," through his scarf as he dropped into the passenger seat. He hunkered down with the bridge of his nose deep in his coat. Only his eyes and forehead showed between the thick woolen scarf and his white African desert pith helmet.

His teeth chattered as he asked, "Why the hell would someone live here? Is it this cold in Muh-waukee?" He loved making fun of my accent, even though I didn't think I had one.

I grinned. "Colder. And there's m-m-more snow 'cause it's by the lake."

"Why the hell would someone voluntarily live in these Arctic conditions? Are you all mad?"

I gave him one of my patented useless shrugs. "I dunno. Just born here I guess."

"You're not a bloody oak tree, you know. You can move any time you like." Easy for him to say. I tried to leave Milwaukee and wound up in frigging Iowa. I released the clutch and eased onto University

Boulevard, then left onto Pammel around the north end of the campus.

We passed a series of barns that made up the School of Agriculture. He let out a tortured moan. "Did we really just pass something called the Ruminant Laboratory?"

"Who's Ruminant? Do you know him?"

"Just drive." He pouted silently the rest of the way.

Minutes later, I pulled up in front of the College's Guest House. De Prorok took two deep breaths and dashed for the warmth and whatever comforts it offered, leaving me to spend the next twenty minutes or so hauling projectors and boxes to the icy steps, then inside the entrance way. I stacked them there so I could reload for Moline in the morning.

I had just managed to pull my feet with their two pairs of wool socks out of my boots when a voice boomed down the stairs. "Brown, are you done?"

"Yeah," I said, as I stepped into a frigid puddle of melted snow, feeling the thick wool slurp it up like a sponge.

"Come join me."

After throwing my overalls onto the bed in my tiny second floor room, I went up to the third floor. The count's room was large enough for a bed and chair, making it the Presidential suite of the establishment. He stood with his back to me, wearing a silk robe of some kind and staring out the window. In his hand was a glass with a thin layer of something amber in it.

"How do you think it went tonight?"

I thought about it. "Pretty good. They liked it a lot."

"Better than Grinnell?" He turned to look at me and knocked back the rest of his drink.

"Yeah, sure. They clapped louder, and they stuck around longer."

His glass hit the table with a solid ca-thunk. From the pocket of his robe he pulled out a bottle and refilled his glass. Then he poured one for me and held it out. I took it without thinking.

I didn't drink much, except for beer. For a German kid in Milwaukee, that was more like a sacrament than actual drinking. As for booze, well it was illegal and I didn't need that kind of trouble. Second, the few experiences I'd had with hard liquor hadn't gone very well. Moderation wasn't taught in our home. People used to say, "Have a drink and be somebody." I was always afraid that someone was my Old Man, so I usually declined.

De Prorok examined his glass. "Templeton Rye, they call it. Not bad stuff as homemade hooch goes. And it's from here. When in Rome, eh? Kind of like drinking cognac in Cognac or champagne in Champagne, I suppose. Honestly, how can people live in this climate and ban alcohol? If I were king, I'd make it mandatory."

He lifted his glass in a toast I nervously returned. I took a little sip, hoping the outside of my mouth didn't show how much the inside of my mouth burned.

"Brown, why do you think it went better tonight than last time? Except for that harpy of a reporter, dragging up old business. But why was it better than Grinnell?"

I didn't know what he expected me to say. "It was weird. I mean, you said the exact same stuff the exact same way, but they sure seemed to eat it up."

His eyes lit up, or maybe it was the rye. "Because they weren't distracted. Everything worked tonight, so they could stay with me. No breaks in concentration. Last time they'd be in Algeria one minute, then wiggling their bums in hard gymnasium chairs watching someone turn a slide upside right the next. I couldn't sustain the magic."

He rattled on, explaining about rhythm, and how a good lecture was like a Beethoven symphony, which seemed like a stretch to me, but I didn't like long-hair music much more than I liked lectures.

"You can't have crashing symbols and pounding drums for ninety minutes, you need gentler movements and slow, dramatic builds, but they can't be interrupted. I mean, you need the big horns and all to keep people awake and excited." Tonight, according to him, it flowed. Even if Ames was just some cow-college town, it worked. And if they all went like this, well soon it would be real cities.

"What cities?" I asked.

"Would you believe New York City? There's talk of Carnegie Hall in the spring, maybe June. Would you like to see New York, Brown?" My sudden dizziness was only partly due to the rye.

We talked about what worked (the unveiling of the tomb seemed to really grab them) and what didn't (that jazz with the robe and the sword looked kind of goofy). He watched me over the lip of his glass as we spoke, listening like I knew what I was talking about, which was completely ridiculous because I didn't know nothing from nothing and knew it all too well.

"Your glass is empty." So it was, and he fixed that little problem immediately. I should have stopped him, but he was in the middle of a story about Madame Rouvier. She was the rich lady with the boobs popping out of her dress in the first movie. At least that's how I remembered her. He recalled her fondly as the one person in all of North Eastern Algeria who could iron out all the permits for their trip.

"A charming woman, Denise, but not subtle," he

said cryptically.

"Did her husband know about you two?" I asked, in that subtle way only an inexperienced, slightly drunk nineteen year old could manage.

"Brown, I'm married. Happily so, if there is such a thing. She was too, although certainly less happy. No, I never slept with Denise Rouvier, much to her great disappointment, I'm sure."

"Then why did she help you?"

"Because I charmed everything but the pants off her. Charm, Brown—you should try it some time." Yes, he'd flirted, intimated, cajoled, stroked fingers while reaching for green beans, and stood far too close for propriety's sake, but he swore up and down her virtue remained intact. At least it was as of the time of his departure.

"Is that why you always kiss the girl's hand when you leave?" I was thinking about the way he treated our escort. "I thought for sure, you know, with the blonde at Grinnell. Maybe not so much with the pudgy one here…"

"I'll let you in on a secret, Willy. American men think everything is about either sex or baseball. Flirting isn't about sex. It's a game. A fun game, too, if you learn how to play it properly." My blank stare began to irritate him a little.

"Seduction is complete when you know the other person has given up and you can get what you want from them. Sex is merely the reward for your hard work. Or the price you have to pay. In the case of Denise Rouvier, it would have been a very high price, believe me."

"How do you do that? How do you know how to talk to people like that?"

He took another sip of his whisky, and threw his head back for a moment, silent. "How did you know how to handle the lantern projector the other night, when whats-his-name couldn't manage?"

I didn't see the connection, but he refused to let me off the hook so I just mumbled, "You just feel it. Say it slides real easy. If you push too hard you can knock it off k-k-kilter, or break something so you need to be gentle with it. Sometimes it needs a rough p-p-push. You can tell just by feel." Anyone who'd ever worked with machines knew that.

"So you know how things normally work, then you adjust based on how it feels, right?" Yeah, that was about it.

"Same thing." He took a big swallow. "It's exactly the same damned thing." It sure didn't feel like the same thing at all, but then I wasn't as smart as him.

We talked in easy circles for a long time. The conversation would drift off for a while. We'd gab about Wisconsin, or the South of France, but it always came back around to the lecture that night. Yes, it had gone well, but there were two things that really bothered him, and he couldn't let them go.

First was that damned reporter. "Why did she have to go and spoil everything? People were having such a good time, and she tried to bring it all… down. Why do some people always feel the need to revisit dead issues? I mean, it's settled. Why can't they just give me credit for doing my bloody job?" I had no answer for him, but I don't think he really expected one.

The second bone he continued to gnaw was the mess with the robe. The real props and relics just didn't generate the excitement of the movies and pictures. "What I really need to do is bring out a real, honest-to-god Tuareg. Scariest people I've ever met, including…" he winked at me as he polished off another drink, "Madame Rouvier. You should see King Akhamouk. Impressive as hell in the flesh. The robes, the swords, all very romantic and exciting. And I wouldn't need to haul around all this projection gear."

I wouldn't have said anything earlier in the evening, but the Templeton truth serum was working its magic on me. "It all looks a bit... girly. The Arabs in movies always look scarier."

That drew a contemptuous sniff. "Arabs are a small, suspicious, superstitious people. Scary with a dagger if your back is turned, but not someone you'd worry about in a real fight. The Tuaregs, though, are much, much bigger. They're all about my height. Or yours."

He stopped and looked me up and down. "Jesus, you are a big one. How tall are you, anyway?"

"About six feet and a bit, I guess."

He sat straight up. "Right, and you're bigger across the shoulders than I am, like he is. Wait!" He leapt to his feet, swayed a second while he corrected his balance, then stumbled over to the trunk with all the robes and props. "Stand up, Brown."

I managed to get to my feet on the second attempt. I wondered what he was doing. Then the light slowly dawned. No way. "Unh uh."

"Oh come on, I'm making a point here." He threw the blue robe over my shoulders, and pulled it down over me roughly, while I wriggled like a four year old trying to avoid getting his jammies on.

Finally, he tugged the burnoose into place, then he attempted to wind the turban around my head—the whiskey making a complicated act even trickier. In frustration, he wrapped it around his own head, then pulled it off and placed the finished product atop my big Kraut cranium. It was just like my Old Man would knot my tie around his own neck, then slip it over my head to finish it up.

He gripped my shoulders and spun me towards the mirror on the wardrobe door. Facing me was a six-foot tall, pale, slightly the worse for drink Tuareg warrior. I didn't look much like the scourge of the Sahara. I looked like Fatty Arbuckle in a Christmas pageant, and told him so.

"Hmmmmm, you're right." He inspected me head to toe like a critical haberdasher, then reached into the box and pulled out a scrap of cloth the same deep blue as the robe, lined with beadwork and small metal wires along the top and bottom. He examined it thoughtfully, then wheeled around and held it over my mouth as if to chloroform me.

"Hold still, dammit." I wanted to stamp my foot and pout, but settled for shaking my head. He grabbed me by the turban long enough to connect the veil across the bridge of my nose. Then he wheeled me back to the mirror. Except for the bloodshot peepers, my reflection looked more like a denizen of the desert than it looked like me.

With a final flourish, he handed me the sword and showed me how to take up a warrior's stance; feet apart, sword upright in the middle of my body. "Take a couple of good swings with it," he said after taking a couple of long steps back.

I mimicked the moves he'd made on stage earlier. I had to admit, it looked pretty terrifying until the blade snapped and fell limply to one side. There was an awkward silence, then he said, "Well, yes, whiskey has been known to do that," and he erupted in laughter.

I looked at the broken flyssa. "Has that ever happened before?"

He wiped a tear of laughter from his eye. "You tell me. How well do you hold your liquor?" I didn't get it, which made him laugh even harder. I didn't know what I'd done that was so funny, and this was starting to get uncomfortable.

He plunked down in his chair, cackling wildly as he poured himself yet another drink. I quickly yanked the turban from my head, letting it unspool in an undignified pile at my feet and then de-robed. I was determined to get out of there while this was still the most humiliating thing to happen.

"Aww, and you make such a fine Tuareg, Brown. The Akhamouk of Ames. The mightiest warrior in all of Iowa," he chuckled.

We made vague plans for the next morning, and I made slow, deliberate progress down the stairs, careful not to wake whoever had managed to sleep through our performance to that point.

When the bed stopped spinning, I drifted off to sleep watching snow fall outside the window. I made a mental note to fix the fake sword before our next stop in Moline. I also had the nagging feeling I'd agreed to do something else for the Count, but couldn't remember what it was. It probably wasn't a big deal, I decided, and passed out cold.

Chapter 8

Touggart, Algeria
October 16, 1925

"Ack, ack, ack, ack."

Bradley Tyrrell, millionaire business owner and philanthropist, squatted in the mud making pretend machine gun noises, while Martini and Pond watched and nodded approvingly.

Martini managed something like a smile. "Très bien. Let's do it again. Alonzo, allez-vous."

In putting the expedition together, De Prorok decided a machine gun would be a good thing to have. For some reason, ammunition wasn't an equal priority. In order not to waste what little they had in rehearsal, they pretended to fire into a group of imaginary rampaging Tuaregs and made the most convincing noises they could muster.

Another thing they lacked was any kind of fighting experience. Pond had been an ambulance driver in the War, his experience with weapons limited to avoiding them whenever possible, and picking up the remains of those who couldn't do the same once the firing ceased. Tyrrell had seen a lot of movies and once met someone on a business trip to Chicago who knew someone who had met Al Capone. Martini served with a French artillery unit in *La Guerre Mondiale*. That made him commanding officer.

The two Americans clumsily disconnected the gun

from the collapsible stand and loaded it back in Lucky Strike. Then, on Martini's command, they hauled it out again, reassembled it and Pond took his turn firing imaginary bullets into the hypothetical attackers. "Ack, ack, ack, ack."

Pond knew he looked ridiculous, but the optimum time to learn the use of this contraption wasn't when swarming tribesmen and rampaging camels were bearing down on you. For that reason, they decided to take the morning and practice, rainy as it was.

It was fairly hostile territory, in its own way. They were surrounded by bemused locals.

"Can I try?" a young boy called in Arabic.

"C'mon, give me a turn," yelled another.

"Agggh, you got me," shouted the littlest one, spinning wildly where Tyrrell's phantom projectile hit him and he fell, giggling, into a puddle where he was immediately dogpiled by his friends.

The elder locals were far less amused. They sat in front of their houses, sipping coffee and shouting obscene jokes about the Americans' guns shooting blanks that brought howls from the youngsters who didn't get the joke but appreciated any mocking of foreigners.

Alonzo looked down at his bleeding and blistered fingers. The gun was an old St Etienne with very finicky works—probably as much a danger to the operator as the people on the muzzle end. He was already in a bad mood, waiting all day for news from home, and this wasn't helping. He had work to do, real work. "Why us? Why do we get the gun?"

It was Martini who pointed out that the options were more than a little limited. Who did they want to bet their lives on? The Count? Monsieur Reygasse? Did they want their lives in the hands of the Renault mechanics? Or fat Barth the photographer?

"But you know, the cars can drive faster than any camel born, we could just outrun them," Tyrrell said with uncharacteristic churlishness. Martini nodded. "D'accord, as long as we're on the road and not stuck in the sand. Then…" he gave a most eloquent shrug. "Encore, please."

They were saved by a loud, piercing whistle from Chapuis. "Post's here."

Pond and Tyrrell re-packed the St Etienne and the stand along with the unopened ammo box with considerably more speed and gusto than they'd managed to that point, wiped their hands on their pants, and hustled back to the hotel in higher spirits. Alonzo watched over his shoulder as Martini carefully locked the vehicle and informed the children in curse-laden Arabic what would happen to them if they touched anything. Then the little Italian wandered off in the other direction, enjoying the chance to be alone.

De Prorok sat at a table in the lobby of the hotel with a short glass full of brandy and a thick stack of envelopes, addressed in a host of languages, in front of him, sorting them by recipient. Each Renault driver had a letter, Martini had none—but then the Italian had no family he was aware of. Hal Denny had two or three letters, none of them official looking. Brad Tyrrell received only a couple of postcards, sent from friends in Europe apparently having a swell time and wishing he was with them. Three envelopes awaited Alonzo Pond; a thin one from Dorothy, Pond's new flame back in Wisconsin, one from his parents in Janesville, and an ominously bulging packet from the Logan Museum.

I wish I knew how to make Lonnie happy. He's not a bad sort, if a bit serious about everything. And God only knows what he's reporting back to Collie, de Prorok thought. Beloit College's support was important for this trip, even more critical to his plans for the next few years. There had to be a way to make the little American get fully onboard. Far better to have Pond as an ally than an enemy, and they were off to a demonstrably shaky start.

He examined his own stack of mail. An imposing manila envelope clearly marked Beloit College lay on top, and he quickly moved it to the bottom of the pile. The same with what was probably a scolding letter from his mentor, Professor Gsell. Why ruin a nice afternoon until you absolutely had to?

He picked up the expensive-looking embossed envelop, slit the seal with his thumbnail and opened it up. Alice's round, girlish handwriting filled the page:

October 14, 1925
Paris

Dearest Byron,

How are you? The girls and I are well and missing you terribly. Little Alice smiled at me today, although Annie says that's only gas, and she's too young. I told her the baby is every bit as smart as her father and is ahead of the other children, and she just laughed. M-T misses her Papa something awful, and has been very naughty, but she is two and they say that's what they do at that age. I don't know.

I hope you've solved your little problem with the local suppliers. Daddy agreed to wire the money, but he was awfully cross about it. I know that when you come back such a success he'll appreciate you more, like I do. Please try to be nicer to him, you'll win him over and he'll come around.

Mother is looking forward to having us for Christmas, and I have to admit I'm looking forward to going home. To Brooklyn, I mean. I like Paris, but the only person I can speak English with is Annie. The rest of the staff speak English reasonably well, but insist I speak in French to learn, then make fun of me because I'm so awful. They think they're helping but it just seems mean.

I don't mean to complain, I just miss you so much. Sometimes I wish I were with you in the desert, like back at Carthage, instead of sitting here by myself changing diapers. Mary says she's coming over in a few weeks, then will go back to NY with us. Won't that be nice?

Be safe, and come back to me dripping with gold and diamonds and glory like you promised.

All my love,

A

Byron felt a glow that was only partially from the brandy. He really did miss Alice and the babies. The details of the household, which used to bore him to tears, seemed absolutely charming at this distance. For the first time in a while, she sounded like the Alice he married; the spunky New York heiress who was game for anything. She was such a good sport she spent her honeymoon at a dig in Carthage, eating camp food and shoveling sand into a sieve. She found it all great fun, and loved being the center of attention, especially by the press.

No one could possibly love being Countess de Prorok more than Alice de Prorok *née* Kenny. Unfortunately, just as the fun was beginning, she came down with two off-setting conditions; an itch for travel and a suddenly swelling belly. For a while, she seemed to resent Byron for her plight, but his last visit home, and this letter, seemed to bode well for their future.

Her father, however, was a different matter. Like

all fathers-in-law, Bill Kenny thought Byron beneath his daughter. Like all sons-in-law, he found that an insulting notion, but when your only yardstick was money, completely reasonable. Oh well, that will change soon enough. *Let the nouveau-riche bastard complain when we find the treasure, and I come home with the digging rights and the income that goes with them. Let's see if Mr. "I'm good friends with Al Smith" lords it over me then.*

He looked over the rest of his mail. One letter bore very good news—an offer to speak at Grinnell College, wherever the hell that was. Byron checked the address again. Iowa, he knew, was somewhere near Chicago, so maybe he could string a decent run of dates together and make it worthwhile, although the idea of the Midwest in January was less than enticing.

The second letter was less encouraging. JH Finley, the president of the National Geographic Society was all up in arms because Byron had another speaking engagement in Virginia around the same time as the one he had booked with them. It was all petty nonsense, of course. The two lectures were on different topics, and was he supposed to turn down good money because of the Society's territorialism? It would all work itself out.

He took another contemplative sip, hoping it would gird his loins to read the letter from Gsell, when angry American voices echoed over the stone tiles. Looking up, he saw Pond and Tyrrell sandwiching a harassed looking Hal Denny between them. Pond was gesticulating wildly, while Brad looked on shaking his head from time to time.

"Look, I can't help what they do in New York…"

Pond was having none of it. "Not one real mention in over a month? Come on."

"That's a piss-poor excuse, Hal, and you know it." Brad was the calmer of the two, but only by a few degrees. That wasn't like him, and Byron knew he'd have to intervene.

Byron listened for a moment, trying to figure out what waters he was about to wade into, and what lay beneath them. The answer probably lay in that package he'd avoided, but maybe it was better to claim ignorance in this case. Finally, he couldn't delay the inevitable any more. He put on his best conciliatory smile, took a single deep breath and stepped in. "Gentlemen, something I can help with?"

"As a matter of fact, Byron, there is, although you've probably been made aware of it by now," said Brad with obviously forced composure. Tyrrell was taking charge, and Pond was happy to let him do it. He took a step back, happy to be out of the line of fire.

"I was just telling Hal, here, that the College and the Museum's involvement are at least partly based on publicity. We're supposed to get a fair mention in every single article—you know that's the deal we made—well, George Collie just wrote that in Denny's last four articles... four of them... We've gotten a single line. One. And that just a throwaway."

Denny piped up, his face turning scarlet. "And I told you..."

"Really, I had no idea. Hal, is that true?" Byron asked as calmly as he could.

The writer took a step back so he wasn't sandwiched between the two taller men, having to look upwards to speak. "I can't control what they do in New York. That's what I'm trying to tell them. I submitted the stories, I'll show you the drafts, but the copy people... they butcher stories all the time. I have no control over what makes the paper. Hell, I don't control much of anything."

Byron knew if Denny did have any real say in

things he wouldn't be here now. He also couldn't afford to irritate either Beloit or the Times, and blast it if every bloody thing he did seemed to annoy someone. *Why couldn't everyone just play nicely?* "I understand your dilemma, must be awfully frustrating for you. And Brad, I haven't read the letter from George yet, so this is the first I'm hearing about it, although I'm sure it's in there. You're right, the Logan and Alonzo… and you… deserve a full mention in all articles. I know Hal'll make every effort." He couldn't resist a quick confirming look down his nose at the sweating reporter, and offered a sympathetic smile.

Tyrrell was visibly more relaxed now. "Thanks for that. Hal, I know it's not your fault, but we do need to make sure all our needs get met. I know you'll do your best."

Byron had an idea. "Hal, would it help if I wrote a note to Carr Van Anda?"

Denny visibly blanched at the name of the mention of the Times' imperious Editor in Chief. "Jesus, Byron, that's not necessary. Let me see what I can do first." De Prorok cursed himself. As usual, a genuine offer to help was misinterpreted. Why did everyone always think the worst of him?

"Of course, Hal. I'll leave it to you. Brad, Alonzo, will that work for you? You know our relationship with the Museum is important, and there's so much future work at stake, for all of us. Really wonderful stuff, I'd hate to see a simple misunderstanding gum up the works. We'll all watch out for each other." He gave his best deal-closing smile, and Tyrrell returned it in kind.

Pond watched as both men lit their pipes, obviously more satisfied with the outcome than he was, but nodded as well. He was glad Tyrrell was here to take care of the business end of things. If only he could get on with some real work, it might make everything more bearable.

"Alright then, I believe the sun is over the yardarm, time for a drink. Pond, will you join us?" He knew better than to ask Denny, who preferred to sulk in public. Besides, he probably had to make some strategic changes to his next dispatch.

"No, I have things to do. Thanks anyway." Alonzo knew he'd need to cool off, and a walk in the light drizzle might just do it. He turned and left the hotel, twisting his neck to get rid of the tension. Getting rained on seemed somehow apropos given the news from home.

First of all, while de Prorok seemed to have deep pockets—or at least long arms to reach into other people's—Pond was having trouble getting paid. Somehow the Logan found it easier to get money from Beloit, Wisconsin into the hands of some local Arab for baksheesh than it did to put it in Pond's bank account only twelve miles away in Janesville. Bills were stacking up, and while no one was complaining—yet—all this drama was so unnecessary. As usual, he'd made all the proper arrangements for money to come in and find its way to the right hands. Why was it so difficult for people to just do their jobs?

Then there was the letter from Dorothy, full of the usual news from home and questions about his work. She was becoming strangely insistent on knowing his exact return date. Was she getting antsy? Was there someone else? He had no way of knowing, and he didn't much enjoy that feeling.

He was also concerned because he couldn't give her an answer. Up until now, he assumed he'd head home, at least for a while, as soon as their work here was done. He even floated the idea of a series of lectures (at a hundred bucks a pop) past Dr. Collie.

Now, not only did they have no plans for any lectures, they wanted to send him to Poland in the spring.

Poland? Jeez Louise. Yes, there was good work being done at a Paleolithic site near Boruska Cave, but he'd already been gone six months. How much longer would Dorothy wait? And damn it all, if he wanted to spend the summer sifting arrowheads, dodging mosquitoes and drinking bad Polish beer, he could have stayed in Wisconsin.

He kicked at a puddle, imagining just for a moment it was the seat of the Count's pants, which made him feel marginally better. The village of Touggart was so small he had to circumnavigate it twice before he felt fit for human company again. His mood wasn't lightened when he realized he had to go to that stupid banquet tonight.

The feast Reygasse promised before they got stuck in Stil was rescheduled, and the whole village was buzzing with preparations. While the idea of another night in a decent bed and a good meal were never completely unwelcome, he itched to be at the real work.

Despite Pond's misgivings and Byron's overindulgence, the departure banquet was a huge success. Reygasse presided over a feast straight out of the Arabian Nights. Lamb, rice dishes and all kinds of fruit and sweets were washed down by what seemed like gallons of tea and wine, depending on the consumer's adherence to his religion, were presented, shared and eagerly devoured. There were toasts, counter toasts, and the now traditional singing of "How Do You Do, Harry Jones?" And dancing girls, real dancing girls, aplenty.

Chapuis and Belaid both suggested moderation, but were roundly ignored by the rest of the Expedition. Who knew when such luxuries would afford themselves? The general gloom over yesterday's misadventures was quickly banished.

That feeling of optimism lasted for about five minutes after Byron opened his eyes the next morning. First of all, he was mildly hungover. Not unusual, but hardly what he needed to face the day. Second, it was raining. Then there was the bill he got presented for last night's festivities.

"You mean we have to pay for a banquet in our own honor? Hardly seems right."

Reygasse offered that condescending smirk of his. "These are poor people. Their hospitality would have been quite meager if we hadn't offered to contribute. And don't forget we cancelled the night before, which meant more food and more work for them. Besides the Caid can be most helpful given the problems we've had with the suppliers."

Byron signed. More unforeseen expenses meant more hastily written begging letters to Beloit, Algiers and Paris to be posted before they left. Besides reflecting poorly on his management, it was outright embarrassing. It also raised the stakes on their success. The results had better be worth it.

Still, it couldn't be helped. "This has to stay strictly between you and I, Maurice." He couldn't risk losing the faith of the Americans, nor the sponsorship of Renault. For certain, the less Denny and the Times knew about any of this, the better.

He paid with a promissory note on his bank in Tangiers, knowing this meant another whinging letter to his father-in-law. Maybe he'd get Alice to write it. She certainly had Daddy wrapped around her finger. He presented the check to the Caid with a deep salaam.

His checkbook got thrown with the other files into

his trunk, papers scattering everywhere. Then he refilled his flask with brandy and dragged his gear down to the waiting cars.

It was raining—again—when they left Touggart for Ourgla. The unexpected monsoons pitted the road, in places washing it out completely. This made for a very slow, winding and bumpy trip. Passengers in all three cars regretted the previous night's rich food and plentiful drinks. The good mood, unlike the thick black clouds, quickly burned off. Most of them spent the early part of the day hungover and extremely nauseous. Twice they had to stop while someone emptied the contents of their stomach on the side of the road.

By noon, though, the desert floor was mirror-smooth and the Saharan sun chased the clouds back to the Atlas Mountains where they belonged. By the time, they stopped for lunch in the village of Tamacine, they found the first real indications of traditional desert living.

There was entirely different feel than the French and Arab influences that now dominated North Africa. The people here were decidedly darker, a small percentage of them African blacks. They were either share croppers, free servants, or slaves, depending on who you asked.

Taking advantage of the break, and eager to shake off the last of his hangover, Tyrrell pulled out his hand-held movie camera. "Lonnie, let's take a walk." Pond grabbed his little Kodak and followed.

Pond relaxed as he walked. "This is more like it."

"You really need to learn to relax, Lonnie," the older man said.

"Easy for you to say, you're on vacation. This is work for me."

"It could be worse, buddy. You could be those

guys." He pointed to the village center, where a crowd stood watching as two coal-black men climbed to the lip of the well. He pulled out his camera and slowly turned the crank. One of the men plugged his nose, blew out for a moment, then sank into the dark water, quickly followed by his compatriot.

Pond found the palest face in the crowd and asked in French, "What are they doing?"

An old man answered in an extremely fractured version of that language. "Cleaning the well. They dive to the bottom to get rid of the silt and sand." As Brad continued to crank away, the elder explained that only a few people could hold their breath long enough to do this job, and most go deaf from the pressure of being so deep under water. More importantly, well-diggers usually died early from the rarest cause of mortality in the Sahara, drowning.

As interesting as Pond found that, the villagers were even more fascinated by the Americans. Children demanded the white men take their pictures, so Pond herded them to Lucky Strike and let them clamber all over her. Suddenly, he got an inspiration.

"Brad, hold my camera for a minute." He dug in the rear of the car and pulled out an old Beloit College blanket, which he tied across the back of the vehicle. Then he got a pennant and tied it to the roof.

"There, that way any time Barth gets a picture of us, they'll have to give the College some publicity. Go ahead, take a picture of her."

"Good idea, Lonnie. They'll love that, especially with the car swarming with Negroes." Pond briefly shooed all the children away until Tyrrell got his pictures, then let them climb back aboard, giggling and jumping up and down, fascinated by the bouncy springs.

A hundred meters away from the village, Chapuis

and de Prorok stood looking at a pile of sand. "Louis, exactly what am I looking at?" The guide took the Count by the arm. A few steps to the right revealed the stripped and rusting carcass of an old Ford automobile.

Byron peered closer. "What is it?"

"The car we used when we made the Timbuktu road. She finally gave up the ghost on the way home and we left it here. We called her Eloise."

You drove in that all the way to Timbuktu and back?" He moved closer. The desert winds had driven sand up the east side of the wreck, but it was clearly visible from the back side. "On those skinny tires?" A few vulcanized shreds clung to four thin rims.

"Oui, and only four of them. Never got stuck in the sand once. Twelve tires on those big bitches and we can't stay out of the mud."

"Is it the cars or the driver?"

"How often has Martini gotten stuck?" That was answer enough, and he knew the Renault people wouldn't like it much. The little Italian was a treasure. Something of a local legend, in fact. When word got out he was available, Chapuis couldn't snap him up quickly enough. Still, protocol demanded he drive the last vehicle.

Nobody understood the power of titles, rank and job descriptions better than the former Byron Khun. His title, while honorary and of dubious pedigree, served its purposes when needed. It opened doors closed to many in archaeology, and impressed the people who really mattered; sponsors and investors. It had certainly kicked down a few doors between him and Alice, hadn't it?

Growing up among the sons of privilege, he knew there was precious little noble about nobility. He was just as comfortable with the diggers and locals on the

Carthage sites as with the leaders. He often preferred to spend his time with them—except that as Muslims, most of them didn't drink, a decided negative. Good men like Chapuis, Belaid, even the underappreciated Martini, were worth five of anyone he'd gone to school with. He trusted them as if his life depended on it, which of course it did.

Unfortunately, the way the world worked, he knew that the Renault Brothers, the government officials, and university presidents of the world had the power to grant or deny the work those good people did. Money and status were the only keys that opened those particular gates. No matter how good any of his team was—and they were very good at what they did, even Reygasse—none of them would be here if not for him using what little leverage he had as the mortar between all those separate bricks.

"When we find Tin Hinan, we'll make sure he gets his due, Louis. Thank you for bringing him on."

"If those two Renault idiots can keep us alive that long, eh?"

Dear God yes, he thought. *Just let us stay alive long enough to rub everyone's noses in their success. The Adventurer's Club, the Royal and National Geographic Societies, even the big universities would all have to support me then. No more mucking about with bloody cow colleges like Beloit.* Audiences would pack his lectures, the fees would flow, and he'd make even more discoveries. But first they had to finish this blasted trip and get home in one piece.

"Okay, let's mount up and get to Ourgla." Chapuis nodded, put his fingers in his mouth and whistled for everyone to return to the cars.

Two hours later, they pulled into the walled town of Ourgla. The "Sultana of all Oases" was everything they'd been promised. Byron poked his head out the window to get an unobstructed view unlike anything they'd seen since leaving Constantine. Instead of squat mud brick, the buildings were bright white and clean. Date palms and other trees grew everywhere, providing shade and splashes of bright green that shone even brighter now that the sun was out in full force. It was a shame they weren't staying here.

In the back seat of Lucky Strike, Brad stopped blowing his harmonica to enjoy the sights. "That hotel sure looks comfy."

Pond didn't bite. "Time to get to work, old timer. A little camping might do you some good. Too much city living will kill you." Tyrrell took one last silent longing look at the town as they passed through the southern gates and into the desert beyond.

Chapuis led them to a spot in the shadow of the Gara Krima. Pond looked around him eagerly. The rocky crag jutted out of the desert floor to about two hundred feet, just like the mesas in the Southwest and Mexico. At the top, he could just make out the rough remains of an ancient Libyan fort, the latest in a long line of warriors and hunters to find this spot over the last four thousand years.

The campsite itself was surrounded by a semi-circle of low, thorny bushes, and at night the circle would be completely closed off by moving the three vehicles into position. It was an easy walk to the first dig site. There was water too, he'd been told. Strangely enough, it was at the top of the mound, in the upper reaches of the rock, although how that happened or how anyone had managed to find it was mystery enough for a lifetime.

Pond climbed out of Lucky Strike, stretched his short legs and looked around, happy. This was the real beginning of his work, and about damned time. He noticed the colored layers in the rock face and pointed them out to Tyrrell.

"See the lines in those rocks, Brad?" The older man nodded. "That's why they call this place Earth Sister of the Rainbow. Years ago, this would have been a very different place. Plenty of water."

"Thank you, Doctor Pond. Can't resist being the teacher, can you?" Brad smiled. He enjoyed the younger man's enthusiasm.

"Not a doctor yet, although if I get any real time to study places like this I will be soon enough. There are at least three sites right near here. Paleolithic and Neolithic. It might take years to really study this place properly."

"Better be nice to de Prorok then. He's going to be your landlord." Tyrrell laughed harder than Pond at that idea. The idea of being tied to that blowhard for the next three years didn't sit very well, but it couldn't entirely spoil his mood either.

Nope, it was time to get down to work. He knew roughly what he'd find. Reygasse and the Musée Borde had sent plenty of samples from the region to Beloit in exchange for artifacts from the Americas, mostly Ojibway and some Cree. They swapped flint for flint and axe for axe, although the quality of what found its way to Beloit was nowhere near what went to Tangiers.

A big part of his job was to determine if that inequity was because the sites didn't offer much, or if the good stuff was being kept from non-European scientists. Alonzo certainly had a theory, but it was hardly scientifically proven. Nor was it charitable to his French counterpart.

Each team set to unloading its own vehicle. From Lucky Strike came the machine gun, digging tools and large wooden trunks for storing and shipping artifacts. The relics would be sorted, catalogued and shipped back to America from the coast.

Hot Dog contained Reygasse's equipment. It was much the same as the Americans' except larger, which Pond figured meant the fifty-fifty split would have to be carefully monitored. It also contained much thicker, more comfortable looking bed rolls than the rest of the group had.

Sandy, the Count's car, contained mostly camera equipment, Denny's typewriter, and de Prorok's personal, very well-worn, digging equipment. Barth stacked his mountain of gear in the relative shade of the thorn bushes and wiped his forehead.

The Count checked the cache of supplies left for them in a niche at the mountain's base. Exactly as planned there were two boxes of food, plenty of water and a couple of tents. On closer examination, however, he found the food was all the same—tins of prewar bully beef. The odds of ptomaine were small, but so were the dining choices for the next few days. Also, a closer examination of the tents revealed they were one short. Whether this was an oversight or yet another form of unofficial taxation wasn't immediately clear.

"Monsieur Reygasse, a moment please." Byron hoped he sounded calmer than he felt. He stood with his back to the rest of the crew as the older man approached with some trepidation.

"Maurice, you told me the people who handled our supplies were dependable."

"They are. We've used them many times. What's wrong?" In answer, de Prorok held up one of the ancient cans.

"This is what they left us. And we're missing other gear as well, including one of the tents and some gasoline."

"Pas possible… they're completely reliable."

"Apparently not. What am I supposed to tell the

others?"

Reygasse looked at him incredulously. "Why say anything? We're not far from Ourgla, we can get more supplies there."

"With what? We have no more money. Those bandits you hired have already bled us dry," he hissed through tightly clenched teeth. Byron towered over the Frenchman, and for a moment he enjoyed the surge of power it granted him. The moment passed, though, and all he felt was tired, betrayed and a little frightened.

Reygasse idly kicked at some gravel with a well-polished boot while the Count continued. "Everyone's depending on me, and probably regretting it. I trusted you. How is this going to look when the *fichu* New York Times writes that we failed because I couldn't get the equipment delivered properly?"

"Please, let me talk to the local Caid and see what's happened. I'm sure it's a simple misunderstanding." Reygasse's tone implied he was offering an olive branch, and Byron was happy to grab it.

"And talk to the other suppliers while you're at it. Make sure the same thing isn't happening at In Salah and Hoggar. I'm tired of looking like an incompetent boob." He put his hands on his hips and took a couple of deep cleansing breaths.

He wondered how his mentors, especially Gsell, would have handled this. Those sites were always poor and struggling, and lacked the prestige so appreciated by academia. Yet they consistently turned out important findings on a fraction of the budgets some of the sites squandered. He also had far less trouble with the Arab diggers than most. What would he have done in this spot?

"I trusted you to make the arrangements, Maurice. I trust you to make it right." Byron had been on the receiving end of this same lecture many times, and he knew how much it stung.

Reygasse sucked noisily on his lower lip for a moment, nodded once and spun on his heels, returning to the rest of the group. De Prorok stood for a few moments more, looking at the pathetic cache.

"Everyone, a word please?"

Without drama or embellishment, which took some restraint, he explained the situation. Water wasn't a problem, and the petrol situation was, for the moment at least, manageable. The news about the endless supply of canned beef was greeted with numb acceptance. Byron knew many had been in the army and were used to hard work on poor rations. Those who didn't had no idea what it was like to eat the same meal twice a day for a week. Ignorance was bliss.

As he expected, the real griping was about the tents. Barth and Denny staked their claims to one of them because of the delicate nature of their gear; typewriters and film equipment couldn't just be stacked like cordwood. The Renault drivers complained the loudest, proclaiming that they were professionals, and demanded to be treated accordingly. Reygasse claimed a spot without deigning to explain why.

"No problem, here," Pond chimed in. Now that the rain's stopped, I'm actually looking forward to sleeping outside. Right, Brad?"

Tyrrell had the good graces to simply offer, "What the hell, I'm on vacation."

Byron clapped his hands together. "Excellent. I know I'm looking forward to sleeping under the stars. Just like at Carthage, it'll be rather pleasant, and probably have fewer vermin than those last few hotels, eh?"

Amid all the squabbling, he noticed Chapuis, Martini and Belaid simply picked up their bedrolls and calmly scraped out shallow spaces on the lee side of the vehicles. Then they set to making dinner.

The simple meal was quickly devoured. Between the novelty of eating outdoors, the excitement of finally getting to work, and the loss of their breakfasts due to hangovers and bad roads, everyone had a healthy appetite.

After dinner, Escande pulled the shortest twig and took the Count, Hal Denny and Reygasse into Ourgla. Denny needed to find someplace he could file a story. De Prorok and Reygasse were on an unspecified mission, but nobody would miss them. The rest of the team settled into an early night of muffled conversation, quiet contemplation and Tyrrell playing more Stephen Foster on his mouth organ.

Chapter 9

Moline, Illinois
January 28, 1926

"Bloody Lutherans. They sure know how to suck the fun out of life, don't they?" The Count was bored and more than a bit ornery. He pouted out the window, blaming his boredom on Moline's strict adherence to liquor laws. The fact it had snowed about a foot and a half since we left Ames the morning before, and nothing across a three state area was moving, didn't seem to factor into his thinking at all.

We'd taken a last minute booking at Augustana College, a bastion of Scandinavian propriety technically situated in Rock Island, but only a couple of miles away. The nice Swedish lady who booked him made a point of putting us up in Moline, which seemed to matter a lot to her. Moline had the good jobs, a Republican city council and a really nice hotel, the Leclaire. Rock Island had the stockyards, Democrats and Negroes, hence most of the fun.

Besides the enforced sobriety, two things made him edgy. I suspected the primary reason for his misery was the cable from his wife, Alice. The Western Union telegraph laid crumpled up on the night stand. For about the third time since its arrival, he picked it up and reread it.

Dear B stop Must return to Paris with mother

and girls early stop
  Will explain later stop Don't worry
  Love A

"Don't bloody worry. What else am I supposed to do? She just packs up and leaves with no explanation? I was going to be there in two more days. What was so bloody important she couldn't wait?" Thankfully, I knew I wasn't supposed to provide the answer, and just let him go.

Close quarters didn't help. We shared a room, because this was a last-minute booking at half his normal rate, and the budget was unforgiving. Neither the college nor de Prorok were about to spring for an extra room, so we had a perfectly functional cot brought up. I didn't mind spending the night in. I was exhausted from the strain of keeping the car on the road for almost ten hours in driving snow. I needed the shut eye.

When we left Ames on Tuesday, the roads were already socked in, and no sane person ventured out. Driving in the snow was all part of the deal when you lived in Wisconsin. But in a strange car, running on about three hours sleep, with a Jim Dandy of a hangover, over a hundred and eighty miles of unfamiliar road in drifting snow, it was enough to make a smart guy reconsider his employment options. If he had any, that is.

When we finally got in, the hotel was able to scrounge us up a couple of sandwiches, one of which cost me almost seventy-five cents with a Coke. That left me less than two dollars, but I wolfed it down and we settled into our night's confinement. The Count was still talking when I passed out.

Now it was Wednesday morning, with nothing to do but worry and complain. "Will anyone show up in

142

this mess?"

"Probably. Snow's stopped, and we won't get any more for a while."

"How can you possibly know that?" he snapped.

"Doesn't smell like snow," I said with a shrug. That at least changed the topic of conversation. Now he pummeled me with a whole series of questions: What did snow smell like? Can anyone smell snow or is it a special gift like using rheumatism to predict rain? How can you tell between the snow on the ground and when it would fall from the sky?

"I never thought about it. Anyone from home'll tell you, you just kind of...feel it in your nose. You say 'smells like snow,' and everyone knows what you mean." Jesus, anyone who lived with winter could tell when a good snowstorm was brewing. For a smart guy, he sure didn't know much sometimes.

This at least got him off the topic of Alice and the babies. He set off on some wild story about Arabs in the desert who can smell water a mile away, like a camel. I agreed maybe it was the same thing, kind of.

Blessedly, the phone rang. Mrs. Carlson, the lady from Augustana, was inviting him to lunch with some of the board members. I knew from the look on his face he'd rather poke his eyes out than go to some fancy luncheon—those people drank iced tea even in January—but his voice didn't betray the horror in his eyes. And it would beat being cooped up in our room for a couple of hours.

I could use some air myself, frigid though it might be. Maybe a bowl of soup and a sandwich that didn't cost a king's ransom would be good. Besides, what's the point of being in Moline if you didn't see Moline? Through the window I could see downtown coming to life, if not exactly bustling. It might even be fun.

I figured I'd give him a head start so I didn't have

to deal with his crummy mood or Mrs. Carlson. De Prorok bundled up as best he could, took up his walking stick and waved goodbye. The notion of escaping confinement eased the black cloud hovering over him.

While I waited, I took a few minutes to look at the sword that cracked and wilted during our debauch in Ames. It was a lost cause. I'd have to pick up some more pasteboard while I was out and about. The blade was pretty much shot.

I turned the phony *flyssa* over in my hands and took a good look. The Count explained there were several kinds of Tuareg swords. Most looked like you'd expect a sword to look; straight blade, with a cross shaped handle and some kind of engraving on them. These were more ornamental, and a whole lot more interesting. They had a curved blade like a scimitar, only smaller. Certainly from an American audience's view it looked more intimidating, especially because they were made of bronze, rendering them far less durable, but they looked like gold in the desert sun— or under auditorium lights.

I wrote down what I'd need: card stock, pasteboard, maybe some glass beads and metal wire. I kept careful track of everything I spent on supplies, so I could present my boss with an accurate bill. I was out of pocket about a buck at that point. Some of his materials were in really poor shape and certainly wouldn't last much longer unless he—or rather I—did something about it. I shook my head for the millionth time. How could someone whose clothes were so perfect be so sloppy about the tools of their trade?

When sufficient time passed, I dressed for the weather and stomped down the hall. Getting into the elevator, I decided to conduct a little experiment. "Hello, Arthur."

That got me a surprised smile and a big, "Morning sir." Sir. Me. God bless name tags.

Once downstairs, I wrapped my muffler around my neck, obscuring my face. I heard a feminine laugh from near the desk and looked over. There was a tiny woman in a thick fur coat. I couldn't see anything else, except she was blond. Five'd get you ten that was Mrs. Carlson. The Count towered over her and gallantly offered his arm. He gave a jaunty wave to the desk clerk. "Thank you Andre, I'll be back later, please hold any messages."

"Of course, sir." Everyone in the lobby watched them leave; the maid polishing the furniture, the shoe shine boy, who was at least fifty, and the three businessmen chatting right in front of the door. Even the guy on the lobby couch looked up from his copy of the Dispatch. I could just make out his brown felt hat and cheap winter coat.

I'd seen that hat before. Twice, in fact. Once in Grinnell, on that first night, then again in Ames. The hat wasn't particularly noticeable, just the same crappy Dynafelt millions of guys wore. It had a high, dented crown with light finger-sized marks where sweaty hands put it on and took it off. It had a ribbon band, the same color as the rest of the hat. Nothing special.

What made it stand out was the face beneath it. It was the same fleshy, pig-eyed, unevenly shaved mug, for sure. Whoever he was, he checked his watch, pulled out a small notebook and scrawled something in it. Then he walked over to the picture windows facing Nineteenth Street and looked out in the direction the Count and the lady had gone.

He wasn't as tall as I'd thought at first, maybe five eight or nine. His eyes—bloodshot and small for his face—followed the pair for a minute. Then, I guess because he figured they had enough of a lead, he bundled up and headed out into the street himself.

I had to find out who this joker was, or at least what he wanted with de Prorok. I counted ten Mississippis and followed him. I forgot to thank the doorman, Reggie, and reminded myself to do that when I got back.

It was cold as hell and got even colder when some snow fell from the awning and went right down the back of my neck. I quickly brushed it away, frantically seeking the brown hat. Even with everyone wearing hats, it was so beat up it shouldn't be hard to spot.

It wasn't. He stood with his back to the plate glass window of a restaurant, smoking a cigarette. Mostly he looked up and down the street. Once in a while, though, he'd peer into the joint, stare a little longer than normal, then turn back to the street. Passersby hugged the walls to avoid falling ice, and Mr. Brown Coat was gradually forced to stand flush against the corner, where he had to strain his neck and balance on one foot to keep eyes on his prey.

Right about then I wished I smoked. It would have given me something to do and a reason to be standing out on the street. The warmth would have been welcome too, because it couldn't have been twenty degrees out with the wind whipping up from the river. I knew between the cold and the blond company the Count would be at least an hour, and if Whosits was keeping an eye on him, he wouldn't be going anywhere either. *Good, I hope he catches pneumonia out there*, I thought.

While he froze his tail off out there, I figured on getting the stuff for my repair project, a quick bowl of soup, and get back to work. I knew the odds of getting a decent German "*suppe*" were slim in this town where everything had been thoroughly de-Europeanized, but even chicken noodle and white bread would fill the hole on a day like this.

I passed the watcher on the other side of the street. Either he didn't notice me or was too smart to let on. At the end of the block I turned back to take one last look just in time to see the maître d' come out of the restaurant and chase him off like some kind of bum. Good.

Forty minutes later I greeted Reggie at the door of the Hotel Leclaire. He returned my greeting as he swung the door open. "Yassuh, sure is bitter cold out there, Mister Brown." A sir and a mister in the same sentence were probably overkill, but it did help warm me up.

By the time I got to the third floor, I was able to move my fingers again. The radiators gurgled away on high, and I stripped off my coat and scarf, whistling my way down the hall. The Leclaire was a nice hotel, and the carpets were plush and spotless, except for where my muddy boots left wet brown prints. My mother would've swatted me with a broom if I tracked snowy mud into her kitchen. I'd never spent the night in a place quite so nice—even if I was freeloading on a cot—but no one said a word to me. A guy could get used to this.

Pulling the big brass key tag out of my pocket, I opened the door. Then I stopped whistling. The Count's bureau was side open and two of his carefully hung shirts lay on the floor. The chest of drawers was left half opened, contents scattered carelessly. The little jewelry box with his onyx cufflinks and tie pin lay on the bedside table open, but everything seemed to be there. The trunk of lecture materials sat wide open, with everything pulled out of its compartments. Whoever had done this was looking for something, and didn't find it the first place they looked.

"Bloody hell," boomed a voice from behind me.

De Prorok stood in the door jamb, scanning the room in a panic. I thought for sure he'd be furious about his clothes. Instead with a choked cry, he threw his stick on the floor and went straight for the crate. He dug to the bottom and throwing things, including his precious piece of Shackleton's sled, aside. Under the false bottom I'd built for him, he found his metal case and inspected it. The lock was still in place, intact.

"I'll tell the front desk to call the cops," I said.

"No." The way he said it left no room for argument.

"Why not? Somebody just robbed us."

He shook his head. "They didn't get anything important," he said, stroking the metal box.

"How d-d-do you kn-n-ow? Look at your stuff." He simply shrugged. He placed the box on the bed, then picked up a shirt and gave it a quick shake, then placed it on a wooden hanger.

"What was he after?" No answer. "I think I kn-n-now who it was."

"Brown hat and coat? Kind of…" The Count waved his hand in circles in front of his face.

"You knew?"

"He was following me today. Kept looking at me through the restaurant window, like a dog at a pork chop."

I figured I'd best tell him everything. "He was in Ames, too. And G-g-grinnell."

De Prorok looked surprised but said nothing as I continued. "At first I thought he was a reporter or something. Then when you left, I saw him in the lobby writing in a little notebook, and he followed you out."

My employer sat stone still on the edge of the bed, silently stroking the metal box. At last he gave a small sigh. "I think I'll see if I can get these shirts pressed.

See if you can get everything reorganized for tonight, will you, Brown?" He rose, ran his hands over his trousers as if pressing them and added, "Sorry about the bother." Then he stalked out of the room with his shirts in one hand, the box under his arm and didn't say another word.

I looked around the room, unsure where to start. A panicky look under my cot revealed that my bag hadn't been touched. No surprise, since the flaking brown leather and rope handle didn't exactly scream, "X marks the spot—treasure inside."

After everything was properly stowed and checked, I was at a loss as to how to fill the time. I sure wasn't leaving this room again until it was show time, and who knew when the Count would return? I pulled out the sword and began tinkering, really getting lost in my work.

I was working on the paint job when a voice boomed out, "How's it going?" Except for the long smear I made when he scared the bejeebers out of me, it actually didn't look half bad.

De Prorok hung two pressed shirts in the wardrobe. There was no sign of the box. "It's in the hotel safe til we leave."

"What's in it?"

"I've already told you, it's personal. Nothing of any intrinsic value. Certainly nothing worth all of…" he gestured around the room, "this." He peered over my shoulder. "Very nice."

I held it up to the light. "It'll be okay from the stage. Be better if it were really metal, though. I also fixed the con-n-nection to the v-v-eil." He put a fatherly hand on my shoulder.

"Lovely job, Brown. Top notch. What do you say to an early supper, eh? My treat."

I should have been suspicious when he offered to

buy. I figured out why about halfway through dessert when he reminded me of a promise I'd made him in Ames.

I vaguely recalled the conversation, my memory not being solid gold at the best of times and three shots of Templeton surely didn't help. I thought about telling him he remembered it wrong, but that wasn't true. In the week I'd known him, he never forgot anything—not a name, a story or a drunken promise.

"It won't work," I said, trying to weasel out of it. "You kn-n-n-ow I c-c-can't talk in p-p-public." Just the idea thickened my tongue to the bursting point.

"You don't say a word. Just stand there wearing the burnoose and the tagelmust," he paused, pointing to his head. "Oh for... the turban. You remember. Anyway, just stand there for a few minutes while I talk about it, looking all... I don't know.... Tuareg-y, I suppose."

"I c-c-can't," I offered weakly.

"Of course you can. You can be silent as the grave. You did promise you'd at least try it." He had me there. "And, of course, you haven't been paid for this week, have you?"

That's how, forty minutes or so into the lecture, I found myself standing behind a curtain waiting to make my debut. I was stuffed into that Tuareg getup: robes, turban and veil hastily tossed over my white overalls. In my belt was the fake flyssa.

I risked a peek out at the audience. Short notice and two days of snow resulted in only half a house— maybe a hundred folks—but that crowd looked awfully big and scary. Come on, I thought, let's just get this over with.

Onstage, the Count was in perfect form. "Now, to give you an idea, I want you to imagine you are an Arab nomad. You're alone in the desert; only you, your camel and the spirits of the Djinn." He looked out to the second row at a skinny, bow-tied gent with a Chester Conklin moustache. "You, sir. Would you be willing to help me for a moment?"

The guy offered token resistance, but his wife, the audience and his ego combined to send him onstage, where the Count shook his hand and gently guided him by the shoulder to stage right. He stood facing de Prorok, his back to where I stood.

"Now, then. Your name, sir?"

"I'm Doctor Allen Lundquist." I already knew that, because it had been my job to spot someone the right size and with a connection to the college. This goofus taught Scandinavian literature and was some kind of big deal.

"Now then, Dr. Lundquist. How tall are you, sir?"

"Five feet, seven inches tall." He wasn't, not by a long shot, but the audience allowed him the white lie.

In his spell-casting voice, the Count painted quite a picture. "Imagine, then. You're only five six, like the average north Saharan Arab..." Over the guy's head he gestured to me.

I took a deep breath and wandered onto the stage, my cheeks burning and heart trying to sledgehammer its way out of my chest. I kept my eyes glued firmly on the doctor's back, not daring to look out at the audience, taking baby steps so I wouldn't faint.

The poor sap on stage kept his eyes glued to the Count, even when the audience started to laugh. I moved as quietly as possible until I was about two arm-lengths away, then pulled the sword from my belt and held it straight in front of me.

"And you have heard nothing but the hot Sirocco winds, and the rustle of sand, but suddenly you turn around..." de Prorok grabbed him by the shoulders and spun him around so he was nose to sword tip.

The dignified Dr. Lundquist nearly crapped himself. In front of him stood this six foot specter in blue robes and a veil, holding an evil looking brass blade mere inches from his nose. The audience went crazy, laughing and hooting. Frat boys shouted, "Atta boy, Professor," and, "Let's see you flunk *him*."

The Count rapped his walking stick on the stage and moved between us. "Yes, the Tuaregs average over six feet tall, towering over their neighbors, especially on camelback. They are neither Arab nor Negro, but a white race. Their culture is full of mystery, and wonderful music. And dance…"

He caught my eye, gave a wink, and turned towards the audience. "Perhaps our warrior prince here would favor us with a dance…" The crowd loved the idea, clapping enthusiastically. I hated it, and without thinking stuck the sword in de Prorok's face, my eyes bulging in panic over the veil.

"Or perhaps not," he said to the audience, and they laughed even harder. He gave me a friendly wave and shooshed me away with his hand. I gratefully complied, nearly stumbling over my big galumphing feet in my rush to leave the stage.

He vamped for time as I desperately pulled the robes off, tossed them on a chair and crouch-walked back to the projector. I stayed low, trying not to crunch any innocent feet on the way back to my post.

While he droned on about King Akamoukasomethingorother, I took big gulps of air to calm myself. That had been nearly as awful as I imagined. I just about managed to achieve normal respiration when a big hand slapped me on the back. I almost slapped back, but some grinning galoot just said, "Good job, kid. That was great." I gave a polite nod and an involuntary grin.

The rest of the lecture flew by. There was the usual

outpouring of appreciation from the locals, and the usual flattery and thanks. I didn't even look at the crowd when my name was mentioned, just waved and stared down at the table, although the ovation was much bigger than last time. My cheeks burned as usual, but I had to admit, I also kind of liked it.

There were the usual questions from the crowd. What's next? (Back to Algeria, perhaps King Solomon's Mines.) Where are the jewels? (In Paris or in Algiers where they belong.) Is there a Countess? (Sadly for the questioner the lovely Alice awaited him in Paris.) Throughout, strangers reached out to touch my arm and thank me while I squirmed like a five year old in church. Why couldn't they just leave me alone to do my job?

I looked around for about the hundredth time but didn't see any brown hats or pig eyes. I did see the Count bounding over to me, eyes blazing with a happy madness. "Brown, that worked a treat, an absolute treat."

He babbled on about how it worked better than he ever thought, and how clever I was to threaten him with the sword—he hoped I would, of course—but oh didn't they just eat it up, and we'd have to find a way to do that in the future, and it worked better than he dreamed, and on and on.

"Finish up, Brown. We're going to celebrate. Our last night and all. Hurry up." He looked for all the world like a six foot toddler waiting to be taken to the zoo. He did everything but stamp his foot.

At last I was done, and found him puffing steadily on his pipe, talking to some fat guy in an expensive suit chomping on a huge bratwurst of a cigar. I dragged the heavy crate next to him and let it drop louder than absolutely necessary. Without saying a word, I pointed to the white helmet still perched on top of his sweat-matted hair.

"Oh, yes, of course. Hardly winter wear is it?" He handed it to me with a chuckle.

The big guy shook his head. "You really wear that stuff?" I looked at him more closely. What I took for fat was mostly muscle, pretty much connecting his ear lobes with his shoulders. The hand holding the cigar was both perfectly manicured, and had scars across the knuckles. Dollars to doughnuts he wasn't associated with Augustana College.

The Count seemed happy to have an audience, even if it was this guy. "Absolutely, although pith helmets don't serve much purpose in the snow. They make a lot more sense when it's a hundred degrees out and the sun is frying you to a crisp." The mope just took another puff on his cigar and shook his head in amused disbelief.

"Mr. O'Malley is taking us out to celebrate tonight. Our reward for a job well done, eh?"

I'd rather have settled for getting paid and going back to the hotel, painfully aware that the loose change in my pocket was all I had to my name until I got paid the last ten bucks de Prorok owed me plus what I'd spent on supplies. Going out with this guy seemed like no way to hang onto my money. "Let's get this stuff b-b-back to the hotel, then you go," I suggested.

"Come on, kid. Live a little." O'Malley gave a good natured growl. "This is a hell of a town. Not like it was when Looney ran things, but you can still swing a good time if you know where to look." He looked like the type who knew exactly where to look.

Without a vote, it was determined I'd drive the Count and our equipment back to the Leclaire. We'd change into more conventional clothing and O'Malley would swing by and pick us up and we'd paint the

154

town. With any luck I'd be able to wriggle out of it. I didn't mind a good time, but this smelled really, really bad. Way worse than snow.

Chapter 10

Near Ourgla, Algeria
October 18, 1925

The proposed headline read, *"American Makes Important Discovery – Stone Hatchet Found in Sahara."* Hal Denny had done his best to cobble the last couple of chaotic days into something interesting for the Times by letting the world know that the Franco-American Expedition of the Sahara had final found something newsworthy. Even if was only a palm sized, pointed black rock. The find was credited to Alonzo Pond of Beloit College's Logan Museum.

"But I didn't find it, Byron, you did," Pond said, stabbing his finger at the typewritten pages.

De Prorok took a slow, deep breath. This was the petty nonsense Gsell had warned him about; the price you paid for the glamour of being the boss. While Byron had been involved in plenty of these arguments over who gets credit for what, primarily as an instigator, he'd yet to deal with anyone wanting their name removed from a discovery.

Worse, it had been his own idea to credit the find to the American in the first place. Now his gesture of goodwill was getting thrown back in his face. It was so simple; offer an olive branch to the Logan by giving them credit, while at the same time applying a balm to Pond's wounded feelings. God knows the poor bastard deserved something for putting up with

Reygasse's nonsense the last few days.

"I don't want or need credit for something I didn't do," Pond stubbornly continued. "Why would you allow Hal to write something that wasn't true? You don't do science that way." Byron didn't bother telling him that small concessions and omissions were bad for science, but exceptionally helpful to funding. Now wasn't the time to rehash that discussion, and it never seemed to sink in anyway.

Pond knew that his vehemence was two parts righteous indignation and one part petty jealousy of de Prorok, but was past caring. After two days grappling with Reygasse over every piece of flint and broken cockle shell, the smug son of a bitch waltzed in and practically tripped over a flawless axe head sitting under a stone overhang. How had he even seen it? De Prorok was the luckiest digger he'd ever seen. It wasn't fair.

Pond eventually left, and the Count patted Denny on the shoulder. "With that one minor exception, it's quite an accurate accounting. I like how you took all the bits about the cockle shells and barnacles and such and drew the conclusion the Sahara was under water at one time. That's important stuff."

"If you say so. Not exactly Tut's tomb is it?"

"Patience, my friend. This is only the beginning. If there was water here, there was a totally different kind of life. Maybe even a different civilization. If there was enough water…"

Denny groaned. "Chrissakes, Byron. Atlantis is not buried in the middle of the Sahara. Let it go."

The reporter's impatience with his current pet theory didn't deter de Prorok at all. "But Hal, what if it was, eh? Can you imagine what a discovery like that would be worth? Schliemann and Carter, both Geographic Societies, Maurice Reygasse, and Beloit bloody College could collectively kiss my arse." He was only half kidding.

"Until that glorious day of jubilee, who do I say found the rock?"

"Give it to Pond, and from now on we ask forgiveness, rather than permission."

It wasn't strictly ethical, he reasoned, *but not a mortal sin*. While he might take the odd shortcut, he knew good work when he saw it. That's why he didn't begrudge Pond and Reygasse their passions. They were uncovering important information about the desert and its peoples. Let them have their moments of discovery and glory. He could afford to be benevolent and share the credit at this stage. His real prize lay in Hoggar when they finally opened Tin Hinan's tomb. *Still, what if they did find Atlantis?*

Denny nodded. Then pointedly asked, "No other edits?"

"No, none at all." He knew what Hal referred to, and was initially upset at the recounting of the rains, the lost supplies and, especially, getting stuck in the mud. "You're a journalist, you're recording what you saw. I can't interfere with that…" He gladly would have if he could, but he couldn't, so…. "Besides, think of the story as we go. All these mounting obstacles, the readers fearing for our safety… it'll make the final victory seem that more, I don't know, dramatic. No, Hal, you're doing fine. Thank you. And give my best to Carr."

This was their last night here in Ourgla, then on to the Legion outpost at Hassan Ifel, or Hassi Inifel, or Sin Ifel, or whatever they bloody called it this week. Most Algerian villages had several names depending on who was looking for it and how bad their pronunciation of the local dialect was. Besides the fort, there was a bordj, or a rough inn there, and they wouldn't have to sleep on the ground. They'd even be able to rustle up a decent sponge bath.

With the teams out at the dig sites, he had the main campground more or less to himself. Some quiet would be good as there was one more important job to do, and it was critical to his long-term plan; to document each site and who wanted to dig there in the future. When it was his job to administer all this next year, he could match the right people with each site. And, of course, the price charged would depend on how badly they wanted it. That happy thought kept him occupied until the teams came back for dinner and arbitration of their petty squabbles.

The next day, they settled in for the five-hour drive to Sin Ifel. Brad Tyrrell picked out the notes of "Peg O' My Heart" on the harmonica while Pond stared out the window, trying not to dwell on his disappointment. There was great digging to be done, he just hadn't really had the chance, and it gnawed at him. At least the desert was beginning to look like his vision of the Sahara. It was an hour or more between evidence of human habitation, and the ground was alternately sandy and mirror-flat, or tall jagged heaps of stone.

"Monsieur Pond, you know what we call this?" Martini asked from the front seat as he steered wildly around a huge stone.

"No, what?" Pond was grateful for any conversation because it usually stopped Brad from playing.

"We call this Michelin Land. The tire company built it to sell more tires."

Tyrrell nodded. "They're smart, the Michelin folks. They managed to convince Renault to put twelve tires on their trucks instead of four. That's a hell of a salesman pulled that off."

Pond laughed. "Not as good as the guy with the bully beef concession around here. You'd think Byron could have gotten a few cans of something else. Even beans would be good."

"Easy for you to say, I have to share a back seat with you," the older man added, then blew a low flatulent sounding note on his Hohner.

Ahead in Sandy, Byron watched as they approached the village. Cresting a small dune, the walls of the Foreign Legion fort glared white and blinding in the afternoon sun. As they drew nearer, it was obvious only a skeleton crew remained. The rest of the force had taken the fight out of the rebel tribes and moved on to battle better armed, more serious problems like insurgent Arabs and Communists in the cities to the north.

He sent up a quiet plea to the gods or the djinns or whoever would listen that the provisioners remembered to leave water and gasoline as instructed. A few cans of something other than bully beef would probably be too much to ask as well, but if they were granting small favors, he'd take it.

For once things were precisely as expected. Fuel and food were stacked in a shaded corner of the bordj when they pulled up. The proprietor, a wiry Arab with a shoe brush moustache excitedly pointed it out. His manner suggested both a deep pride in his own integrity and an even deeper desire that honesty be remembered to the appropriate authorities. Byron happily assured him he wouldn't be forgotten.

By three in the afternoon, everything was counted, stacked and stored. Everyone but de Prorok seemed perfectly happy to have themselves a rinse and a siesta. Byron walked around the bordj, needlessly re-inspecting everything, gratified that for once all was in order, but bored. And, he knew, inaction was seldom his friend.

Trying to settle his thoughts, he pulled out the list he'd compiled of all the shots he wanted for his new lecture tour. He wanted to build the sense of mystery and tension up to the inevitable triumphant discovery of the tomb.

When people thought of the Sahara, they conjured images of blowing sand, S-shaped line after line of drifting particles burying, uncovering and reburying anything foolish enough to challenge its will. Men clawing across the dunes to their death, that's what people expected—practically needed—to hear from desert travelers. Unfortunately, they'd been met with all that blasted rain and mud. Reality could really muck up a good tale.

But now that sun was out in full force, and things were returning to normal. He thought about the dunes they passed on the way into town. If he, well Barth, pointed the camera correctly, it could create that lonely arid visual he needed to create the man-against-the-elements tableau he was looking for. He jumped up. "Barth. Henri? I have an idea…"

"But it's so late in the day, maybe tomorrow… the morning light would be better," he protested meekly.

"Nonsense. Late afternoon, long shadows on barren sands. It'll be perfect, and you know it."

"But Chapuis isn't here…"

"God's sake man, we don't need Chapuis for a glorified walk in the park do we?" Henri Barth mopped his brow with a grimy handkerchief. There were no decent fans in the boarding house, and he was a wet mess. He couldn't imagine how close to boiling his Swiss blood would be out on the dunes.

"An hour. Two at the most. Come on, man, daylight's wasting. Please?" Twenty minutes later the Count and Barth, along with a still camera, a handheld movie camera and several rolls of film bounced along in Sandy, Escande at the wheel.

"Here you go, perfect, right here." Sandy pulled to the side of the road by a marker proclaiming two miles to Sin Ifel. A large dune petered out right at the road's edge. De Prorok leapt out and ran as best he could up the steep slope to the top. From there he could see the road, of course, but turning his back to the trail, he faced what looked like hell's waiting room… a sea of sand, broken only by jagged islands of rock and one bare, thorny tree. Low dune after dune led to an infinite horizon. He looked and saw his shadow spreading yards ahead of him to the east. That meant the sun was directly behind him, an impossible landmark to miss. This would be easy.

"Henri, come up here, you have to see this!"

With a shrug of defeat, the Swiss photographer followed the already fading footprints up the sand bank to the crest. He didn't bring any equipment with him, harboring the faint hope he'd be able to talk to the Count out of this madness.

When he got to the crest, de Prorok could tell he'd won. The view was perfect, Barth's protests be damned. Barth might—indeed did—complain a lot, but in his more honest moments he'd tell you that the Count had a good eye for what worked on film. The films they'd done in Carthage made both their reputations. They were by far the best anyone had gotten from there and the audiences, especially American audiences, loved them.

A light breeze moved sand around, but it was hard packed and easy to walk on. He barely left a print. It would be easy walking once the equipment got here. He turned to Barth, who was already mentally framing shots.

"Where's your gear, man?" Byron snapped at him.

"I didn't want to haul it all the way up here if we weren't..." His head dropped in defeat, and he yelled down the dune, "Escande, can you bring my gear up here please?"

From the road, Byron could hear the driver. "Come get it yourself, you lazy Swiss pig." That was hardly going to raise the esprit de corps.

"Come on, Henri, I'll help you. We'll get a good days work in, eh?" He gave the photographer a slap on the shoulder hard enough to spin him around. Then he skittered down the dune to the car and was already half way up with a load when he passed Barth, still making his way gingerly down the hill.

Several minutes later, Barth emerged over the lip of the dune soaked with perspiration, red-faced and puffing. He put his hands to his knees for a moment, then stretched and weakly took up his tripod. The Count was already a hundred yards ahead of him and widening the distance.

"Allons-y, Henri. Just over that next dune will be perfect." Then he strode off, still looking through his binoculars.

"What's wrong with right here? It looks good to me."

"Trust me, Henri. I know what I'm doing."

By the time Barth caught up to him over the next dune, Byron had the shot he wanted. He looked north through his fingers, forming an imaginary camera lens. Then he made a quarter turn west and framed that shot, too. It was perfect.

Pacing off three steps, he turned. "I'll stand here, you shoot me this way, with me looking into the sun like it's morning, see?" He turned. His face changed ever so slightly, taking on a dreamy appearance. His voice changed, becoming the voice of the lecturer, the narrator of the adventure film. His extended arms and flat palms helped paint an entrancing, exotic picture.

"As sun rises over the Sahara, you see the miles of trackless desert before you… and this is where you pan all the way around, Henri, three hundred and sixty degrees you see. That sense of loneliness. Wouldn't do to have the road behind you like there's an easy way out… And at the end of the day…" He spun slowly clockwise until he faced away from the late afternoon sun. The shadows stretched far ahead of him, "…still nothing but sand, rock and fear."

Barth gave an involuntary chuckle and Byron knew he had him. Sand, rock and fear was a good line. They'll eat it up. Damn, he was good at this. Maybe he should direct films.

De Prorok helped Barth set up the tripod and mount the camera, more from a desire to get things going than to be of assistance but either way in ten minutes they were snapping the first stills. Tall and tanned, his teeth gleaming in the sun, hair dark and only slightly moist from perspiration under his pith helmet covered in a brand new white cloth, he felt for all the world like the Hollywood version of the dashing young archaeologist. Henri dutifully snapped the pictures as the Count suggested, acknowledging they were, indeed, perfect.

Byron stood, hands on his hips, completely satisfied with the way the afternoon had gone. It wasn't a waste after all, and he knew with what he'd get at Tamanrasset he'd have enough to satisfy him until they reached Hoggar and Tin Hinan.

In the fading afternoon sun, he noticed—about 300 yards to the southwest—a lone tree and the darker half-moon of what looked to be a cave. Without waiting for his companion, he strode off to investigate.

"Byron, where the hell are you going?"

"Henri, where's your sense of adventure? There's something up there." Byron sometimes regretted his lack of consideration towards Barth at times, and he knew there was no arguing with him when he got like this, like a hound with the scent of a rabbit in his snout. With another helpless shrug, the photographer followed, lugging his equipment as best he could.

By the time Barth caught up with the Count, the younger man was on his stomach, frantically clawing at the sand and throwing it behind him like a tall, thin badger. "What are you doing?"

"Come here, you won't believe it. Honestly, I had no idea…" Barth bent close enough to see inside the aperture, curious as to what his employer was babbling about. He saw a black patch on the floor, sharp rock fragments all over the floor, and white scratches contrasting with the darker rock of the cave. If the sun weren't so low in the sky and shining right in, he's not sure he would have seen them at all.

He set down his equipment and came in for a better look. Two long fingers held out a flat, pointed black rock. "Look at this, a campsite, I'm sure of it. Pond will absolutely lose his mind." De Prorok put the projectile in his pocket and continued sweeping the floor of the cave with his fingers. "Get some pictures of this, Henri. Oh I wish Denny were here to get it all first-hand…"

Barth took some stills, and a few feet of film with Byron's feet sticking out of the half-buried niche, his head lost inside the hole. He had to stop, though, because there was no longer enough light. Sundown had snuck up on them.

"Byron, what time is it?"

De Prorok was slithering backwards out of the cave as he answered. "I don't know, why… Oh, it's later than I thought."

"We'd better get back, Escande will be looking for us."

Byron nodded. "Right you are. Got a bit carried away there, but what a stroke of luck."

Barth wasn't listening, though. He was looking around in what dim light remained, gathering all his equipment. "Which way?"

Byron paused for a moment, turned back to the cave and held his arm out at forty-five degrees. "We came at it from that direction. Sun was low over the dunes there, so that's west. We had the sun to our backs, remember those shadows?" Barth nodded, pretending to remember any of that. "So that way."

"You're sure?"

"Henri, have I ever steered you wrong?" After thirty minutes or so, Byron regretted asking the question. They were no closer to the road that he could tell, and it was now pitch black.

In fact, he'd steered them very wrong. Damned if he'd let Barth know that, though. Damned man was such a worry wart.

"What if they don't find us? We didn't bring any water with us?"

"You didn't? I did." Byron held out a canteen to his partner, who untwisted the top and took a deep swig of lukewarm water. That stopped the whining for a moment. Byron used the time to think. The packed sand that made walking so easy also didn't form deep prints, so even if they could see where they were going, there wouldn't be much of a trail to follow.

"Let's just stop for a moment and get our bearings. Have a seat, Barth." Byron was worried about his friend. Henri wouldn't stop pacing back and forth, and from the sniffling Barth was close to panic, if not actual tears.

"You said this would be an easy run, Monsieur.

You said it would be a few weeks of easy work, and now look what you've done. I don't want to die out here."

"And you won't, my friend. Chapuis and Belaid won't take kindly to losing us. They probably have a party out looking for us already. Remember, I have the checkbook."

"That's not funny."

"Yes it is. You know it is. Why do people always lose their sense of humor when things get tight? That's when you need it most." Those were the last words between them for a while. Byron let Henri stew and sniffle while he looked up into the night sky looking for some kind of giant arrow pointing them home. The full expanse of the Milky Way trailed off in either direction. One thing about being in the middle of nowhere. It was a hell of a view.

"Do you see that?" It was Barth who saw the beacon first. He grabbed Byron by the sleeve and pointed to two pillars of light shining into the sky. He wiped his face on his sleeve to clear the tears and snot.

De Prorok was about to ask what he was talking about when he saw the lights as well. "Ah, bravo, Henri. See, we'll be fine." He gave his panicky companion three comforting pats on the shoulder and headed towards safety, lugging most of the equipment.

The Count carried most of the gear because in his panic Barth threatened to ditch it in order to conserve his strength. Tearfully, the photographer worried they were surely lost and would have to survive in the wild for days until rescue came or he was forced to kill the Count for food. Besides, those damned pictures were the reason they were in this mess.

Calmly, Byron tried to explain what a shame it would be if they'd gone to all this trouble for nothing. Sure enough, they'd be fine. Wasn't he always lucky?

"Lucky I don't kill you," was the sobbing reply.

"Hallllooooooo there," de Prorok shouted towards the light. No response. "Hallllloooooooo… ahoy there."

They heard a faint, "Thank God… over here. Escande, they're here." He picked up the pace, stepping quickly towards the voice, then slowed down again so Henri could stay in sight. The poor man had been through a lot today.

Greetings and hugs were exchanged all around. Belaid and the driver took all the gear and a softly weeping photographer down the dune to the car. Louis and Byron stood at the top of the dune.

"Are you okay, Monsieur?"

"Perfect, yes. Oh Louis, you should see what we found… a cave… Even you didn't know about it. Not my thing of course, but Reygasse and Pond will have a whale of a fight over it." He dug into his pocket and proudly displayed one of the arrowheads.

Chapuis stared at him, dumbfounded. "You could have died out there, Monsieur, two miles from your bed. For a god damned piece of rock." Byron braced himself to answer, but counted to five instead and simply nodded his assent.

"You're right, Louis. Bloody stupid of me." He looked down towards the road. In order to create a beacon, Escande had driven Sandy up the steep hill so the headlights shone to the heavens. Now they had to get him back on the road. They heard tires spinning in the sand with a plaintive whine before they grabbed the road bed, and Escande had Sandy back where she belonged, pointed to In Salah and bed. "Still, we got some great pictures, absolutely grand. And a site even you didn't know about. I do have the damnedest luck."

Chapuis shook his head and bit back several

possible harsh responses. That was certainly one way to look at it.

The next day, after a short and blessedly uneventful drive, they found themselves at an oasis called Oued Aoulguy. While Pond and Reygasse engaged in a race to see who could find anything worthwhile near the dried river bed, Prorok squinted up at the surrounding rocks. There were stories about these hills, but he couldn't remember exactly what they were.

He spotted discoloration high up in the rocks, but he wasn't sure. He grabbed a hold of two projecting stones and pulled himself up. It wasn't a shadow. "I wonder what this is. Writing, maybe?" he shouted back, ascending rapidly.

A moment later, de Prorok called for Chapuis, then Belaid, and finally even Reygasse and Pond surrendered the field of battle to see what was causing all the ruckus. Now they all stood on a flat hilltop, with caves and taller rocks behind.

De Prorok stood, hands on his hips, examining the rock wall. On the wide mesa in front of it, all around and up as far as they could see were inscriptions, symbols, and scratches clearly made by human hands.

"Well? What is it?"

Belaid ran his finger over the scratches in the rock and grinned. "I'll be damned. You see this big one here? It's a sandal. And the little sandal next to it, they're connected, no?" Everyone nodded impatiently. "That means they're tied together forever. They're to be married—fiancées, see?"

"What about this writing here?" Pond pointed to a fainter set of marks.

"It's the same thing: so and so loves so and so, this person and that person together forever…"

"But they're in different languages."

Belaid nodded, pulling thick moustache hairs off his tongue as he excitedly explained. "Yes, see here, it's Arabic, obviously. That's fairly recent. Down here is Tifinar, and these are much, much, older than that."

This was news. Arabic they expected to find. Even Tifinar, the written language of the Tuaregs going back to the fourth century Berbers, before the Muslim invasions a hundred years later. Belaid patiently pointed out the sheer number of inscriptions of all ages. Scratched into rock, written over, and gradually covering the whole face of the mountain.

He squinted momentarily, then snorted as he read one strange set of scratches. "This here, it's a billboard. A woman claims she has the best love spells of all. Can make any man fall in love, any woman desirable."

"How come this one only has one shoe?" Pond was on his belly, studying a lone shoe with lines of script encircling it. Belaid looked carefully, then took a look over the steep drop-off. "This one is sort of sad. It says his beloved betrayed him, and he came here to throw himself off the cliff."

An embarrassed silence descended on them for a moment. They all looked over the precipice, imagining what that drop would do to a badly lovelorn young man.

"So all of this is basically..."

"Damn it Byron," laughed Tyrrell, "You've found the only Lover's Lane in the whole Sahara Desert."

De Prorok beamed. He stood and looked out over the desert floor below. His voice took on the story-teller tone. "For thousands of years, young Tuareg and Libyan lovers have come to... What do we call this? Love Mountain, Belaid, what is that in Arabic?"

"Jabal Al-Hubbab, more or less."

"To Jabal al-habb...whatever it is, we'll figure

something out… to pledge their troth and seek eternal love. The lonely seek assistance from sorceresses, those beyond help seek to end their pain." Barth shook his head and pulled out his camera. The boss was wound up, and would want as many pictures of this as he could get. "…Older than Islam, before the Berbers and Tuaregs, from the time of the most ancient Libyans, young hearts sought what everyone the world round seeks: their soul mate, their one true love, in the bitter sands of Jabal al- Habbab, the Mountain of Love."

He ended his reverie at the edge of the cliff, arms spread wide to greet the afternoon sun. Reygasse shouted "Bravo" and the Americans applauded enthusiastically.

This time, no one begrudged the Count his pictures and film. Henri followed Byron's commands, getting the best angles he could with both still and movie cameras, without going too near to the edge. He'd already almost died once this trip, no sense tempting fate.

The others climbed down to help Reygasse and Pond get back to their cutthroat game of hide and seek with the Stone Age.

Remaining behind for a moment with Barth, Byron ran his hand over the ancient graffiti, guiding the camera lovingly over the inscriptions. He thought of Alice and smiled. Their sandals had been joined for three years. She was a lovely girl and game enough. But she looked so tired when he left, with one baby barely two and the other only a month old. She deserved better.

While Henri carefully brought his gear down, when no one was looking, Byron pulled out his jackknife and slowly etched "Byron et Alice, A.D 1925" into the soft sandstone.

Chapter 11

Moline, Illinois
January 27-28, 1926

We compromised, which meant the Count pretty much got what he wanted. I'd come out with them, and he'd pay me. Well he'd pay me five of what he owed me. Apparently it was all he could spare until the banks opened and he could cash Mrs. Carlson's check. It seemed the "bloody Lutherans," were also sticklers for generally accepted accounting practices, and wouldn't pay in cash.

That's how I found myself in the back seat of a '23 Lincoln, sharing a bench seat with Mrs. O'Malley. The Count rode shotgun as the big guy pointed out all the cultural high points of Rock Island, Illinois. These seemed to consist mostly of pointing out which ethnic group lived where. There was some overlap between the Shanty Irish and the Negroes, and the Wops apparently were coming in droves because of the good jobs at Deere, and you know how those guys are with their hands.

"The Little Lady dragged me to that shindig tonight, but I'm happy I came," said O'Malley as he maneuvered the icy streets. "Normally, I let her go to that cultural jazz by herself, but this was better'n the pictures. Imagine Jack and Lizzie O'Malley showing a real honest-to-Christ Count the town. Ain't that something, baby?"

Lizzie O'Malley sat beside me, all blond marcelled hair with her mink coat bundled up to her chin and stared petulantly out the window. This seemed to amuse Jack O'Malley.

"You married, Count?"

"Byron, please. Yes, but Alice has had to return to Paris unexpectedly."

"How long since you seen her?"

"A month and a half, far too long."

O'Malley let out a whistle. "Bet it is. I can't get Lizzie here to let me off the leash for a couple of days' business trip to Chicago, let alone a month and a half. Ain't that right, honey?" Mrs. O'Malley just pulled the coat tighter around her.

After a few minutes we pulled up in front of an apartment building that took up a whole block. The bottom floor contained a small candy store, and a plumbing supply store. Most of the windows were blacked out, which seemed strange for a business. O'Malley led us through the candy store—oddly enough open at this late hour—to a room in the back and knocked twice on the door.

I'd been to speaks before, but this place was a world away from the basement rathskellers and shabby Kraut beer joints back home. White-jacketed waiters bustled around, and there were tablecloths. Instead of plant workers, shop girls and off duty cops sneaking an illicit warm beer, there were banker types in ties and pretty girls in short dresses sipping cocktails. I was painfully aware of being the worst dressed guy in the joint, and that included the staff.

One of the waiters shooed some lesser mortals away from the corner table and ushered us over. I could feel envious eyes examining us and kept my gaze downward, worried I'd be exposed as a fraud and unceremoniously expelled.

I was invisible. All eyes were on the Count who couldn't have stood out more if he'd worn his pith helmet and desert getup. I felt stares burn right through me to gawk at the tall, exotic stranger.

In a voice designed to be overheard, O'Malley roared, "Jerry, a little somefin' for me and for Count Porok here." Lizzie rolled her eyes but didn't correct him.

"Willy, can I get you somefin? Come'on, it'll put hair on your chest." To appease him, I asked for the first thing I could think of. I ordered Templeton on the rocks like it was my usual, which given my limited experience I guess it was. He nodded and gave the order without even pretending to order something else. Back home, we'd ask for a "Special Coffee," or a "House Speciality." This place was classy. And obviously well protected.

A chain-smoking Negro piano player was doing his thing in the corner. I don't know if he was any good, but he sure played fast. When he finished his song, nobody applauded, or even seemed to pay much attention. He was just part of the furniture here— functional and moderately expensive but mostly beside the point.

De Prorok was in the middle of a long, rambling description of what it was like to live in Paree, going on about his house in the Rue Alfred Dehodencq and how Alice and his two little angels were there now, waiting for him. O'Malley was drunk enough to commiserate, in that maudlin Irish way, that we're all 'nuttin without family," and how he treasured Lizzy and their kids. It seemed like a good time to go to the can.

I wound through the crowd and past the piano and its cloud of grey-blue smoke. Looking everywhere but where I was going, I bumped into a short brunette.

175

Actually, brunette doesn't even come close to how coal-black, and obviously dyed, her hair was. She had it cut in a bob, and looked just like Colleen Moore in "Flaming Youth," if Colleen Moore was barely five feet tall and still had baby fat and badly rouged cheeks. Her cigarette ash fell on my coat, and she brushed it off casually and laughed. I checked for scorch marks. This was the only coat I had and I didn't need some stupid girl ruining it.

"Ooops, sorry about that," I mumbled and hurried on.

I was in less of a hurry on the way back, certainly in no rush to join the Count and the O'Malleys. I felt like I did at any party; oafish, barely tolerated and eager to be somewhere else. I gawked around, taking everything in, and tried desperately to look like I belonged and probably failing miserably.

"You were in there long enough, were you draining it or playing with it?" The short girl I'd bumped into said from her stool by the bar. I just shrugged and tried to move on but she put her small hand on my shoulder, bright red nails digging into the cloth. "Aw, I'm just teasing, ya big galoot. Where you off to in such a hurry?"

My mouth flapped open and nothing came out. Then I pointed my chin towards the corner table and nodded.

She gave out a brassy, braying, haw haw. "Big and dumb, just like I like 'em." Before I had a chance to even get offended, she stuck her hand out. "Jacqueline." She pronounced it Jack-a-leen. "What's your handle?"

I knew the answer to that one. "Willy. Braun."

"Hiya Willy. Good tameetcha. You here with O'Malley?"

"Sort of, yeah."

"Oooh, a big shot. Whaddya do? You don't look like the normal muscle."

I mumbled something about working for the guy in the white suit, and being from Milwaukee, keeping it as simple as I could while looking around the room for an escape route.

"What about you? Are you here alone?"

She puffed herself up. "Why not? I'm free, white and twenty one." Well, she was two out of three, but I didn't say anything. Not that I got a chance. For the next fifteen minutes I didn't get a word in edgewise. I learned how she was from across the river in Bettendorf, Iowa, originally, and how she was working in an office here in Moline, but only til she could get to Chicago, because really that's where everything was going on and didn't I think the piano player was great and she saw Jelly Roll Morton once in St. Louis, and a bucket load more until my head spun.

"You gonna buy me a drink?" I sure hadn't planned on it, and I needed all the money I made this week, but soon I was a buck and a half lighter, and we both had fresh drinks. My rye and rocks sat mostly untouched on the bar, while Jacqueline sipped some kind of yellowish gin cocktail. We clinked glasses, and I watched her thickly painted lips leave a red smudge on the rim of the glass.

She wasn't really my type. I was more into the goody-goody Italian Catholic types who didn't much care for big dumb Germans, but she was the kind of girl I sometimes attracted. At the very least, it was a distraction from hearing about dear Alice all night, and I relaxed a smidge. I was even beginning to enjoy myself.

I was pretty sure I wasn't drunk on the one rye, but I felt a bit woozy and disconnected. Here was this pretty girl, pretty enough at least, in a strange city, in a classy joint, and she was talking to me. It got even stranger when I realized she was leaning against me, her breath warm on my neck and her hand on my arm. "You're a nice guy, Willy. It's hot in here. You wanna go outside for a minute?"

At first, I thought she needed the air because she was drunk, or even going to be sick, but she was awfully steady on her pins as she led me by the hand out the back door. Dimly, it occurred to me she might have another reason for being away from the crowd but I knew that couldn't be it.

As soon as we were outside, she turned and wrapped her arms around me, burying her face in my chest. It was awfully cold out. I guess I needed instructions, because she looked up at me. "Don't you want to kiss me, dummy?"

The idea hadn't occurred to me up til then, but it suddenly held some appeal. I leaned down to give her the kind of nervous, chaste kiss I always started with, because it wouldn't be the first time things had ended before they even got started. The way she kissed me back let me know that wasn't going to be a problem and for one panicky moment I wasn't sure it would have been possible to move too fast for her. She crushed her lips against mine.

I pulled back, partly to breathe, and partly to look around to see if we were being watched, but her lips hungrily chased mine so I kissed her back out of self-defense. She moaned and opened her mouth, her tongue grazing my lips, and I uncertainly followed suit. I could taste a mix of gin and lipstick and tobacco, but it tasted better than any of those things. I wanted more.

Her coat hung open, and her hands parted mine so I could feel the heat of her body against me. Her breasts pressed into my ribcage. I pulled her closer yet, and her legs clamped my left leg between them with another little, "mm-hmm."

Among the million things streaking through my mind at that moment, I remembered something the Count had said about people and machines; that you tested and they'd tell you how to handle them. I pulled her against me, tighter than I would have normally dared. Her small frame shivered against mine. I guess that worked.

Maybe she was one of those projectors that needed a firm hand. I ran another test. Running my big clumsy paw upwards, I hesitantly cupped a breast. Instead of being rebuffed, she gave a happy chuckle. I squeezed tentatively, didn't get socked for it, so I squeezed a little harder. That elicited another happy noise, so I did the same to the other breast, feeling the nipple harden under my touch. It rubbed through her dress against my palm. My fingers closed on it, giving it a soft pinch.

"Yessss," she breathed with a sound that went right to my crotch. Embarrassed, I realized how hard I was. She could feel it too, and ground against me, instead of pulling away like I expected. I pinched even harder, and she pulled back quickly.

"Ow."

"Oh, Jeez, I'm sorry…." She saw the stricken look on my face and smiled wickedly.

"You can pinch'em, just not so hard, ya big lug." I took her at her word and picked up where I left off. She nodded as her tongue wrestled with mine.

I began conducting all kinds of experiments. I ran on hand over her bottom, gently at first, then cupped it firmly. This caused a slow, circular grinding against my thigh. I grabbed harder, and she ground more enthusiastically.

My hands were everywhere, testing, probing,

assessing pressure and acceptance. I was so involved in my explorations, I forgot about the throbbing below my belt for a moment. What happened if I did this? Too hard? What about this, then? I guess I scored more hits than misses, because she squeezed my leg between hers, and met my efforts with enthusiasm.

She started breathing louder, making little steam clouds in the cold air. Her lips peeled away from mine to take short gulps of air and then plunge back, tongue first. Her hips pressed harder, the circles tighter, the pressure more insistent. Her moans became shorter and higher pitched, and I watched myself from someplace outside, fascinated and surprised as hell.

She gripped my hand by the thumb and slowly brought it down her body and under her dress. I could feel cold skin, but also a heat and dampness through the silky smoothness of her panties. My eyes opened wide, searching hers for confirmation this was really okay. She opened her mouth to speak. What would…

Then the door behind us flew open, sending us both stumbling out onto the sidewalk. "Brown, oh my God, I'm so sorry…"

The Count stood in the doorway, bundled up and ready to go. Jacqueline pulled her coat around herself and looked away to avoid his stare. I stood there with my lips covered in lipstick, my coat and mouth both open to the elements.

He managed to tip his hat. "I'm frightfully sorry my dear, I was afraid something had happened to young Brown here." Something almost had, but that moment had just sailed past and waved goodbye. "I'm afraid we're heading back to the hotel. Would you like to…"

"I guess…" I looked from him to Jacqueline's face. Her lipstick was almost gone, and mascara drips ran down those chubby, baby cheeks. She bit her lip and nodded. Without saying another word, she pulled her coat tighter around herself and slinked inside, brushing past the Count without another word.

"I truly am sorry, Willy. Do you want to…?"

"No, I'm good. We should be getting back." I wiped my mouth on my sleeve, took a deep breath and followed him inside. I looked around for Jacqueline, but she probably sought sanctuary in the lady's room. The O'Malleys stood dressed and impatient, ready to go.

De Prorok grabbed his walking stick, offered our waiter a quick, "Thank you, Alex," and we passed through the door back into the candy store. O'Malley held the door for us. As I passed he leaned in conspiratorially, "I see you met Jack-leen," but not another word was said until we were back in the Lincoln and on our way back to the Le Claire.

We passed silently through the lobby and up to our room. Soon enough, I lay on my cot in the dark, listening to the Count snoring lightly and wondering what the hell had just happened.

Morning came early. De Prorok was already on the phone with New York. Now that Alice wasn't going to be waiting for him, he had to make new arrangements. He sure didn't want to stay with his in-laws without the buffer she provided. He needed to cable Paris, to see what new plans were in the works. Plus he was setting up an appointment with his new booking agent, the mysterious Lee Keedick.

He was so caught up with all that I had to remind him, once gently and once much more strenuously, that we had to get to the bank if we were going to make his eleven o'clock train. He owed me five bucks, plus one and a quarter for supplies, and I'd be damned if I wasn't going to get my money. My Old Man taught me a few things.

We took care of things right in the middle of the bank. "There you go, Brown. We're square, yes?"

"Thank you, sir." I hoped I sounded appropriately business-like. He let the "sir" slide.

After the bank, there remained only one thing to do. I delivered my boss and his gear to the train station. He was going on to Chicago, then back to New York. I had to return the car to Cedar Rapids, then it was home to Milwaukee. I'd written Mama to tell her I was returning for a visit only. She was thrilled. She didn't mention the Old Man's reaction.

"We're still on for Milwaukee in February, yes? We have a lot of work to do." Again with the "we." I promised him "we" sure were.

"Is it any warmer in Milwaukee than it is here?"

"Not really." Actually, it was frequently worse, but why tell him that?

The Count looked me in the eye. "You were an immense help, Brown. Really. Couldn't have done it without you."

I felt an unreasonable and unfamiliar feeling of pride start at my toes and shoot up til it nearly erupted out the top of my head. True, anyone could have done what I did, but no one else had. I waited tracked until the conductor called the, "All aboard." He gave my hand one last shake, offered a jaunty wave of his walking stick and stepped up into the first class compartment.

On the way back to the car, I kept a close eye out for brown hats and chubby brunettes, but didn't see either one.

Chapter 12

Tamanrasset, Algeria
November 2, 1926

At five foot two and a half inches, Alonzo Pond was used to feeling shorter than most people. Standing in front of the King of the Tuaregs, who was almost six and a half feet tall, and rode on a seven foot camel, he was absolutely dwarfed.

Standing as tall as possible in his cleanest desert garb between the much taller de Prorok and Tyrrell, he was still a shrub between two pines. At least those guys cast a little shade, for which he was grateful. It was only nine o'clock in the morning, but the desert sun announced its intention to make up for all the clouds and rain the past few weeks.

The King and his half-dozen envoys grabbed the cross-shaped pommels of their saddles and threw their legs over, alighting on the sand with surprising grace for men so large. What was doubly impressive to the young American, they managed it while wearing ankle-length robes and huge turbans which never budged an inch. Black veils covered every face, leaving only a narrow slit through which mahogany-brown eyes surveyed the world. All seven of them wore swords; King Akhamouk sported one on each hip. The first blade was a long, straight sword the other a jeweled flyssa, its wicked curved sheath jangling noisily as he moved.

Pond watched carefully as de Prorok demonstrated the correct way to greet the King. Akhamouk of Akhmenal held his hand out, palm down. The Count took two steps forward, bowed at the waist, gently gripped the royal fingers and lifted them up, kissing the back of his own hand. "Allah salaam alaikum."

The King smiled. "Alaikum salaam." He moved on to greet Reygasse, dressed as expected in full military regalia. His Highness spoke to the Marshall in very good French, and moved down the queue to Alonzo. There was a moment of confusion when the King, obviously briefed about American customs, offered his hand out to shake Pond's, and the shorter man nearly bowed into it. Quickly gathering his wits, and terrified how he'd tell Dorothy if he messed up, he shook the huge brown hand, then proffered the ceremonial fake kiss as well, just to cover all the bases.

It must have gotten the job done, because Akhamouk grinned down at him, patted him on the arm encouragingly, and moved on to greet Tyrrell, Chapuis and the rest of the entourage. The rest of his men worked the receiving line as well, offering polite head nods and smiles.

The exchange of gifts began. The Count gave the King a truly impressive hunting rifle, complete with a scope, over which the Tuareg made appropriate gushing noises. Out of the corner of his eye, he saw the Legion commandant shift uncomfortably, and fight to hold his tongue. Packages of sugar, salt and tea were doled out with great ceremony.

Pond offered the runt of the litter, who stood only about five eleven but almost as wide across, a pocket knife with a six inch blade. The happy recipient beamed and thumped Alonzo on the shoulder, drowning him in a stream of words, smiles and salaams. He opened and closed it half a dozen times, showing it off to his compatriots. Pond nodded and smiled back, wondering if the guy had ever heard of a magical place called Woolworth's, since that's where the knife came from.

"Okay everyone, let's adjourn to my offices please." The Commandant, de Beaumont politely but firmly tried to shepherd everyone out of the sun into the relative cool of his command center. As the party broke up, he leaned over de Prorok and hissed, "The rifle is one thing, but you had to give him a scope? You'd better hope none of us wind up on the wrong end of it."

The Commandant arranged for both chairs and cushions for everyone's comfort, depending on their personal preference. De Prorok thought that was an excellent touch. Beaumont was, by all accounts, a generous host as well as an excellent commander. The Count liked him, and thought the feeling was mutual, the gaffe with the rifle scope notwithstanding. This was a relationship worth tending.

As Reygasse went into his standard, "The Government of France Sends its Greetings" speech, Pond leaned over to the Count and whispered, "Would they mind if I took their picture?"

De Prorok realized what a terrific picture it would make: the modern White explorers and the Tuaregs meeting indoors, blue robes against stark white walls, medieval and modern. They'd eat it up. "Please do, wish I'd thought to invite Barth."

"But isn't there a… taboo or something… about Muslims not wanting their pictures taken? I don't want to cause an incident."

Good old Pond, thought Byron, overthinking everything. He grinned, "Tuaregs aren't too fanatical about their Islam, Lonnie. In fact, the Arabs call them 'The Abandoned People' because even Allah doesn't

185

really want them, and the feeling's quite mutual. They're just Muslim enough that the Arabs leave them alone, and Algerian enough the Legion won't shoot as long as they don't shoot first."

While Belaid translated the King's conversation with Reygasse, Pond held up the camera to the two warriors in the colorful robes and gestured that he wanted to take their picture. He was assured everything was fine when one of them put his arm around his partner and offered a cheesy, if mostly toothless, smile. Then Pond turned his camera across the room, and King Akhamouk stopped in midsentence to strike a regal pose on his cushion, remaining perfectly still until he heard the camera click, then picked up where he left off.

At last the deal was struck. The Expedition would spend the next thirteen nights in the Tuareg camp, which currently sat fifteen kilometers from the fort at Tamanrasset. Beaumont attested to the harmless nature of the expedition, which seemed to reassure the King. Byron liked the man more and more.

"Thank you, Commandant. I appreciate your efforts."

"Not at all, happy to help," said the Legionnaire. "All in the name of science. I hope you find what you're looking for. Oh, one thing more," he looked uncomfortable. "I'm afraid you should leave the machine gun here."

"You're sure?" Byron was perfectly happy to do so, since it meant more room for gasoline and water. "Can you ensure our safety?"

"D'accord. If they bother you, it will bring the full fury of the Foreign Legion on their heads. You will be as safe as in your own back yard." The way Beaumont sat back in his chair folding his arms over his chest said that agreement was likely ceremonial. The decision was made and irrevocable.

"If you think it's for the best. You're the professional after all."

The Count caught up Belaid on the stairs, and they stopped to talk on the landing. "Is she there?"

The interpreter chuckled. "Oh yes, I heard from her last night. She's there, and everything's set."

"Will they tell us, do you think?" Byron asked, looking Belaid right in the eye. The slim interpreter pursed his lips and nodded. "When was the last time you saw her?"

"Six months or so, last time I was through. So far everything she's told me is true, which is more than I can say for when we were married."

Byron slapped him on the shoulder in appreciation. "Almost there, my friend. Almost there."

Ninety minutes later, the three cars bounced off the broken creek bed that served as a road onto the flat, hard sand of the camp. Pond grabbed his notebook before the car even came to a halt and began scribbling furiously.

What he presumed would be a small group of nomads was virtually a village of three hundred or so light brown tents, laid out in concentric circles, with a well as the center point. Most of the tents were just one large piece of material, mostly camel hide, pegged to the ground at the back and supported by poles at the sides and center. The openings faced away from the wind, and were less than three feet high. That made them tricky to enter, but kept the inside of the tent out of the direct sun, and allowed the minimum amount of blowing sand to find its way into the stew pot.

Five tents had been set aside for the Expedition team. De Prorok claimed the largest for himself, Barth and Hal Denny, thinking it best to keep an eye on his chroniclers. Reygasse claimed a tent for himself to no-one's surprise, the Renault drivers bunked together, as did the Americans. Chapuis gladly threw in with Martini, the two desert hands choosing to be as far from the action as possible. Pond realized one of them was unaccounted for.

"Belaid, what about you?" he asked.

The Caid gave him a sly smile. "Don't worry, Monsieur. I have made other arrangements."

Five minutes later, those other arrangements arrived in the person of the former Madame Belaid. A woman boldly strode into their camp and greeted the interpreter with a smile and a soft peck on the cheek. Unlike the men of her tribe, she was unveiled. Her raven-black hair was wrapped in a French-style scarf made of cheap but vibrant green silk. Gold earrings dangled almost to her collarbone and framed a strong, symmetrical face. Pond thought she might be thirty years old, and every year of hard desert living showed around her striking grey-green eyes.

She slipped a possessive arm around Belaid with a smile that took some of those years away, but made her seem no less formidable. The guide held out a hand to de Prorok, speaking in slow, clear French for her benefit. "Monsieur le Comte, may I present my wife… former wife… her name is Tadêfi. It mean 'Sweetness.'"

"As it should Belaid. Whatever possessed you to let her go?" Tadêfi laughed at the obvious, but no less appreciated, flattery. Like all Tuareg women, she had the right to marry—or divorce—anyone she wanted. After three years of living up North, she returned to her own people, leaving Belaid with a broken heart, but full visiting and conjugal rights.

Byron bowed deeply. "I understand we have you to thank for this?"

"It was nothing. It makes the French happy, and your gifts have been most appreciated." She shook her sleeve and a large silver bangle slipped to the end of her thick, bull-strong wrist and work-hardened fingers.

The Count bowed again, "If I'd known how lovely it would look on your delicate hand, I'd have given you two."

"We're not finished yet," she countered playfully, giving Belaid a punch on the arm for looking jealous. "We still need the exact location, but I'm sure we'll find out soon."

Byron allowed his disappointment to show. "He won't tell us?"

She shook her head. "He can't just come out and tell strangers where Our Mother sleeps, but he'll give you enough hints that even this one..." she gave her ex-husband's arm another squeeze, "...can follow. Of course another gift or two might not hurt your cause at all."

After some small talk, she turned and half-dragged Belaid towards her tent. De Prorok chuckled, feeling a momentary tinge of concern for the man's wellbeing. He knew how Alice got when he'd been gone for any time, and she was no Tuareg between the sheets.

The next several days were a frenzy of picture taking, movie shooting and fanatical note-jotting. Barth recorded hundreds of feet of film; children playing, men and women dancing, even a few domestic scenes, although Byron knew his audiences didn't care much how these people lived day to day in ways so much like theirs. They wanted to see how American lives were so different from—and superior to—others.

While Brad Tyrrell cranked away taking movies for his private collection and played endless games of tag with the children, Pond went about his work with the determination and focus he put into everything he did. Each trinket he picked up or traded for was catalogued in small, precise handwriting along with when, where and how it was obtained.

A normal mortar and pestle were obtained by trade for a small hand mirror. A pair of sandals, the straps almost eaten through, was merely picked out of a trash heap. These were the mundane items of everyday life for these people, but he found them exotic, and hoped the folks in Beloit would, too. They weren't gold, but gold didn't have anything to say about real lives in the real world.

He noticed that the older members of the village were the hardest to deal with. They were suspicious of the visitors, although they seemed to find the odd white men harmless enough. They often refused to sit for pictures, or demanded so much in trade for their posing it was easier to look elsewhere. They also showed very little interest in European or American goods, unlike the younger generation of Tuaregs.

The difference between generations was evident in the everyday life of the camp. In the tents of the newer families Pond found modern cooking pots, and the occasional canned food item. Simple but beautiful handcrafted sandals and jewelry were traded for modern conveniences with little thought.

On their fifth day there, Pond saw an item he coveted. A young Tuareg bride walked across the camp bouncing a necklace of polished brown stones held together by delicate gold wire off her lovely brown chest. He got caught staring a bit too long, because the husband glared at him and demanded to know if there was something Pond wished to tell him.

Given that Alonzo was the shortest person over the age of thirteen in the encampment, he immediately called for Belaid to assist in the discussion before things took an uglier turn. While anger and jealousy might be universal languages, salvaging the situation without bloodshed would require linguistic skills he didn't possess.

After a series of shouts and growls, the explanation was clear. "He wants to know why you were looking at his wife."

Pond blanched. "I wasn't looking at his wife... I mean I was... she's quite lovely but..." he gestured to his own collar, "I was admiring her necklace. It's beautiful." Belaid relayed the message.

The young woman shyly fingered the item and allowed herself a proud smile, while her husband turned the heat on his rage down to a simmer, still glaring down at Pond. He rattled off a few sentences to Belaid, who relayed them in French in a much calmer voice. "He wants to inform you that if you try to steal it he'll kill you. There were more details if you want them."

"No, I get the message, thanks. Please tell him that I only admired it very much and would love to acquire it. How much do they want for it?" Belaid got about halfway through the translation when the couple began arguing in particularly heated fashion.

"He said no," the interpreter explained, "and then she said it wasn't his to give, and she said hell no. He said, 'what do you mean it's not mine'? And..." he finished the sentence with another shrug. Marriage was a universal language.

By now they had an audience. A couple of older Tuareg women shouted angrily, then the men. De Prorok watched, concerned, from the periphery but said nothing. Reygasse stood several feet outside the circle, smiling smugly and lighting a cigarette, thoroughly enjoying the show.

"It is... comment est-ce que vous dites... an

heirloom?" Pond nodded that was probably the right word, so Belaid continued. "Her mother, her mother's mother and so on... has worn that necklace. It's part of her trousseau. You understand trousseau?" He did understand, in fact his recent letters to Dorothy contained more veiled talk of trousseaus and dowries than discussions on the finer points of paleolithic anthropology.

At last it was explained that he didn't want it for himself, or for his own woman, although he did allow himself a quick fantasy of presenting it to Dorothy, but for the Museum. This elicited a long detailed explanation of what a museum was and why anyone would stand in line or pay money to see things like shoes and necklaces and camel bridles. Finally, it was agreed there was no harm meant, no damage done, and Pond was, indeed, an insensitive ass. Everyone but Alonzo Pond seemed satisfied with that summary of the situation.

That night, after Tyrrell introduced another of the master works of Stephen Foster to their hosts, and choruses of "How do you do, Harry Jones?" were sung in a hodgepodge of languages and varying degrees of musicality, Pond, Chapuis and de Prorok were left alone beside their fire.

Each savored the silence, their eyes drifting aimlessly from the sparks rising in the smoke, to the insane number of stars above, then to the other fires dotting the tent village. The night was cooler—not cool to be sure—but less oppressive than it had been all day.

Belaid appeared out of the darkness, and whispered in Pond's ear, "Monsieur, someone wishes to speak to you about a private matter." The Count raised an eyebrow, but said nothing. He merely pulled out his pipe, tamped some tobacco in and lit it with a twig from the fire, enjoying the solitude. Pond and Chapuis got up and followed into the darkness. They were met by a tall, unusually thin, young Tuareg warrior.

"Monsieur, the young man has something to show you." He gestured to the warrior, and from inside his robes he produced a necklace similar, albeit a few stones lighter, than the one he'd tried to purchase earlier that day. "He says he's willing to sell it to you."

"Why? I thought these were family heirlooms? Did he steal it from someone?" Belaid asked him if he wanted to rephrase the question, since accusations of thievery often ended in swordplay. Eventually the story emerged: it belonged to the wife, who desperately wanted to go to the North, Constantine most likely, although her dream was Algiers. They were willing to sell it for the right price.

At first, Pond tried to talk the young man out of it but eventually the image of the necklace mounted on a white base behind glass at the Logan, his name prominently featured on the descriptor card, not to mention how irate Reygasse would be, overcame his better nature. They agreed on an extortionate but not unobtainable price. It would take several days for the money to be wired to Tamanrasset, but he'd go into town and pick it up. They had til then to change their minds.

The young warrior agreed, slipping the necklace back into his robe and slinking away into the dark.

"Thank you, Belaid."

"D'accord."

When Pond returned to the fire, Chapuis turned to him. "You know, I think you are here just in time."

"How's that, Louis?"

"Fifty years ago, we'd have been dead before we even smelled this place. Ten years ago, a couple of us might have been allowed in, but no cameras. Trading only, no money—not francs or silver. Tomorrow, who knows what this will look like?"

Pond looked around the village as they slowly made their way back to the fire. "You know the same thing happened at home. The Ojibway, the Sioux, they were warriors, too. Wanted nothing to do with us. Then they made peace—they had to, of course. Now the only way to see their way of life is to look at old pictures, or buy moccasins by the side of the road." He thought of the arrowheads, baskets and beadwork he'd personally shipped to Reygasse's museum in Algiers.

"That's why you're so good at this, Lonnie. You know what's at stake," said De Prorok from his spot on the ground. Pond sniffed derisively. "No, really, you're very good. Careful with your documentation, absolutely meticulous…"

"That's the easy part."

"No, it's not. Not at all, I'm absolute rubbish at it. At the real work, that is."

Pond sat down, and the two men looked at each other, then away in embarrassed silence.

"How's your Dorothy, doing?"

"Fine. Very well, I think."

"Is she proud of you?"

"I think so, as much as she understands of the work, although she tries. What about Alice? What does she think of what you do?"

De Prorok puffed philosophically for a moment. "She loves being the Countess, almost as much as her mother likes her being the Countess, and the babies of course." Three slow, wet sucking puffs on his pipe-stem later, he added, "She's an awfully good sport about it all. Oh, Pond, you should have seen her at Carthage. She'd never held a shovel before and she's out with the diggers, and whisking off artifacts like a maid with a feather duster. Until then I think she thought I showed up in my lecture outfit and just picked things out of the dirt. But she just dug in. Do both of you a favor. Before you marry that girl, take her out in the field."

"If I ever get home, they're talking about sending me to Poland in the spring."

"Won't happen," De Prorok declared. "Plans are in motion, Lonnie."

"What plans?"

"It's still not official, of course, but I think I'll be granted exclusive administrative rights to this region for the next three years. It's all but signed. Reygasse has the paperwork in motion, just waiting on the desk jockeys in Algiers. The Logan, of course, will have first choice of sites. This could be very good for you."

"What does that even mean, exclusive rights?" Damn it, Pond didn't sound nearly as excited as de Prorok thought he should be.

"Someone has to administer the permits, decide who digs where, what they can take, what stays here with L'Institut. All that red tape nonsense and, of course, there are fees to collect." He raised a conspiratorial eyebrow and let that sink in. "Naturally, you and the Logan are first in line, and you'll get the family rate. What do you think? Would coming back a couple of times beat spending the summer in a Polish swamp?"

Alonzo looked up into the star filled sky and let out a satisfied sigh. "I'm sure it would." A minute or so with the fire crackling providing the only sound, he asked, "Do you think it will still be here a few years from now?"

"Not like this, not like it was. That's why they need us, here, Pond. To document it and share it all. Get it down while there's still time. I've seen it at Carthage.

They get caught between the Mullahs and the French... neither fish nor fowl. They'll have to make choices and none of them pretty, but going back to their old ways isn't one of them. Someone needs to tell their stories after they can't."

"We could just leave them alone."

"We'd be the only ones who did." Pond couldn't argue.

By the fifth day, the Count was bored out of his mind. He and Barth filmed or snapped every interesting move anyone in the village made. Most of them twice, just for coverage. He wanted to move on and find Tin Hinan's grave but didn't yet have the information he needed.

"When will we get the location?" he demanded of Tadêfi.

She didn't much care for his tone of voice. "The Boka will tell you when he tells you. But you might find out tonight, assuming you mind your manners and open your big stupid ears." Belaid tried to stifle a snicker, thoroughly enjoying his role as neutral translator.

At last, an invitation came from Akhamouk to attend a special feast. The special entertainment was to be the Boka, a shaman and storyteller. Besides being a historian, the old man was a "friend of the *Kel Essuf,*" the silent, lonely spirits of the desert. They spoke through him in the form of stories.

Byron's mood brightened considerably. Maybe this was the word he needed to move on. Not that things were unpleasant. In fact, they were settled into a kind of mind-numbingly happy routine. Reygasse and Pond had reached a détente now that there was enough material for everyone. They were even sharing observations. Notepads were filled, replaced, and filled again. There was good, solid, anthropological work being done. It bored him to tears.

At dusk, everyone began to gather. Each family brought something to be shared, even though the King was supplying most of the meal. He could afford such largesse, because he was feeding everyone with gifts the Expedition gave him earlier. No one would ever accuse Akhamouk of being less than open-handed.

Byron waited, impatiently sucking on his pipe, through the requisite speeches and several rounds of their new nightly ritual, "How Do You Do, Harry Jones?" Women sang lovely, haunting songs full of dazzling moonlight, disappointed lovers, and bloody murder. Most of the blood shed belonged to unfaithful or cowardly husbands. Tuareg warriors were afraid of nothing, it was said, but Tuareg wives.

Finally, the Boka stood up and let out a long ululating cry. An expectant hush fell over the crowd. He moved closer to the fire, to the center of the circle, extending his arms to welcome the *Kel Essuf* to speak through him.

Pond scribbled as best he could in the firelight. The Boka was an old man, egg-bald under his turban, wrinkled and stooped, but still imposing. He wore a white robe, with a thick sash around his waist, and from the sash dangled a black skin bag full of stones.

Belaid translated for Byron and the others. "On special nights, the Boka reaches into the story bag. Each rock represents a certain story. You never know what stories the *Kel Essuf* want to be told each night. Whatever he pulls, that's the tale he tells."

He explained no one knew on any night whether it would be a romance, a recounting of great bravery in battle, or hilarious stories of torture befalling unwary desert travelers who didn't properly fear the plainly superior Tuaregs.

They watched the Boka thrust a bony hand into the bag and pull out a large white stone. "Tonight," he announced, "we tell the story of our Queen, Tin Hinan, Berber Saint, Mother of all Tuaregs." The crowd oohed and aahed in surprise. This story hadn't been told since Akhamouk's ascension to the crown. Belaid explained that rulers tended not to care much for tales that glorified their predecessors. They often failed to shine in comparison. Random selection or not, this was one of the most loved, and least told, stories in the shaman's repertoire.

De Prorok looked across the fire, and could tell by the relieved look on Tadêfi's face this was no coincidence. She returned his gaze and gave an imperious nod. He quickly called Chapuis and Belaid to his side and pulled out a notebook, even though he could barely see to write.

At the top of the page, he wrote, "Story bag?" *What a marvelous gimmick*, he thought. *The audience would eat it up*. He had so many great stories now, it was hard to fit them all in. What if he could leave it to random chance, or better yet, plan certain stories and make it look like random chance? It was a plan worth exploring. But that could wait. He forced himself to focus on the matter at hand.

Alone in the circle, the old man bowed low to the King and the royal family, then straightening as best he could, put out his arms and slowly spun around. He looked skyward, and called for the help of the Kel Essuf. "Help me do honor to the story of Our Mother, Tamenukalt, Tin Hinan, and how the Tuaregs came to be the most feared warriors in the world."

Byron watched, in awe, as they apparently complied with the humble request. The Boka's wide white eyes shot open and his spine stiffened. His chest expanded and his voice, stronger and more virile than before, boomed out over the assembly.

Always looking for tips to be a more effective speaker, Byron sat spellbound as the crowd was regaled with tales of Tin Hinan's beauty and her bravery in the face of the Muhammedan invaders. He sat bolt upright on hearing that last detail. He knew most modern versions of the story anachronistically portrayed Tin Hinan as a dutiful, if very independent minded, Muslim woman. That detail was a clear message; the Boka's way of promising he'd get the real story tonight. Including, hopefully, clues to her final whereabouts.

As the shaman sang, danced and screamed the story the *Kel Essuf* wished to share, Byron, Chapuis and Caid Belaid compared notes, discussing in hushed tones what was relevant and what wasn't. By the time the performance ended in wild applause, drumbeats and open weeping, Chapuis was satisfied he knew their destination.

"I know the place. It's not that big a surprise, pretty much where we thought it was. The thing is, there's more than one tomb up there. We have to find the right one. I have people up there who can get us what we need."

Byron nodded. "Good, I'm losing my bloody mind here. Belaid, thank your wife for us, please."

The Caid gritted his teeth and smiled. If he expressed his gratitude to her much more, there'd be nothing left of him.

"Alright, gentlemen. We'll leave in three days."

February 18, 1926
Brooklyn, New York

Byron,

I hope you're well and staying warm. I know the audiences are eating you up. How's that new boy working out? I hope he's better with all that equipment than you are. Ha ha.

I wish things were going well here, but to be honest, they're not. My family is being quite awful lately. Not with the girls and I, they are being very sweet as usual, but about you. Some of it is left over from Algeria—mostly about the money, which is more than I thought it was, but also the lawyers are involved, and you know how they are. Daddy says this is your last chance to come clean about anything you might have or know. Do you know what he's talking about? I told him you didn't even bring the girls souvenirs from your trip, let alone gold or jewelry but he's being a grumpy old bear about it all. Mary, of course, is on his side as usual.

Also, someone from the Brooklyn Eagle called, and you know how nice they've always been to us. This reporter woman was so rude! They are trying to twist everything so you look like a big faker and I set her straight, but I don't think we'll be in the society pages in the Eagle for a while.

Since you've added another week or two onto your tour, I'm thinking it might make sense to take the girls back to Paris sooner than we planned. Annie is furious, of course, but really I can't stay and listen to people say such horrible things, especially when they're not true.

Byron, I feel so alone and scared sometimes, I need you to tell me that what they're saying is all lies and we are going to be alright. You know that I will always stick by you, but I need to hear your side of the story.

Since I'm going to be traveling, I need to ask you for more cash. I don't dare ask Daddy or Mother.

Will you wire that directly, or should I contact Lee Keedick?

Please write soon, Darling. The girls send their love.

Love,

A

Chapter 13

Milwaukee, Wisconsin
February 20, 1926

The sword hit the floor with a ringing clang that echoed around the cellar workshop. I picked it up with a few choice words, loud enough to feel better, but not so loud Mama would hear me. I didn't really want to get chewed out this morning.

The Count's train arrived in less than four hours, and I wasn't done yet. Painting and polishing the tin took days longer than expected, and now the blade had a big nick out of it. I wanted it to be as perfect as possible, and was making my usual hash of things.

I gripped it in two hands, feeling the leather grip solid in my palm. It made a satisfying "swoosh" as it sliced the air. On stage, the lights would bounce off it, impressing the bejeebers out of the audience. While the Count rattled on about "fierce Tuaregs," and "bloody duels of honor," this would look more like the real thing, and less like a cheap prop.

Out of the blue, something odd occurred to me. If it was real, the sword would have been used for gutting missionaries and beheading intruders. It would hardly be in pristine condition. Remembering my boss's motto—a good story beats the hell out of reality any time—I grabbed a ball peen hammer and gave it a couple of more whacks, knocking another small notch out of the blade and dimpling the metal.

Now it looked like it had seen a lot of Arab neck bones and missionary spleens.

Amazingly, the little glass chips along the "T" of the hilt hung on. I was afraid they wouldn't—gluing glass is notoriously tricky and I sure didn't have a jeweler's delicate fingers—but all five of them held in place, glinting white, green and blue.

I wrapped the sword in an oily rag and carefully placed it in a brown cloth drawstring sack, along with assorted bits of copper wire, colored glass and pieces of tin and other scraps I'd managed to scrounge over the last couple of weeks. I didn't know if I'd need them, but it wouldn't hurt. God knows I wouldn't be traveling with much else. But I would be traveling. Out of Milwaukee for good.

More importantly, I'd be out of this house. Away from my father, away from everything that smelled like cabbage, and cheap pipe smoke, and fried sausage fat. Even mama's hugs smelled of *sauerbraten*. The very German-ness of it all threatened to suffocate me.

Rather than the clean, bright colors the rest of America favored, and folks like my Aunt and Uncle eagerly adopted, I was completely surrounded by heavy curtains, carved dark wood and ever-present reminders of a Bavarian existence I never knew. Decorated porcelain plates with "*Gott Segne Unsere Heimat*," in heavy Gothic letters, embroidered tea towels with stags and fir trees, and little figurines of milkmaids and hunters covered every flat surface. Like most of my friends, also the children of immigrants, our home was packed with yearning souvenirs of countries our folks had been all too eager to flee.

But after a few weeks of being able to breathe, I was back, however briefly. And paying for the privilege. I'd barely put my bags down and managed to squirm out of my mother's embrace when he started in.

"Sho, you're back. Didn't find a job in the Promised Land?" He looked over his glasses at me, but didn't bother getting out of his chair.

"Only for a couple of weeks. Then I've got a full-time job, Papa." Mama smiled dotingly, and was about to ask for all the glorious details, but she never got a chance.

"Until then?" Gerhardt Braun never let a potential silver lining spoil a big, black cloud. "You're going to live here for free?" That had been my plan, truth be told, but now he was making a big deal out of it. I was too exhausted to fight. The bus had gone Cedar Rapids-Dubuque-Fort Dodge-Madison-Milwaukee, stopping at every wide spot on the road along the way. I needed a bed, a sandwich, and some motherly head-stroking.

"How much?" I pulled out the eight dollars I had left to me, which fortunately was in large-sized notes, instead of coins and looked more impressive.

"A dollar and a half a week," his chin jutted out, daring me to take a swing at it.

"Oh, Papa," my mother moaned.

"Okay, fine." I peeled off three bills and thought about throwing it in his face, but instead handed it pointedly to my mother while looking at him. At least she'd get to see the money, and he'd have to ask her for it before drinking it away. "But I get to use the workshop."

"What for?"

"Work." I knew he couldn't really argue that one.

I knew I'd miss those three dollars, and if the Count was late, which his last letter indicated he might be, it would cost me a buck and a half more, but short time work wouldn't really be a problem. One thing about the Old Man's employment record, he knew every foreman and straw boss at every factory in Milwaukee, and most of them knew me by association. I could pick up a day's sweeping here, or filling in on a loading dock there, enough to save a little. They all respected the Old Man as a hard worker, and knew the apple wouldn't fall far from the tree. They'd take a chance on me, even if they couldn't hire my father, who was known far and wide as "The Crazy Kraut."

It wasn't his being German, specifically, or even his drinking that bothered them, although booze usually factored into the inevitable dismissal. It was his politics. Gerhardt Braun was a committed Wobblie, and while he took pride in his work, that same pride sooner or later resulted in a challenge—often of a physical nature—to an authority figure. That resulted in yet another job in yet another factory and another extorted promise to "just keep his head down and do the work." It didn't all make much sense to me when I was younger, but then a lot about him didn't make much sense.

Like how the other fathers Americanized their names. What was the harm in that? Slava Boycic was, "Sam," and Giuseppe Iaccobucci, Maria's father, was "Joe." Yet Gerhardt steadfastly refused to become a Gerald, or better yet, a Jerry. It only dawned on me after the War that being a German named Jerry might not exactly be an asset when seeking employment. He grudgingly allowed me to morph from Wilhelm to the more palatable Willy, although he couldn't understand why a real man would deliberately give himself a baby's name. Wilhelm was a perfectly good working man's name. I had been named for his father, after all, not the *Gottverdammter* Kaiser.

So I job hopped and tramped my way through the next two and a half weeks. There was another, completely unexpected advantage to my working so many jobs. I was able to scrounge scrap tin from Mallory's Cannery, blobs of colored glass scraped off the cement floor at Wisconsin Glassworks, and thin copper wire which soon became sword blades, beads from Tin Hinan's tomb, and devices to secure Tuareg veils behind big Kraut ears.

Everything was fine until the Count's letter arrived a week ago, telling me the schedule had changed and he wouldn't be in the Midwest again until his arrival on the twentieth. That meant another buck and a half, but the worst part was explaining my late departure.

Mama smelled my disappointment, but couldn't hide her happiness at my being around a few more days. Explaining my presence meant telling the Old Man exactly what I was doing. That went about as well as I expected it to.

"Vass is dis 'projection technician'? You're an engineer all of a sudden? You vent to college in Cedar Rapids?"

"N-n-no, but you see the Count, de Prorok, he does these... scientific lectures..."

He almost pissed himself at the idea of me and science in the same sentence.

"Imagine," he clucked, "My Villy working with a Count. Such a big shot."

"Count? What kind of Count?" he demanded. To him, rich people were a problem. European rich people were worse, and aristocrats the source of all evil in the world. In his drunken moments, he admitted his biggest gripe about the Great War was it had crippled the nobility, but ended before finishing the job.

"So you're just going to travel around doing this big shot's dirty work? Are you going to wipe his royal arse for him too?"

"Gerhardt, please..." Mama knew better than to

get between two butting rams, but maternal instinct is a tough thing to ignore. I stepped between them, pulling myself to my full height. She sighed and moved to the neutral territory of the kitchen, where she pretended to dry dishes but could still hear everything.

"Yes, a Count… well, he's really an American, but… the p-p-p-oint is, he wants me to go with him as he travels around. For two weeks at first, but then it'll be p-p-permanen-n-nt."

He knew better than to believe in the idea of a permanent job. The idea of me with such a beast was beyond his comprehension. "You won't last t-t-t-two weeks." He deliberately spit out the "t"s as he often did when reminding me of my many limitations. "People like that don't hire people like you out of the goodness of their hearts. They use you while they need you and then kick you to the curb. Then you'll come crawling back to your mama to take care of you. Scheisse," he shook his head.

I accepted my mother's weak hug from behind as I sat there, flushed and sweating, determined not to give him the last word, but of course he got it.

Now I stood hours from my escape. Today the Count arrived, and I had to get him and his gear to the Pfister. He was speaking on Monday, then things really kicked off. First to Chicago, then on to Rockford, Madison, and Beloit. After that was probably St. Louis, but then New York, Philadelphia, and dear Jesus anywhere other than Milwaukee. I wouldn't come back with my tail between my legs. I couldn't.

"Brown!" a familiar voice slashed through the crowd at the Lake Front Depot. The gleaming silver tip of his walking stick waved over the heads of people disembarking the Hiawatha from Chicago. The multitude parted as the Count strode towards me, hand extended. He gave my arm a squeeze and almost pulverized my hand with the greeting.

"So good to see you my friend." He looked around with a conspiratorial smile. "Seems remarkably civilized for a... what did you call it? Frozen shit hole?"

"Well, it's no D-d-des Moines." I smiled.

He threw back his head and launched a laugh over the heads of the crowd. "Touché, but what is, Brown? What is?"

I managed to find us a taxi and a driver willing to lash the larger cases to his trunk and take a short fare. The Pfister was only five blocks away in Saturday traffic, and the extra dollar tip was sufficient inducement to defy the laws of gravity and risk running afoul of Milwaukee's finest.

On the way, de Prorok babbled on about his travels, and how good it was to see me again, and how he hadn't been able to find anyone to fill my rather large shoes (not to mention the Tuareg costume), and damn did it never get warm here, and he still hoped Alice would reconsider and join him, and did he mention I looked well?

We pulled up the front of the Pfister hotel, but a uniformed doorman waved us away before the cab even came to a complete stop. "Gotta bring those bags around back, can't bring them through here."

I was going to argue with him, but I felt a less than subtle grip on my arm. "Of course, which entrance? I'm sorry, your name is..."

"Percy, sir. Sorry, rules, you know."

"Of course, Percy. My man will bring them around. Where would you like them?"

As Percy tipped his cap and gave directions to the

freight entrance off Mason Street, I said nothing and pouted. Apparently I was just "his man." Percy had a name, I didn't. Three minutes later, I was banging on the back fire door of the Hotel Pfister, surrounded by gear and luggage.

The door opened up, and a Negro porter came out, slapping his arms for warmth. He gave me a silent but friendly enough nod. "This all?"

"Yeah," I answered. "They wouldn't let me come through the front."

"Know how ya feel. Let's get this inside." We each grabbed an end of the biggest trunk, and in three trips. "Close this door, tight. Sometimes it don't close right. I'll go get us a cart and get it upstairs for ya."

"Thanks." I was going to ask his name, but he was already around the corner and gone. I turned back to the door, gripped the handle and prepared to pull it shut, when it flew out of my hand and burst open.

Standing in the doorway was a pig-eyed, red faced, stocky guy in a brown coat, hat and scarf. "Hi kid. Figured it was time we finally had us a little talk."

I looked around frantically for either an escape route or some assistance, but saw neither. The guy took a step inside, and pulled the door solidly shut behind him. "Relax, I just want to talk for a minute."

I held my breath as he reached into his coat, but all he pulled out was a business card, and held it out to me with two fingers. I took the card and studied it. His name was printed on it, *Joseph Havlicek, Investigator,* but what really got me was the big black eye staring up at me. This guy was a Pinkerton.

Most people would be relieved to know he wasn't a real cop, but most people weren't raised by radical socialists. The Pinkertons were just above the Bogeyman and just below the Rothschilds on the list of the world's terrors. What had the Old Man done now?

"Thought we'd have a little chat about your boss."

"The Count?"

He snorted. "Okay, the Count, de Prorok, whoever. What do you know about him?"

"Whaddya mean? He's an archaeologist. He goes around giving lectures." I didn't know what this guy was looking for.

"So why's an archaeologist keep muscle around? I mean does he really need a big guy like you to watch a few rocks and projectors?"

He thought I was the muscle. He was not just scary, but out of his ever-loving gourd. "I'm n-n-not... I just run the p-p-projector and help with the lectures."

His tiny eyes never left my face, and I knew he could see every bright red capillary and drop of sweat on it. I wondered if I could make a break down the hall, but he slid his foot over a few inches and pressed it hard against mine, pushing it back against the wall, pinning me in place. If he wasn't a cop now, he had been once.

"Okay, let's try this. I'm going to ask you some questions, and then I'll leave you alone. I really don't want to get you in Dutch with the boss." He took my terrified silence for assent. "Have you ever seen him with anything really valuable? Anything he's trying to keep hid?"

"N-n-nope, nothing like that."

"A lot of people don't believe that." The calmer his voice got, the scarier he was.

"Like who?"

"People. Some here, some in other countries. They think he has something that don't belong to him, and they'd like to get it back. No questions asked, you see, but the sooner the better. The longer it takes, the more trouble he's in. You sure he ain't hiding something?"

I shook my head.

He leaned in even closer and I could smell the cheap cigar on his breath. "You sure? You'd tell, me, right?"

"I said no, Goddammit." Just to give myself a little breathing room, I shoved him away. It was nothing much but he bounced off the wall behind him, and his eyes widened.

When you're my size, people can confuse blind panic with aggression. Sometimes that works to my advantage. Sometimes. Havlicek was trying to decide which this was. If he guessed that I really had no idea how to fight, I was in a world of hurt.

"What's going on?" a familiar voice echoed down the hall. The Count and the porter stood there with a rolling metal cart.

"Nuttin' at all. Just having a word with Mr. Braun here. Pleasure to meet ya. I'm Joe Havlicek." He stuck his paw out but the Count declined the offer. "Okay, we can do it that way. I represent some people who are looking for stolen property. They seem to think you know where it is."

I'd never heard de Prorok's voice sound so icy calm. "What is it I am supposed to have taken?"

"I think you know the answer to that."

"I don't have it. Never have." His voice was flatter and calmer than before.

"You know they won't believe you. What am I supposed to tell them?"

I heard a clock tick. An elevator dinged somewhere behind the wall. De Prorok's answer was almost as quiet, "It doesn't matter. I don't have it." He gestured from the porter to the gear. "Percy, let's get this loaded if you please. Brown, are you coming?"

"Yes sir." I stepped over Havlicek's foot and ignored the little voice telling me to step on it just for grins. The Pinkerton just stood and watched, then shrugged and put his hat on, adjusting it carefully.

"We'll talk again soon, I'm sure." He opened the door and a blinding shaft of sunlight and bitterly cold air burst into the dark hallway. "You know where to find me, kid." Then he was gone.

Not another word was spoken as we loaded the gear onto the cart, wheeled it to an elevator, rode to the seventh floor, and Jasper opened the door to 706. Once inside, the Count tipped him fifty cents. "Thank you, Percy."

"Thank you, sir. You gentlemen have a pleasant day," he said with the same smile he doled out a hundred times a day. The door closed behind him with a quiet snick. I waited for de Prorok to say something—anything—but it was awfully quiet for the longest time.

The Count just stood looking out the window. The bright winter sunshine lit up the room, but left him a solitary, lean shadow, staring out at the tarred rooftops of downtown Milwaukee and the star encrusted surface of Lake Michigan. He lit his pipe and blew a long, slow cloud of smoke before he finally turned to me.

"Pinkerton?"

"What? Uh, yeah. Havlicek... Joseph Havlicek." That got a nod out of him, but it was a completely insufficient answer. "What's g-g-going on? What are they looking f-f-f-or?"

"Treasure, Brown. They think I have some of the Tin Hinan treasure. I'm not sure what they think I have. Jewels, precious metals, maybe the Holy bloody Grail. Christ, I don't know what all."

"And you don't?" The disappointed look he gave

me stabbed me in the gut.

"Willy, I may be… I am…a lot of things, but a thief is not one of them. Yes?"

The best I could choke out was, "Yeah, sure. Of course. Will he come back?"

"I shouldn't be at all surprised." He took another long look out the window, then turned to me. His face had transformed back to his usual peppy self. Clapping his hands together and rubbing them vigorously, he gestured to the pile of gear. "Do you know I didn't have a single competent assistant while you were gone? Just dreadful."

He opened the box of slides, and I saw them all jumbled together. He waved his hand vaguely in that direction. "You've got your work cut out for you, I'm afraid. But you are on the clock."

That thought made me smile, and I threw my coat on the bed, eager to get back to work. Then I saw the cloth bag. "Oh, I made something…" Oh God, what if he hated it? "It's n-n-not very g-g-good, but I…" Finally, I reached in and took the sword by the blade, holding it out to him like a dead fish.

"What's this?" His long fingers reached around the hilt, grasped it and then took an exploratory swipe across his body. "Oh, Brown. This is quite marvelous…" He took a step back, then went into the bent-knee pose the jokers in his films struck before dancing. He beamed happily, hopping forward a few steps then back, waving the sword like a maniac.

He clipped the lampshade, and I had to make a diving catch, but he didn't notice. He just kept humming merrily to himself, completely oblivious to the trappings of the hotel room or anything else.

"You made this yourself, Brown? I'm gobsmacked. It's perfect. The weight is a bit wrong, of course, but then this is… tin is it?" I nodded, feeling a warm and very unfamiliar swell of pride. "Clever. They'll never know from the stage. Especially when you're all..." He waved his arms to indicate my being dressed up like a big pale idiot.

"You know where this will look especially good? Under the lights at Carnegie Hall." He must have seen the shock on my face because he plopped his keister on the bed and slapped his palms on his knees. "I was going to save the surprise, but what the hell. It's not official of course, but I have officially signed with a booking agent. Lee Keedick—you've heard me mention him—and he says we are penciled in for a lecture there in June. Imagine, Brown, we could be doing all this at Carnegie Hall."

He went on and on, but I was fixated on the "we." Grinning, he leapt to his feet. "Yes, we have engagements all the way through the end of the spring, before I have to go back to Paris, and then Algeria again. How'd you like to stay on through the end of the tour? St. Louis, New York, Philadelphia... the people at the Smithsonian haven't confirmed yet, but Washington's a given..."

All those names buzzed around in my head. It was really happening. The big cities back East might as well have been Budapest or Timbuktu, and I was going to see them. But what happened after that?

The happy buzzing was replaced by a nagging question. "What happens after that? When you're gone?"

He stopped sucking on his pipe long enough to wave it at me. "Damn it Brown, are you always this negative? This is good news, man. We'll figure out the details. These things always work themselves out."

That sure hadn't been my experience, but I just bit my lip, gave him a nod and turned back to the box of jumbled lantern slides. If I was back on the clock, I'd best hop to it.

"Tomorrow I won't need you, but Monday of course is our lecture at Marquette. Then Tuesday we're off to Chicago." "We" were leaving Milwaukee for good on Tuesday.

Sunday morning I took Mama to church. It was the first time in ages, and we both knew it would be the last for a long time. I let her wheedle a completely empty promise out of me that I'd go once in a while, just to stay on God's good side. She also tearfully demanded to know when I'd be back, and I was vague enough to comfort her but no one could accuse me of lying in church, either. I wasn't much of a believer, but I never stepped on cracks in the sidewalk.

It took a lot of time on Saturday to get everything in proper order but it was worth it. Monday's lecture was the usual rip-roaring success. The sword was a big hit, although it was heavier than I thought and I almost de-nostril-ed the Count when he attempted to get me to dance. I guess both the audience and the speaker caught a whiff of danger, because it got a bigger laugh than ever.

The only thing different was the question period. The questions were mostly the same, but the way people asked them sounded, I don't know, more hostile. An older guy from the Sentinel asked, "The papers say you might still have some of the jewels. Can we see them?"

I didn't hear the answer, because I was scanning the crowd to see if Havlicek had put him up to that, and if I could spot him. I looked for a familiar hat, and I saw one, but not the hat I was expecting. This was wasn't brown. It was red and black checked wool. It didn't belong to Joe Havlicek. It belonged to my Old Man, and he was heading my way.

I could feel the coals in my cheeks blaze brighter. I

stood there half dressed in my desert warrior costume, with my white overalls showing. I wished the floor would cave me in and carry me away to a quick, if messy death, but I didn't have that kind of luck.

He came to within three paces of me, then gave me a very slow once-over. "Nice get up."

I had no response. I knew exactly how ridiculous I must look to him. Up until this moment I'd managed not to think about it.

"Brown, who's this?" I cringed, and didn't turn around. I could feel de Prorok over my shoulder. My father raised an eyebrow at the "Brown" but said nothing.

"It's my father. G-g-g-gerhardt Braun, Count B-b-byron de P-prorok." I think I remembered to make a vague gesture of introduction.

The Old Man started to remove his cap, but remembering his role as representative of the proletariat, he pulled it further down on his head. The Count held out a perfectly manicured hand, and my father waited just long enough to reciprocate to send a message of extreme disapproval.

"*Herr Braun, Sie haben einen feinen Sohn.*" His German was flawless, of course as he complimented my father on his fine son. It also had enough of a Prussian undertone to it I knew it would irritate the hell out of the Old Man.

"My English is perfectly good, Herr de Prorok." In all his years of embarrassing me, this was going to be the worst yet. It was like watching two cars speed towards each other, but unable to do anything except watch and hope for survivors.

"Indeed it is. You must be very proud of your son. I've not found anyone else like him." My father ceded a small shrug. At least he didn't argue the point. With one more clap on the shoulder, he nodded to the Old

Man. "Well, I'll leave you two. Willy, let's get packed up, please. I'd like to get back to the hotel as soon as possible."

I nodded, then turned back to the full brunt of my father's most severe over-the-glasses glare. He held it until I was sure it left a mark. I could feel my back stiffen and I stood as tall as I could. That gave me about three inches on him, and I needed every one of them. Hopefully he couldn't hear my knees knock through the robes.

"This is the job you want?" He flicked the robes with his fingertips. "This is a good job for an honest man?" The disappointment dripped from his lips like acid.

"Yeah. Yes it is."

"For how long?"

"Maybe for good." That got a contemptuous snort from him.

"He'll work you like a mule then dump you soon as he's done. Probably in the middle of nowhere. Then what will you do?"

"F-f-find another job. Isn't that what you always do?" He actually flinched at that, but it was all the satisfaction he'd give me. It might have been enough.

"When do you leave?"

"Tomorrow. Chicago."

"Does Mama know?" I nodded, not breaking eye contact. "If you go, you're gone for good."

I nodded my head, as confidently as the swelling lump in my throat allowed. He gave a single nod and turned away. I waited a moment, realized he wasn't going to look back, then went back to packing up film cans and straightening pictures.

Chapter 14

Chicago, Illinois
February 23, 1926

It was only a hundred miles as the crow flies from 13th and Keefe to Union Station in Chicago. I wasn't a crow, and it may as well have been a million miles. The moment my feet hit the sidewalk on Canal Street, I felt I'd really left Milwaukee for good.

To a nineteen year old lunkhead, Chicago was something out of a movie—maybe Safety Last with Harold Lloyd. I remember watching him hanging from that clock tower high above Los Angeles and not being able to feel my feet. I felt the exact same tingle just looking up at the skyline around me. We had tall buildings in Milwaukee, but only a few, spaced out over a few blocks downtown. People really worked up there every day. Not people like me, of course, but people.

Count de Prorok was in no mood for my open-mouthed hick act. He hailed a cab while I stood looking around generally being a serious navigation hazard to the hundreds of other people on the sidewalk. When the hack driver opened the trunk, he grabbed me by the arm. "You are joining me, Brown?" I turned beet red, mumbled an apology and squeezed in between the cases and trunks as he directed the cabbie to the Allerton, at Michigan and Huron.

The Count laid his head back on the seat and stared at the ceiling, just like he'd done the whole train ride down. That left me to take the bullet and make nice with the cabbie. His babble interfered with my gawking, but he was relentless.

"This is the year, I swear to God. Seventeen years the Cubs have stunk but this is their year, don'tcha think?"

"Yeah, probably." I knew anything I said was irrelevant, it just gave him a chance to reload.

"I mean, dey got Hack Wilson, for Chrissakes. If you can't win a World Series with Hack by-god Wilson, what do ya gotta do?"

"I don't know."

"Seventeen years. You'd think they'd win one soon just by accident."

It was like that all the way to the Allerton. We arrived and, just like at the Pfister, I was dropped off in the alley with our stuff. I had a few uncomfortable moments alone with the luggage looking around frantically for brown hats that weren't there, then a few more when I realized I was surrounded by more black faces than I'd seen in my whole life. The porters and kitchen help took their smoke breaks by the loading dock, apparently. Still, Arthur the porter, once he got over the surprise of being asked his name, was a good guy and got our gear up to 803 without incident.

We knocked, but the Count didn't answer. I stood there for a moment like a moron, not sure what to do, even after Arthur used his passkey to crack the door and extended his palm. I had never tipped anyone at a hotel before, and had no idea how much was enough. I reached into my pocket and found two quarters and a paperclip.

Fifty cents must have been pretty generous,

because he gave me a gap-toothed smile and an enthusiastic offer of girls or booze, whatever the boss or I might be looking for. I gave him a smile that I hoped was worldly and amused, rather than horrified, and declined his kind offer, but yes, I knew where to find him if I changed my mind. It seemed a lot of people at the Allerton changed their minds after a lonely night or two.

The Count stood at the window, looking south towards the river and the Loop. Pipe smoke formed a blue halo around his head that renewed itself every minute or so with another silent puff. He seemed oblivious to my banging around as I stacked the cases in the corner, and put my one flaking brown suitcase at the foot of my cot. Not a word was said, the gurgling and sputtering of the radiator and faint footsteps out in the hall, muffled by carpeting, were the only sounds.

Just to make myself useful, I snapped open the case with most of his artifacts in it. "What will you need tonight?" I asked, hoping like hell that list didn't include me. He had dinner plans with several of the money people from the Oriental Institute, and I wanted no part of those shenanigans.

One thing I'd learned in our time together, I was Gerhardt's son enough to feel a discomfort bordering on loathing around rich people and college eggheads. The primary function of the Institute was to play matchmaker between both those groups. Throw in some wrinkly nun school teachers and it was my idea of hell on earth.

Without giving me his full attention, he pointed vaguely at the case. "The makeup pot. The Venus is good. I just need enough for a quick show and tell... And you may as well give me my helmet, too."

"It's snowing out. You're really wearing this?"

He laughed. "No, but I'll bring it. What is it with people? No matter how much money they have, or how powerful they are, they all act like children and want to try on my pith helmet?" I knew why. I'd tried it on myself the first time he left me alone with it. I wanted to see how I looked as a famous explorer. One look in the mirror cured me. I immediately realized I no more resembled a dashing desert explorer than I did a Tuareg king.

"Because they want to imagine what it's like to be you."

"They can't possibly imagine what it's like to be me," he snapped. Then, realizing how petulant he sounded, he added, "They don't know how lucky they are not to get lice from that damned hat."

I scratched my head as I asked, "You've had lice?" For some reason, the idea struck me as ludicrous, even though almost everyone I knew had them at one time or another, and in springtime half our school had smelled like kerosene and Life Buoy. On the other hand, if I were a pest, that head of wavy dark hair was prime real estate, and with a penthouse view.

"Live in the desert long enough, you'll catch everything but the clap. Live in the city long enough, you'll probably catch that, too." He managed the first real smile I'd seen in days. "You'll have to watch yourself in New York, Willy. You barely got out of Moline with your virtue intact." The idea of getting out to see Chicago was far more exciting than arguing whether my virtue was technically intact or not, so I chose to focus there.

"So you won't need me tonight?"

"No, go out and explore the Windy City. Try not to get yourself machine gunned. We have that luncheon tomorrow before we head to Rockford, so don't be too late."

"Yes, Mama."

He didn't miss a beat. "*Und keine madchen nach hause bringen,*" he squawked in an old woman's voice.

"You don't bring any girls home either, young man," I smarted off before I realized what a crappy thing it was to say. Despite his shameless flirting, there was only one girl he wanted to bring to this room, and she was a long way from Chicago.

He let it slide with a quiet, "I'll try to control my baser urges."

After the obligatory but completely hollow offer to stay with him til he left for his appointment, I jammed two dollars in my pocket. The rest of my savings I shoved in a sock, rolled it up tightly and squished it to the bottom of my suitcase with the rest of my worldly goods, then under the rollaway bed flush against the wall.

One advantage of being broke most of the time is you learn to kill time creatively. The two best ways to do that; street cars and movie theaters. Back home I'd often just pick a line and ride it from one to the other, watching the neighborhoods change like the seasons. Dirty cramped tenements to bungalows to mansions, then inevitably back downscale as the lines petered out just like winter to spring, to summer, to fall. All for a dime.

Even in Cedar Rapids, I was intimately familiar with the Sixth Street South West and Third Street North East lines as they ran through downtown. Here my destination was the Clark-Wentworth line, which ran an unfathomably long way through the city. My goal was to ride it as north as made sense, and as far south as I dared, which according to Arthur, wouldn't be far.

I wandered up Michigan Avenue to Chicago, then across to Clark. It was late afternoon, and the

Magnificent Mile was alive with the lady shoppers in furs, and professional men in suits, ties and thick wool overcoats. I must have looked like one of the servants, just gaping and staring, and not a particularly bright or useful one.

Once on the streetcar, though, I fit right in. Working our way north, I was amazed to hear the languages around me change abruptly. Downtown it was English, of course, in a variety of accents and volumes but eventually it would switch to mostly Swedish, then a mix of Bohunk languages, even Syrian and Yiddish, then back to English as the tram chugged and clanged north towards the better suburbs.

The neighborhoods bewildered me. At home, there might be a block or so where people clung to the Old Country—which ever country that happened to be— but here it went for what seemed miles in any direction. A dizzying array of restaurants, stores, and signs in strange script beckoned and repelled me at the same time. Would I even know what to order in a Chinese restaurant, or a Syrian place? The Count would know, but he wasn't here to guide me. If I wasn't going to starve, I'd best learn to feed myself. I took it as a challenge to try something exotic and foreign-sounding.

Left to my own devices, I finally chickened out and found a German place where at least I knew what I was ordering. I was disappointed to find out that, besides being the most expensive meal I'd ever ordered, the food was no better than I'd find on Keefe Street, or even in my own Mama's kitchen. It left me feeling cheated, and determined to be braver in my food choices from then on. At least as much as possible. I heard Orientals ate cats, and sometimes served them to unsuspecting Americans. That much adventure I wasn't up for.

Losing track of time, I rode north, then south again, farther than Arthur suggested was wise, I was proud to note, then high-tailed it back downtown. I found a movie house playing "The Sea Beast," with John Barrymore and Dolores Costello. Turns out, it was really Moby Dick, but it was still pretty good. I don't remember any women when I read it in high school, but then I usually enjoyed the movies more than the books.

I sat in the dark, feeling awfully smug when the projectionist messed up a reel change, and I joined with the audience hooting and hollering when the whale appeared on the screen. I thought about how Ahab wouldn't stop til he found that creature, and he risked everything for the girl, Esther. I never much liked Barrymore, or any of the pretty boy actors for that matter, because they didn't look or act like anyone I knew. But watching, I recognized the look of wild enthusiasm when he spoke about that whale. It was the same look I'd seen on de Prorok's mug when he talked about Carnegie Hall, or "digging rights," or "making the world forget Howard Carter ever existed."

I wondered if Countess Alice had long hair like Dolores Costello. I'd seen her picture but I couldn't remember. That was something else I thought about alone in the dark. The good girls—Lillian Gish, Mary Pickford, Dolores Costello in this picture—all had long hair in ribbons. Maria Iaccobucci had hair like that: thick Italian tresses that my chewed-up knackwurst fingers would never get to run through. The bad girls—Theda Bara, Vilma Bánky, heck even Jacqueline from Moline—had their hair bobbed. The movies told us we were supposed to like the good girls, and in the movies I did. What wasn't to like? They were sweet, and nice and usually gave their all for their man without complaint. That was the movies. In real life they scared the bejeezus out of me.

In real life, I liked the bad girls. Or at least they seemed to like me. They were either bad or the maids, telephone operators and garment workers in my neighborhood who just wore their hair short because it was easier to manage when you had real work to do. Surely long hair would get all tangled in an operator's headset, and when you had to be at work at the crack of dawn, did you really have all day to brush it out? Most of them, in my admittedly limited experience, weren't bad. Just practical.

The movie let out about eleven, and I stepped out onto Halsted Street. Traffic was light, mostly taxis running north and south. Small, dry flakes of snow spiraled to the ground. It wasn't really cold for February, just a little breeze blowing east towards the lake, which made it almost balmy. I decided to walk back to the hotel, although I could have gotten a cab.

I smiled at the very idea. I could get a cab. Hell, I could do anything I wanted. Here I was in a big city, money in my pocket, no one sitting at home waiting for me. I could get rip roaring drunk if I wanted, which I didn't. I could see another movie, or walk back to the hotel, or grab a cab and head for the fleshpots of Calumet City. I wouldn't, of course, and whether that was my upbringing, just good sense, or a lack of cash wasn't really the point. I could do it if I chose. I had a choice.

Walking down the street, I whistled an old German tune Mama taught me, but that didn't seem right, so I switched to "Sweet Georgia Brown," which gave me a beat to walk to and quickened my pace as well as my pulse. It sounded so much more Chicago, and more modern. And a whole lot like me, which made me indescribably happy.

This was uncharted territory, being responsible to no one by myself. I was in the second biggest city in the country, where I only knew one person, and he was a stranger here himself. I could have been in Cairo, or Marrakesh and someday I might be. Even the familiar seemed exotic and alien. Maybe I should be the one wearing a pith helmet, I thought. I actually laughed out loud from sheer joy, but no one heard and neither I nor they would have cared if they did.

About a block from the Allerton, I saw a newsstand, and stood there scanning the headlines. According to the Daily Herald, there were immigration raids on Dago neighborhoods after another body was found in Cicero. Forty one bodies, they said, including this guy Orazio. Mama said the Italians would never amount to anything, but the ones I knew were alright. Some, like Maria Iaccobucci, could redeem the entire race single handed.

I was lost in bloody images of tommy guns and thoughts of long dark hair like Dolores Costello's when I was jerked back to reality by a familiar voice.

"Hey, kiddo. How's it going?" Havlicek grimaced against the cold, which only made his eyes squintier and piggier than normal. "Where's your boss?"

I hugged my coat tighter around me and shrugged like an idiot. Havlicek rolled his eyes. "Will you give him a message? Jesus, Braun, I'm just the messenger here, don't bust my chops. Tell him he has a visitor. Bill Kenny wants to see him first thing in the morning."

"Who?" Apparently the depths of my ignorance continuously surprised the Pinkerton.

"He'll know, but first thing means first thing, no matter how hungover the son of a bitch is." He waited for me to respond. I think he thought I was stalling. In reality, I had no idea what to do.

"T-t-tell him yourself," was the best I could muster.

"Why'dja think I was standing out here? If I could find him I wouldn't be freezing my heinie off. Figured you'd know better than I would. Now you been told and I can go to bed. Remember, first thing." He spun on his heel, hunched his shoulders and headed up Michigan Avenue. I don't know if the wind had shifted from the west to east off the lake, but for the first time that night I felt really cold.

Finding the Count was going to take some work, but I had a pretty fair idea of where to start. Arthur wasn't working, but a couple of the other black guys on duty remembered a tall, skinny, rich guy asking for the location of the nearest speak. I got the same discounted rate for the information as de Prorok had, but it still cost me some of what I had left in my pocket. I dashed out and over to Wabash.

Even with the password, it took some doing to get in, dressed like I was. Through the metal grill, I told the guy I was just looking to find my father, who had left Mama crying at home. It was a story I'd told before. That earned me a terse, "You got five minutes to find him and get the hell out."

The pounding of a piano and the din of drunken conversation made it impossible to pick out even the Count's foghorn of a voice, but I found him by following an equally obvious clue. Over against one wall sat a crowd of well-dressed folks. One of them was a bottle blonde wearing a short red sequined dress and an off-white pith helmet. With less than my usual grace, I bulldozed through the crowd towards them, bumping into enough people I caught the eye of the bouncer, who cut off my approach.

He was taller than me by about an inch, but had me by about thirty pounds of pure muscle. The guy looked like a slab of beef with eyes. A vise grip that hurt even through my winter coat brought me to a halt about ten feet from the table. I was close enough to recognize the back of the Count's head, but not close enough to get his attention.

"Help you?" He grunted exactly like I imagined guys like him in the movies sounded.

"I just need to get my f-f-f-friend," I said, waving frantically to the back of de Prorok's head.

"Don't think so." I couldn't fight this guy, I didn't have enough money to bribe him, and I suspected my limited charm wasn't going to get the job done, but I did have a stroke of luck. The blonde saw me and the bouncer, and quickly called the rest of the group's attention to what promised to be an entertaining, if only a one-round, fight.

"Brown, good to see you," honked a welcome voice.

"You know this guy?" the gorilla grunted.

"Indeed," he slurred, wrapping an arm around my shoulder. "My assoshiate. Join us Brown…"

"We have to go." I grabbed at his arm.

"In a moment. Allow me to introdushe you…"

"No." He looked at me, furious, but I finally had his attention. "Who's B-b-bill Kenny?"

"What did you say?"

"Kenny. Bill Kenny. Havlicek says he wants to talk to you."

His face blanched. "Now? Oh my God. Is it Alice? The girls?"

"Who is he?" I shouted.

"He's my father-in-law… did he say what he wanted? Oh, blast, where is…" He turned and scrambled to gather up his coat, briefcase and scarf. "There, okay, let's go…" He gave a half-hearted wave to the group at the table. I reached over, grabbed the helmet from the girl's head, and muttered an apology as I put the hat under one arm, my employer under the other, and dragged him towards the door.

As we hit the cold air on Wabash, he combed his fingers through his hair over and over again. "Okay, let's go find him. Oh, God, shomething's happened to Alice… or the babies…"

"He says he wants to talk in the morning, first thing."

"In the morning, he doesn't want to talk to me right away?" I shook my head, then took his arm and maneuvered him in the direction of the hotel. The walk certainly wouldn't do him any harm. I quickly checked his bag to make sure he had the Venus and the makeup jar. The snowy streets were nearly deserted, so nobody would see me trudging up Huron street holding a bag, a pith helmet, and the arm of a slightly inebriated European aristocrat. I almost wished someone would, just so I could confirm this was really happening.

"In the morning…" he muttered, "so it's not about Alice… at least nothing serious. Even he wouldn't make me wait on that." He stopped suddenly. "What's this got to do with Havil…whoever?"

"Havlicek. I don't know. Says Kenny is his boss."

The look on the Count's face was the same I used to have in math class—an unhealthy mix of confusion and panic. I took a few more steps homeward in hopes of luring him back to the hotel. He followed meekly, muttering to himself. "What the bloody hell is he doing here?" and, "sanctimonious bastard," were about all I could decipher.

Walking drunks home wasn't a new experience for me, although I'd never had to deal with one as tall as I was. We managed to get back to the Allerton, up the elevator, and down the hall without bouncing off the walls and doors. Once inside, he shrugged me off and staggered to the bathroom to splash cold water on his face. After a moment, he caught me watching in the mirror, and slammed the door.

Not knowing what else to do, I did what I always did in the presence of bellicose drunks. I stripped down, got into bed, turned off the light and pulled the blanket up to my nose. Then I turned my face to the wall, ignoring the voice in the bathroom and pretended to be asleep. After an eternity, the door opened, the light clicked off and I heard the Count get into bed.

Chapter 15

Chicago, Illinois
February 24, 1926

We both pretended to sleep most of the night. I must have dozed off towards dawn, though, because when the phone rang I nearly jumped out of my skin. The Count moaned, and I leapt up to answer it.

"Morning, kid. How is he?" Havlicek sounded awfully chipper this morning. The son of a bitch was enjoying this.

"Fine," I said looking at the moaning, rumpled form on the bed.

"Swell. We'll be at your door in thirty minutes. Get him up and human."

De Prorok sat up and rubbed his eyes. I nodded to him and said, "Half an hour. Right." Then I hung up as quickly as I could.

"Half hour. I heard." He looked around, as though searching for clues to his next move. "Call downstairs for a pot of coffee, and lots of sugar." As he swung his feet to the floor, he added, "Thank you."

I just nodded and pulled a clean shirt and underwear from my suitcase. "You probably want me gone for a while, so I'll just grab breakfast downstairs, or…"

"No, please. Stay. I… stay. But first, coffee."

I rang down to room service, which wasn't nearly as glamorous as I thought it would be, told them to hurry, then took my clothes into the bathroom. I didn't need a shower nearly as bad as he did, so I splashed cold water on my face, ran a washcloth under my arms, then gestured to the room. "All yours." He was already brushing past me with his clothes in hand.

Fifteen minutes later, came the rattle of a cart and a brisk rap on the door. "Room service." I opened the door and let the guy in. He couldn't have been much older than me, but was all shiny brass and dazzling teeth.

"Anything else you need, name's Andrew."

"Thank you, Andrew, that will be all," bellowed a voice from the bathroom. "Brown, take care of Andrew here and pour me a cup. Three sugars."

I'd be damned if I was paying for this tip, too, so I grabbed a quarter off the bedside table and gave it to him while ushering him to the door. "Great, thanks… like I said, name's… And…" The door closed on him with a click.

The man standing in front of me was not the same wreck who'd stumbled into the bath a few minutes earlier. The bleary eyes were now sharply focused and his clothes were perfect. He took a long sip of his steaming coffee, and let out a satisfied, "ahh." I don't know how he did it. I hadn't had a drop last night, and felt like five pounds of horse crap.

He calmly took another gulp, then took the long stem of his pipe, tamped tobacco in it, and turned towards the window where he struck a match and took two long, slow, sucking puffs. He tuned everything out, just inhaled through his nose and exhaled clouds of cherry flavored smoke while staring out at Huron street. I may as well've not been there, and wished I wasn't.

Bang. A single sharp rap on the door rattled the walls. De Prorok took a step back and two to the left, finding a blank patch of wall to lean against. He crossed his arms in a false but convincingly casual pose. Then he pasted on a smile and nodded at me to open the door.

When I pulled the door open, I was face to hat with Joe Havlicek. Behind him stood a solid, balding man in a very expensive glen check suit. They both pushed past me into the room, the detective's look dared me to try something, and the other man never spared a glance at "the Help", striding to the center of the room. His blue eyes were locked on the Count.

Bill Kenny was one of those guys who carried himself like a self-made man and wouldn't let you forget it for a single minute. His forehead was high but he still had plenty of hair carefully slicked back with something that smelled of vanilla and Vitalis. He wore his suits in such a way you'd swear the price tag was attached to the sleeve so you'd know it was new and expensive.

"Bill, what a pleasant surprise," de Prorok stepped forward, his hand extended in greeting. It wasn't accepted.

"Byron." Just one word, flat and expressionless. His voice was deep and sounded like money and class.

"I didn't know you were in Chicago. I missed you in New York, but I'm delighted you're here. Coffee?"

"We need to have a chat, you and I." There was nothing explicitly threatening in the words, just a cold, hard fact stated in the coldest, hardest way. I had heard that a lot from teachers, parents—all kinds of adults—but never heard it said with such calm, core-shaking, absolute authority.

De Prorok gestured to one of the brocade chairs and pulled the other up to the table and lowered himself into it, casually crossing his legs and sitting back. "By all means. Ahh, but where are my manners?

William Brown, my father-in-law, William Kenny. Bill, this is my assistant, Willy."

I stuck my hand out, and he gave it a brief pump. "Pleasure," he said gruffly, "but if you don't mind, this is a family matter."

"No, Brown, stay." He nodded at Havlicek. "If this one stays, so does he."

Kenny sighed. "As you like, Byron. I'm trying to save you embarrassment."

"A bit late for that, isn't it?"

Kenny shrugged. "Fine." He waved his hand at the operative, who produced a manila folder from under his coat. Kenny snatched it from him without sparing the Pinkerton a look. "You've met Joe Havlicek, I presume?" It wasn't really a question.

Unsure what to do with himself, Havlicek looked around, then plunked himself on the end of my cot, casting sideways glances at me. I leaned against the wall, crossing my arms and forced myself to stay focused on him. His occasional sideways glances my way were oddly satisfying. I liked making him nervous.

"I've had him following you since you got back to New York in December."

Byron nodded. "Does Alice know?"

"As a matter of fact, she does." I saw the Count wince like someone stepped on his foot, but he remained stoic. "In fact, I've suggested she stay in Paris until we had this chance to talk."

"She never mentioned any of this to me."

"I don't imagine she would. I'm her father."

"And I'm her husband, which you'd think would count for something." Byron poured himself another cup of coffee. His hands shook so badly he nearly spilled it, so he placed it into the saucer and left it there. He leaned back to lock eyes with the older man. "What's this about, Bill? I'm not cheating on Alice."

"I know that. I'm a bit surprised to tell you the truth. This'd be easier if you were."

"What would?"

Kenny leaned forward, his hands gripping the arms of the chair. "I'm letting you know the gravy train stops here. This is about you being a screw up, and a fake. I'm tired of it, and I'm damned if I'll let my daughter and grandchildren suffer any more than necessary because of your… your lack of character, let's call it."

It was the first time I'd ever seen de Prorok speechless. Confused, his eyes darted from the folder on the table to Havlicek, but the detective sat stone-faced. He looked back to his father-in-law again. "I don't understand."

"Which part don't you understand, screw up or fake?" The icy tone was gone. Real anger oozed out of every pore. My boss sat back, rendered mute. Kenny was just getting warmed up. "Do you have any idea how much money you've cost me in the last three months?" De Prorok shook his head. "Of course you don't. Ten thousand and counting. What do you think of that?"

"Bill, it can't possibly…"

A well-manicured hand slapped the tabletop. "Don't tell me what's possible, God dammit. Thousands, just to pay your debts in Algeria. I should have let you rot there. Then there's the lawyers in Paris, and my people are still dealing with the American Embassy, the Algerian authorities, the French…"

"The Algerians are dropping the charges. There was nothing to…"

Kenny's eyes popped at the interruption. His voice was becoming more strident, and the façade of class began to fade away. He was a New Yorker, first and foremost, and you could only cover that up for so long. "They're droppin' the charges because I have the best lawyers in Europe, not because they believe a woid… word, whatever, of your bullshit story."

"It's not…" He was interrupted by a raised hand. He obeyed, exactly as Kenny expected.

"Let's start at the beginning. Who are you?" He flipped through the papers in the file, not finding what he was looking for. "Joe, where's the damned birth certificate… Oh hell, here it is. Never mind."

Havlicek started to rise, then sat back down again. He said nothing, just held his hat in his hand, twisting it over and over like a steering wheel. Bill Kenny looked from the paper to de Prorok.

"Born Francis Byron Khun, in Mexico. American citizen. Date of birth, October 1896, exact day unknown."

"I told you that years ago. And it was the seventeenth, for the record."

The additional information didn't slow Kenny down. "At the age of eight, your mother and father separate. She takes you to Europe, but leaves your brother and sisters with your father. Only you, not the other kids. Any idea why?"

"I was eight. I didn't get a vote. And I didn't ask. I always assumed I was her favorite."

"Huh. Well, I wondered, what kind of mother leaves her kids behind… Joe, what did you find out?"

The Pinkerton stood at parade rest—feet apart, hands clasped behind his back. For the first time he looked like the cop he once was when he was still a respectable citizen.

"It's all a bit muddy, sir. We had a heck of a time finding out anything, then sorting rumors from fact… a lot of rumors. For a while, there was a story he was a Hungarian Jew, but that went nowhere."

238

De Prorok snorted. "How disappointing, Havlicek. You'd love that, I'm sure. But no, I'm not a Jew. You could have just asked, Bill. Or would you like to inspect my cock personally? I'm sure Alice would tell you. She apparently keeps nothing from her precious Daddy."

I thought I'd successfully stifled the laugh, but all eyes turned my way for a moment. I offered a quick, "Sorry."

Byron had regained some of his calm. "So if I'm not a Jew, what am I?"

Kenny leaned back comfortably and asked, "Who's Oscar Straus?"

"I'm sorry, who?"

Havlicek was happy to volunteer. He rocked back and forth on his heels. "Oscar Straus. Austrian. A pianist and composer, one of those long-hair types. When the subject's mother arrived in Europe after the divorce, she spent a lot of time in his company with the boy." He paused for dramatic effect. "The best information we have is he could be the subject's real father. Khun found out and kicked them both out."

De Prorok glared at him. "Bastard."

"You or me?" the detective smiled back, obviously pleased at his little joke. He went on reciting his findings like a fifth grader afraid he'd forget his oral report, "Educated in England, eventually moved to Switzerland where they lived with the maternal grandmother. Formally adopted by her brother and allowed to use the honorary title Count de Prorok. Started using it when he attended university in Geneva."

Bill Kenny stared daggers at his son in law. "You've been getting a lot of mileage out of that phony baloney title ever since, haven'tcha?"

"I told you all along it was honorary. I never lied

about that. And Alice certainly seems to enjoy it."

"Yer not above using it every chance you get, though, are you? That's how you got to be in charge of that trip last fall."

Byron's hands stopped shaking long enough to pick up his coffee cup. "Bill, you of all people know in business you use every advantage you can. I notice you don't use your Lower East Side voice when you talk business with the Governor, do you?"

"Yes, well let's talk business, shall we? How much money do you actually have? Because I have a list of people from here to Timbuktu that say you owe them money."

"A temporary problem, I assure you."

Havlicek chimed in. "You weren't planning to sell any stolen jewelry to help solve that problem, were you?"

The Count glared at him. "That's the second time you've accused me of that. What exactly is it I'm supposed to have stolen? I'd love to know."

"Come on, Byron. Is it so hard to believe? You know everyone thinks you took more from that stupid grave than you claim."

De Prorok leaned forward, placing the cup on the table and spilling coffee on his pants. "I didn't, and it's a bloody insult. Oh blast…"

"Bullshit. You took the bones, the beads, and a bunch of other stuff. They practically had to strip search you before you left Algeria. The Times wrote what a great treasure you found… but you only turned in some useless rocks and trinkets. It's not much of a stretch to think the real goods are somewhere else. The other answer is that you lied about the treasure in front of the whole world. Not exactly a ringing endorsement of your honesty, is it? So how are you going to pay your bills, besides mooching off me that is?"

"You really want to know, Bill?" The Count stood up, slapping at the coffee stain on his pants, and went to the artifact case. He popped it open and dug through it wildly, throwing the contents everywhere til he found the false bottom and removed the metal strongbox. "This is the key to our... mine and my family's... Alice's future."

Havlicek and I both leaned in to take a look, and were equally disappointed when he opened it and all we saw was paper. First there were snapshots; one of his mother, one of Alice, one each of the girls, then one of the entire family, taken when he was home after Algeria. The only other article in the box was an official looking letter. He put it on the table in front of Kenny, carefully avoided any spilled coffee, and deliberately smoothed it out.

"Here, see this? It's a letter from Maurice Reygasse and the Algerian Government. It gives me full administrative rights to the Hoggar and Touggart Territories. All those sites we found? They're mine. If anyone wants to dig there, they have to pay for the rights. To me. Me, Bill."

The triumph on his face lasted only a moment. He could see none of us understood what he was saying. "Look, for the next three years, I effectively own every archaeological site in the North Sahara. Beloit College... Pond is dying to go back. That's two years at least... at seventy-five thousand dollars a year. The Oriental Institute, Michigan State University, the Smithsonian, the National Geographic—and the Royal Geographic..."

"When was the last time you heard from Reygasse?" The ice was back in Kenny's voice. The way he asked the question scared me more than his yelling.

It obviously threw the Count off as well. His voice cracked. "Three weeks or so. I'm expecting a letter any time now."

Kenny shook his head. "Afraid not. You've made such a mess of things, he's rescinded his offer."

"What do you mean… rescinded? He can't…"

"Part of the price of clearing up the hash you made over there was promising the Algerians you'd never darken their door again. They don't want you. The American Embassy refuses to grant any expedition rights or support if you're in any way involved. Those letters are worthless."

De Prorok paced back and forth, running his fingers through his hair. His voice became shriller. "It's not true. In fact, I'm getting Beloit's commitment to two more years when we're there next week. I spoke to Collie just last week from Milwaukee…"

"It won't…"

"It will," the Count shouted. "It bloody will. Those rights are worth at least a hundred and fifty thousand dollars a year for the next two years. At least. I'll pay off all my debts, every penny. To you and everyone else. Then I can set myself and my family up for the future. With that and my speaking fees…"

Kenny harrumphed. "Do you really think you can support Alice and the girls in Paris on two hundred dollar lecture fees?"

"For a start, yes. Lee says we'll be in Carnegie Hall by summer. The book is almost done, and has publishers chomping at the bit for it. And that's just a start. If I can get funded for Abyssinia… I know the National Geographic is interested in my theory on King Solomon's mines."

"Finley and the Geographic are washing their hands of you. They all are. You're a God damned cancer, Byron. No one with any credibility will work

242

with you. You're an incompetent, thieving fraud."

"I am not a fraud," he shouted so loudly the room shook. "My findings are solid. We proved it to that committee. We even won over the French papers…"

"With tests I paid for. And I had to go all the way to Tunis to find an expert that'd swear the body was even female."

The Count was sweating and shaking, his eyes bugging out of his head. "That… that's the most important find in the last five years. And I found it. Me. And there'll be more. I've told Alice this. I've told her. She knows everything."

"Yes, she does. Which is precisely why I want her out of the way."

"What are you going to do, Bill? Have one of your boys moider me?" Byron loved to poke fun at people's accents, but his timing was awful.

"Go ahead and make fun you pompous bastard. They're not coming back until this is settled."

"Settled how?"

Kenny sighed, straightened up and looked directly at de Prorok. "They're staying at Saint Hulbert until we can work out an annulment."

Byron's voice dropped to a cracked whisper. "On what grounds? We have two children, so it's not that. What about them?"

"Misrepresentation and fraud. We've already started the paperwork. Al Smith is very good friends with the Cardinal, and he owes me a favor or two."

"You can't do this."

"You can't stop it," the older man countered.

"I can. I'll have Beloit's contract next week. I'll pay back every penny…"

"You won't get a dime from them. And even if you do, it doesn't mean Alice is going to put up with the shame of it all. The lying, the drinking, the whole shebang. The ride's over." He stood up and closed the folder.

De Prorok took a couple of heavy breaths. He rubbed an arm over his eyes to remove the water welling there. He looked up at the ceiling to gather his thoughts, paused, then spoke. "What if I can get the Beloit contract?"

"You won't." The way he said it, no one had ever been so certain of anything, ever.

"But if I do?"

Kenny thought for a moment and nodded. "Business is business, I'll grant you that. You have to finish this tour…God knows you need the money. I expect to see you in my lawyer's offices the week you get back. No later than the seventeenth. If you have a contract from a reputable organization, we'll talk."

The Count nodded solemnly. I wanted to puke on his behalf.

"Oh, and Joe here is going to stay on the job until you get back to New Yawk, just in case. And if you suddenly remember any souvenirs…" he turned and pinned me to the wall with a piercing stare, like he expected me to drop to my knees and confess, "…either of you, Joe'll be happy to claim them."

Kenny didn't say another word. He just picked up the folder and handed it over to Havlicek, who shoved it inside his coat and gave me a pig-eyed smirk that made my blood boil. I wanted to punch him right in his fat face. I wanted to kill him with my bare hands. I never hated anyone as much as I hated him at that moment.

But not as much, I could tell, as Byron de Prorok hated his father-in-law.

Chapter 16

Near Abalessa, Hoggar Province, Algeria
November 4, 1925

Byron knew this was probably not a good idea, but in the battle between his good sense and his need for action, good sense lost out more times than not. He couldn't wait any longer to find Queen Tin Hinan. The need to dig was like a mouse inside a wall; steadily scritch-scratching away until it was all he could think about. It was time.

As dawn grabbed a bare finger hold on the horizon, he spoke to his chosen crew. Belaid and Louis Chapuis, of course would be invaluable, along with Brad Tyrrell. Byron asked him, "Last chance to back out. You're sure you want to come, Brad?"

The American grinned. "I didn't come all this way to give piggybacks to little kids all day. But won't Alonzo and Reygasse be upset they weren't invited?"

De Prorok nodded gravely. "Probably, but we aren't even sure the site is where we think it is. No sense interrupting their work here until we have something solid. We'll find the tomb, and if it's worthwhile, we'll move the whole crew out there. Besides, we don't have enough supplies for more than one car right now."

They didn't have enough by a long shot. The damned provisioners had left them short of just about everything. Petrol, water, non-beef canned food were all running out. The fact he had to put the arm on the College for more funds meant he couldn't very well exempt Brad Tyrrell from the action, but he was a good man and another set of hands would be welcome. The others could collect the new supplies and join them.

"You're not bringing Hal Denny or Barth?" asked Louis Chapuis.

"No sense. No room, for one thing. We've only one vehicle, but also, we don't know what we'll find. I'd rather have them arrive to a triumph, if you know what I mean, than watch us scramble in five wrong places before we find anything." Plus the whining would make a hard situation even less bearable.

The others nodded in agreement. Good. Only one major decision still to make. "Who do we get to drive us out there?"

Four voices answered in chorus, "Martini." That was easy, and not at all surprising. The little Italian had proven to be the best mechanic, most resourceful driver, and less of a pain in the ass than the more prestigious Renault men. He'd commandeer Lucky Strike and get on the road as soon as possible.

"Alright, then," the Count clapped his hands together. "Let's get a move on, gentlemen. Her Majesty awaits."

In less than an hour, they'd loaded as much gas, food and water into the vehicle as they could scrounge. De Prorok's last act was to write identical notes to Alonzo Pond and Maurice Reygasse, both already out in the field at this early hour. He briefly explained where they'd gone, a return date of a week, even though they only really had supplies for four days, and approximate coordinates to meet them at as soon as the rest of the supplies arrived. Then they were off the eighty mile drive to a vague destination somewhere south in Hoggar Province.

Lucky Strike bounced along as Martini navigated the dry river bed and spewed an endless stream of curses. The targets were, depending on the moment, the heat, the desert, and the Renault car. "More tires, more trouble," he muttered.

Tyrrell pulled out his harmonica, but stopped when his seatmates groaned. "Please, Monsieur, no more Oh Suzanna."

"You don't like Stephen Foster?" the businessman asked, slightly offended.

"He's an acquired... and particularly American taste, Brad. Hold on, we're almost there. Then you can serenade the scorpions all you'd like."

Unlike a lot of Americans, Brad Tyrrell seemed to know when to cater to foreigners and put his harmonica in his breast pocket next to the pipe. "Fine. Philistines. No appreciation for fine art." Chapuis and de Prorok laughed, the others didn't understand English. "What exactly are we looking for, Byron?"

"A mountain, well, a hill actually. Perfectly rounded so it should stand out from the others. But don't stare out the window too long. You can burn your eyes quite badly."

"Really?"

"Mmm-hmm. You see how Chapuis and Belaid rest their eyes every couple of minutes?"

"Hmmph, I just thought they were as bored as I am."

Byron saw Chapuis open his eyes long enough to get his bearings. "Stay to the left fork, here Martini," he ordered. Once a sergeant, always a sergeant, Byron thought. Martini knew how to take orders though, and like all grunts throughout history preferred direct orders to hints, nudges or suggestions. It provided cover if anything went wrong.

As to staying on their present course, well where else would they go? The old dry riverbeds led inexorably south and east. Years ago, floods starting in the Atlas Mountains ripped through the land and eventually petered out in what was now desert. The terrain reflected that history. Heading what was once "upstream" meant running the wrong way against punishing rocks. Like so much else in life, it was easier to go with the flow.

Byron laid back against the seat, helmet over his eyes, daydreaming of Alice, of returning to Paris in triumph, of throwing his success in his father-in-law's face. He didn't pay much attention to the little conversation going on in the car. Most of that was Chapuis talking to himself, anyway.

Like most scouts, he'd just blurt out, "Okay, where's that damned other river?" or, "There should be a well here," or, "Lying bastards said there was a camp." Byron tuned it all out until he heard Louis slap Belaid on the arm.

"Belaid, what do you see there?"

The interpreter wiped sandy grit from his eyes and peered towards the distant horizon. "Hills, not much else. What am I looking at?"

"Do you see something, Louis?" Byron sat upright, willing his eyes to see something of value.

Belaid obviously saw something he didn't. "The close one, it's uhhhh," the caid drew with his hands in the air, indicating a vague roundness.

"Martini, do you see it?"

"D'accord."

"Can't you step on it a bit?" asked de Prorok. Martini just shook his head.

"Steady speed saves gas. We don't have much left, have to make it last, so… No, Monsieur." The car continued at a steady fifteen miles an hour, which satisfied everyone but the Count, who knew better than to complain. It was always best to let professionals do their jobs.

"Speaking of gas. Supplies are on their way to the camp, though, right?" Tyrrell asked.

"Getting nervous, Brad? Supplies should be at Tamanrasset in two days, Maurice and Pond will join us in three. With a little luck, we'll have found our Queen by then." Byron offered that with far more confidence than he felt. Nobody needed to remind him that if there was one thing the expedition lacked so far, it was good, old fashioned luck.

Among his daydreams was the occasional, fleeting vision of being discovered years from now, his desiccated corpse clinging to a sarcophagus. Pyrrhic victories weren't really victories to anyone but historians.

Continuing south, the outline of the hills came into sharper focus. They were too small to be true mountains, but they loomed high over the flat desert floor. Perhaps a mile ahead was a smaller hill, and as Belaid noted, it was rounder than the others.

Martini stopped the vehicle on solid, stony ground about two hundred yards away. For a moment, the only sound was the sizzling of water in the radiator as the car cooled down. Finally, de Prorok was able to croak out a question.

"Chapuis?"

"I think so. Yes sir." Belaid shrugged in silent agreement.

The Count let out a whoop and clambered out of the car. He reached back in and dug around, finding a pair of heavy binoculars. Holding them to his eyes, he scanned the hill slowly; top to bottom, then side to side, then back the other way.

Trying to control the excitement in his voice, he

said to Louis, "It hasn't been touched in a long time. No graffiti, no signs of any activity whatsoever. Why's that do you suppose?"

Chapuis grinned. "Maybe it's taboo?"

"Quite right. And why's that? Who built it, do you suppose?"

The guide squinted. "The locals are Haratin… Negroes, mostly slaves or ex-slaves, probably. They didn't build anything like this. Neither did the Tuaregs, though they might have repurposed an old structure. It's old… ancient Libyan, maybe?"

Byron switched to English for Tyrrell's benefit. "So, Mr. Tyrrell, we have what's an old holy site, with a heavy taboo on it, in the middle of nowhere. Why do you suppose that would be?"

Brad responded to the cocky grin on de Prorok's face. "Well, Professor, could it be the Queen's tomb?"

"Because it's the Queen's bloody tomb, Brad. We found it. Don't you feel the tingle?" Byron was almost giddy.

"What I feel is my old bones aching. There's gotta be twenty tons of rocks there. We can't do it ourselves." Byron didn't blame him for being worried. And the poor fellow was essentially on vacation. They'd need help.

The Count nodded. "We'll need diggers… a dozen, two would be ideal. Louis, there's a Haratti village nearby, you said?"

"Yes, but what will we pay them with?" The question hung in the air like a bad odor, more an accusation than a request for information.

"We have the cash for the supplies…" Byron offered.

Chapuis shook his head. "The most useless thing in this part of the Sahara is actual money. We barely have enough food and water for a couple of days, and we need our tools... They'll want something in trade."

"Yes," de Prorok admitted. "The prudent thing would be to send word back to Tamanrasset, then wait for Reygasse and Pond to arrive. We can always go back." He looked from face to face and saw what he hoped to see, a disappointment at being so close to their goal, and an itch to prove themselves. "Or... we can find some goods to trade, to at least get us started until the others arrive."

They quickly took inventory of what they'd managed to throw into the car before their ill-conceived, hasty exit. Cooking pots, hand mirrors, grooming items of all kinds became expendable. Byron smiled as Brad Tyrrell slipped his harmonica under the back seat of the car, lest it come a casualty of the mad scramble for tradable goods.

The negotiations with the Haratin didn't go as smoothly as he'd hoped, but why would they start now? Nothing else on this cursed trip seemed to go his way. The Chief was reluctant to help. If they could find workers willing to help the crazy white men move tons of rock, which was unlikely, and pay them enough, which seemed doubtful, there was the matter of breaking the taboo on the mountain. The place was holy to their Tuareg overlords, although no one in the village could recall why, or what was buried there, or even if it belonged to the Tuaregs in the first place. Still, why chance it?

The fear of how the Tuaregs would react prevented Byron from just sending word back to Tamanrasset. If word got out they were despoiling the grave of the Mother, no one could confidently say what the response would be. When Byron presented a hypothetical situation to King Akhamouk, the sovereign had been extremely articulate on how they'd react, and it was enough to quash the conversation then and there.

Byron and Belaid wheedled, cajoled and outright prevaricated but finally managed to secure the services of fifteen men, each of whom would provide their own food and water, for six days. This was an ambitious commitment, given they only had three days, maybe four days of anything to eat and drink. Gasoline was out of the question, with luck they had enough to get back to the site that night. Eventually a deal was struck, and the Expedition returned to the Tomb Site, as they optimistically called it, to set up camp.

Work began the next morning. After the trip to the village, the car was running on vapors at best, and they weren't going anywhere until rescue arrived. With no driving to be done, Martini set to work maximizing their meager rations and circumstances. By the Count's reckoning, they had three days worth of supplies, which he deduced could be stretched to five with the miracle working driver in charge. If everything at Tamanrasset was on schedule the others would be here in three days, so Martini counted on five at least. This meant extreme rationing. Water would be a problem, of course, and the little mechanic dug in the dry riverbed until he found a trickle of water, which could serve as an emergency well in a pinch. They might make the insanity last a week. After that, he didn't dare speculate.

Standing two-thirds of the way to the top of the mound, Chapuis, Tyrrell and the Count tried to figure out the best plan of attack. "How many chambers, do you think?" the American asked.

"Eleven or twelve, depending if that one there is one big room or just the dividing wall's collapsed."

"Should we start in the center and work our way out?" Louis wondered.

"No, let's start at the top and work our way down," countered De Prorok.

"Why's that?"

"Why not?" which was reason enough to begin in earnest. The first day, all they accomplished was the moving of rocks, large and small, from the top opening and the most obvious entrances. Every hour or so, something would happen to cause a work stoppage. A large black scorpion scuttling out of a crevice became a sign of the gods' displeasure at their work, and the workers would throw down their picks and levers, threatening never to return until Chapuis or Belaid, and sometimes both, cowed them into getting back to work.

This was nothing new to De Prorok, having come to the conclusion years ago that it took four reluctant locals to do the work of a single motivated white man on a dig. Tyrrell muttered darkly he knew some anti-union boys in Chicago who could set things right in a hurry.

The archaeologist just continued grabbing rocks and moving them until he bent over one and carefully dusted it with his palm, then with a whisk broom he kept strapped to his belt.

"Brad, come here. See this?" The American peered down. The edges of the rock were rounded, but not in the perfectly smooth way of river stones. These had been carefully formed. "This is amazing workmanship, and it's not local. I don't even think it's Tuareg. Looks Roman."

"Did the Romans ever come this far south?"

"Not as far as we know."

"So if it's not Roman, what could it be?" De Prorok started to answer but never got the chance. "And don't tell me Atlantean, because you know it's not. Jesus." Tyrrell had less patience than most for the

Count's obsession with the Lost Continent. Byron chafed at the skepticism. At least Pond would have engaged in the debate.

"Killjoy. Still there's definitely something here, and it's very old, and not Haratin nor Tuareg, so someone or something important was up here a long time ago." What a find if it turned out to be Roman, he thought. He would be as famous as Schliemann, and much richer. The German had been complete bollocks as a speaker and no writer at all.

That night's dinner consisted of beans and thin coffee. Martini jealously guarded the supplies, and saw to sleeping arrangements for everyone. Still, the rumbling of stomachs didn't keep anyone awake, and they were all asleep as soon as the sun went down.

Day two continued in much the same way. Short, intense periods of moving rocks, followed by breaks for every possible pretense from the heat to the warning cries of Djinn, telling them to leave the mountain's spirits in peace.

By day three, the work was slower. Partly this was because they'd found nothing of any value other than worked stone. An unexpected lightning storm, which the locals deemed a harbinger of upcoming death and Djinn vengeance, drove everyone to shelter for a while. More depressingly, the supplies were almost completely gone, and there'd been no sign of relief.

Martini was reduced to digging in the river bed, getting enough of a trickle for a single cup of coffee, brewing it, and then repeating the process so that everyone at least had coffee for breakfast. They were reduced to one bowl of corn meal and beans a day. The laborers were eating marginally better than the white men, which seemed to the locals—who'd never witnessed such a thing—another sign of madness and an exceptional bad omen.

By day four, everyone was hungry, tired and out of sorts. The white men took turns looking out for signs of relief or a caravan, as much out of an excuse to rest than any real hope of rescue. Still, they continued to work, uncovering caves and hollows of worked stone. The work kept their minds occupied and not obsessing on their growing hunger and thirst.

The locals were almost completely useless by then. They spent the day sitting in groups alternately grumbling spitefully and shaking their heads in bewilderment at their crazy employers. Byron had never understood those overseers who beat, starved or physically abused their charges, but he was beginning to come around to their way of thinking. He was about to commence another round of begging for help, when he heard Chapuis' voice.

"Monsieur le Comte? I think you want to see this." Surprised at the unusual formality, Byron turned towards the scout. Pinched between two filthy fingers was a light blue stone. Turquoise. The first rock of any color other than brown they'd seen since their arrival, and might have been the most beautiful thing either of them had ever seen.

"Brad, Belaid, Martini, come here," he croaked from his sand-choked throat. Even a few of the workers now craned their necks to see what had caused the excitement but could make no sense of the tall white man's fuss over one colored rock.

Now digging and sifting wildly, they found a blue glass bead. It was roughly chipped on all sides to round it off. Then a reddish-brown piece of agate, polished and smooth. Each discovery propelled the hungry, exhausted men to another feverish round of digging, sifting, whisking and picking.

Finally just as the sun was about done for the day, their shovels clanked against more stone, but this was no ordinary rock. Three tall slabs of rock, one dovetailed into the next, formed a barrier to what was apparently a chamber.

De Prorok ran his long, thin fingers lovingly over it, probing the seams, looking for carving or any clues as to what lay on the other side. He reached down for a pry bar, but Brad Tyrrell put a fatherly hand on his shoulder. "Byron, let's rest for the night. It's almost too dark to even get down to the camp. We'll open it in the morning."

He was about to object, but a quick look down the steep slope to the campsite and the exhausted faces of his team and he simply gave a heavy sigh and nodded. The men gathered their tools and groped their way down to where Martini had dinner, such as it was, waiting for them.

Exhausted and hungry as they were, sleep was a rare commodity that night. For some it was hunger, and aching bones. For Byron de Prorok, it was the thought of what might lie beyond the rock portal. Exhilarating as the thought was, there was a far more compelling reason to remain alert. The drums started a couple of hours after midnight.

For the first time since their arrival, they could hear *toboles*, large drums for communicating over long distance, from the village at Abalessa. Their steady throm-throm-throm echoed off the mountain behind them.

Brad Tyrrell finally asked the question they'd all been asking themselves. "What's that all in aid of?"

"Nothing good, I'm afraid," said de Prorok.

Belaid, never one to soft-sell the truth said simply, "They're letting everyone know we're here, and we're vulnerable."

The American squirmed. "We've been here four days. Why now?"

Chapuis chimed in. "They wanted to see what we were up to. Now they're hedging their bets. They know we have no more food, and we can't drive away, so they can kill us pretty much any time they want."

The American wrinkled his sunburnt forehead. "Why would they do that? We're not hurting them."

"Partly because they can, and partly to score points with the Tuaregs. When we weren't finding anything, it did no harm to dig here, and if we found what we were looking for, we'd protect them. Now that we've actually found something, they're worried Akhamouk and his people will be angry with them. So they gain face by killing us, or better yet, telling the Tuaregs we're here. Then it's out of their hands." Belaid laid out the scenario without visible emotion. Byron couldn't tell if it was stoicism or resignation.

Martini's soldier instincts buzzed like hornets. He was never big on "I told you so," but he sorely regretted leaving the machine gun back at Tamanrasset. He shot de Prorok a silent accusatory look, but said nothing. Like all good soldiers, he blamed the commanding officer, and reserved the right to complain bitterly when the time was right. For now he just sat silently.

The crackling of the fire nearly concealed the sound of a kicked stone from behind them. Chapuis leapt up and ran to the car. He pulled out his rifle, shouldered it and fired into the darkness over de Prorok's head, seemingly in one motion. Panicked whispers filled the air and the patpatpat of sandals retreating on the sand once again were replaced by the ordinary stillness of the desert night.

The rest of the night was spent in fitful sleep and continuously changing sentry duty.

At the first hint of dawn, Martini dug for coffee water. As he crouched in the arid river bed his eyes swung back and forth, searching for signs of trouble, but everything was quiet. Even the flies seemed to hold their breath. By the time the rest of the team rose, there was enough hot coffee-colored liquid for everyone. That would have to suffice for breakfast.

As daylight bounced off the hills, a handful of the Haratin workers arrived for duty as if nothing were wrong. Today's work was too important to risk a full-blown confrontation, so Chapuis simply barked orders as usual, demanding they grab pieces of lumber, pry bars, and the tire jack from Lucky Strike and climb to the great stone doors.

"Are you a praying man, Brad?"

"When the mood strikes."

"How's it striking you at the moment?" Byron gave a crooked grin and nodded to Chapuis and the workers. With a barked command, crowbars, jack handles and boards were pried into every seam and groans of effort filled the morning air and bounced off the rocky surface of the mound.

The first push gained nothing, but the second effort was rewarded with a loud crack and the left-most stone popped out of place. Belaid and Martini quickly jammed stones and lumber in the opening to prevent it closing and reloaded for another stab at it. This time the slab fell forty-five degrees to the left, leaving a black, yawning gap in the rock.

Everyone froze in space, the silence broken only by the buzzing of the ever-present black flies. For several seconds, nothing moved and then a large brown-black python slithered harmlessly from within. Seeing the serpent, the remaining workers shouted in terror, threw down their tools, and ran away. Translating as he ran after them, Belaid explained they thought the guardian of the tomb had come to kill them for their impertinence.

No amount of hollow threats or equally worthless offers of payment could entice them back. The members of the expedition were finally, truly, on their own.

De Prorok paid no attention to the scurrying workers. His sole focus now was getting inside the cavern. After ensuring that the snake—a harmless but nearly five foot long python by the looks of him—had fled the scene, he took a single deep breath and ducked inside.

His eyes adjusted quickly as he scanned the room and his initial excitement quickly ebbed. The chamber, and it was obviously crafted for some purpose, was so full of sand, he could barely move. The loose, dusty grit had blown in over the years, further burying whatever lay here.

Tyrrell stuck his head through the door. "You okay, Byron?" The only response was a nod as the Count continued to look around. He knelt and ran his fingers through the sand, letting it sift through his hand. Something remained behind, and he examined it.

"What is it?" the American asked breathlessly.

"A date seed," he responded, with more excitement than Tyrrell thought a mere piece of fruit should create. "Louis, we have date seeds, lots of them. Brad, get me a sieve, please."

Handing it to him, he pled ignorance. "What's the big deal about some date seeds?"

"Because," Byron began as he scooped up a sifter full of sand and slowly shook it back and forth, "In tombs like this, it was common to provide plenty of food for the journey to the afterlife. Since this was sealed, we can assume it wasn't someone's house, right? No one lived here."

Tyrrell nodded. "Then it makes sense this was a

tomb." He let out a triumphant whoop as he picked two items out of the screen. One was another date seed, picked clean by ants and polished smooth by shifting sand. The other was a small, round piece of turquoise.

That small blue-green stone momentarily extinguished any exhaustion or hunger. For the next several hours, the men formed a demented bucket brigade; passing handfuls of sand to each other until they were outside the cavern. Then they were carefully sifted, and small treasures put carefully aside. More date seeds, turquoise, and the occasional roughly rounded agate comprised the rapidly growing stash.

Each took a shift inside the cavern, scooping handfuls of dust and grit, and sifting. Periodically one of them would take a break for a tiny sip of dirty water, or to climb up a few dozen feet and look fruitlessly for any sign of rescue.

Eventually, the antechamber was cleared, only to reveal a smaller chamber directly underneath. This one too, was under a layer of sand, but one much thinner, and the rewards were more frequent. Beads, semi-precious stones, animal skins and the remains of baskets full of dates saw daylight for the first time in hundreds, maybe thousands of years.

Louis Chapuis was taking his shift in the chamber when he froze, bent over. His shoulders began to bob up and down and De Prorok could hear a soft but very clear sob. "Louis?"

"Gold, it's gold, sir." He held up a necklace, crude filaments of gold wire keeping small fish-scale sized pieces of gold in place. "Thirty years in the desert, I've never found gold before. I didn't think I ever would."

"For God's sake, let us see," Tyrrell shouted from outside. The Count and the scout emerged, blinking into the late afternoon sun. Gently, the necklace passed from hand to shaking hand. It was badly tarnished, and had very little precious metal in it, but there was no mistaking what it was.

"It looks like some of the work we found in Utica, Brad. Carthaginian style. It probably came from the north at some point." De Prorok lay back against a flat-faced rock. The strength rushed out of him and he was temporarily unable to stand. He just reclined there, his long legs stretched out in front of him.

De Prorok thought he could die happy at this moment, then feared he might, as two large shadows fell over the team. They shadows belonged to two of the biggest Tuareg warriors he'd ever seen.

How they had arrived unseen was no mystery, but their intentions were. They stood there and said nothing. The exhausted, thirsty men looked back in awe. Both warriors were over six and a half feet, wrapped head to foot in blue. Their faces were veiled, revealing only their dark, kohled eyes. They carried ancient carbines strapped across their shoulders and daggers on their forearms. They both carried a lance with a vicious iron tip.

The Count weakly raised a hand in greeting. "Hello my friends, what brings you here on such a hot day?" then allowed himself a small exhausted giggle.

The two tribesmen, looked at each other, then back at the tomb and the exhausted expedition members. One looked like he wanted to say something, but no words were spoken. Both men turned and calmly walked down the hill, climbed aboard their kneeling camels and headed at a slow trot towards the northeast.

"That's not good," Chapuis muttered as he continued to wave farewell.

"What's not? They're leaving aren't they?" De Prorok didn't much like his tone. *What does he know that I don't?*

"Abalessa is the other way. They're heading to Tamanrasset. If they get to Akhamouk before help gets here, it's all over."

Belaid picked up a smooth stone and put it in his mouth to generate a little saliva and ease his thirst. "There'd better be gold in there, otherwise this is an asinine way to die."

Chapter 17

Rockford, Illinois
February 24, 1926

The good thing about the afternoon lecture in Rockford was it left us little time to dwell on the morning's disastrous meeting with Kenny. We packed up, got picked up by a Rotarian from Rockford in a LaSalle, drove mostly in silence, checked into the Chick House—which was actually nicer than it sounds, slightly—and went on to the Rotary do.

I was shell shocked. It didn't help that Havlicek was there waiting for us, making no effort to be inconspicuous. In fact, he seemed to take great pleasure in waggling his fingers at me in greeting, although he never approached us or directly interfered. He may as well have. I was all thumbs, missing a couple of cues like some kind of amateur. Not badly enough for the audience to notice, but plain enough that I earned the daggers the Count shot me from the stage.

De Prorok, on the other hand, never missed a beat. It always seemed that the worse things were, the closer to perfect he was onstage, never fumbling a word or stepping on his own jokes. He was bulletproof. He was completely, flawlessly, dashingly, infuriatingly brilliant. Until he came off stage that is.

He rushed towards me and I braced myself for the tongue lashing I knew I deserved. "Willy," he said, which was strange because he always called me Brown, "do me a favor and get all this stuff back to the hotel please. I need to find a Western Union office." He spun on his heel so fast that a pocket-sized notebook fell to the floor, but he just kept walking.

A little mystified, I picked it up and put it with the projection gear. Then I saw his pith helmet lying on a stool, and scooped that up as well. The Venus sat on a table next to a half-drunk glass of water. He'd left a trail of relics, props and debris from the projector to the backstage door. I shook my head and gathered them up.

I looked at the Venus in my hands, taking a really long look at it for the first time. It was just a rounded, rough piece of rock with four scratches where the girl parts should be, but he sure acted like it was important. Until he had better things to think about, then it was left lying where anyone could pick it up. The only other Venus I remembered was in a painting, and she looked pretty hot to trot on that clamshell. This one was built more like Mrs. Kaczmierek, the old Polish woman across the street from us. Of course, the thought of seeing these specific parts of Magda Kaczmierek was mildly horrifying. The statue was short and squat, like her, but at least the old bat had a face, such as it was.

Why was he so careless with things that mattered so much? And there was no reason to carry it around everywhere. It would be easy enough to copy, especially if people didn't really know what they were looking at. It was the same with the sword. He could just as easily use a dummy, and keep the original safe. I made a note to get some supplies from the hardware store.

Back at the hotel, I carefully stacked all the equipment for a quick escape tomorrow. There was a quick "shave and a haircut" knock on the door. I was afraid it was Havlicek, and considered not answering, but a young voice came through the door. "Cable for de Prook."

I opened the door to see the desk clerk. Unlike in the nicer hotels, he wasn't wearing a uniform or a nametag, just a ratty sweater vest like mine, although without all the little wool pills all over it, and a tie. "Are you de Prook?"

"Prorok... no, I'm his..." Jesus what was I? I could never get my tongue around "projection technician", "frie...assistant. I'm his assistant. What can I do for you?"

"Yes sir. Just got this cable for Mr. De Proo..rok. From Paris. France," he added, just in case I might confuse it with some other Paris. It took the yellow envelope from him, then realized I was on the hook for a tip and made a mental note to start dunning the Count for all the money I've spent. Like the man said, a deal was a deal, and this expense wasn't part of our arrangement. I pulled out a quarter and saw Pete's eyes crinkle up in a smile. Pocket change went a lot further in Rockford than in Chicago.

"Thanks, what's your name?"

"Pete, sir." The 'Sir' didn't even faze me anymore.

"Do you know where there's a hardware store nearby?"

"Sure do. Anything you need, I can..."

"Nah, I'll get it. Then I reached into my pocket for another quarter. "You wouldn't happen to know where a fella could find a drink, maybe after hours?"

He looked around suspiciously, then leaned in. "You looking for a good time? I know a girl..."

"Nah, just sometimes I like to go out at night... if I get bored or something." He exchanged my fifty cents for some fairly useless directions to both a hardware store and a respectable speak, but Rockford wasn't that big a town, the kind of place where "a piece" is considered an accurate measure of distance. If I had to track the Count down later, it wouldn't be tough.

As it turned out, I didn't have to chase the Count that night, because no sooner had Pete left, when he burst through the door and threw his walking stick and coat onto the floor.

"Lost my damned notebook…" The panic in his voice was palpable. I nodded to the cheaply stained pine bedside table. "Thank God, Brown. You're a peach, an absolute life saver. I need to get a cable to Paris and couldn't find the… oh never mind. We have it now, eh?"

"Are you okay?" I asked.

"Never better, why?" It was a whopper, but he nearly pulled it off.

"A telegram came for you… from Paris." The words were hardly out of my mouth when he ripped the envelope from my hand.

"Is it from Alice?" He tore it open and read it, his shoulders slumping a bit. He read it a second time, smiling. Whatever it was, wasn't horrible at least. "Not bad news, though. Not in the least. Do you know what this is?"

I hated when he asked me that. In three weeks of working with him, I'd never once guessed right. This time, he didn't really expect an answer because he just kept talking. "This is from a friend of mine at *L'Academie des Arts et Sciences* in Paris. Brad Tyrrell and I are being awarded the *Palme d'Or* this year."

"Congratulations." I had a vague idea who Tyrrell was, he'd been on the Sahara expedition, and no idea whatsoever what the Academy-days-whatever was, but an award was usually a good thing. After the day he'd had, he deserved to get tossed a bone of some kind.

"Congratulations indeed. Y'see, this is actually a very high honor, in some circles at least. Extraordinary achievement in the sciences, and all that. Yes, it'll help a great deal." He could tell I didn't have the foggiest clue what it all meant and he was getting impatient. "Don't you see? If Tyrrell, and by extension Beloit and the Logan, are winning international prizes, they won't want to cut ties with me. It'd be a scandal. They'll sign the contracts just to maintain face. I'll get the contract... and that bastard," and I knew exactly which bastard he meant, "can go piss up a rope. Anyway, it's good news, Brown."

He looked around the room and saw the Venus on the table. "Thank goodness you found her. I was afraid I'd left her behind."

"You almost did."

He picked it up and stroked it affectionately. "Lovely isn't she?"

I shrugged. "I s'pose. Why do you t-t-travel with the real thing?"

"What do you mean?"

"Well, it's v-v-v-valuable. You should be more careful with it. You kind of leave stuff behind, especially when you're... you know."

"I can't just leave her behind. She's all I've got from that trip."

"What do you mean, all?"

He sat on the end of the bed, running his long fingers over the smooth grey stone. "I mean it's literally the only thing I have. Most of what we found was confiscated before I left, or stayed in Africa with Reygasse or in Paris at the Institute. I barely escaped with the clothes on my back and all the film and snaps. They're the only things of real value I have left."

"But you said it was the greatest treasure since

Tutan—that Tut guy."

He barked out a laugh. "It is, but it's been a bad few years for archaeology. The good news is, no one's really found anything worth a damn since Howard Carter, so technically speaking it *is* the best of a pretty shabby lot. Plus the New York bloody Times said so, so it must be true." He shook his head like it was the funniest thing he'd ever heard. I didn't get it, though, because I always thought if the Times said it, it had to be true.

"It's a souvenir, I guess. Certainly it's useful, I mean people love to touch things that are old or from exotic places. And it's stone. Even I can't break it."

I thought of all the pictures he took with him that he never showed, or how he traveled with that stupid piece of wood from Shackleton's sled. He traveled so much, but he never went anywhere without it. It reminded him of his past. What had I brought with me? Two changes of clothes and that bag of odds and ends. Sure as hell nothing that reeked of Milwaukee or home. Why would I?

"Honest Injun, there's no jewels, or treasure?"

His eyes hardened. "Et tu, Brute? We've discussed this. Do you think me a thief?"

My eyes dropped to the floor. "N-n-no sir."

"Right then. Ask me again and you'll get the sack. Understood?"

"There's something else," I said. "You owe me fifty cents for t-t-tips." I explained why, and he ponied up good-naturedly.

"Good on you, Brown. Never let the little debts pile up. Although, over-tipping is a bad habit. Looks gauche." He gave me a silver dollar and told me not to worry about the change. Then he pulled his pipe from his breast pocket, stuffed it with some cherry wood tobacco, struck a match with his thumb and lit it. "Oh, and stay sharp. No more slipups like today, eh? Everything hinges on our being perfect, especially at Beloit."

He didn't wait for a response, just gathered up his notebook. "I have to find the Western Union office…" and he was out the door.

The next few days were a blur; packing, unpacking, identical lectures then repacking. Madison, La Crosse, Eau Claire. I saw very little of my boss. Sometimes he was gone at dawn and didn't come stumbling in until late. Sometimes it was because he'd kick me out of our room when he was on the phone.

I never really knew what was going on. All I got were glimpses of notes scribbled on telephone pads and snatches of telephone conversations.

"Reygasse, Maurice Reygasse, see voo play…"

"St Hulbert, Paris, France… yes France. The country… Oh for…"

"Please, Operator. Try again… I know she must be…"

The lectures were perfect. The other twenty-two hours in the day were starting to wear on both of us.

One morning in Eau Claire, Wisconsin, as he poured his third sugar into his coffee, I handed him a brown paper bag. "It's n-n-not very g-g-good."

"What's this?" He opened it up and pulled out a grey plaster copy of his Venus. "Did you do this? It's wonderful."

It wasn't. He was just being kind, it was slightly lopsided for one thing. "It needs another c-c-c-oat, but I thought we could keep the original safe and use this one onstage. I made two copies."

"Good thinking. Yes, fine, fine." He fixed his eyes on me until I squirmed. "It's really quite good you know."

"Really?" I hated the way I warmed whenever he gave me a compliment. Like a girl brown-nosing a teacher. Hated it but kind of liked it, too.

"Mm-hmm. In fact, I know some reputable artifact sellers in Carthage who could take lessons. You've got a career in art forgery if you want it. What else are you working on?"

"Nothing really. Well, maybe a couple of things, but they're not ready to show you yet."

He accepted that, and took a couple of more slurps of his coffee. "You know, it's much warmer here than in St. Louis. Do you have a lighter jacket?"

"Not really."

"You're really going to have to do something about your wardrobe. I'm getting quite tired of that grey vest. I'm sure the moths are, too. You really should think about it, now that you're Mr. Moneybags and all." He smiled and slipped me an envelope. It was payday. A week since I left Milwaukee.

"Clothes maketh the man, Brown. You should think about that."

I must have made some incoherent grunt, promising to think about it. Really, all I could think about is that "we" were going to St. Louis.

South, where it was warmer than Wisconsin.

Away.

Wednesday the 3rd dawned sunny and bright in Beloit, despite being colder than a well-digger's ass. The view from the Grand Hotel wasn't much, but the recent snow was still a pure white, blown into a hard crust that sparkled in the cold sunshine and blinded you if you stared too long.

I was worried the Count would wind up with a dog and cane, the way he kept staring out the window for long periods of time, saying nothing. He was as nervous as I'd ever seen him, puffing pipe smoke like a coal train. His mouth ran non-stop. Without a reason, he'd just start yakking and couldn't seem to stop himself. He'd apologize for "going on so," then just keep going.

It didn't get any better after lunch. We went out, and he picked up the Beloit and Janesville papers, expecting to read about the upcoming lecture. Nothing. Not a word. Well, there was a small notice in the "Upcoming Events" but hardly enough to draw a crowd.

It was the same around campus. On one of my exploratory walks that afternoon, Beloit not being big enough for street cars, I didn't see any signs or posters advertising the lecture. The campus rag, the Round Table, did have a small article, but certainly didn't make a big fuss. If this was so darned important, why were they treating the Count's visit like it was some state secret?

The longer the day dragged on, the more nervous he became. Usually, the closer we got to show time, the calmer and more confident he grew. I swear he actually got taller and better looking in the hour before he took the stage. Today, though, he was a sweaty shaky cartoon of himself.

"Remember, this is important. You'll be meeting all kinds of important people. Do try to make nice. And for God's sake, talk to them. Don't just grunt like some kind of gorilla." What was I supposed to say to that? I stuck out my lips, scratched my arm and made oooh-oooh-oooh noises until I got a laugh out of him. It struck me it was the first time I'd heard him really laugh in three days.

We arrived at the chapel in the center of the campus two hours before the start time, as we usually did. No one really paid much attention, in fact I had to find a janitor in another building to unlock the back door so we could get our gear inside.

Once inside, de Prorok looked around. "Not exactly the Great Hall, is it?" The chapel was lovely, but small. "Rather thought they'd be making a bigger to-do."

"Byron, about time. Good to see you." A tall, good looking guy with a high forehead, a moustache and glasses walked up the aisle of the chapel, his hand extended in greeting.

"Brad, by the Dickens, great to see you." The two men shook hands and the Count quickly called me over. I recognized this guy from the pictures of the Expedition. It seemed strange seeing someone in the flesh you only knew from pictures. I guess it would be like meeting Lon Chaney in person.

"Brad Tyrrell, this is my traveling companion and projection technician, William Brown. Brown, Brad Tyrrell, one of the stalwarts of the Sahara Expedition." We shook hands briefly. He was tall, nearly as tall as I was and built half way between the de Prorok and I—not as whippet thin as my boss, but less of a lunk than me. He had that calm, rich guy assurance about him and a smooth, baritone voice.

"Nice to meet you, young man."

"A... pleasure... sir." I may have sounded slow, but at least the words came out right. So far so good.

"Byron treating you okay?"

"Yes sir." Short and sweet, that was the watchword for tonight. I was consciously avoiding "m"s and "p"s.

"And what does a projection technician actually do? Wait, don't tell me... your job is to keep Byron away from his own equipment so he doesn't show upside down pictures, am I right?"

"That's a...bout it, yessir."

"Fine, fine. Glad he's got someone to keep him out of trouble. Well, don't let me keep you. I'm sure you have plenty to keep you occupied." He smiled, then turned away from me in that way businessmen have of dismissing you even while you're still in the room.

As I puttered, I heard them talking, so I puttered even more quietly.

"Brad, have you received your notification about the Palme d'Or yet?"

"The what? Oh, yes, thank you. It was very kind of them. I'm very grateful. Listen, I need to talk to you about a couple of things before tomorrow's meeting."

The Count was obviously only half listening. "Doesn't this seem like an awfully small venue? I mean, the College, especially the Logan, was such a big part of the expedition, you'd think they be making more of an effort to fill the hall, don't you think?"

Tyrrell's voice flattened out, and I had to strain to hear him. "Yeah, about that. Look, Byron. You have to know the college isn't too happy with you right now."

"Why ever not?" I wanted to know the answer to that one, too, and caught my finger in the slide mechanism of the projector. I sucked the pain out of the digit, and strained to hear. It was getting easier, because that foghorn of a voice ratcheted up the volume.

"We have brought the world's attention to this piss ant school..." Even he realized he was shouting, and in an empty, echoing chapel to boot, because he dropped his voice dramatically as he went on. "This piss ant backwater cow college. Do you think the New York Times would even know Beloit, Wisconsin, existed if not for me?"

Tyrrell's voice was getting flatter and smoother. "I know that, but you have to admit things have gone a bit sideways in the last few months."

"Oh, what things?"

"The school had to bail out a ton of money, for starters…"

"Which they'll get back when they sign the digging rights. My God, they'll save fifteen thousand dollars the first year alone."

"Yes. If they sign." We both froze hearing that.

"Why wouldn't they? Pond is having the time of his life over there, playing in his sandbox and counting arrowheads and creating his precious little catalogues. Why would they risk all that?"

"They'll explain it all at the meeting tomorrow morning. Please, Byron. As your friend, I'm asking you to step carefully. They'll want to know you have all your bases covered with Reygasse and the Institute. If there's anything you're keeping from them, anything at all… For Chrissake the Algerian government is still calling you a grave robber." The Count was about to protest, but Tyrrell put his hand on his shoulder, momentarily silencing him. "It just doesn't look good, is all."

The older man paused, then asked another question in a quieter, sadder way. "Why did you have to charge them for this speech tonight?"

"What do you mean?" The Count's voice was getting louder again, and jumped up an octave. "It's only two hundred and fifty dollars. And I really didn't have a choice. Lee, you've met him in New York, Keedick, insists on getting his pound of flesh. And I have overhead," he gestured over to me, the Overhead. "Why are they pulling this nickel and dime nonsense now? Was I supposed to do this for free?"

"Actually, yes. They might have seen it as an act of good will. A thank you for all their support and all that. Now it looks like you're just in it for the money."

"I *am* in it for the money. Some of us need the damned money. We're not all millionaires, you know.

274

I have a family to support, God damn it, Brad."

"Alright, take it easy. We'll talk some more and maybe we can figure out a plan of attack when we meet with President Maurer and Collie in the morning."

"Can we talk to them tonight?" Byron asked.

Tyrrell hesitated. "They're not coming tonight. We're meeting in Maurer's office in the Middle College tomorrow."

"Not coming?"

Brad Tyrrell shook his head. "Afraid not. I'm introducing you tonight. Okay, you fellas get set up, and we'll see you right at eight o'clock. He gave de Prorok another pat on the shoulder and walked up the aisle to the main chapel door. He brushed past Havlicek, who'd been eavesdropping from the last row of pews.

I don't know if the Count saw the detective or not. He just looked at me and barked, "I'll be back in a bit, Brown," and stomped out of the chapel through the rear. I couldn't avoid the bastard, though. He strutted up the aisle, hands in his coat pockets, hat pushed back and a big cheesy grin on his mug.

"How's it goin' kid?"

"What do you want?" I asked, without looking up from my work.

"Just sayin' hi. We're going to be seeing a lot of each other, might as well be friendly about it." I had no intentions of being civil, so I put the first reel—the departure from Constantine—on the projector and threaded the film carefully while doing my best to ignore him. It would have been easier to ignore a snowball down my pants.

"Seriously, what's wit'you?" He sidled up to me and looked over my shoulder. "Hmm. You do good work, gotta hand it to you. You know your boss is in big trouble."

"Why don't you leave him alone?" I managed it without stuttering, but did sound like a whiney little kid. "What's he ever done to you?"

"To me? Nothin'. Look, I respect bein' loyal to your boss. I got a boss, too, who doesn't much like your guy. You gotta admit, de Prorok ain't helping his own case much."

I didn't have to admit a damned thing, at least not to this guy. "He didn't steal anything. Get off his back."

The detective opened his coat. It was getting warm in the chapel already. "Maybe he did, maybe he didn't. It's not really my business. I follow and report. It's a job, kid. Like yours, just a job."

It wasn't just a job. Not to me. I slowly stood up and leaned into him. I had him by a good four or five inches. "I'm not a kid."

He did exactly what I knew he'd do; what bullies always do, he backed up a step. I was beginning to get a feel for him. Some guys just need a firm shove on the carriage. I let myself enjoy the moment when he took another step back.

"Whatever you say, Jumbo. It's your funeral."

"So are you going to follow us all the way to St. Louis?"

His voice changed. He was just talking to me, man to man in that cop way they have when they want you to relax and say something stupid. "If that's what it takes. Look, either I get something on him, or my boss quits paying me. It ain't personal."

I thought about the hours de Prorok spent moping over Alice and the babies. I remembered him smiling like a trained chimp at all the meetings with college presidents' wives and Rotarians. All the miles he traveled through the snow to bring people a little fun and maybe teach them something, the fights with bookers over money, and having to get to the bank before leaving for the next town so I could get paid. Havlicek was wrong. It was very damned personal. I couldn't tell him all that, though. I just said, "He's a good guy."

"You believe that, don'tcha? Look, Willy. It's Willy, right?" I nodded. Suddenly he was trying the fatherly approach. That was probably the least likely way to win me over, but he couldn't know that. "He's a fake. He's Billy Sunday in a jungle suit. Trust me, get out while the gettin's good."

"Thanks for the advice. S-s-see you in St. Louis." Damn, I'd almost gotten out of it without stuttering.

He shrugged and put his hat on. "Your call. If you can think of anything that'd help us out, Mr. Kenny is a pretty generous guy. He'd probably make it worth your while."

I wasn't going to sell the Count out. The very idea was infuriating. First of all, I was no rat. Secondly I didn't see why everyone hated him so much. Sure he was working angles, but who wasn't? And who was he really hurting? And really, what choice did I have? Byron de Prorok was my ticket out of… well, just out.

I hated feeling so useless. I couldn't really do anything to help the Count out of his situation, it was all beyond me. But Havlicek…there had to be a way to get rid of him, at least. I knew somebody smarter would have figured something out by now. De Prorok didn't have the luxury of someone smarter, he was stuck with me. So much for hiring the best.

That night at Beloit College the Count was as good as I'd ever seen him. From the moment Brad Tyrrell introduced him and he hit the stage in a spotless desert shirt, jodhpurs and pith helmet, he had that audience of professors' wives and spoiled frat boys eating from his hand. Of course, we'd stacked the deck in his favor, too.

Ordinarily, he didn't deviate a word or two from his normal lecture. This time, we'd gone through every slide and photograph and made sure every picture of the car—I think it was Lucky Strike—showed the Beloit College banner. It got a rousing cheer every time it appeared on screen.

He spent a lot of time up front, maybe too much time, thanking the Logan Museum, and the College, and President Maurer, and President Maurer's mother, and Governor Blaine and Calvin Coolidge, and God himself. Even though the big shots weren't there, plenty of people from the College and Museum were. Normally, these academic guys would beam proudly when they were mentioned. Tonight the faculty that bothered to show up just squirmed like the Father'd called them out during the homily in church.

I clicked one of the slides into place, and showed the whole Expedition. Some frat boy with pomaded hair behind me shouted, "Hey, it's Lonnie Pond."

Another one hooted, "Yeah, Little Lonnie!"

Three times the Count's walking stick banged the platform. "Yes, that's Alonzo Pond. Beloit College— and all of you—should be very proud of him." His brow crinkled and he stalked to the front of the stage, pinning the loudmouth to his seat with a fierce glare. "Alonzo Pond rode three days on a camel, risking danger and even death, to save every man on that expedition from starvation and drought. He may be 'Little Lonnie,' as you so charmingly put it, but a better man… and a better representative of this institution… you'll never find." A hush fell over the room.

Then I saw him silently count to four, and a smile reappeared on his face, and his voice rose. "In fact, he represented all of you so well, that Tuareg and Arab tribes across North Africa know the Beloit yell." He threw his head back, held out his arms and shouted, "Ole Olson, Yonny Yonson…" Before he was done, the frat boys joined in. "On Beloit. Wisconsin." Then they started again, and the whole crowd took up the chang. "Ole Olson…" Over and over it went until the chapel's walls shook.

By the time we were done for the night, the place was in an uproar. The frat boys loved him, the Professors' wives thought he was adorable, and he was the king of Beloit. Even I got my share of pats on the back and invitations to parties, providing I brought along my "A-rab getup."

We didn't, however, get an invitation from the college president. Likewise nothing from the Logan Museum, or even the student body president. On a normal night, there was a whole conga line of people eager to bask in the reflected glow of the famous Count de Prorok. Tonight, not one person of any importance offered anything other than a mild, "good job." No Faculty Tea, no brandy with the president.

De Prorok was dumbfounded. He'd worked with these people for over a year, and not one person wanted to join him for a friendly chat or an illicit glass of, "the good stuff." We were left alone in a chapel to pack up and kill an exciting night in beautiful downtown Beloit.

By the time I hauled the stuff back to the room, he was already pouring a glass of Templeton for himself. He paced back and forth, not acknowledging me for a long time, just muttering, "Oh shit. Oh Christ, Oh bloody, bloody hell."

I didn't know what to say, so I said the worst thing I could have, given the circumstances. "Maybe it's not that bad." His lip just curled up in a snarl.

"This is all Bill Kenny's fault," he said. "He's turned Alice against me, and now he's trying to ruin me with my colleagues. But he won't. Not for long. You heard them tonight, Brown. I was great. I'm too good at my job to be denied." He paced and drank, then drank and paced some more.

"They've got to sign those digging rights, tomorrow, Willy. Without them, I'm ... they must at least agree to them in principle. I know Bill wants the signed agreement, but if we can at least get a verbal commitment... Brad Tyrrell understands, and I know he's trying. I wish Alonzo were here. He knows exactly how important those sites are to the Logan, but he's still over in In Salah counting arrowheads and kissing Reygasse's arse."

A question had been nagging at me, buzzing and banging against my brain like flies caught in a windowpane. "If he's already in Algeria, why do they need you?"

De Prorok stopped pacing. I swear the earth stopped spinning for a moment. His eyes slowly widened like camera lenses. "What do you mean?"

I wasn't sure myself, but now that I started asking, I couldn't let it go. "Why do they have to go through you to dig there?"

"Because I have the..." He dug the strongbox out and pulled out the papers. "These are the digging rights to all that part of Algeria. Touggart Province. Hoggar. Right here." He crunched the papers in his fist, then in a panic, laid them on the table and tried to smooth out any creases.

"Where'd you get those rights from?"

"From Maurice Reygasse, on behalf of the Algerian government. No one can legally dig there without legal authority."

"Couldn't the college just go right to him?"

"After all I've done for them? They wouldn't. It would be a scandal. And I'm giving them a huge discount—sixty thousand dollars a year instead of seventy-five. They have to." His voice was getting high again. Then it dropped almost to a whisper. "They just have to."

No, I realized. They didn't. And if they didn't have to, they wouldn't. He was... we were...well and truly screwed. Then I could see he realized it as well, as he dropped his head into his hands and sobbed like a baby.

"Alice... I just... Oh Christ, what am I going to do...? That bastard..." I could just make out the occasional word between the blubbering. I stood over him, not knowing what to do. Pat him on the shoulder? What would that do, and who the hell was I to be comforting anyone?

Figuring he needed his privacy, and being completely incapable of offering any real help, I went for a long walk. I didn't go back upstairs until the light went off in our room.

When we got to the President's office in the morning, a very nice, older secretary greeted us warmly. "Good morning, Mr. De Prorok. The others are waiting for you, I'll bring you right in."

"Who exactly is in there?"

"Well, President Maurer, of course, and Dr. Collie from the Logan. And Bradley Tyrrell, I believe." Then she stepped smoothly between him and me. "Just take a seat, young man. I'll bring you out some coffee while you're waiting."

"It's alright, Brown. 'Tis a far, far better thing I do. This won't take long." He followed her into the office, gave me a weak smile and a thumbs up, then closed the door with the marble glass window in it behind him and gave me a motherly smile.

"Cream and sugar?"

I sat there in a heavy upholstered chair, surrounded by dark wood paneling covered in photographs and certificates designed to make you feel unworthy, straining to hear. It was all incoherent mumbling at first, then the voices would get louder and finally someone would remember their manners and it would get quiet again. I did manage to hear some of it.

"But I have legal authority…"

"We will not be allowed into Algerian territory if we have anything to do with…"

"But the New York Times…"

"Alonzo Pond was nearly arrested because of your carelessness…"

"What do you mean embarrassment? We were awarded the Palme d'Or…"

"Yes, I'm afraid it is, final…"

At last, the door opened. President Maurer held the door and offered his hand to the Count. "Byron, I'm truly sorry it's come to this. We really do wish you the best. Good luck." He really looked like he meant it, too.

De Prorok stood perfectly straight, and I could hear the strain in his voice, but the smile was nothing short of perfect. "Of course, Irving. I understand. All an unfortunate misunderstanding, of course, but business is business and all that. Perhaps another time."

Brad Tyrrell emerged from inside, putting on his coat. "Byron, wait. I'll walk you down."

"No need, Brad. Brown and I are all ready to go. We have a train to catch." I was already holding the door for him and he brushed past me with as much dignity as he could muster, which was considerable given the circumstances.

As the door closed behind us, I heard Tyrrell's drifting down the hall. "Stay in touch. Give my best to Alice."

Chapter 18

Near Abalessa, Hoggar Province, Algeria
November 13, 1926

Byron de Prorok scratched his itching cheek and studied the northern horizon. Even at twenty nine years old, his facial hair was embarrassingly sparse and he knew he must look an ungodly mess. Certainly, he'd never grow a great professorial beard like his hero Gsell. He desperately wanted to shave, but knew Martini would probably shoot him if he tried to use any of their precious water for such a wasted effort, as well he should.

He squatted in the slim shadow provided by an overhanging rock, at least as well as his long legs would allow. His pants bagged at the waist. He'd lost weight he couldn't really afford to lose and was glad they'd traded away all the mirrors so he didn't have to look at himself. Vanity wasn't the only reason he didn't want to face his own reflection. For the first time, he admitted to himself he may have just killed them all.

The banging and grunting of men working in the burial chamber a few yards away were the only sounds other than the incessant buzzing of flies. Even hungrier than they'd ever been in their lives, everyone continued to work, if only to keep their minds occupied. De Prorok knew how lucky he was to have every man jack on his team, and how badly he'd failed them.

Chapuis and Belaid he knew were proven campaigners. Discovering Martini was pure luck; they'd have been in a lot more trouble if not for the little magician. He looked at the man trudging towards him. Even poor Brad Tyrrell, who was essentially here on holiday, never complained or shirked any of the hard work.

"Byron, you okay?" Tyrrell's voice ricocheted off the stones.

"Never better."

"Yeah, me too." The older man plunked himself down in the dust beside the Count. Once more adjusting his hat to provide a tad of relief, they sat there in companionable silence, sucking on pebbles for the precious saliva it generated.

Byron needed to say it to someone. "Brad, I'm awfully sorry about…"

"Bah, don't. A little tough slogging, but I'll be home for Christmas and this will all be a great story to tell the grandkids." Byron winced. Home by Christmas, the last words of too many men.

Brad Tyrrell looked at him. "You've done okay, you know."

"I'm an ass."

The American snorted. "Well, I never said I'd hire you. Frankly, you couldn't organize a gang bang in a whorehouse."

"Thanks ever so much."

"Relax. I'm just saying, you've got a lot to learn. It's only natural for Pete's sake. This is your first time in charge. But you've also had the dirtiest luck I've ever seen. Completely snake bit."

"Always been like that, Brad. It's my fate, I suppose. Just when I think things are going my way, they turn to shit."

"There's no such thing as fate, Byron. You're smart, ambitious... God knows you work hard at the things you work at. It's all you really need to succeed."

The younger man shook his head with a sad grin. "That may be the single most American thing I've ever heard."

Tyrrell ignored the barb. "You just need to work smarter. Take fewer chances. No one's ever taught you that part, I'm guessing."

De Prorok shrugged in response. "The lesson's never stuck, at any rate."

"Well, remember this. You were right. She's here. We—you—found her. Speaking of which..."

The Count nodded and stood, joints creaking and stomach growling. "Yes, I'm on duty. Thanks, Brad." He patted Tyrrell on the shoulder at a loss for anything more profound to say.

As he neared the tomb opening and bent down to enter, he heard Louis Chapuis' voice. "Monsieur, come look. Vite, vite." He looked to see the guide waving his filthy kepi wildly and shouting, as best his parched throat allowed.

From their perch high on the mound, they could see for miles. In the far northeast, three small objects moved across the desert floor towards them. Byron squinted into the blinding midday sun. "Are those pack camels?"

Trying to tamp down his excitement, he grabbed the binoculars and trained them on the fast moving figures. The lead camel, laden down with jugs and crates, was piloted by a Tuareg he didn't recognize. The second camel's jockey was much shorter, and bounced around awkwardly, legs flailing, unable to maintain their place on the animal's neck. The third camel, tied behind the second, had a roughly made platform balanced atop the cargo, and its rider lay face down across the platform, in danger of being bounced off any time.

"God damn, I think that's Lonnie Pond." Byron handed the binoculars to Tyrrell, who grinned broadly.

"Has to be. He's the only one too short to ride a camel properly. Louis, can you tell who's on the stretcher?" He handed the binoculars back to Chapuis.

"I'm not sure. Denny, maybe?"

Christ, I've killed the Times reporter, he thought. Then he joined the others in a mad, whooping, scramble down the rocks to meet their rescuers.

They arrived at the desert floor just as the unlikely caravan halted at the campsite. Pond's camel bent her front knees and the American gingerly stepped off. Byron wrapped him in a dusty bear hug, while Tyrrell slapped him on the back.

"Lonnie, you are a sight for sore eyes," the other American said, but he was already looking to the injured rider on the third camel. "Denny, my God, what's wrong? Are you okay?"

Pond made an attempt at discretion by whispering, "It's saddle sores. Byron he'll be…"

"It's what?" Byron's voice honked.

"He said it's saddle sores, you asshole. Now get me down from heah…" Denny moaned, sounding every bit the angry New Yorker. Everyone knew that whether it was a horse or a camel, saddle sores were very serious things. Bloody blisters and exposed raw flesh could be agonizing and became easily infected. They were no laughing matter, although that didn't stop non-sufferers from having their fun anyway.

Their guide, a toothless, fearsome looking Tuareg, gave a quick "tuk tuk," and dismounted with ease, jabbering away a mile a minute in Tamasheq. He calmly guided Denny's camel to a gentle, or as gentle as such a lumbering beast could manage, kneel, while

Chapuis peppered him with questions.

Martini and Belaid each grabbed a corner of the blanket Hal Denny laid on to form a sling and helped him to the ground and then gingerly to his feet.

De Prorok asked the reporter, "Any permanent damage, Hal?"

"Just let me get my damned feet under me. Jesus." Once the journalist was safely on the ground, and able to limp under his own steam, the men began to unload more precious cargo. Cans of water, gasoline and motor oil were piled next to food stuffs. No one had ever been so glad to see chipped beef.

Pond winced and tested his legs with a few tentative steps. Brad Tyrrell offered an arm and helped him to a perch on a nearby rock. "You okay, Lonnie?"

"Yeah. I hate camels. My legs are too damned short to really get a good grip." Both men paused, then allowed themselves a snorting laugh of relief.

Byron's relief at their rescue was only momentary. He approached the Americans and quietly asked, "Where's everyone else? Is everything okay?"

Pond nodded. "The supplies came three days ago but Reygasse was away on some damned fool errand, and one of the trucks has a cracked oil pan. Denny and I threw everything on camels and came as fast as we could. Maurice should be here with the cars and the rest of the gear... wait. What day is it?"

There was a momentary clamor as everyone tried in vain to recall the day of the week. Finally, Pond counted them off on his fingers. "We left Saturday, I think, so that makes today... Monday? He should be here late today, tomorrow for sure. Assuming he got back on time, that is."

"Fine, fine..." Now that things were on the upswing, de Prorok couldn't wait to share the really important news. "Lonnie, Hal, guess what? We found

289

her. Tin Hinan. We found the tomb. Really, come and see, it's quite…"

"Byron, don't you think that can wait a bit?" Tyrrell motioned with his head to the rest of the team who were practically chewing through the crates to get to the food and water inside.

"Of course, yes. Apologies. Monsieur Martini, prepare the feast, if you please." As everyone but Hal Denny scrambled to assist, de Prorok rattled on to the only person who couldn't get away. "Seriously Hal, the Times will be beside themselves. The greatest discovery in the history of the Sahara. We did it."

Once throats had been soothed and stomachs appeased, the team swapped stories. Pond listened skeptically as de Prorok told his version of events. To hear him tell it, things had been tight but not dire. The gauntness of his face, and the embarrassed glances of the other men suggested otherwise, but Pond didn't push. Brad would give him the skinny later on.

Denny was the storyteller, so Pond let him relate the rescuers' tale. The message from Abalessa arrived late Friday night, and the supplies arrived soon after. The problem was, there was no way to get to the tomb site; Reygasse and Hot Dog had gone on some mysterious mission and wasn't due back til Monday. The other car, Sandy, was down with a damaged oil pan, and it would take two days to fix, so Pond and Denny decided to take as much as they could throw on a couple of camels, and head out. The others would catch up when they could.

Of course their guide, Yeddir, spoke no English, so they had no real idea how far it would be, when they'd arrive, or what shape anyone would be in by the time they got there. Two greenhorns and a guide who couldn't communicate with them carried gas, oil, water and food across eighty miles of Sahara in hopes of finding the right needle in an impossibly large haystack.

Denny warmed to the tale with the telling, convinced it was front-page stuff if he lived to tell it. He'd already written it in his head. His injuries weren't to the part of his body required for typing.

Chapuis looked worried. "Did you pass anyone, or tell them where you were going?"

Pond knitted his brow. "Not really. A couple of Arab traders, but that's it. Why?"

"Because if Akhamouk gets word of what we're doing here, we're in hot water." The party members looked at each other, half of them not understanding just how much hotter the water could get.

De Prorok didn't want them becoming fixated on the negative, now that things were finally looking up. "Lonnie, care to take a look at what we've found?" He bounced on the balls of his feet, eager to share the find with someone who could really appreciate what he'd... they'd... managed to do.

Pond sighed and tried to ignore the burning in his thighs. "Of course, let's get a look at the lady. Can't think of anything I'd rather do."

Pond's short legs had trouble keeping up with de Prorok at the best of times, and after three days on a camel these were hardly the best of times. The Count would scamper up the hill, then turn back and wait impatiently, then dash ahead some more and wait, all the while keeping up a constant stream of chatter. "Wait til you see the chamber. It's worked stone.... But not Arab or Tuareg. I swear, it looks Roman... can you imagine Romans this far south? Really extraordinary.... And the gold... real gold, Pond, like the stuff I pulled out of Utica. And gemstones... Carmelite mostly but I'm sure there's more..."

Pond grunted appropriately, hearing only half what

was said. He was too busy concentrating on not having a heart attack or falling off the mountain.

De Prorok continued his manic monologue, "…and here we are, home sweet home." With a triumphant sweep of his arm, the Count indicated the chamber opening.

"What's all this?" Pond asked, pointing to a crate covered in blankets. De Prorok flung back the blanket.

"Ta da. This is the best stuff we've pulled out so far." His long fingers gently lifted the gold necklace for inspection, then scooped up a dozen or so colored stones, letting them slowly filter through his hands, his face ablaze with the fever of discovery.

Pond thought he'd seen that same look on a housecat that drops a mouse at her master's feet, expecting praise for such a fine offering. If the son of a gun expected oohs and aahs, he was going to be as disappointed as the cat. "Have you catalogued all this?"

"Not yet. Haven't had time, have we? Too busy digging…"

"For Chrissakes, Byron, you know you have to document everything in real time… Oh for… Let me take a look. Pond ducked into the darkened chamber, allowing a few seconds for his eyes to adjust. The afternoon sun came in over his shoulder, striking the back of the chamber and offering just enough light to confirm his worst fears.

What he saw both excited and horrified him. The front half of the chamber had been shoveled or swept clean of dust. On the floor were dried remains of the animal skins that once carpeted the tomb. Against the far wall was a platform of decomposing wood, still covered in a thick layer of sandy grit. On top of the platform, sleeping under a blanket of silt was a body.

The skull, neck and most of the chest lay exposed along with a few bones that must have been feet and toes. Crowning the skull was a metal circlet, probably a crown, but it was too dark to tell what it was made of.

That was the exciting part, and he couldn't deny the hot tingly rush of excitement building, but he wasn't going to let that get the best of him. The scientist in him was horrified at what wasn't there; markers and notations for each artifact should have been everywhere. "Damn it, Byron. Haven't you documented anything?"

De Prorok suppressed an urge to scream. *Did the little bastard always have to be so tight-assed about everything? Can't he see what we have here?* He took a deep, calming breath before responding. "Well yes, photographic documentation, I mean. Brad had his movie camera, and he and I both have our little Kodaks. We've been taking snaps as we go, best as the light lets us. We figured we'd restage everything when Barth gets here and… What's wrong?"

"What's wrong? Honestly? You know better than this. I mean, Brad has no clue, he's an amateur, but you… You've corrupted the site. Jesus… we don't even know what all this really means."

"What it means, Pond, is that we have discovered a Roman burial chamber deep in the desert, with the remains of a real queen that many thought was just a myth. We've got Carthaginian gold and…"

"You don't *know* any of that. You've got worked stone, I grant you, but we don't know, really know, who worked it yet. You have a body of someone important, but you don't really know who…"

"Of course we know…"

"No, we don't," Pond found himself shouting. "You don't know, you're guessing. Do you even know

293

that's a woman lying there?"

"Of course it is," Byron frantically tried to wedge himself in beside the fusspot American. "Look at that crown, the necklace. Would a man wear those?"

Pond forced himself not to take the bait. Egyptians buried their dead with belongings of both sexes. Tuaregs were a complete gender mystery, with the men going veiled and kohling up their eyes while the women ran the show. Since no one really knew how old this tomb was, or whose body they were looking at, nobody—especially a pea-brain like de Prorok could be really sure. It was a great story. It was piss poor science.

Pond flinched as de Prorok clapped him on the shoulder. "And now you're here to add a little rigor to the proceedings. Now we'll have her dug out in no time, eh?"

"Yeah, well… we'll have to get started, I suppose. But everything has to be by the book."

"That's a lad. I'll get everyone rounded up and back at it." Pond was older than de Prorok by two years, and it galled him to be treated like a child, especially by that overgrown adolescent. Still, if this place turned out to be what it seemed, well he'd have to just swallow his pride and get on with it.

Sweep by sweep, handful by small handful, the body was revealed. The pages of Pond's notebook slowly filled with each entry: *wood (unkn) segment from platform (?) 6 in.* Then the piece of rotted wood was dusted, marked and set aside.

As they worked into the next day, Pond became increasingly excited, and de Prorok's enthusiasm waned. Pond began to feel the familiar rhythm of the work: dig, dust, analyze, record, then dig some more. The Count, on the other hand couldn't help but be disappointed.

No carved sarcophagus, no golden images. The bracelets, armbands and crown were made of brass or some other lesser metal. A few glasslike beads, their faces roughly formed, provided most of what little glitter there was. The only thing someone could really call treasure was one tarnished gold necklace and a pile of semi-precious stones—mostly Carmelite and polished agate—not much return on all their suffering.

The only statuary was that silly round female figure—most likely a fertility fetish of some kind. Interesting enough in her way, but it was hardly Tut's death mask. As a purely anthropological discovery, it had value, no argument. As a career-making treasure trove, it stank of disappointment. Again.

He ducked low to see inside the cavern. Pond was bent over the body, examining the skull with calipers, muttering to himself, lost in his work.

De Prorok harrumphed loudly. "What are you doing?"

Pond adjusted the screw, double checked the numbers and noted them in his book. Looking up, de Prorok could see his forehead wrinkled in confusion. Brown dust mixed with sweat left muddy streaks across his brow. "Byron, how sure are you this is Tin Hinan?"

De Prorok knew that tone, and he didn't much care for it. It was the sound of a professor laying a trap for an obtuse student. Still, he pasted on a casual smile. "Well, every source says she's buried here. This mound has been a holy site for fifteen hundred years or so. Who else would it be?"

"I don't know… it's just… Look, the body is shorter than most Tuareg males, so it's easy to assume it's female. The cranium…" He went on as if explaining to a reluctant freshman. He held the calipers against the exposed skull, "…is consistent

295

with a female. That's all good."

Then he moved down the body. "But the pelvis… it's too narrow. What if this is a teenage boy, rather than a woman?"

De Prorok shook his head. "No. Unh-uh. I mean, I'm not doubting your measurements…" He hoped his voice sounded more convincing than it sounded in his own ears, "Not at all. But consider this." He scrunched his eyes shut for a moment, gathering his scattered thoughts as he so often did before launching into one of his theories. "We know that Tin Hinan died young, and childless, far as we know. Yes?" Pond nodded patiently. "So… we have someone shorter than a Tuareg male. Lots of body jewelry… like the dowry necklaces we saw in the camp." His eyes lit up. "The figurine…"

He grabbed the fetish statue and practically shoved it under the other man's nose. His long fingers traced the breasts and the scratches indicating a rather prodigious vulva. "Don't you see? This is probably some kind of, I don't know, fertility goddess, judging from the… breasts and… what if this was buried with her to help her bear children in the next life?" He nodded, expecting a similar nod from Pond but got a winkled forehead and a shaken head instead.

"It's possible, sure. But…"

"There you go, then." De Prorok felt better. There was nothing like converting a skeptic to get the blood racing again. Of course, it all fit if you wanted it to. It was just a matter of squashing those pesky doubts that could paralyze you if you let them. Occam's razor, *lex parsimonaie*, was one of the cardinal rules of science after all. The simplest answer was usually right. He believed that, when it suited him. Why ask a lot of inconvenient questions? No one else would.

He still heard some of those doubts in Pond's

voice, although weaker. "There's something about her pelvis that bothers me…"

The academic in Pond was frustrated by the haphazard nature of the entire operation. De Prorok seemed awfully sure of himself, but then he thought Atlantis might be under their feet, too. Was he right, or just lazy? It would be a whole lot easier if he was right. If.

When the sun sank too low for the light to enter the tomb, Pond and de Prorok headed back to camp. They passed Chapuis, cradling his rifle in his arms and chewing what was left of his finger nails. "Louis, something wrong?" De Prorok felt obliged to ask, although he wasn't sure he could stand hearing the answer.

Chapuis looked up at the Count. "The drums have started up again." De Prorok just nodded.

"What's that about?" Pond wanted to know, or pretended to. The knot in his stomach told him he already did. It tightened a bit when they neared the bottom of the hill. Martini, Brad Tyrrell and Hal Denny were loading gear into Lucky Strike.

"Lonnie. Great. We're going back to Tamanrasset to see if we can find Reygasse, and maybe get some assistance out here. Denny needs to file his story, so he's coming with. We'll be back in the morning if everything goes right."

"Yes, God knows everything's gone right so far." Pond wasn't entirely sorry he let that slip, but de Prorok didn't hear him. He was too busy in conference with Hal Denny.

"Byron, take a look at these stories…. Which do you like best?" The reporter held three pieces of paper out for the Count's inspection. De Prorok read each in turn.

Daring Rescue on Camels Saves Prorok Expedition
Tomb Yields Proof of High Civilization in Sahara
Jeweled Skeleton Found by Prorok in Tomb of Goddess

A long, slender finger pointed to the last one. "That one's rather hard to resist, isn't it? Well done, Hal."

"I like that one, too. Almost makes coming out here worth it." He placed extra emphasis on the 'almost.' "I'm not looking forward to sitting in the car for eighty miles, but it beats the hell out of a camel. They'll eat it up at home. This is huge, Byron. It'll be the making of you."

Chapter 19

Near Abalessa, Hoggar Province, Algeria
November 13, 1926

That night nothing happened, but they couldn't have slept much worse if it had. The drums from the village thrummed steadily all night, drifting over the still desert like a faraway radio station. There was no sign of incursion—Chapuis' rifle and his willingness to use it proved a strong deterrent, and now that the white men were no longer starving and thirsty they made a less tempting target.

Alonzo Pond slept well as he always did outdoors. Years of camping in open spaces meant he could make himself comfortable and nod off almost anywhere. He did lay awake for a while, hands clasped behind his head and dreaming of speaking fees and a girlfriend suitably grateful for his safe return. He also mentally composed his report to Dr. Collie and the Museum, and hoped he could strike the right balance of excitement and scientific neutrality.

The discovery of Tin Hinan, if indeed it was her up there, was icing on an already rich cake. From a strictly anthropological standpoint, the paleolithic discoveries they made along the way were more important, if not nearly as glamorous. He just couldn't share de Prorok's enthusiasm, not without a lot more study. He liked the man, who wouldn't? But his abundant charm couldn't cover up his complete lack of professionalism. How could anyone go through life that completely sure of himself? It wasn't natural. Pond envied the man despite himself.

Byron de Prorok slept less than the others. Conflicting emotions battled in his head: pride at the discovery, impatience to tell the world, fear that he might be wrong. More than anything that night, the voices in his head told him he'd wind up like Gordon at Khartoum—lauded, respected, remembered as a hero, but not there to enjoy his own fame.

He accomplished the obvious goal. After all, the tomb was here, even if the actual treasure was less than he'd hoped for. It was an important find, and he'd milk it for everything he could. After all, he had the ear of the world's most important newspaper and that would shut up the doubters at the Royal Geographic Society—let them deny him membership now—and the Renault vehicles had survived the trip. Maybe they'd give him one of those new luxury models the drivers were raving about, a Vivasix. Alice would love that. But first he had to get everyone home safely. The nagging voice in his head, the one that sounded like his Grandmama, told him he was damned lucky no one had died. Yet.

Unable to sleep, he arose and joined Louis sitting like a gargoyle above the camp on a thumb-like outcrop of rock. The stones groaned and popped as the heat of the day turned to chilly night. De Prorok jumped at every noise. Chapuis was an old hand, though, and could separate the normal sounds of night from real danger.

"Monsieur, you should get some sleep," he said once he lowered the rifle he had aimed at the Count's chest.

"Mmmm, yes I suppose so." De Prorok swept a spot clean and sat down heavily. "What do you think he'll do? Akhamouk, I mean?"

"He won't be happy, that's for sure."

"I don't imagine so. But he wouldn't actually come after us, would he? It'd bring the whole Foreign Legion down on him. Beaumont doesn't strike me as the kind to let them get away with it."

Chapuis sucked his teeth thoughtfully. "The smart thing would be to complain a lot but not do anything. He's trying to keep his people alive. Survival is more important than honor, when it comes down to it."

"Is it? I'd think honor is worth fighting for. I know Akhamouk thinks so."

Chapuis looked away towards the village at Abalessa. "Then we're screwed."

Morning didn't so much break as shatter into existence. One minute everything was cloaked in the grey-blue of early morning, the next the sun played a merciless reveille. Pond stretched and groaned himself awake, momentarily missing the cold rain that tormented them earlier.

The men allowed themselves a leisurely and abundant breakfast. Belaid took over the cooking duties from Martini, which meant the coffee could double as battery acid, but at least there was plenty of it. They also allowed themselves the luxury of a shave. Most did it to avoid the itching of sweaty follicles and vermin. De Prorok wanted to look good if—no, when—Barth arrived with the camera gear. These pictures were his treasure. Let others worry about the bones and stones. The real money lay in movies and pictures.

With nothing better to do, Pond and the Count puttered around clearing one of the outer chambers. The work wasn't terribly rewarding. There was nothing of any value compared to the main chamber—to Byron's mind that was more evidence the body in there was important as it could be—and Pond's insistence on cataloguing every date seed and dried rat dropping meant it was not only unrewarding, but painfully slow as well.

It was a blessed relief when they heard Belaid's voice ring out. "Monsieur, the cars... Three of them... Come see."

They emerged, blinking, into the sunlight. To the northeast, they could see three miles out on the desert floor, and three small figures making a black dotted line that moved towards them along the white stone riverbed.

Lucky Strike, the Beloit banners flying as if it were on its way to a football game across campus, instead of across the Sahara, led the way at exactly twenty miles an hour. The other two cars followed closely behind, laden with crates, kegs and jugs and arriving in a chorus of "aaooogah" horn blasts and hoorays from the men.

Before Lucky Strike even skidded to a full halt, Maurice Reygasse opened the door and stumbled, out of the vehicle. He wore his digging uniform, still bright white but with fewer jangling medals. He ran up to the Count, grabbed him by the arms and offered a quick kiss on each cheek. "Byron, is it true? You found her?"

The Count beamed down at the shorter man, still clutching his arms as if he might run away. "Oui, Maurice. And she's beautiful. Would you like to meet her?" They turned towards the hill, then de Prorok turned back to Henri Barth and shouted, "Barth, get your equipment if you would. High time we captured this properly, don't you think?"

The rest of the team hustled to unload the gear, starting with the cameras, while Belaid ran behind them, urging them not to take more than they'd need for one night. "We won't be here long. We need to get gone as soon as we can. Put that back, we won't need it…"

De Prorok, Reygasse, Pond and Brad Tyrrell approached the burial chamber. For a minute, they stood silent, the only sounds the buzzing of flies and the exasperated puffing of Barth lugging his equipment up by himself. The Count took off his helmet, laying it on a rock, and put on the soft beret he used inside the tomb. He gave the Frenchman his most welcoming grin, looking over the shorter man's shoulder to make sure Barth was ready to capture the moment. "Ready? May I present Tin Hinan, Mother of all Tuaregs." He bowed low and gestured for Reygasse to enter.

The scene had been carefully staged for a one-time performance in Reygasse's honor. Neatly laid out at the end of the platform were the necklace, a tiny gold column about an inch and a half long with no apparent purpose, one earring and the fertility fetish that de Prorok playfully called, "the Venus." That was it as far as anything one could realistically call treasure.

Beside the body were a small wooden plate, a glass bowl lined with what might be silver, and a glass cup left behind to nourish the departed soul in the next life. Date pits abounded, as did smaller items that might be grape seeds, or fossilized rodent droppings.

The skeleton itself rested on a platform of rotted, woven wood that barely held together to supports its burden. Each arm sported metal bracelets, seven on one arm, eight on the other. The metal was dull and heavy, most likely lead instead of something more valuable and glamorous.

Reygasse stood silent in front of the display for the longest time. Just when de Prorok thought he might explode from anticipation, the Marshall turned to him with tears in his eyes. "We've made history, you and I, de Prorok. This changes everything we thought we knew about the Hoggar…" He wiped a tear away with this sleeve, leaving a muddy strip. "Do you realize what we've done? The tomb of Queen Tin Hinan. She was… is… real. It's a treasure, a real treasure."

Finally, the Frenchman let out a "Vive le France" and threw his hand in the air, banging his knuckles on the low stone ceiling.

De Prorok ignored the "we" and joined, because it felt so good to shout. At last, someone else understood exactly what he'd—they'd, he had to remember—accomplished. No nit-picking about procedure or permissions, just the pure joy of discovery.

He allowed himself the moment of triumph, then cleared his throat. "Maurice, we have to get the pictures and get out of here. There might be… uh… some unhappy locals."

Reygasse bit his lip. "Yes, we heard there was trouble. That's why we left before dawn, in case anyone tried to stop us. Is it as bad as Denny says? You know how Americans are, always looking for Indians to fight." De Prorok just nodded. Yes, it probably was. Having Maurice as a representative of the Government would certainly be a help, but no guarantee.

They watched Barth scramble around trying to wedge himself and then his equipment into the little tomb. At last he came out, sweating and filthy. "I'm sorry Monsieur, there's no way to get any usable film in there…. There's no room, and it's hot. It's like trying to film in hell."

De Prorok was in too good a mood to have it spoiled by mere reality. He patted the fat man's arm good naturedly. "Let's get the outdoor shots, and we'll figure something out. Just give me a moment to prepare."

The preparations took the form of changing into a clean shirt and replacing his filthy beret with a pith helmet whose cloth covering had been replaced by cloth so white Reygasse could have made another uniform out of it. When he was as movie-star ready as circumstances allowed, he and Barth planned their shoot. First, were several snaps of de Prorok and Reygasse surveying the opening, their faces looking appropriately solemn and academic. These were followed by movie film of the two men emerging from the chamber, positively glowing with the aura of scientific discovery.

Tyrrell and Pond were included in the shots as well. Brad was his usual good natured self. Pond was considerably less so.

"This is all a fake. It's ridiculous." Pond had taken Brad aside to vent his frustration, but he was overheard anyway.

"Pond, please." De Prorok had just about had it with the American's priggishness and nay-saying. "We know what we found, we're just trying to document as best circumstances allow. We aren't faking the discovery, for Lord's sake, we're just telling a story people will want to hear. What would you like us to do?"

"Telling the truth would be a nice start." Even while grousing, he followed Barth's orders to smile and shake Reygasse's hand in simulated congratulations. The little weasel hadn't been anywhere near the discovery, but you could bet his name would be all over it.

"Be nice, Lonnie," Brad hissed. "The Museum will be thrilled. Collie's practically wetting his pants and he doesn't even know the final results yet. And think of all the work you'll have. This'll make your career too, you know. Enjoy it for God's sake."

"Is that the College representative or the ad man talking? What have we really done here? Jeez, Brad, think about it. Everyone knew this was Tin Hinan's gravesite. They've known it for hundreds of years. We didn't discover anything, really. And what have we got? This great treasure is a few minor pieces and a body we can't even prove is who we say it is."

The older man swallowed his frustration and put a paternal hand on his shoulder. "That's something, though, right? I mean the one thing—right or wrong—about history is nothing really happens until someone officially confirms it. So we've confirmed it. We've done our job. Declare victory and go home."

A voice cried out, "Pond, we could use some assistance." He turned towards the chamber and saw the burial goods carefully lined up with Barth taking close-up shots of each item, then picking them up and grouping them for more snaps.

"What the hell are you doing? Byron… what…"

"Evidence, Pond. Can't very well take pictures in the dark, can we? Now help us with the body."

Pond shook with anger. The clown was finally taking things way too far. "You can't pull a body out of the ground and expose it to the elements, it'll turn to dust. Damn it, even you know better than that."

"Then help us do it right, damn you."

Pond couldn't stand the thought of their discovery turning to dust and blowing away on the desert wind, so he grudgingly supervised the transfer of the body from the tomb. The wood couldn't survive the move, even if the bones did, so they slipped a blanket under the platform and lifted the whole thing. Being the shortest, and fate having its little joke, Pond and Reygasse were responsible for the hard part: getting her to the opening. From there, de Prorok and Chapuis lifted her through the door in to the sunlight and the Twentieth Century.

The retrieval was filmed by Barth, who was ecstatic at the way the light played off the bones and shadows fell dramatically across faces. Pond just watched in horror. They shouldn't move the body at all, and if they did—and it was clear they were going to take her for further study—the bones and artifacts should be coated in gum arabic, or diluted shellac. Candle wax might do the trick, if they had enough. As it turned out they had enough to cover the skull, both arms and the pelvis. The rest was up to the gods, who had not exactly been on their side to this point.

Once everything was safely stowed, Byron heaved a sigh of relief. The only decision remaining was when to leave and where to go. Originally, they were heading in different directions. Reygasse and his car would go to a paleolithic site west of Tamanrasset. Pond was to go to another, just outside Alouef.

He, Brad Tyrrell, Hal Denny and Barth were heading home. After all, Tyrrell had been promised he'd be home for Christmas, and God knows the man had been a trooper but he'd clearly had enough. With Tin Hinan found, Byron's own interest in staying around vanished like a mirage. All he could think about was spending a little time with Alice, the babies, and the public acclaim he'd earned after all this foolishness.

Chapuis had a different idea. "We'd best leave all together, and as fast as we can," he stated with calm assurance. "The Tuaregs know we're here, and they won't be in a forgiving mood if we take their queen for a joyride." Belaid agreed with more energy than he'd ever shown about anything, which was enough to convince any doubters.

They settled on getting to the garrison at In Salah, where the Legion was posted and could provide cover while they made further plans. If luck was with them, and wouldn't it be nice when that was no longer part of the equation, they'd only have to camp out one night on the way. The renewed thomp-thomp-thomp of drums from the village sealed the deal.

The caravan was loaded in record time, and the Expedition set out for home. With the path known, and the excitement more or less over, things reverted to their natural order. Sandy, with Escande behind the wheel, took the Count, Denny, Barth and Queen Tin Hinan, took the lead. Hot Dog, chauffeured by a sullen, homesick Chaix had Reygasse, Chapuis and Belaid. Martini was relegated to the rear with Lucky Strike, two Americans, an unfair share of the equipment, and the Beloit College banner and pennant flapping in farewell.

The caravan shot along the riverbed, then onto the rutted road that ran through Abalessa to In Salah. As they neared the village, they could hear drumming again over the noise of the Renault's engine.

As usual, it was Hal Denny's voice that dragged de Prorok out of his daydreams and back to the real world. "What the Christ is that?"

All along the village side of the road, a small crowd of Haratins gathered. Most held spears, a few brandishing ancient carbine rifles. A few bright blue Tuareg robes could be seen mixed in the crowd, their owners sitting atop camels. Drums beat and weapons waved in the air, but that all ceased as the line of vehicles drew closer.

The crowd fell silent, and turned as one to witness the crazy white men coming towards them, rather than wait on the mountain to be slaughtered. One of the leaders stomped angrily to the middle of the road and held his hand up, seeming to demand they stop and fight like men.

In the lead vehicle, Escande tightened his grip on the wheel and gritted his teeth. De Prorok sat upright, his hand on the dashboard, his teeth gritted to prevent screaming like a little girl. Denny scribbled furiously in his notebook as neatly as the rocking of the car permitted.

"Easy now, try not to kill someone," the Count said as calmly as he could.

"I will if they will," countered the driver, flooring it.

"This is amazing stuff. Forget articles, there's a book here. Assuming we live to write it, of course." Byron was sure Denny was only half joking.

The car got much closer to the elder than either party expected before the old man jumped out of the way and Sandy shot past, followed by the other two vehicles and outraged cries and wails from the villagers.

As Lucky Strike shot past the crowd last, Pond and Tyrrell stuck their heads out the windows and looked back. They could see two camels piloted by rifle-waving Tuaregs half-heartedly chasing them, then shrinking into the distance until they were just angry black dots against the light sand of the road bed.

Laughing in relief, they slapped Martini on the back and began the Beloit chant: "Ole Oleson, Yonny Yonson, on Beloit. Wisconsin." Martini joined in the laughter, feeling confident enough to drop back to an appropriate twenty miles an hour and pointed Lucky Strike northeast towards In Salah.

November 14, 1925
9. Rue Alfred-Dehodencq, XVI
Paris. France

Dearest Byron,

I hope this letter finds you well and happy, my darling. By now you will, of course, have found your Queen and will be too rich and famous to ever talk to us again. Don't forget your Countess. Ha ha.

The papers are just full of your adventures. Did you really find all that treasure? I hope you bring home a little something I can wear around the house. Maybe just a simple tiara I can wear with my housecoat! It sounds so wonderful, and I'm so proud. I wish I was with you. Do you remember how much fun we had in Carthage? None of my friends ever had a honeymoon so swell.

Your last letter sounded a little sad. Does Daddy miss his girls? They surely miss you. M-T is walking now, well, running around like a wild Indian, actually. Thank goodness for Annie or I don't know what I'd do. Annie is being terribly grumpy, she hates France and wants to go back to New York. I admit, I get a little homesick, but wait until you hear me parle français.

Mary is coming over and will come back to New York at Christmastime with us. I know you don't like my sister, much, but that's only because she's such a mother hen to me and our chicks. She really does like you, you know. Please try to get along with her this time.

Daddy says the funds have been wired and everything is fine. Just contact Mr. Langham as soon as you can. Apparently, it's quite a lot of money and he's very concerned about it. You know what you're doing, of course, but you know how Daddy is.

I will leave you to all your important work, and I know you'll be home in two weeks! I can't wait to see you. The girls and I will cover with you kisses and give you breakfast in bed and treat you like a king, because you are the King of the Explorers now that you found the Queen.

All my love,

A

P.S. Try to bring home something for the girls this time. Just a little souvenir. They miss you too.

Chapter 20

In Salah, Algeria
November 24, 1925

The telegram read:

> *To: Maury Chef Cabinet Gouverneur General*
> *Palais Ete, Algiers*
> *Comte Prorok has discovered a magnificent*
> *prehistoric treasure*
> *Very rich and unique*
> *Will donate to the general government*
> *Respectfully, Reygasse*

De Prorok smiled and nodded. "Wonderful, Maurice, well done. Don't you think we should send a copy to the Logan Museum as well?" Letting the Americans know the same time as the French was a small bone to throw them. Their money had been— still was, if he was being honest—absolutely crucial to their success. But at least it was official, the world was learning of their triumph.

The Count, Maurice Reygasse and Hal Denny stood sweating in the telegraph office, swatting at flies the size of bats. The men crowded around a table fine-tuning their cables and trying to keep the papers from blowing around.

By virtue of rank and ability to speak whatever pidgin French the telegraph operator worked in,

Reygasse was the first to tell the world of their success. As he worked with the operator to get the news out, de Prorok and Hal Denny went over the copy one last time.

Byron barely recognized himself in the stories. He felt nothing at all like the dashing, intrepid, heroic figure in Denny's accounts. In truth he was haggard, underweight, miserable and, good Christ, he needed a drink in the worst way. Still, the sins Denny committed were of omission, not commission, and both of them could live with that.

The Times would get exciting accounts of their discovery, albeit the value of the relics was slightly exaggerated. Page One would come alive with the saga of Pond's camel ride to their rescue, even though none of that would have been necessary if de Prorok had planned correctly, or the sandstorm that held them up a day and a half before they could make In Salah, necessitated by their sudden cowardly dash for home, or the brave French Legionnaires escorting them from the barren wastes into civilization, despite the inconvenient fact that escort was only necessary because of the carless plunder of a holy site and de Prorok's bold-faced lies to the Tuaregs and their King.

Denny ran his finger over the page. "Is sepulcher with an 'er' or an 're'?"

"Isn't that what you have editors for, Hal?"

"I don't trust those idiots on the copy desk. This stuff is pure gold; I want them to keep their grubby mitts off of it." Denny's mood hadn't improved even though the saddle sores were pretty much healed.

"Next," muttered the telegrapher, extending a gnarled brown hand. Denny slipped a thick stack of typewritten pages across the chipped formica. "All of this?" Denny nodded and the agent moaned in despair, and mopily returned to his keypad, dit-dot-dashing the news to France, then to London, and across the Atlantic.

De Prorok thought about how the Times would describe their entry into In Salah: the cars arriving amidst gunfire and loud cheers—exactly as he'd imagined it would be. That was only an hour ago, and everything had turned to shit since then.

A stack of angry cables and letters from Beloit, New York and Constantine was his welcome home gift, each more demanding than the last. He expected Commandant Beaumont to be all smiles and congratulatory cheek kisses, instead there was a terse demand that the Expedition's leaders meet him in his office at "the first available minute," which basically meant he was already late.

The Count straightened his shirt and pants, using two fingers to pick at them, unsticking them from his chest as best he could. "Alright Maurice, let's go face the music."

Four doors down from the telegraph office was the mud brick building that served as local headquarters for the police, the Legion, the tax collection unit, the Bureau of the Interior and anyone else responsible for keeping a lid on things beyond the civilized—meaning French—cities of Algeria. The various departments and bureaus couldn't agree on much, but at the moment they were in accord on one important point. They each wanted their hands on Byron Khun de Prorok, and all of them expected their own pound of flesh.

If the Count was sweating before, he was positively drenched now as the meeting with Beaumont went from bad to worse and from worse to the sixth level of hell. He was hunched over on a hard, straight-backed chair, elbows digging into his knees. Reygasse stood beside him, occasionally clapping a hand to his shoulder in whatever negligible comfort he could offer. Beaumont himself sat behind his desk, leaning forward from time to time. Sitting cross-legged on a cushion and occasionally puffing on a hookah, but otherwise silent, was the local Caid, a picture of serene confidence in a snow-white burnoose.

"My hand to God, we're not hiding anything." De Prorok desperately tried to control the whiney tone of his voice, which emerged whenever he was confronted by authority.

"I'm afraid he's right," the Marshall said. "You've seen everything we have."

Beaumont was unimpressed. "My men are getting shot at for a few bones and some rocks? That's the great treasure you've been bragging about?"

"It's not about treasure, damn it." The Count's voice rose another third of an octave before he paused to bring it back down. "It's about the discovery itself... the Queen of the Tuaregs... Maybe proof of Romans or Carthaginians all the way south to Hoggar. Do you have any...?"

The soldier slapped his palm on his desk, scattering several papers and a dozen flies. "Well, the current King of the Tuaregs wants his grandmamma back, *tout de suite*, along with all the gold you stole."

De Prorok tried to answer, or at least made a vague croaking sound, but Maurice Reygasse gestured that he'd handle it. Putting on his best logical-bureaucrat voice, he spoke. "Commandant, the only gold found was that one necklace, and that tiny bead, which you know are now the property of the Government." He pronounced the last two words very carefully, not being subtle about the importance of the stakeholders. "The bones must go on to Paris for verification and further study. The turmoil is unfortunate, but..."

"Unfortunate? You're lucky you didn't wind up

buried up to the neck and fed to the ants."

The chieftain, having had enough of trivialities, sat straighter on his cushion, calmly smoothing the wrinkles from his robe. "None of this answers the important question, Messieurs, which is, where is our money?"

De Prorok's eyes shot fire. "We don't owe you any money. You and your... co-conspirators have robbed us blind from the beginning. You should have enough by now to buy this country back twice over."

"You have proof of these payments?" Beaumont leaned forward hopefully.

The Count sniffed, "Of course not. When you're in the middle of the God forsaken Sahara, there aren't a lot of notaries around certifying transactions." He could tell by the pained expression on Reygasse's face he just said something wrong. Again.

"Gentlemen," the Marshall said calmly, "would you give me a moment with my young friend here?"

The Legion commander shrugged. "Maybe you can talk some sense to him." The look on his face suggested great skepticism on that front. The tall Arab stood as well, gave a serene salaam and walked out, confident things were going his way.

As soon as they were gone, de Prorok slumped forward, running his fingers through his hair. "Maurice, this is madness..."

"Stop whining. You really don't have receipts, or records of payment?"

"Do you really keep track of all the baksheesh you pay, and all the last-minute deals you make?"

Reygasse threw up his hands. "Of course. Bribery is a cost of doing business. You track your payments to whom and for how much. Without documentation it's your word against someone else's. Even if you have it, it's still your word against theirs, but paperwork tips the scales in your favor." De Prorok sat open mouthed, while the Frenchman continued his lecture. "Paperwork is the life blood of any rational society. It's why the French colonies thrive while the British Empire crumbles to bits."

"But they're really going to take his word over mine… ours?" de Prorok asked incredulous.

"Byron, my boy, Beaumont and the government will have to deal with the Arabs and the tribes long after you're safely back in Paris. Why would they take your side?"

De Prorok shook his head, sweat flying everywhere. "And where are we supposed to get this money from? Can the Ministry help us?"

Reygasse chuckled at the notion. "And why would the French government pay to get you out of trouble with the Algerian government, which gets all its money from the French government? Grow up." He saw the pain on de Prorok's face and eased up a bit. "How much do they want?"

De Prorok stood up and grabbed some papers off Beaumont's desk. "Thousands. Look…" He shook the papers under Reygasse's nose. "Several hundred to suppliers for materiele dropped off to difference caches, most of which you'll recall never arrived, permit fees… We had all the approvals before we left."

Reygasse snatched the papers and looked for himself. "Approvals from whom?"

"Rouvier's office. In Constantine." De Prorok could tell from the Frenchman's reaction that was every bit as bad as his gut told him it was.

"Did you have it all in writing?"

"Most of it. I had it on good authority the rest would be rubber stamped before we got to Tamanrasset."

"Who was that authority?" Reygasse asked, flinching because he already knew the answer.

"Madame Rouvier herself. Denise…" As the words flew out of his mouth, the Count realized the enormity of his miscalculation and his shoulders slumped. "Christ, this is bad, isn't it?"

"Let's think about this. Without the proper papers, you don't have the protection of the government. Without protection from the government, you are on your own to deal with the locals to strike your own deals. That seems to be where you are. Surely you went through the same foolishness in Carthage?"

De Prorok sat back down on his chair and blew a heavy sigh at the ceiling fan. "I never dealt with any of this piddly crap. Professor Gsell or one of his assistants dealt with the permits and such."

"Well, that 'piddly crap' is your best friend if you're going to be the Regional Administrator. Get used to it."

The mention of his future income soothed de Prorok's soul a little. "Alright, so right now… today… how do we fix this?"

Reygasse's patience was at its end. "Do I have to wipe your ass for you, too? Who always has money? The Americans."

De Prorok bit his lip and shook his head sadly. "They won't like it. Collie at the Logan is still furious with me for the advance I took at El Kantara."

"That was before about a million dollars' worth of publicity in the Times. Do you want to stay here the rest of your life?"

"No, I have to be in Paris next week."

"Then talk to Tyrrell and Pond. Tell them you'll give them a break on the digging rights for next year. Little Lonnie is already wetting his pants to get at those sites. He's a pain in my ass, but they trust him, and he knows the value of what we've found out there. I'll handle Rouvier on my end, you get the money from them. Of course there's always your father-in-law…"

"Out of the question. Alright, I'll speak to Brad." He had to admit, Maurice had a point. But those weren't the only problems. "What about the Caid?"

Reygasse smiled and patted Byron's shoulder. "My friend, his people haven't gone anywhere in a thousand years. You're the one with the timetable. He can afford to be patient. And he knows Beaumont wants him happy. Get the money, the rest will sort itself out."

"You're sure."

"D'accord."

Outside, a horn blew a deep "a-oo-gah" as children and chickens scattered. Martini piloted Lucky Strike to the side of the caravanserai that served as headquarters. Alonzo Pond and Brad Tyrrell emerged, stretching their legs after a long day digging, sifting and cataloguing. Pond was giddy with delight. Tyrrell was just tired.

The older man groaned and stretched his long legs. "How do you do it? You looked like a five year old in a sandbox."

Pond knew where this conversation was headed. "It's just what I do, Brad. What real anthropologists do. The work needs to be precise. It's what separates professionals from the amateurs." He didn't need to name names, and Brad was tired of him bitching about it anyway.

A voice boomed from the doorway. "Gentlemen, can I buy you a drink? That's thirsty work you've been doing."

Tyrrell smiled. "I do believe I need something to cut the dust, Byron. Pond?"

Some of the glow left the shorter man's face. "Sure, why not? Give me a minute. I'll meet you inside." As he climbed the stairs to his room and splashed water on his face, he allowed himself to indulge the dark thoughts he usually kept under wraps. When was the blowhard going to leave, already? He got his damned Queen, such as she was, and he obviously had no interest in the real work that needed to be done. The idea of having to come to him hat in hand every year for the excavation rights wasn't a particularly pleasant one, but it beat the hell out of having to work with Reygasse.

To be fair, Byron had brokered an entente of sorts. At first, Reygasse tried to claim every promising site for himself on behalf of the government, doing everything but peeing on the fenceposts to mark his territory. Thanks to Byron, Pond had been able to leverage the Frenchman's almost pathological obsession with American Indian relics into a tradeoff for at least a few good sites, along with solemn vows not to interfere with his collecting. The Count might be incompetent, but he wasn't vicious. He was also, it pained him to admit, damned good company when he wanted to be.

Entering the café, he could see his two companions engaged in conversation. Neither of them were smiling, and both had pipes in their mouths, puffing smoke towards each other. Tyrrell's voice was the loudest, which couldn't bode anything good.

"Bottom line, Byron. What are we going to have to come up with?"

The Count ignored the question for the moment, and waved to Pond with a smile a little too big for the surroundings. "Ah, Dr. Pond." Pond was technically still a graduate student, and de Prorok only used that name when buttering him up.

"I was just telling Brad here that we've hit a bit of a snag." The Count launched into a brief explanation, sparing many of the details he'd shared with Tyrrell and leaving out much of the worst news. Brad Tyrrell was the business man, and knew the right questions to ask. Pond had a pretty good head for business, although little tolerance for it, and it was clear that "snag" was something of an understatement.

"…and so there you have it. None of us can leave or really get back to work until the blackmail's been paid—of course that's not what they're calling it—and the paperwork's cleared up." De Prorok looked from one of the Americans to the other, awaiting a response. Tyrrell was lost in thought, Pond visibly fought to contain a deep rage. Fortunately, the older man spoke first.

"We'll handle it, Byron. Give us a day."

"Thank you, Brad. It's most embarrassing, but we'll clean it up and start fresh, eh?" De Prorok thought he was through, but as he turned to go he heard Pond's voice, icy cold through gritted teeth.

"You've screwed this up from the beginning, you know."

Tyrrell held up a hand. "Lonnie, you don't…" Usually, when Tyrrell spoke, Pond demurred, but after six weeks the dam finally burst.

"From the start, it's been a disaster. Logistics have been horrible. Running out of food… and gas… and water…"

"But everyone's safe and sound in the end aren't they? Really, I…" If de Prorok thought he was going to get a fair hearing, he was going to be disappointed.

"Sure it's alright. Now that we're back. Somehow we've been lucky. And I'm supposed to be representative of the Museum. How's it going to look for me that I have to go back and beg for more money? You've never thought about how that might look…"

"I'll handle that conversation. You don't have to worry about it," Tyrrell interjected.

"That's not the point, is it? Paperwork, logistics, food… running out of gas, for crying out loud. Not to mention the mud and the… Christ, it's been a complete horror show."

The Count's face red and his eyes bulged as he, too, reached his boiling point, and his deep baritone echoed off the inn's walls. "Disaster? Was finding Tin Hinan a disaster? Tell me, Pond, exactly how many times the Logan was in the New York Times before I arranged it? I'll tell you, exactly none. Same with Beloit bloody College. Nobody'll ever confuse it with Yale, will they? For that matter, how many graduate students get their names on the front pages around the world? Your career is made, you ungrateful little prick. Do you know how many years of digging Ojibway arrowheads it would take to build a CV like the one you've got now?"

"I don't care about the New York Times. You nearly killed us you asshole."

"Okay, Lonnie. Enough." Brad reached his hand to clasp the younger man's bicep. "Byron, you'll hear from us tomorrow. Let's get this settled, and everyone goes on their merry way. There'll be time and blame enough for everyone when the dust settles."

The Count's face had returned to its natural color. "Thank you. Yes." He straightened his pith helmet and tugged the wrinkles out of his shirt while he inhaled deeply and let it go with an audible "whoof."

"Pond, I… I'm sorry." Then he strode away, looking straight ahead and ignoring the smirks and whispers around him.

"Sit down." Tyrrell's voice had the authority of

command to it and Pond obeyed. "Feel better, do you?"

Pond grinned as he took a seat. "Yes, actually, a little." The after a moment he added, "Sorry about that."

The older man leaned in, the weight of his elbows rocking the rickety table. "Look, de Prorok is in over his head. This was his first command, and he screwed the pooch. Everyone knows it, including himself. Maybe especially himself. The question is, what are we going to do about it? We can argue and fight and blame him, or we can solve the problem and move on."

"So he's going to get away with it? The College has to pay for his cockups? Again?"

"In the short run, yeah. Look, if someone doesn't pony up, you can't dig because the permits will be held up, and the Legion won't protect you. Nobody, not you or any other scientific expedition will get any kind of help or support from the locals if they don't see their money, right? And… and this might be the biggest thing… Byron won't leave until it's all settled. How much are you enjoying his company?"

This got a snort of laughter from Pond and he could feel his shoulder muscles unclench. "I just… incompetence shouldn't be rewarded."

"It won't be. You don't think there will be consequences? Trust me, he's going to take it in the ear. And, to be fair, it's not all his fault. Poor S.O.B's been lied to and snowed since the beginning. Didn't really know what he was getting into, Just naïve… a green pea. I've seen lots of guys like that… ya see them in business all the time. Smart, talented, but they have no business being in charge. He needs a boss to keep him in line. Not everyone's cut out to be king."

"But we'll have to deal with him for the next three

years. Can you imagine?"

The older man took a long, slow puff on his pipe and blew a smoke ring as big as his head. "You have to admit, it won't be dull. Let's see what happens next year and cross that bridge when we get to it. Okay?"

By the next afternoon, peace returned to In Salah. Brad Tyrrell, on behalf of Beloit College and the Logan Museum, agreed to monthly installment payments. They'd be wired to Alonzo Pond, who was staying behind to work at a nearby site. With Pond in charge, there would be no question of records being kept straight or payments skipped. The chieftain didn't know or care what a Beloit, a Museum or an America was, he only knew that each month the little scientist would pay him until the account was settled.

Not everything went smoothly. For a brief moment, it looked as though Pond might lose his Tuareg necklace, but he had the appropriate paperwork, and that appeased both Beaumont, who needed to keep things official, and the Caid, who didn't give a camel's fart if the Tuaregs were happy, as long as his money came and he was happy to let Pond off the hook as a gesture of good faith.

De Prorok on the other hand, had a practically new Flyssa confiscated, along with some glass beads that probably came from the Tin Hinan site and a small shiny button he'd lifted from Pere Lavigerie's gravesite. They let him keep the piece of wood from Shackleton's sled once it was plain that the scrawled handwriting was in English and couldn't have come from Algeria. He was leaving with the clothes on his back, the body of Queen Tin Hinan, and a few relics that Reygasse had already claimed in the name of France. His treasure was now just a figment of the New York Times' imagination.

Reygasse personally took responsibility for the

administrative paperwork. He used the phrase "on my word of honor," about three times, and the Legion commandant was fine with that, since Reygasse was a Frenchman. With the onus now switched to someone the Commandant could trust—or at least locate, if it came to that—the Count de Prorok was free to leave Algeria.

He made an executive decision to leave immediately in Lucky Strike, along with Brad Tyrrell and Hal Denny. The cursed oil pan in Hot Dog was leaking again, and the two Renault drivers decided to stick it out together until they could both get home. Chapuis, Belaid, an inconsolable Henri Barth and thousands of feet of film would depart the next day with them.

There was no farewell dinner, no final toasts, and no ceremonial send-off. It had the feel of a family visit gone on far too long. Everyone wished each other well, and mostly meant it, but there was more relief than pain at parting.

"Well, Byron, are you ready to go?" Tyrrell was already inside the stifling vehicle as his companion stood with his hands on his hips, taking one last look at the little village.

"I suppose so, yes… Monsieur Martini… Allez-y…" He ducked into the front seat and slammed the door shut. The little Italian stepped on the gas, and they headed north amid weak shouts of "Bon Voyage," and, "See you in the Spring," the skitter of stones spitting out from under tires, and a harmonica playing "Oh Suzanna."

Chapter 21

Paris, France
December 1, 1925

Baby Alice spit up on Byron's shirt for the second time that morning. He couldn't get up to do anything about it, because two year old Marie Therese had taken up a happy permanent residence in her daddy's lap. Since it took two days for her to come near him without screaming, he just let her snuggle warmly against him.

In French, he said "Alice, dear... please." His wife's only response was a happy chuckle. She handed him a clean diaper to wipe himself with and kissed his forehead. Her dark curls framed her face, and she looked lovely, if a bit tired. It wasn't, "I've been in the desert for two months and anything would look good, pretty." She had two babies in diapers and was still the lovely, vivacious, naïve young lass he'd married. Parenthood and marriage suited her much better than him, although God knows he was trying his best.

"You'll have to change your shirt before you go. Annie, please take the baby." She handed her gurgling, wiggling namesake off to the nanny. "Marie, you too, little one. Go with Miss Annie." De Prorok smiled. Her French was atrocious, but as always his wife was game. It was kind of adorable to watch her struggle so.

He slipped into English as he always did when they were alone. "You don't think I should show up at the

Embassy with baby throw-up on my shirt? I would think it's rather a good look. Makes me appear very respectable and domesticated."

"Here. Let me..." She slapped his hands away and undid the shirt studs. She took a moment to stroke his chest hair through the gap. "I'm sorry I've been so tired, darling."

"Well, you do have two babies. I don't know how you do it. I've been home a few days and I'm ready to dash screaming for the door."

She grabbed his shirt front and looked him square in the eye, pretending to be angry. "You'd best not, buster. I have you for another ten days before you go gallivanting off."

"Whoa, Tiger. It's hardly gallivanting. You girls will be with me. Then we'll all be in Brooklyn for Christmas. That'll be nice, and I can get home between lectures." He knew Alice was homesick. She had only the nanny, a good Irish New Yorker, for real company. Otherwise she was alone in a little house in a second-class Parisian suburb.

"Well, Mary will be here in a few days. That'll keep me company until we get home. But then, Monsewer le Compt, you are all mine." Mary was her belligerent older sister, self-proclaimed defender of the family honor, and a royal pain. He wasn't sorry he'd be shipping out as soon as she arrived.

"Absolutely," he said, wrapping his hands around her waist, then stroking her firm bottom through her skirt. "We can leave the girls with Grandmama and you can come with me. Washington, Atlanta, we'll make a honeymoon out of it." Given that they'd spent their real honeymoon in a dig outside Carthage, he figured he owed her that much. He very much wanted to be alone with her. They could hit a few of the big Eastern cities, then he'd deposit her at the family manse and head off for the wilds of Grinnell, Iowa. Wherever the hell that was.

Alice wiggled under his touch. "I still don't know why she insisted on coming over so close to Christmas, we're going to be there in a few weeks anyway."

Byron agreed it was a good question, but who knew what went on in that woman's mind. The whole family, aside from Alice, were a mystery to him. His father-in-law, Bill, was an open book. A rude, boorish, terminally bourgeois book, to be sure, but usually you knew where you stood. Her mother Mary was a complete cypher, silent as the tomb. As to their impending visitor, well that was a veritable Ibsen drama of sibling rivalry and repression.

Close proximity to family was something he'd largely been spared. He remembered something Tolstoy said, "All happy families are alike; each unhappy family is unhappy in its own way." He looked around him and wondered if any family was really happy. He felt like his could be, if he could break free of the Kennys.

"Maybe she wants to make sure I'm really putting you on the boat and not keeping you prisoner in decadent, evil France." She gave a playful scream as he pulled her into his lap and pressed her against his bare chest. Alice gave a quick look around to see if little eyes were watching, then gave him a deep, warm kiss.

"I'm sorry it's been so rough on you. It's so unfair," she whispered, stroking his face.

"Hopefully, today will put it all to rest. It's just good to be home with you... and the girls," he added quickly.

Both of them pointedly ignored the stack of Paris newspapers at their feet. Since his originally triumphant arrival, things had gotten sticky. The local press was equally divided between effusive praise and scathing attacks, depending on their politics.

Les Temps, the house organ for anti-colonialists and left wing academics was being particularly rough on him, and wasn't done quite yet. Of course, they'd attack anything Reygasse and the establishment supported, and a chance to stick it to the New York Times was raw meat to the jackals. Le Matin was also sniffing around.

De Prorok could appreciate a good story. Someone in Algeria obviously leaked the fight over missing relics and angry locals to a socialist reporter in Paris who couldn't wait to fan the flames. Anything supported by the French government, the union busters at Renault and the Americans must be guilty of something.

He desperately wished he'd found all the gold and gems they thought he had, although that was largely his own fault. The wild tales he told Denny, and continued to tell anyone who'd listen, were just that, stories. He never expected his harmless exaggeration to be taken seriously. When he couldn't produce the fabled treasure, though, it was either admit to a few fibs or criminal smuggling.

The treasure, or lack of it, was only one problem. From Africa came complaints of grave robbing, a ridiculous charge but hard to argue with, since he was clearly in possession of the Queen's remains. Some of the anti-Reygasse crowd even spread the rumor that the body wasn't Tin Hinan and probably not even female. Fortunately, the top people in Algiers backed his claims, but rumors lingered.

The icing on the cake, though, was that someone had gotten the American embassy involved. That was the real problem, since lawyers meant money—money he didn't have—and that meant asking Bill Kenny for help. True, he had the best lawyers on the Continent at his disposal, but their crude methods, more Tammany Hall than Assemblée National, seemed counterproductive. The mood was turning nasty with cables and charges flying across three continents but things were finally returning to a simmer. Christ alone knew what it cost, and he knew there'd be an accounting at some point.

By then, though, he'd be able to support Alice and the girls. Between the digging rights, the books he planned and the lecture tours, he'd control his own destiny. Until then, he was just the ne'er do well son in law. It chafed him, but for the moment—and only for the moment—the family's involvement was a necessary evil. That too shall pass.

"Well, back to the salt mines," he declared, pushing her off his lap.

"It'll be fine. Daddy says Mr. Langham is very good."

"He is, really. I just wish he'd be a bit more tactful. State Department types are really just pencil pushers at heart, and they rather like being the face of America. They really don't care much who your father knows in Albany. I can see it in their beady little eyes."

"Even Al Smith?" Alice was every bit as proud of her father's friendship with New York's governor as the older Kennys, never missing a chance to drop the name. If he was honest, Brad Tyrrell and Beloit College had proven more helpful in the end. Beloit's president Maurer and his friendship with Calvin Coolidge trumped Bill Kenny and Al Smith every time, although he'd never admit it to his wife.

"We'll get it all wrapped up today, I promise. Oh, did I tell you, I got a cable from Lee Keedick about a deal with some film producer in Hollywood, California. Hoag and Somebody or other." He expected more of a reaction than he got. "Really, Lee is going to be a great asset."

"Well, if he can get you Carnegie Hall, I'll believe it. Daddy says he's a bit of a shyster."

Byron gave her a smile that brushed away any doubts. "You leave that to your brilliant husband." She smiled up adoringly. Those eyes warmed Byron to his core.

Things did go better after that. The charges by the Algerians were dropped, more from exhaustion than satisfaction. L'Academie formally announced its findings on behalf of Count de Prorok and the Expedition. There was even talk of a Palme D'Or for him and Tyrrell. The State Department grudgingly admitted everything seemed to be in order, and as long as the French were happy, they were content to let things slide, although not without keeping his dossier, bulging with notes and letters about his character, close at hand.

The morning of December 15th was sunny and cold with the wind blowing off the harbor at Le Havre. It stung the faces of the de Prorok family as they leaned over the rail, but couldn't dampen their excitement. Alice and Byron, Count and Countess de Prorok and the girls waved to no one in particular as they waited for the SS Leviathan to set sail. Annie and Mary stood behind them shaking their heads and huddling together for warmth.

Byron wrapped a reassuring arm around Alice's trim waist and squeezed. She'd been strangely quiet since her sister's arrival, but that was just the stress of traveling with small children, a nanny and a royal bitch of an older sister. He only had to pack his film, pictures and a small trunk of belongings. Living life out of a suitcase was nothing new to him. The biggest snag came when he tried to find his piece of Shackleton's sled. Alice had put it aside, deciding he didn't need to drag it halfway around the world. He corrected her as gently as he could, and stored it away, wrapped carefully in two pieces of newspaper like he had for fifteen years.

Alice snuggled close to him, her fox fur collar tickling his nose. "Isn't it exciting, Darling? The New York papers are already buzzing about our arrival. The Brooklyn Eagle wants an interview, just as soon as the Times is done with you. Wait til you see the welcome we get. And Christmas with the whole family, it'll be wonderful."

Byron kissed the top of her head. Well, all of her family. No, his family now. "The new tour will be a corker, Alice. Everything is coming together."

Alice looked up at him, her eyes strangely watery, he thought, but maybe it was the cold salt air. "Really, Byron? It's going to be okay?" She needed assurance, which he gladly gave her. *Why couldn't she see what he saw?*

"Of course, this is just the beginning of great things for us, sweetheart. Everything is going to be swell, you'll see." Byron de Prorok looked off to the channel, and New York beyond that, and America further still. The future he always dreamed of was finally his; a golden career, a beautiful family, financial stability—all of it. It was so close he could reach over the rails and grab it by the scuff of the neck.

"Nothing can stop us now, Alice. Nothing."

Chapter 22

Chicago, Illinois
March 5, 1926

The Count crumpled the telegram into a ball and threw it at the wall of Mrs. Cudahy's boarding house. To say he threw like a girl would be an insult to the girls I knew, who could at least get it home from the infield if they had to. "Omaha and Grand Platte. Garden spots of the plains, I'm sure."

I tried to put a good face on it. "It's work at least." And it was better news than the wire that awaited us upon arrival yesterday. That one had been from the National Geographic Society in Washington D.C:

> *No room on schedule spring or summer stop*
> *Chance something in 27*
> *JH Finley, President, NGS*

Whenever the Count cussed, it didn't sound like real swearing, just genteel annoyance. This time though, he let out a string of words that would have gotten him a mouthful of Life Buoy if Mama heard him. The gist of it was, John H Finley had his head firmly up his own arse. I'd have laughed, but the look on his face told me it wouldn't be a good idea.

We shared a room in a boarding house on South Dearborn. Lee Keedick, the omnipotent agent, used it for his other show business clients—mostly opera singers and long hair types—when they were in Chicago. It helped keep down expenses.

That was going to be the way of things now, especially that money was going to be tight. When someone else was footing the bill it was the Pfister, or the Allerton or the Palmer House. When it was on the Count's dime, it would be boarding houses and shared rooms. That was fine by me, but it bothered him deeply. He must have apologized three times since we arrived the day before.

"It's only temporary," he explained at least twice. "Only until we get the money straightened out again." It didn't bother me much, but I could see embarrassment, or maybe even shame, written on his face.

Then I asked him for the third time. "We're still going to St. Louis, though, right?"

"Jesus, Mary and Joseph. Yes, we're going to bloody St. Louis. Don't have a lot of choice in the matter do we?" At least I still had a job.

As boarding houses went, this one wasn't bad if you didn't count the Irish biddy running the joint. Colleen Cudahy had a beak like an eagle and a brogue so thick you could smell peat smoke. Her nose wasn't nearly as sharp or deadly as her tongue, which could take an eye out from across the room. I learned that the first day, when I tracked mud into her parlor.

She wasn't shy about sharing information either. Apparently the last two young men Mr. Keedick arranged to share this room did not keep to their separate beds, and she let it be known in no uncertain terms that wouldn't be tolerated. Not in her house. She knew how those European types were. Degenerates, the lot of them.

"You look like a good lad," she confided to me that first afternoon, "but I don't trust that fancy one.

Too pretty by half, and prob'ly English, from the sounds of him. They're all queer, that lot." It took a very involved conversation with my employer to understand what it meant and what had her so riled up. I guess I wasn't pretty enough to be a suspect, and for once I was glad.

The widow Cudahy's inability to keep a thought in her head for more than five minutes without sharing had one big advantage. I knew Havlicek was watching the house. Well, not him, since there were twenty-four hours in a day, but another guy, younger and even shorter by the sounds of it. He'd come around asking about the Count, then tried to take a room, but the widow Cudahy had that uncanny Irish ability to smell an informer, and enthusiastically sent him on his merry way. Poor guy was probably still picking broom straw out of his hair.

The ride down from Beloit had been two and a half hours of silent hell. De Prorok sat and moped, occasionally sipping from a bottle he got from God knows where. Somewhere around Elgin, he began to perk up and by the time we got to Union Station he found his second wind. Since then he managed to keep me hopping.

The first order of business was to go through all the slides and pictures, and pull every photograph we added before the Beloit speech. Anything with the school's name on it should be replaced with something more dramatic, or at least Beloit-free. To be absolutely precise, he told me to burn them, I assumed it was just the anger and the brandy talking, and placed them in a separate box.

I was also responsible for procuring the train tickets, which could wait for tomorrow. What couldn't wait was finding a cleaner to do something about the Tuareg robes and turban. Apparently my stage fright literally oozed from every pore, and the costumes were getting awfully fragrant. I didn't know any place in Chicago one would find a laundry with twenty-four hour *burnoose* and *tagelmust* service, but he assured me I was smart enough to figure it out.

His duties consisted primarily of making phone calls, sending telegrams to Maurice Reygasse in Paris that were doomed upon transmission, waiting for word from Alice and having dinner—and drinks— with his friend at the Oriental Institute. Some muckamuck from Michigan State University was in town, and he might get them interested in the work the ungrateful bastards at Beloit didn't want to pay for. Not for the first time, I wondered how having someone else pay for dinner and getting drunk could be remotely considered work, but that's why he was the boss.

His being occupied freed me up for the evening. Sharing a room meant I had little time to spend on my tinkering, and I had some things I should probably work on, but "The Black Pirate" with Douglas Fairbanks was opening. To see a Fairbanks movie opening night seemed like the kind of luxury only a free man with cash in his pocket could enjoy. A guy could get used to that feeling.

I wandered north on Dearborn, whistling happily while walking underneath the thundering train tracks into the Loop, and was surprised how fast you could feel at home in a place after only one visit. A guy could get used to Chicago, I supposed, but there were so many other places. St. Louis next, and New York, maybe Boston. Lost in my daydreams, I stepped off the curb into a slushy puddle right up to my ankle. I wondered if he had anything planned in Florida.

My evening consisted of a great pirate movie and a plate of egg foo young, which I was proud to order all by myself but was disappointed to find out was just an omelet covered in brown gravy, but at least it was cheap. My soaked wool sock refused to dry, and rather than risk pneumonia I headed back to old lady Cudahy's.

I hadn't even finished banging my shoes clean on the wooden stoop when the door flew open. "'Bout time you got back, boyo. You need to do something about him." I had a pretty good idea who "him" was.

"He's carrying on something awful up there. You'd best see to him. And calm him down. Honest people need to get their sleep, y'know."

"Yes, ma'am, I'll see what I can do." I took the stairs two at a time and banged on the door.

"Mr. De Prorok…."

A loud, thick voice shouted at me through the thin white panel door. "Piss off, Brown."

It wasn't really an option, with an old Irish woman standing right behind me, cutting off retreat. I opened up anyway and closed the door behind me, nearly nipping her beak as she peered in to see what was going on.

He sat on the bed with his elbows on his knees, a half-empty pint bottle on the bedside table, and a pipe smoked in the ashtray sitting atop a mountain of dead ash. His eyes glistened with tears, bloodshot and burning like someone had circled them neatly in red ink.

"Are you alright?" I asked, for lack of anything intelligent to say.

He sniffed, which was more answer than the question deserved and handed me a yellow piece of paper. It was from Western Union. I unfolded it to see:

To: B de Prorok
Not coming to New York
Send money as agreed
A

"It's true, Brown. She's not coming back. She's choosing him over me." He looked up for a response, any response. Getting none, he dropped his face into his hands and wept. Deep gasping sobs wracked his body.

I held the paper out to him, but he was too busy crying to notice, so I put it on the bed, carefully pressing it flat. I couldn't stand to see him like that, and seeing grown men cry wasn't something that happened in my neighborhood, so I was completely useless to him. I looked around the room. On the rickety round table near the window the lockbox lay wide open. The letters and official papers were scattered all over, wrinkled where they'd been balled up, then pressed flat again, probably more than once. There were pictures of the little girls. The picture of Alice de Prorok, all soft curls and adoring puppy dog eyes, lay beside the overflowing ashtray. A water ring, although probably not water, marred one corner of the photograph.

Because I didn't know what else to say, I managed to pour gasoline on the fire. "It'll be okay."

He looked up at me, the red coals in his eyes blazing. "How? Exactly how is it going to be okay?" It was a fair question, and one I didn't have the answer to. My oafish shrug only infuriated him. "Yes, well I don't know either. I'm ruined. All of it… my family, my career the digging rights, they're all gone. And why? What have I done to deserve this, eh? What have I done that's so God-damned awful?"

"Well," I began, trying to sound like I had a clue

what I was talking about, "you'll see the girls all the time."

"No, I bloody won't. He'll get them…" I knew he meant Kenny, there was only one "Him" in de Prorok's world at that moment. "He'll take them and hide them in Brooklyn, and won't let me see them, just to be spiteful. I know that miserable son of a bitch will…"

His foghorn voice blew at full volume and a small Irish fist banged on the door. "Ye knock it off in there, or I'll call the police. We got honest people tryin' to sleep that don't need this nonsense." I felt like asking her to name one, but opted for lowering my voice to a stage whisper, as did de Prorok.

"What am I supposed to do? *Je suis fauché.* I'm broke. Completely and utterly busted."

I knew there was broke, and there was *broke.* "How can you be broke? You make two hundred a day?"

His lip curled up like I'd crapped in his hat. "Two hundred a day is nothing. And everything gets sent back to Alice as soon as it comes in. Why do you think we share such glamorous accommodations?"

"It's more than most people make."

"I'm not most people, am I?"

A completely unreasonable and unreasoning rage was building inside me. "No, you're not. Most people work a hell of a lot harder for a whole lot less." The words flew out of my yap before I could stop them, and I knew there were more where they came from.

His lips pulled back in a teeth baring snarl. "Vass de matter, Villy. Vorried about you chob? Worried you might have ta go back ta Muhwaukee and live with Mutti und Papa?" The German "v"s were meant to sting, but not as much as throwing my Wisconsin accent at me. His ear and his aim were both deadly.

"That's not what I s-s-said." Damn.

"But it's what you meant. You need me. Everyone needs me… until they don't. Then they're happy to leave."

"I'm not going anywhere."

"Hmmmph. Because you need me. But you will, eventually. You'll suck the life from me, fifteen dollars at a time and I'll have to start all over again. I've worked too hard to be treated like this. I don't deserve it."

There he was, playing that song again. How hard he worked. Poor him. He doesn't deserve this. Well who does? Sometimes you got what was coming to you. Sometimes you got more, some people did, anyway. Usually it evens out and you still feel gypped. I felt the words bubbling inside me, churning and boiling and I knew I shouldn't let them out because that's how stupid things get said and unretractable words spit in people's faces. They flew out anyway.

"Why don't you deserve it? What makes you so special?" His body sagged, his fingers ran through his hair over and over. "What do you even do? You get on stage for an hour or two every c-c-c-couple of days and talk about shit nobody really c-c-cares about. And they pay you good, and they treat you like a big shot…"

He looked up and gave a long sniff, followed by a longer pause. "Because I have a talent, Brown."

"Okay, you can talk real fancy, b-b-big deal. That's not work."

He couldn't have been more shocked if I punched him in the nose, which was close to happening. We were both getting hot, but while my voice got louder and more spit-producing, he got quieter, his voice dropping to a hiss. It was scary. Like a rattlesnake is scarier than a barking poodle.

"It is a big deal you blithering idiot. It's the biggest

deal there is." He stood, meeting me eyeball to eyeball. "Most people can't do what I do. Look at you. You can't take what's in that big block head and say something without stammering and sounding like a cretin. People write you off, they think you're stupid. And you're not... not by a long shot... You're smart, but it's wasted. The world will never know what you really are... and neither will you, because you can't tell your own story."

He began to pace, his lecture voice emerging, focused on an audience of one. "Most people can't tell their own stories. They piss themselves at the idea of speaking in public, or they can't find the words... so they walk around frustrated and angry at the world. But that's what I do. You see? I tell other people's stories for them. I take history and all those dates and facts and all that boring bullshit science and translate it for the brainless masses in a way they can actually comprehend. Do you think anyone really cares about science or history unless it comes with a good story?"

His voice dropped again as he stood over the table, his finger stabbing the digging rights document over and over. "All those academic prigs, looking down their noses at my work. Do you think those smug bastards would ever get one penny if not for people like me? The almighty Doctor Pond and his bloody arrowheads. Does he really think anyone would give a single God-damned cent if he sits in the desert and digs up rocks just because it's the right thing to do? I get paid so people give a shit. I get two hundred dollars, they get thousands, maybe millions. The National Geographic Society doesn't like my methods, but they by-God are happy to sell their magazines with pictures I took, aren't they?" He stared out the window. His voice dropped, and I realized he wasn't really talking to me at all.

"I earn my money, chum. Believe it. And what do I get in return? Stabbed in the back. Beloit, my colleagues, my own wife. Even you."

"Me? What did I do?"

"You're already planning your escape."

"N-n-no, I'm not." He didn't realize I was working like crazy to find a way to stay.

"Really? You're really staying?" I really was. I nodded in answer. "Why?"

That was a fair question. Why did I stay on with Meyer when his theater burned down and I nearly lost a hand doing it? Why did I stick it out at home when every part of me cried out to go? Because I couldn't leave Mama with the Old Man. Now I was staying with this guy, dodging detectives and pulling him out of speaks and making sure his pictures didn't turn to dust.

"It's my job."

He nodded and laid back on the bed, hands crossed behind his head. "Good night, Willy." I was dismissed from my own room. I left anyway.

Backing out of the room I nearly tripped over Mrs. Cudahy, who just happened to be putting towels away, at eleven thirty at night, within earshot of our room. "Everything okay, dear?" she asked innocently.

"Yes ma'am. Just hunky dory."

"There's no one in the basement room tonight. You can bunk there. One night only, mind ya."

"Thank you, that's very kind."

The mother hen clucked. "Nonsense. It's too late to make other arrangements. But one night only, mind ya." I nodded gratefully, and she beamed like I was the big, lovable, *einfältiges Kind* she never had. "Alright, downstairs with ya then."

While I tossed and turned more than usual, I slept like most nineteen year olds—dead to the world—

until the sun wouldn't be ignored a minute longer. It reached through the narrow street-level window and slapped me across the face until I roused myself. It was above freezing for the first time in days, and I could hear melting show drip-drop from the eaves as I laid under the blankets.

I threw off the covers and stood on the faded fake Oriental rug, wiggling my toes happily. Carpeting was just another reminder I was no longer at home. Feet freezing on bare wood or cold linoleum is no way to start a day.

Widow Cudahy insisted I eat breakfast before "buggering off." This was no great hardship. She always served a big morning meal, on the table promptly at seven, even though most of her roomers were show folks with a very different definition of "first thing in the morning" than she had. I had the whole meal pretty much to myself.

Dearborn Avenue was quiet this early on a Saturday. The sun glinted happily off the puddles of melting slush. A warm breeze, as warm as a wind in March could be, promised an eventual end to a particularly stubborn winter. I didn't bother buttoning my coat, happy to let it flap in the breeze. I was in such a good mood as I waited to cross Adams that I gave a nod to the skinny, dim looking, bucktoothed kid Havlicek had watching the place. The world's worst detective turned away, pretending he didn't see me, and hoping I'd play along.

Whistling "Sweet Georgia Brown," endlessly, I picked up the tickets to St. Louis at Union Station, got the robes from a very confused Chinaman at the laundry who wanted me to model them and headed back to the boarding house. The sun felt good, and we were heading south where it would be even warmer.

Twenty minutes later, I gave a quick "shave and a

haircut" on the Count's door, which swung open on its own. I poked my head in to see the Count at the table, staring at the papers and pictures in front of him. I came in and placed the robes on the bed. It wasn't til I was standing right next to him he looked up. "Do you know she's six months old, and I've seen her for less than three weeks?"

"Who?"

"Baby Alice..." He flapped the photo in my face. "My daughter. My baby girl. She was born just before I left for Africa, and I was home barely a week before I left to come to America. She's no idea who I am. It's no better with my oldest..." This time he held the picture still, talking to it rather than me. "Marie Terese. Look how big she is. Three years old already. Smart as a whip, and didn't even recognize me when I was home last. It took two days just to get her to sit on my lap without crying."

I knew which picture was next in line. He traced his fingers across the picture, silently stroking Alice's smartly curled hair and the lines of her high collar. His voice dropped to a ragged whisper.

"I have to go home, Brown."

"To New York?" I knew that wasn't the answer, but hope wouldn't surrender easily.

"She refuses to come back to New York until her father arranges the divorce... annulment... whatever the hell he's planning. I have to go back to Paris." His voice was low, calm and steady. He'd made his decision. He also didn't say "we."

"But we have to be in St. Louis tomorrow night, don't we?" I could hear the panic in my voice and couldn't do a damned thing about it. "I bought the tickets already..."

"I've already called Lee to cancel. Apparently, I have a nasty case of laryngitis. Can't you tell?" He

346

inhaled slowly, a long ragged breath then let it go even slower. "I'm sorry."

"What are you going to do?" It was the question I should ask, not the one I wanted to.

"I'm headed back to New York tomorrow, then the first boat I can get."

"What if she won't see you?"

"She will if her father doesn't get in the way. That's always been the problem. She's quite reasonable until Daddy gets involved."

"What about Havlicek? If he knows what you're up to he'll stop you… or tell Kenny. Same thing."

"I'll have to find a way to throw the bloodhounds off the trail, I suppose."

"What about me?"

He slowly gathered the pictures together and stacked them, tapping the bottoms on the table so they lined up neatly. He never looked up. "I'm sorry. I'll pay you for the week, of course."

A week? Fifteen bucks and marooned in Chicago, what was I supposed to do? My head spun with the centrifugal force of a thousand questions and absolutely no answers.

"Three weeks," I heard myself say. It sounded like me, but it was Gerhardt's angry at everything, workers of the world unite, Wobblie voice. Let the rich bastards think they own you and they do. "I want three week's pay, and I'm on the clock until you leave for New York."

"I can't pay you for three weeks. There's nothing for you to do. And obviously, I have other places to send my hard-earned money."

He wasn't going to get out of this easily, I was like a dog with a sock. "You already owe me for this week, and you'd expect me to give you a week's notice if I was quitting, right?" He shrugged. "So that's two weeks. You still need to get all your stuff on the train, right?" He nodded. "And I'll get rid of Havlicek for you." Where the hell did that come from?

His forehead crinkled. He stared at me as if trying to see right through my skull. "And how are you going to manage that, pray tell?"

I hadn't the foggiest notion. The tiniest seed of an idea rattled around in my noggin like a pea in a whistle, but it was nothing like a real plan. "N-never mind. If I can get Havlicek off your back, will you p-p-pay me for three weeks?" I don't know how I did it, but I kept my eyes on his, refusing to look away. It was a silly, childish staring contest, but I'd be darned if I'd lose. At last he broke away.

"The train to New York is at noon tomorrow. I have to be on it. Without that... Without being followed."

"You will. Deal?"

He nodded, but that wasn't nearly good enough. I stuck out my hand. "Shake on it. Three week's pay, forty-five dollars cash, if you get on the train without Havlicek following or knowing where you went." His right hand hung at his side for an eternity, but finally he extended it and shook my paw.

With as much dignity as I could manage, I turned and left the room. I needed to think about how I'd pull this off. This called for a long, solitary street car ride.

As we chugged and clanged along Madison Street, I kept asking myself: how would Douglas Fairbanks handle this? It didn't matter, I wasn't Douglas Fairbanks. More like Fatty Arbuckle. Chaplin would do something charming that would send the bad guy packing and still get the girl. I imagined the chasing and the furious bad guy stomping and chewing his hat all to the tune of a tinkling piano and I smiled. By the time I reached Kedzie on the way back, I had something close to a vague notion of an idea of an outline of a plan.

I jumped off the street car and up Dearborn, running south as fast as my winter coat allowed. Fortunately, I found Skinny standing exactly where I'd left him. That meant the Count was still at the boarding house, too. Perfect.

I came up behind him as quietly as I could. Then I leaned in to his ear and shouted, "Hey!" Poor guy nearly messed his pants.

"Jesus H Christ on a crutch, what're ya doin'?"

I pulled myself to my full height and leaned in. "Tell your boss I have something for him."

"Don't have a boss. Don't know whatcher talkin' about." He was loyal, but not too smart. I knew how that felt so I backed off a step and lowered my voice.

"Tell Joe Havlicek that I found what he's looking for. The missing… uhhh… item." I hoped I made it sound mysterious and enticing enough. I must have, because he bit hard.

"Really? What did you find?" Like I'd tell this yahoo.

"Just tell him to meet me at Union Station tomorrow at nine thirty. The door to the platform. We have to catch a ten o'clock to St. Louis." He nodded and repeated the instructions.

I leaned in and lowered my voice. "And tell him I expect to be properly taken care of. I'm going to be out of a job if His Nibs finds out about this." I gestured with my thumb over to the boarding house.

"Got it," he said. I could see that he did. Fear of getting caught doing something sneaky was something this guy could relate to.

I left him standing there as I hustled back to Mrs. Cudahy's. Crossing the street, I nearly got hit by a cab.

That would have ruined my plans, but if this didn't work it might be for the best.

Chapter 23

Chicago, Illinois
March 6, 1926

"He's really going to St. Louis?" Havlicek asked. I held up two tickets in response. "Gotta give it to'm he's a trooper. Show must go on and all that."

It was my turn, "You're really following us down there?" He held up his own ticket.

"If he goes, I go. That's how the game's played. Least it'll be warmer there, right?" It had warmed up a bit, but even a warm March in Chicago is colder than most places any sane person would want to be, and the wind whipped up the platform blowing paper bags, old newspapers, and the occasional expensive hat all over place. The detective shoved his hands deeper into his pockets. "Whaddya got for me?"

I reached inside my own coat and pulled out a shiny black strongbox. "Look familiar?"

His eyes scrunched in confusion. "I thought dere was nothin' in it?"

"Ta-da." I thumbed it open quickly, just to enjoy his reaction. He leaned in and his eyes unscrunched. I didn't have to look, I knew what was in there. It was a small necklace made mostly of smooth red and brown stones with a few blue and green gems mixed in, held together by cheap gold and copper wire, unrecognizable beneath the tarnished patina, all strung together by unsophisticated hands and fit for a barbarian queen.

"I'll be damned. I really thought he was telling the truth. Doesn't look like much, does it? I thought this was supposed to be the find of the century."

I gave my best sad sigh. "Yeah, well he's a bullshit artist, isn't he?" I took my time, carefully thinking out each word and pushing my tongue to the bottom of my mouth to fight the stammer. "Most of what they found was junk, and almost all of it went to the museums in Africa and Paris. This was the only thing he could sneak out." I paused and moved my tongue over my teeth to keep it loose. "He figured the Oriental Institute would pay for it—and they were going to—but the heat's on thanks to you and they won't touch him with a ten foot pole. He's going to try and find some rich geezer in New York or someplace."

Havlicek took another gander at it. He pointed to the stones. "What's that?"

"It's called Carmelite—kind of agate they used in jewelry."

"And that's gold? Looks kind of dinged up." The sap wasn't completely sold yet, and I was afraid he might pull out one of those jeweler's eye-thingies for a better look. We didn't have time for this. I drew on my reserves of panic and hoped I could turn it into the right amount of aggression.

Maybe he needed another push on the carriage. "Jeez, what an idiot." He looked like I'd slapped him. Good. "What does your mom's jewelry look like when it ain't been polished for a while? Now imagine no one's given it a decent cleaning in fifteen hundred years." He whistled in appreciation. He reached for it again, and I nearly snapped his fingertip off slamming the lid shut.

"Time's wasting. He's prob'ly already wondering

where I am. You got something for me?" He gave me a conspiratorial smile, like we were pals or something and reached into his pocket, pulling out a wad of bills. He didn't hand it over, though, just looked at me with his old ex-cop eyes.

"Why now? You been a straight shooter all along. Not real bright, but a good kid. Why now?"

I looked away for a minute, trying to control my breathing, my tongue and my bladder, then turned to him with a shrug. "Like you said, how long do you think I have before the gravy train runs out? Sooner or later he's gonna leave me flat. Might as well get something for it, right?"

"Right." He handed me the money. "Thirty bucks. That's two week's salary, right? Mr. Kenny says to thank you very much. I think he likes you, kid."

I resisted the urge to punch the piker right in the snoot. Instead, I pulled the box closer to my chest. I knew how this particular piece of equipment operated now. "He likes me more than that. What did he really tell you to pay me?"

This got a laugh out of the Pinkerton, and he dug into his pocket, adding another twenty to the roll. "He said fifty. I figured you'd settle for thirty. You're smarter than you look." If he really believed that, I was in big trouble.

Fifty sounded about right. It was a nice round number, and nothing to a guy like Kenny. I took the money, grabbing it tight to control the shaking, and handed over the box. For a moment, I thought he was going to look in it again but fortunately the stream of people getting onto the platform was turning into a mob.

"It's time to go. Luggage is all loaded. He's gonna be wondering where I am. He's waiting in the bar car."

Havlicek snorted. "Where else?"

"D'you always have to bust balls? Yeah, he's in the club car. I don't want him to see us together. Give me a minute, then get in one of the cars ahead of us."

He nodded. "That'll work. Alright." He put the strongbox under his coat and picked up his valise. "See ya in St. Louis, kid." He touched the brim of his hat in salute, and I felt those piggy eyes burn into my back as I grabbed the handrail at the second car and pulled up. I allowed myself one last look back. Yup, he was watching.

As soon as I got inside, I dropped into a seat and leaned against the cold glass. I was panting and sweating, and my hands shook wildly as I felt the wad of bills in my pocket, sure my pants would burst into flame the way it burned there. A fat Pullman gave me a suspicious once-over, but I waved my ticket at him, and he moved along. I leaned back with my head craned to the right as a brown hat and its owner bobbed past the window towards the front of the train. I pressed my forehead to the glass, watching him until he climbed into the first car behind the locomotive.

The conductor waddled to the doorway and hollered out, "All aboard." I stood up, calmly moved to the door beside him, grabbed the railing and stepped out onto the platform, keeping as close to the train as I could. The train started to move, and I headed towards the caboose. I took one last look behind me, saw nothing, and ran like hell.

"Hey, where you goin'? We're leaving," the conductor shouted. Not fast enough for my liking, I thought, and kept running and dodging oncoming traffic until I was safely inside the depot. The only people who paid me any mind were the concerned folks wondering why the big guy was grabbing his knees, huffing and puffing and looking like he might pass out any minute.

"Is he gone?" the deep voice came from behind a pillar.

I nodded and gasped for air. "Yeah... On his way to St... Louis."

"You're sure?" I nodded again because it took less air than talking. The Count allowed himself the first smile I'd seen in three days. "How did you manage it?"

"I just gave him the necklace."

His eyes weren't clear, but they sure got wide. "What necklace?"

"The one you stole in Algeria. F-f-fashioned by crude hands in a savage land," my voice dropped to an imitation of his. He still didn't get it. "The one I was making for you as a surprise."

"He believed you?" I wasn't sure if he was relieved or insulted. Relief won out. "He really thought I stole a necklace and was stupid enough to carry it around with me? How could he believe such a thing?"

"He wanted to," I said. He just nodded thoughtfully. Then I handed him the two tickets. To my disappointment, but not my surprise, he took them both from my hand without looking at me.

His embarrassment lasted only a moment. He gave himself a shake, and his best business smile reappeared. "Well, Mr. Brown. I believe I owe you three week's wages." He handed me a wrinkled stack of fives. I was tempted to count it, but took the high road. Instead I nodded and calmly put the cash in my right hand pocket, where they burned just as hot as Kenny's did in the left.

I couldn't think of anything to say. I'd used up my whole supply of clever, so I just said, "Thank you, Sir."

"Thank you, Brown. Thank you very much." Then he paused, and for the first time, probably in his whole life, the Count de Prorok was at a loss for words. He took a couple of preliminary stabs at a sentence before he could ask me, "What are you going to do?"

It was the first time he'd asked me that, and I fought down the resentment that burned in my gut. "I have no idea," I said truthfully. "But I'm not going back to Milwaukee." That was equally true. "What about you? What's your next move?"

He sighed and straightened his shoulders. "I'll go to New York, from there back to Paris soon as I can get a boat and win my wife back. I can keep my family together, I know I can, if I can just get there before her family... I think if we agree to live here—New York, I mean—that might make Alice happy enough." His eyes didn't believe what his mouth said for a minute, and neither did I, but I nodded anyway.

We slowly walked over to where his luggage was stacked. My battered, flaking suitcase lay on top of the pile. I picked it up and clicked it open, pulled out half the money de Prorok gave me, shoved it inside the socks that served as the National Bank of Willy and pushed it to the bottom of the suitcase. I saw my drawstring bag containing the broken pasteboard sword, the mold for the Libyan Venus, a few beads, glass chunks, and a little copper wire. I shoved the rest of de Prorok's money into that bag. That made forty-five bucks in my suitcase, and another fifty in my pocket, plus what I had in my billfold.

"Can I buy you lunch before I go?" he asked. I knew he'd have to trade the tickets to St. Louis just for fare to New York. Plus, I didn't know what else to say. I let him off the hook.

"No sir, a deal's a deal. I pay my own meals." I

held out my hand. "Good luck."

He took it in both hands. "And to you, Braun. *Bon chance.*"

We stood a moment longer than was comfortable, both of our eyes looking everywhere but at each other. Then I picked up my suitcase and turned my back to him. I figured I could wrangle a night our two out of Mrs. Cudahy. At least meals were included. It was as good a plan as any.

Walking through the rotunda, I studied the big board. Trains were arriving and departing from all over the country. Imagine, being able to just pick a spot and go anywhere you wanted. Then it dawned on me. I had everything I owned in my hand and a hundred bucks in my pocket. I stopped, unsure whether I should continue outside or not.

Through the revolving doors, I could see flakes falling gently to the sidewalk onto Canal Street. People walked past the glass doors, huddled up against the lake wind, one hand holding their collars closed, the other keeping their hats from blowing away. I looked from the winter outside back to the departure board. The heck with it. It was time to go somewhere warm.

Chapter 24

Los Angeles, California
November 22, 1954

Even after twenty-eight years in California I never got tired of the sunshine. I was whistling, "The Nearness of You," along with the radio in the old Chevy and tapping on the steering wheel when I turned off Melrose into the Windsor Gate at Paramount Studios.

"Morning, Nathan." I beat him to it this morning.

"Morning, Will." Nathan had greeted me the same way for almost twenty years—a jaunty good morning and a tip of the cap. The striped wooden barrier lifted up and I drove towards the workshops at the back of the lot.

The front was all studio offices, busy nebbishy guys in suits and ties and secretaries way too good for them. Then were the working lots, where if you weren't careful you could get distracted by all the cowboys, saloon girls and extras dressed as Martians. I remember trying to explain to my insurance guy once that I lost a front bumper to a falling suit of armor. Only in L. A. I suppose.

The prop and set workshops were stashed away at the back of the lot. I pulled into my usual spot. Maury Lewis stood expectantly, holding the papers and a bag of crullers. He couldn't even wait for me to get out of the car before accosting me. "Morning, Will. Whatcha got today?"

I had to think for a moment. "Conquest of Space, I think. You?"

He gave me that smug look he always got when he was working on an A picture. "Starting that Grace Kelly thing today, The Country Girl. Bing's in it, too." Maury always liked to rub it in when he got a prestige assignment. When he got "Sabrina," you'd think he won the Irish Sweepstakes and got to marry Audrey Hepburn as a bonus. I'd be hearing "Bing this," and "Grace that," for weeks to come. "Conquest of Space," was just a programmer George Pal was riding herd on. Personally, I didn't care how big the picture was, just what kind of work I'd be doing on it. Props was a union job, so we all got paid the same no matter what. Maury could have the women's pictures and the big melodramas. I much preferred playing with swords and guns. Hell, we were building some kind of kooky space ship thing for "Conquest," which was way more fun than making sure we had the right kind of coffee cup for Miss Kelly, who was a bit of a brat, truth be told.

I'd been at Paramount for twenty years by that time. I came over in thirty-four, after kicking around at the Sennett studios, then Columbia and RKO until JT got me the job on "The Scarlett Empress," with Marlene Dietrich. I was always good with swords, and some dumb ass had given the Cossacks scimitars instead of shashkas. "Swords are swords," was good enough for Poverty Row, but not for the big time, and I took over that bonehead's job on the spot. I've been here ever since. Some call it luck, but how hard is it, really, to just do your job?

The routine never changed. Maury and I arrived, checked the schedule to see which lazy S.O.Bs we could pawn off on the other, and which hustlers we could claim for our own teams, then we'd work like crazy to make sure everything was set up for the first shot of the day.

Once shooting was underway, there was plenty of down time, which meant shooting the shit over coffee and the papers. I normally looked at the trades and a little local news. Maury was a racing schedule and sports guy. Lately, he'd taken to reading the obituaries, which worried me a bit, but he said there was nothing to it.

I was on my second cruller when Maury sat up and passed the Examiner across the table. "Hey, don't you know this guy?" He stabbed it with his finger. "This guy, right here."

It was Shelley Mazer's column. I usually didn't read him, since he was one of those "Broadway is better than pictures" types, but the words leapt off the page at me:

REMEMBERING "COUNT" DE PROROK

One of the hazards of being an old hand at this business, is you hear about a lot of people you know going to their rewards. I was talking to my old New York agent pal, Lee Keedick, who told me one of the oddest ducks on that pond has just passed…
"Count" Byron de Prorok.

For those of you too young to remember, "The Count" was quite a character: an archaeologist, lecturer, and shameless self-promoter. In 1925, when Lee first took him on, he was fresh off an expedition in the Sahara that saw him splashed all over the front page of the New York Times. His high-society wedding to the daughter of W F Kenny—yes the Tammany Hall Kenny— was all over the papers. I remember my buddies at the old Brooklyn Eagle couldn't get enough of them. Pretty Alice Kenny and her Handsome Count were all the rage at parties, at least on the wrong side of the East River.

He was quite the bon vivant and raconteur; handsome, with

a stupendous gift of gab. The "Count" was the Lion of the Midwest lecture circuit—a real novelty in the minor metropolises of Iowa and Missouri where he made the housewives' hearts flutter wildly. He wrote four books, with titles like "Digging for Lost African Gods," and "Dead Men Do Tell Tales." The problem is that while dead men might tell tales, so do archaeologists, some of those tales very tall indeed. The "Count" was exposed as something of a "fabulist," which is Lee's favorite word for a pathological liar. He could spin a good story, though. Seems his title was "borrowed" from a Polish Uncle, and his claims of finding tombs full of gold turned out to be pretty much as phony as his English accent and his claims of fighting Tribesmen and Italian agents in Abyssinia or uncovering lost temples in Mexico. Pretty Alice Kenny divorced him, leaving his two daughters with his in-laws, and she very quickly remarried an Englishman with a real title and three names. Byron continued to drag his pictures and films around for years, although he never reached the same level of fame despite getting decent reviews at Carnegie Hall, including one from me. After the divorce, he lived full-time in Europe, where he remarried (at last count, according to Lee who quit keeping tally) three times. Old Byron never had a problem attracting the ladies. He'd just put that silly helmet on his head and they'd melt.

To those of us who knew him, it wasn't a big surprise he was the worse for drink when they found him a few days ago, aged 58, on a train bound for Paris. According to Keedick, who still represented him stateside, he was about to begin an American lecture tour on his experiences as a Resistance fighter against the Nazis. Whether his experiences with la Resistance were more factual than his claims of finding King Solomon's Mines, is now known only to the Lost Gods he always talked about.

I remember many a night in New York listening to the Count's amazing tales, believing half of them, and probably giving him too much credit at that. Like most of New York, I hadn't thought about him in years, but I'm sorry to see him go.

The world is a duller place.
SEEN AROUND TOWN
In other news, who was that blond starlet hanging on the
arm of...

The Count was dead. I hadn't thought of him—really thought of him—in years, so I don't know why the idea he was gone seemed so ridiculous.

"You okay?" Maury asked.

"Yeah, fine. Huh."

"You said he was kind of an odd duck." Maury knew the story, or at least the bones of it. Since no living person was actually born in Los Angeles, the "how did you come to California?" story was part of the ritual when you met folks here. Byron de Prorok was part of my story.

"That he was."

I was spared any more discussion by the ringing phone. Apparently one of the plywood gyroscopes had fallen off the wall, nearly decapitating Mickey Shaughnessy. The rest of my day was spent stretching canvas over studs and double toe-nailing props in place so it didn't happen again. Just another day at the office.

I mentioned the Count's passing to Maureen when I got home. It was no big deal, just one of those, "hey, remember that guy I told you about, well he died," stories people tell when you get to our age. She made the appropriate tut-tutting noises and that was that until we shut the house down for the night.

I still hadn't gotten used to things being this quiet. Both boys were out of the house now. Gerry was still at boot camp, and Michael had his own apartment over on Las Palmas. I'd gotten Mikey a job over at Columbia, and he'd managed not to screw it up yet. Time would tell. Maureen always said I was too hard on him. She didn't know what hard was, but she was probably right. She usually was.

I went out to the garage and pulled the string over my workbench, squinting against the glare of the bulb, then pulled an old box off the shelf. After rummaging around a bit, I finally found what I was looking for, an old grey cloth bag. "Hey, Babe, come here for a minute," I shouted out to her.

"What's that?" She leaned into me and looked over my shoulder, rubbing my arm in the playful way married people have if they're lucky.

"I had this with me when I got to L.A...." I opened the string wide and pulled out some wire, some loose glass beads, and then a longer package. Wrapped in two pages of the L.A. Examiner from March of 1926 was a broken pasteboard sword. Two blue beads rattled around loose inside the wrapping. I caught them and pressed them back into place. Not that they'd hold. They never had.

"That's what you had with you? Quite a haul."

"That and about sixty-five bucks in my pocket."

She squeezed my waist and sweetly kissed my neck. "Mr. Money Bags, that's why I married you." She always said that, although there wasn't enough money in the world to make that a fair bargain. I got the much better deal.

I wasn't much of a drinker, so she was surprised when I suggested a night cap.

"Really? What do you want?"

I knew what I wanted. "Do we have any rye?"

"You don't even like rye. I think we have bottle Maury and Sheila brought over two Christmases ago, want me to get that?"

She dropped some rocks in a couple of glasses while I found the Wild Turkey. Templeton Rye no longer existed now that booze was legal, it would have to do.

We clinked glasses, and I offered a quiet, "To the Count," and we each took a sip in silence. I could feel it burn and thought rye wasn't a drink for sunny climates. For the first time in years I sort of missed the snow. Almost.

I laughed at the way her face crinkled as she swallowed, but she was a sport, like always. Curling her long legs under her on the sofa she leaned her head on my shoulder while I stroked her long, curly hair. After a few minutes of that she asked, "So who was this guy?"

"Oh, he was a piece of work," I began. Then I told her about my six week career as a projection technician, and getting on the train for Los Angeles, and then about the column in the paper.

"Was he really with the Resistance?" she asked me.

I finished my drink and put it down a little too hard on the glass coffee table. Then I laid my head back against the sofa cushion. "Probably not, but I wouldn't put anything past him."

The End

Acknowledgements

My fascination with Byron de Prorok began five years ago when I uncovered several of his books in the Half Price Book Store in Wheaton Illinois. He was the perfect subject for my obsession with people who have all the tools for success and still manage to get in their own way. You get no points for guessing why that's of interest.

In the back of those books was an autobiographical essay that set me on this path, so I have to thank Michael Tarabulski, who is the only person on the planet who shares my fascination with Byron (although he's more of an Alonzo Pond guy.) I also have to thank Nicolette Meister, Fred Burwell and the folks at the Logan Museum and Beloit College for allowing the pleasure of rummaging through their archives and taking my research seriously before I did. That goes for the Cedar Rapids and Milwaukee Historical Societies as well.

While I've written a lot of non-fiction in my life, this was my first stab at a novel, and I couldn't have done it without the support of friends and fellow writers. To Teresa Basile, Fiona Stevens, Pat Ryan, the Naperville Writers Group, Ida, Ryno and EJ at the West Suburban Writers Meetup, and my dear Robyn Clarke, thank you.

Thanks to Erik Empson and his team at thebookfolks.com for their hard work bringing my somewhat odd baby into the world.

Finally to The Duchess and Her Serene Highness

who have tolerated me while I scratched this itch, all my love and gratitude. To all of you who enjoyed this book, please stop by my website www.WayneTurmel.com and read my blog showcasing other indy and small press writers of historical fiction, learn a bit about me, and hear about upcoming work. There's another novel on the way.

The Count Of The Sahara is also available on kindle:

www.amazon.com/dp/B01407R2H2

37858381R00221

Made in the USA
Middletown, DE
09 December 2016